RASHIDA T. WILLIAMS

Venom and Sand
A Portal Drifter Novel: Book One
Red Adept Publishing, LLC
104 Bugenfield Court
Garner, NC 27529
https://RedAdeptPublishing.com/

---

1.   http://StreetlightGraphics.com

For C., who excitedly cheered me on through every single episode.

Chapter 1: Silent Partner

Leona

I hated dying. The darkness didn't scare me. I was used to that hollow emptiness lingering in my soul. But I would never get used to the silence. Ever.

My body was hoisted onto a cold wooden bench, and my head slammed against the solid planks. Pain shot through the back of my skull. I would have screamed if I'd had more than a breath left in me. With the very last of my strength, I tightened my grip on the fistful of small gold coins in my left hand.

Two fingers pressed into my neck. There was a subtle vibration in the room, and the faint smell of whiskey filled the air. Voices—I couldn't hear their voices. Panic crept through me. If I lost total control over my emotions, I would be trapped in a state of paralysis until they buried me alive... and my body rotted from the outside in. I clung to the only rational thought I had left.

It's just death.

I exhaled. The pain faded, and I suddenly felt weightless. Time seemed to stand still. My heart stopped. There was no sound.

***

The sharp clinking of coins scattering across the floor rang in my ears. My eyes shot open. A white sheet obstructed my vision.

"The woman gets bitten by a venomous snake, and her first thought is to grab some worthless coins?"

I gasped and sat bolt upright, tearing the sheet off my face. Every inch of my body ached, and I struggled to get enough air into my lungs. Candles illuminated the cramped space, casting shadows on rows of bodies covered in identical white sheets.

"It's an apparition!" a slender young man shrieked.

I spun around, not sure I could take any more surprises. "What? Where?"

The young man pointed at me with his mouth agape. A taller gentleman with a silver-streaked beard stood beside him completely expressionless. I let out a breath.

"You nearly scared the life out of me, you fool." I rubbed my throbbing head with mangled fingers. "Which one of you broke my hand?"

The young man's eyes rolled back in his head, and he fainted. I fixed my gaze on his companion.

"I knew I couldn't run forever." He wiped his hands on a blood-stained apron. "But I didn't think they'd send a trapper."

"That's what happens when you illegally sell body parts off-world, *doctor*." I swung my legs off the table, and my boots hit the floor hard. Gravity always felt heavier after a reawakening. Even the thin fabric of my cotton gown seemed to weigh down my shoulders.

"Your eyes..." The doctor stared at me with furrowed brows. "I've seen you before."

A pungent odor, like rotting fruit, filled my nose as my sense of smell returned. "No, you haven't."

"I remember every inch of my patients," he said. "Two years ago, there was a woman, badly burned, but she had your eyes."

I squared my shoulders. "What happened to her?"

"I suppose you don't want to know the details." He flashed me a crooked smile. "But her eyes fetched me a decent profit."

My heart beat so hard my entire body shook, but my voice remained steady. "Rest assured, you'll be dealt with accordingly."

The doctor looked me up and down. "I suppose she was important to you."

"She was my partner."

His eyes narrowed. "Just your partner?"

My throat tightened, but I choked out the word. "Sister."

He nodded. "And now you're here for retribution."

"*Justice*," I corrected him.

"How exactly does this work?" the doctor asked, inching closer to a tray of rusty medical instruments. "You come here with no partner and no weapons. You think I'm just going to surrender quietly?"

"I was hoping we wouldn't have to resort to primitive methods."

The doctor grabbed a bow-framed amputation saw. "I prefer primitive."

He lunged. The saw almost sliced my face, and I ducked. I scrambled under the table, clutching my injured hand close to my chest. The doctor shoved the table out of his way. My heart raced as I dragged myself across the rough, uneven floorboards.

"Take your sweet time!" I shouted into the air.

Faint rattling echoed throughout the space. The doctor froze. A six-foot snake slithered out of a dark corner and crept between us. His black diamond-shaped markings shimmered in the candlelight. The doctor slowly stepped back, lowering his weapon.

I pushed myself to my feet with my good hand. "What took you so long?"

The snake coiled up in a defensive pose and hissed at me. I didn't flinch. Seconds later, the reptile morphed into humanoid form and towered over me. His sandy-brown skin had only the faintest traces of scales, and inky-black diamonds ran down both sides of his neck. A canvas vest clung to his muscular chest, and a braided whip dangled from a leather holster on his hip.

"I asked if you needed backup three times, Leona." Everett tilted the front of his broad-brimmed hat with a single finger. His bright-yellow eyes blazed with anger. "You ignored me."

I huffed. "How many times do I have to tell you? I'm not telepathic!"

Everett shook his head and tossed me my blade. It bounced off my limp hand and clattered to the floor. I ground my teeth.

"Sorry." He lifted up my skirt to reveal a leather garter belt on my thigh and shoved the knife into its scabbard. "I forgot you were damaged."

The doctor glanced from me to Everett then back at me. "You two are—partners?"

I yanked my skirt out of Everett's hands and pushed him away. "Yes, why?"

"They must have made a terrible mistake," the doctor said gravely. "Trappers are usually so well-matched they work in perfect harmony."

We glared at him. He shrank back. Everett and I were bound together, and there was nothing either of us could do about it. A breach of contract meant termination from the Agency. Sometimes literally.

"I can't work with a broken hand," I said to Everett. "And I'm out of gold."

"Forget it. You already owe me twenty-five pieces."

"I'll pay you after this job. I swear."

He crossed his arms. "That's what you said after the last *three* jobs. You haven't made good on any of your promises."

I stomped my foot. "You cheap—"

"Where did the doctor go?" Everett asked, glancing about the room.

All the bodies were still. The back door creaked open and closed, carried by the wind.

"Blast!" I met Everett's eyes. "If we let another one get away..."

He reached into his pocket and flung a single gold coin in my direction. I caught it in midair and held it tightly. A cool prickling sensation trickled down my body as I absorbed the metal. The bones in my left hand cracked and snapped back into place. Everett shuddered at the sound. Tears stung my eyes, and I blinked them away. The pain wouldn't last long. I dropped the coin. All that remained was the silver. I flexed my fingers. My bones always healed so much stronger.

"Thank you," I said sincerely.

Everett grabbed his whip and headed for the door. "Now you owe me twenty-six."

"I'm sure you won't let me forget it," I muttered.

We rushed out into the night. The doctor was running at full speed across the barren prairie. Everett's long strides were impossible to match, but I pushed myself harder. My heart pounded against my chest, and my vision blurred.

"We have to catch him before he finds a portal!" I yelled.

Everett swung his whip overhead without breaking his pace. Thick clouds formed in the sky, blocking the light of Aadar's moons. The energy in the air shifted. All the hair on my body stood on end. Lightning flashed around us, and a roll of thunder shook the land. Suddenly, Everett stopped and planted his feet firmly on the ground.

"Stay back!" he shouted over his shoulder.

I skidded to a stop. Everett cracked his whip, and a bolt of electricity shot out of it, striking the doctor in the back. He let out a choked yelp then dropped to the ground, convulsing.

The clouds lifted as the energy surrounding us stabilized and the static charge faded. I caught up to Everett, masking my breathlessness with a cough. We cautiously approached the doctor and hovered over his still body. He was unconscious.

"Let's hope you didn't kill him," I said.

"Of course I didn't kill him." Everett placed his whip back in its holster. "I want to get paid."

The world tilted slightly, and I shook off a dizzy spell.

"What's wrong?" he asked.

"Nothing," I said sharply. "We need to get him to the station before dawn."

I took a step, and my legs gave out. Everett caught me in his firm arms before I hit the ground.

"It figures I'd get stuck with a delicate partner who's prone to fainting," he said.

I regained my balance and brushed the dust off my dress. "Reawakening took a greater toll on my body than usual, that's all."

Everett was silent for a moment. "It's not usually like this?"

"No. I always heal quickly once I'm conscious again."

In the moonlight, I could see a flicker of panic in Everett's eyes.

"I'm out of gold," he said. "And my venom is killing you—again."

Chapter 2: Kill Me Twice

Leona

"Don't be ridiculous," I said. "Your venom isn't strong enough to kill me *twice*."

I touched a tender spot on my neck. Two small puncture wounds dotted my throat. I wasn't healing.

"We have to fix you. Immediately." Everett circled around me. "If you die, the Agency will match me with a new partner. You know how lengthy that process is. I might not get paid for weeks."

"Your concern for my well-being touches my heart."

Everett's yellow eyes almost glowed in the darkness as he examined my neck. "The venom is still part of me. I can control it and draw it out of you."

I thought about my alternatives. I had none. "Be quick about it."

Everett held me still. His soft breath against my bare neck caused my skin to tingle. The last time he was that close, he was begging me to come up with a different plan to trap the doctor. I had refused. He tried to warn me of the dangers. I thought I was prepared, but his bite still caught me off guard. The pain was excruciating. All the muscles in my body tensed as I struggled to bury the memory.

Everett hesitated. "You need to relax, or it's going to burn."

"Just do it, and get it over with," I said.

Everett gently pressed his lips over the bite marks on my throat. I gritted my teeth and closed my eyes. A warm sensation spread through me as he began sucking the venom out of my bloodstream. His venom. For a split second, we shared a connection. A single word echoed in the deepest recesses of my mind. *Crotalus.* My veins suddenly felt like they were on fire. I gasped and slipped out of his reach.

"T-this isn't working," I stammered, backing away.

Everett wiped the venom from his mouth. "Well, what do you suggest?"

"We finish the job, we get the gold." I knelt down and grabbed a handful of sand. "I'll live, and you'll get paid."

Everett gave a slight nod. He lifted the unconscious doctor over his shoulder and stood behind me. I inhaled the warm desert air and raised my eyes to the glistening stars dotting the night sky. My vision sharpened as I focused my mind on our destination. The sand heated up in my palm and turned black.

I slowly let out a breath. "Hold on."

Everett wrapped his free arm around my waist. His heart beat rapidly against my back. He hated drifting, but he would never openly admit that to me. I let the hot sand slip through my fingers and fall to my feet. I closed my eyes. The ground swallowed us up, and my stomach dropped. Everett clung to me desperately as we fell through the darkness. Grains of sand whipped past my face, stinging my cheeks. The falling sensation stopped abruptly, and we were propelled forward, out of the vortex.

Everett hit the ground first. I landed on top of him, knocking the air out of his lungs. A stiff breeze sent a chill through me. Majestic trees towered over us, and the sun began to rise over mountains in the distance. I pushed myself up with shaky arms and coughed, accidentally blowing chunks of sand into Everett's face. He glared at me.

"Sorry. I didn't mean to—"

The doctor's limp body landed on my back, cutting my apology short. I crumpled under the weight. Everett grunted and tossed us both off of him.

"You are by far the worst drifter I've ever traveled with!" Everett shouted as he dragged himself to his feet. "We've never had a smooth crossing."

I shook sand out of my ears. "We're alive, aren't we?"

"That's a low bar, Leona. Even for you."

I blew him a kiss. He mumbled something under his breath and scooped up the doctor. In truth, my twin sister had always been the better drifter. Once she committed a location to memory, she could return to the exact coordinates. My landings were always off by a mile—or two.

"We just have to reach the depot before our train leaves." I felt a little queasy as I stood. "We have plenty of time."

A loud whistle sounded in the distance. I glanced at Everett. We took off running toward the station. Rocks and dust went flying in all directions as we scurried across the rough terrain. I would never hear the end of it if we missed our drop. The crisp morning air filled my lungs and drove me forward. I overtook Everett and cleared the tree line. The train rounded a bend at the bottom of the rocky incline. I let out a sigh of relief. We were going back to the home office with our catch. Our first catch.

Everett cried out. I spun around. He fell to his knees, clutching his left arm. The doctor scuttled away with a pair of bloody forceps. I darted after him and tackled him to the ground. He struggled to free himself from my grip as I pinned him down from behind.

"We don't have time for this!" I shouted. My heart was racing.

The doctor grabbed a rock, reached back, and smashed it into my forehead. I shook off the blow and pushed his head into the dirt. My limbs started to go numb, and I suddenly felt lightheaded. The venom coursing through my body was taking hold of me again. The doctor elbowed me in the stomach. I hunched over in pain. He tore himself from my grasp, jumped to his feet, and bolted down the rugged hillside. Everett fumbled with his whip and chased after him, leaving me behind.

A strong burst of wind threw us all into the air and knocked us on our backs. I tried to speak but couldn't catch my breath. A heavy force held us down, making it impossible to move.

"What have we here?" a sickly-sweet voice inquired.

I closed my eyes. I couldn't handle any more embarrassment.

"It looks like we have ourselves a couple of trappers... and their fleeing catch."

Claude and Elsie peered down at me. His blue eyes danced with amusement, and her painted lips curved into a smile. Their clothes were pristine. Like they were headed to a social.

"We'll take it from here." Elsie opened her fist, and the gravity field lifted.

I gasped and sat upright. "You can't—"

"Can't what?" Claude asked with a smirk. "Apprehend a known outlaw?"

Everett crawled next to me. "He's ours. We're turning him in."

Elsie snapped a lace fan open and began fanning herself. "And how are you going to catch him, pray tell?"

The doctor was on the run again. A wave of nausea overtook me. I leaned forward and vomited. Everett clenched his fist.

"You two seem to have a lot going on." Claude turned his back to us and thrust out his hand. A gust of wind threw the doctor to the ground once more.

Elsie gave us a friendly wave. "Toodle-oo."

The two trappers left us to attend to their catch. I staggered to my feet in a daze. Everett led the way to the train station. He spoke in a low voice, but I couldn't understand his words. The world was a blur of colors and sounds. A single thought kept swirling through my mind: *Maggie's going to have my head.*

We boarded the train, and I followed him to our compartment. Tufted seats lined the walls. All I wanted to do was curl up on the soft velvet fabric and let the world fade away.

Everett slid the doors closed and tossed his hat on one of the benches. "And next time one of us needs to check for weapons so we're not caught off guard by a pair of scissors!"

I swayed.

Everett frowned. "Are you listening to anything I'm saying?"

I fell backward between the seats and hit my head on the floor.

"Leona!" Everett rushed over to me. "Are you all right?"

I stared up at him, struggling to breathe. "Get it out of me."

Chapter 3: Broke and Broken

Everett

I accidentally broke Leona. Her thin ivory dress clung to the curves of her body as she lay sprawled across the railway car floor, heaving for breath. Thick raven hair partially covered her diamond-shaped face, and her deep-brown skin glistened with sweat. My venom had spread. Quickly. She wasn't going to last long. Her dark eyes pleaded with mine as words seemed to escape her. I lifted her onto the long velvet bench and checked her pulse. Her heartbeat was weak.

"Everett..." she whispered. "Stop stalling. I don't care how painful it is. Just get it out of me."

Leona was always rushing me. I hated being rushed. She had assured me she could heal from anything, that her body would regenerate with enough gold. And I had been foolish enough to believe her. When I bit her, I didn't hold back.

"I can't just—" I gently touched the fang marks on her throat, and she flinched. "I don't know how to do it without hurting you."

Leona grabbed me by my vest and pulled me closer. "Do you realize the level of scorn we'll face from the other trappers if I die from your venom in a failed attempt to catch a low-level criminal? You'll never work again."

I climbed on top of her and pulled the ruffled sleeve of her dress off her left shoulder. "Try not to scream too loud."

I leaned over her and began sucking her neck. My venom tasted sweet. Leona gasped and arched her back under me. I could only imagine how badly it burned.

I attempted to speak directly into her mind. *I'm so sorry, Leona!*

She didn't respond. I tried apologizing again. Nothing. Her body trembled, and a high-pitched squeal escaped her throat.

The doors slid open, but I didn't stop or look back.

"Well, Elsie, this might explain why they've been so preoccupied they can't seem to set a proper trap," Claude said.

"I declare! I'm not sure I could either."

"Get out!" Leona screamed.

The doors slammed shut. My tongue brushed against Leona's tender skin. She writhed in pain. I had to keep her from crying. I couldn't handle her crying. I grabbed her right hand and held it over her head. She squeezed my hand, digging her nails into my skin.

It's almost over. I spoke more for myself than for her. *It's almost over...*

Leona clung to me as I drew the last of my venom out of her. I could feel the muscles in her body begin to relax. She exhaled and slowly let go of my hand. I lifted my head and met her eyes.

I never want to do that with you again.

Leona remained still but didn't look away. Her full lips were parted as she took in shallow breaths.

Can you hear me? I asked.

"I'm hungry," she said.

I sighed. "We don't have enough money."

I needed to stop getting my hopes up and accept reality. Leona lacked telepathic abilities because she wasn't a pure-blood. Her ancestors didn't originate on Aadar. But that wasn't the issue. As a shapeshifter, I could project my thoughts to a nontelepathic human if I shared a deep enough connection with them. The real issue was something I didn't want to admit. That despite being partners, Leona didn't trust me. At all.

The doors slid open again. Two trappers entered our compartment. I quickly climbed off Leona. She sat up and readjusted her wrinkled dress. Ada and Agnes sat on the bench across from us without saying a word. They were a study in contrasts. Ada was short and round, while Agnes was tall and lanky. Their pants and boots were covered in mud, and by their odor, they hadn't been anywhere close to civilization in days.

"Leona," Ada said. "It's good to see you—alive for a change."

"It's always lovely to see you as well," Leona said with no emotion.

Ada looked me up and down. "And you're getting along with your new partner, I see."

Leona glared at her.

"How many traps have you two successfully set?" Agnes asked, casually picking her teeth with a small silver dagger.

Leona's voice was sharp. "None."

"And you've been together for how long?" Ada asked.

"Eight months," Leona answered.

I glanced at her. Trappers had their own code that I still didn't understand. She acted like she owed them an explanation.

"A regenerating drifter and a lightning-wielding shapeshifter..." Agnes pointed her dagger at us as she spoke. "It seems odd that they would match you two together."

I cracked my neck. The Agency paired individuals based on either their born ability or their learned skill. The best partners had complementary powers, like Claude and Elsie. One could push, the other could pull. Leona and I had no such advantage.

"The Agency doesn't make mistakes," Leona replied after a moment.

"You're right." Ada stared at Leona. "The Agency doesn't make mistakes."

I got to my feet and turned to Leona. "I'll look for some food."

I grabbed my hat and left the compartment before she could respond. She was better at dealing with the other trappers. She had more experience with them. I had been with the Agency for less than a year. Leona had already spent eleven years as a trapper before her sister's... *accident*. She rarely spoke about it, and I knew better than to bring it up—to her.

I maneuvered around loitering trappers in the narrow passageway and opened the exit door. A burst of cool mountain air hit my face, and I cringed. I wasn't fond of cold weather. I crossed the metal platform into the next railway car. The heavy locomotive rocked and swayed along the bumpy tracks as I made my way to the last train car. The holding area. I entered the slip carriage. A wiry guard immediately blocked my path.

"I'm looking for the doctor," I said.

The young man didn't budge.

I bit back my irritation. "I'm here to see my catch."

He arched a single eyebrow. "*Your* catch?"

I handed him four silver coins. He pocketed the money and pointed to the last compartment. I entered the cramped space and slid the doors shut behind me. The spry doctor was seated and handcuffed.

"Have you come to free me?" he asked with a grin. "I like traveling with you and pretty eyes. You're both easily distracted."

I sat across from him and peered into his sunken gray eyes. "Who was Maude's buyer?"

The doctor's face fell. "I don't know what you're talking about."

"Sure you do. You said yourself she fetched you a decent profit."

The doctor swallowed hard. "I was just trying to get under your partner's skin. She needs to lighten up. You both need to lighten up."

I leaned closer. "Who was the buyer?"

The doctor rested his shackled hands on his bloodstained apron. "If I tell you, will you let me go?"

I kept my voice low. "I'll see if I can arrange a deal for you."

He glanced about. "I sold her to a rich off-worlder. He goes by the name of Irving."

"How do I find him?"

"Foreigners and off-worlders know him well. He handles a lot of their transactions. But if he finds out you're looking for him, he'll disappear."

I slowly got up. "That's all I needed to know."

The doctor grabbed my arm with his bony, clawlike fingers. "If you ever want to sell your partner out, I can get you a fair price on her parts."

I jerked my arm away. "You disgust me."

He shrugged, innocently. "From what I hear, the other trappers wouldn't think twice about offing Leona."

The sound of her name coming out of his mouth made my skin crawl. "And that's the last thing you'll ever hear about her."

I collapsed within myself and shifted into snake form. My tail rattled. Before the doctor could cry out, I sprang forward, bit his arm, and released my venom into his bloodstream. Not enough to kill him. Unfortunately. His expression went blank. I shifted back into human form and captured his gaze.

You will forget everything you know about Maude and Leona. I spoke directly into the doctor's pathetically weak mind. *You never knew them. They don't exist.*

The doctor blinked repeatedly. I slammed the door before he could come out of the haze. The guard pretended he didn't see me as I exited the railway car. The doctor's last words replayed over and over in my mind. *The other trappers wouldn't think twice about offing Leona...*

My pulse hastened. I tried to remind myself that the doctor enjoyed toying with people, but that fact did nothing to calm my nerves. I darted up the train, ignoring angry comments and complaints from random trappers I accidentally bumped into.

I reached our compartment. It was locked. There was no sound coming from inside. I pounded on the door.

"Leona!"

The doors slid open. A strong gust of wind almost blew my hat off. The large glass window had been smashed to pieces, and the forest was a blur of greens and browns as we sped through the mountains. Leona stumbled out. Her dress was covered in blood. She yanked a silver dagger out of her stomach and looked up at me.

"We have to get off this train."

Chapter 4: Trust Fall

Everett

"Leona, you're bleeding out." I tried to stop her as she staggered down the cramped hallway of the railway car.

She waved me off, splattering blood on the walls. "It's just a scratch."

"What happened?" I demanded. "Why did they attack you?"

Leona shook her head, as though it was too painful to relive. A wave of guilt washed over me. I had been so focused on getting information out of the doctor, I hadn't picked up on any other signs that she would be in danger.

Leona muttered to herself. Something about a woman named Maggie. I couldn't make sense of anything she was saying. Suddenly, she stopped and banged on the door to one of the compartments. Elsie slid it open and gasped at the sight of her.

Claude jumped up from his seat. "Get them in here and shut the door!"

We crammed into the small space, and Elsie locked the door behind us. Leona collapsed onto the bench. I sat beside her and felt her forehead. Her clammy skin was cold.

"We're out of money," I said urgently. "She needs gold."

Elsie fumbled with their overhead luggage and tossed me a leather purse. I carefully poured some of the gold coins into Leona's hands and held them closed. Her soft fingers felt delicate in my rough calloused hands.

"Thank you," Leona whispered. "All of you."

Both of Claude's fists were clenched. "What happened?"

"I don't know," I said. "Two trappers came into our compartment. I left to find something for Leona—"

Elsie fanned Leona with her dainty lace fan. "Everett left you all by your lonesome?"

Leona nodded without opening her eyes.

"You never, *ever* leave your partner alone," Claude said. "Especially not on a train full of trappers."

I ground my teeth. "We're all working for the same Agency!"

Claude and Elsie exchanged a glance. Leona slowly sat up. All of the coins fell to the ground, depleted of their gold.

"There's a rift within the Agency," Leona said. "There have been reports of trappers going rogue."

"What's being done about it?" I asked.

"The Agency immediately revokes their employment." Claude ran his fingers through his red hair. "But by then it's usually too late. The damage has been done."

Every muscle in my body tensed. "Who's behind it?"

"No one knows," Elsie said. "But trappers have been winding up dead."

Claude put a hand on Leona's shoulder. "We're really sorry about what happened to Maude."

Leona nodded. Her eyes were glossy.

"What would they want with Leona?" I asked.

Elsie shook her head. "There are rumors, but no one has confirmed them."

"They told me..." Leona's voice was distant. "They want to dispose of drifters."

A loud knock made me jump. I grabbed a wool blanket and threw it over Leona. She curled up into a tight ball and didn't make a sound. Without thinking, I shifted into the form of the young guard I saw earlier and blocked her from view. Claude opened the doors.

Two trappers in matching suspenders and flannel shirts stood in the doorway. The Knox brothers. They each held up a bottle of whiskey.

"Have either of you seen Leona?" one of the brothers asked, slurring. "We thought she could use a drink after what happened to her catch today."

They were drunk. Or pretending to be.

"She went to the slip car," I said in the young guard's voice. "Something about wanting to interrogate the doctor they tried to bring in."

The two trappers shared a knowing smile and moved on. Claude swiftly locked the compartment and pressed his back against the door. Beads of sweat trickled down the sides of his face. He clearly wasn't used to being the prey.

I shifted back into my regular human form and stood up. "We need to get off the train before we reach the next station. The depot will be crawling with trappers. There will be nowhere to hide."

Leona slowly removed the blanket. "Will you help us?"

"Of course we will." Claude straightened his suit jacket as though preparing for battle. "There's a bridge over the river just before the first stop."

Elsie gave me a small pouch of coins. "You're probably going to need this."

The train whistled.

"We need to move!" I said.

We rushed down the hallway to the end of the railway car. I pushed the door open. The lush mountainous landscape whipped past. I held my hat close to my head.

"I can slow us down, but only while we're over land!" Elsie spoke over the loud locomotive. "Once we reach the bridge, you'll be in Claude's hands."

Leona gave her a tight hug. "Thank you. For everything."

"Be safe out there," Elsie said. "Don't trust anyone but each other."

Elsie grabbed hold of the iron railing and held her other hand out over the edge of the train. The metal wheels creaked and whined as though the brakes were being applied. Elsie's gravity field slowed the train down as we climbed to the roof with Claude.

The train wrapped around a bend, and a bridge came into view. Below the bridge was a wide river with rushing rapids. We steadied ourselves and prepared to jump. My heart beat wildly in my chest. Leona's eyes were fixed on the horizon.

"I'm so sorry I left you alone," I said.

Leona met my eyes. She said nothing.

It will never happen again. I attempted to speak into her mind. Her expression didn't change. She couldn't hear me.

"Get ready!" Claude shouted.

I blew out a breath and braced myself. Elsie released the gravity field as the train approached the bridge. The train sped up.

"Jump!" Claude yelled.

Leona grabbed my hand. We jumped together. A heavy blast of wind knocked into our backs and sent us gliding through the air over the rapids below. Claude sent out another burst. The sound of the train faded. We fell for what felt like an eternity. I held my breath, and we hit the icy water. Leona slipped out of my fingers. I clawed through the rough waters and broke through the surface.

I gasped. "Leona!"

She burst through the water. "I'm here! I'm all right!"

A wave of relief came over me at the sound of her voice. We swam against the current toward dry land. I climbed out of the river, coughing up water and struggling to catch my breath. Leona dragged herself onto the rocky surface beside me. She reached down and scooped up some of the muddy soil.

"I can't drift while I'm wet," she said.

I stood up and helped her to her feet. "Then let's get you dry."

Chapter 5: Slippery When Wet

Leona

I couldn't stop shivering. The sun seemed to set earlier in the Wispy Mountains than I remembered. Everett was off gathering firewood, but he didn't venture far from me. Neither of us was equipped to deal with the frigid weather. I needed to get dry so we could drift. Preferably to a warmer climate.

Everett returned and piled the logs inside a makeshift fire ring. He'd hardly spoken more than two words to me since the train incident. He seemed lost in his own thoughts.

"I left my matches in my other dress," I said.

Everett barely cracked a smile. He grabbed his whip and swung it overhead. Clouds formed above us, and I felt a shift in the air. There was a flash of lightning followed by a roll of thunder. He cracked his whip, and an electric bolt struck the pit. A spark ignited. He crouched down to fan the small flames. The fire caught and consumed the woodpile.

"I'll find us something to eat." Everett morphed into his reptilian form and slithered over fallen leaves as he disappeared into the forest.

"Anything but rodents!" I called after him.

His tail rattled. I smiled and inched closer to the fire. Drops of water trickled down my neck from my thick curly hair, and my tattered cotton gown was plastered to my skin. I was soaked through. I wrung out as much water as I could then wrapped my arms around my legs. My attention was suddenly drawn to the sky. Melodic whispers emanated from the thin veil of clouds. Aadar was lulling me to sleep. Exhaustion crept over me. I slowly lowered my head and closed my eyes.

A loud *pop* jolted me awake. I had no idea how long I'd been asleep. Everett was sitting beside me, roasting meat over an open flame. His large vest was wrapped around my shoulders. Feathery clouds were painted in a copper hue as the sun's light faded in the distance.

"You woke up just in time for dinner," he said.

The pleasant aroma made my stomach growl. "What's on the menu?"

He handed me the skewer, and I took a large bite before he could reply. The gamey meat melted on my tongue. I moaned. I couldn't remember the last time I'd tasted anything so delicious.

"Rabbit," Everett said.

I tried to slow down and savor each bite, but I was ravenous. It wasn't until I was gnawing on the bones that I realized Everett wasn't eating.

"You're not hungry?" I asked.

"I ate." He tossed the last of the wood onto the small fire. "I don't particularly enjoy cooked food."

"Your future wife will appreciate that about you."

I got a slight chuckle out of him. The fire was warm, but the temperature was dropping rapidly, and my clothes were still wet.

"We should see if we can get a refund on our train tickets," I said.

"I'd rather not have anything to do with trains for a while," Everett replied.

I grabbed a long stick and poked at the logs. "That was a pretty convincing lie you told Harvey."

"Who?" he asked.

"On the train, you told the Knox brothers I was interrogating the doctor."

He shrugged. "It seemed like something you would do."

"No..." I said. "It seems like something *you* would do."

Everett didn't respond. Leaves rustled in the wind, and I wrapped his vest tighter around my body.

"Did you?" I asked finally.

"Did I, what?"

I sighed heavily. Everett was always stalling. "Did you interrogate the doctor?"

He stared into the flames. "Yes."

"I knew it." I rose up on my knees. "What did he say? Did he tell you anything about my sister?"

Everett shook his head. "He knew nothing."

"Nothing at all?" I pressed. "What about a buyer? Did he give you a name?"

"He knew *nothing*," Everett repeated firmly.

I slumped back down. Another false lead. Every time I thought I was getting close to finding answers about Maude's death, the trail would run cold.

His voice was soft. "I'm sorry."

I stifled my disappointment and tended to the fire. No catch. No lead. Nothing but dead ends. I repositioned myself a bit closer to Everett. At least he'd tried.

"How are you feeling?" he asked, gesturing to my abdomen.

I touched my stomach, half expecting to find a hole where the dagger had pierced me. There was going to be a deep scar. I glanced up to find Everett staring at me. I quickly covered myself with his vest, and he looked away.

"Does it hurt?" he asked.

"No. It was just a little dagger. I've had much worse."

"No, I mean..." He met my eyes. "Does dying hurt?"

Random images flashed through my mind. Rope. The well. A bottle of poison. The barrel of a six-shooter. My heart beat faster. Sweat began seeping through my pores. I buried the memories, refusing to succumb to my emotions.

"Yes. It hurts," I replied. "Every single time."

Everett fell silent. We had spent countless nights together, but we had never once talked about anything other than the next job. We were partners, and yet we knew next to nothing about each other.

I cleared my throat. "Does it hurt when you shift?"

He shrugged. "It depends on what I shift into. The longer I stay in a particular form, the easier it is for me to maintain it. But some things hurt worse than others."

I nodded, wondering just how many forms he had taken.

"Plants are near impossible," he added. "I've been trying to shift into a cactus for years."

I burst into laughter, unable to contain myself.

Everett grinned. "I'm serious. It's harder than you might think."

"Well, I hope I'm around to water you when you reach your ultimate goal."

There was no mirth in his gaze. "I hope so, too, Leona."

The flames slowly burned down, and we were left with nothing but smoldering ashes.

"They're going to start coming after you too," I said.

"I know."

"If you want to part ways... I would understand."

He placed a reassuring hand on my shoulder. "You're my partner."

I nodded appreciatively. I wasn't used to relying on anyone except my family. What was left of them.

Everett yawned, and I pushed myself to my feet.

"You rest," I said. "I'll get more firewood."

An icy breeze went straight through my damp clothes as I headed deeper into the forest. I clenched my teeth and started gathering as many branches and logs as I could carry. The less trips we had to make through the night, the better.

By the time I returned to our campsite, the fire was completely out—and Everett was gone. I threw the firewood aside and frantically searched the area. He wouldn't just abandon me. Not after what we had been through. Dusk was falling. I squinted through the remaining light and lifted a nearby rock.

"Everett!" I cried.

He had morphed into his reptilian form and was coiled up underneath the boulder. I shoved it out of the way. He didn't budge.

"Are you all right?" I asked. "Can you hear me?"

I brushed my fingers against his cool scales. He remained motionless. Brumation. I'd completely forgotten that Everett was cold-blooded. The sudden change in temperature left him in a dormant state.

A twig snapped. I held my breath. The forest went silent. I quickly scooped Everett up and wrapped his heavy body around my neck. We were exposed to the elements and the wildlife without any sort of protection. He couldn't move. I couldn't drift. There was only one option. I had to find a portal... or we would never make it through the night alive.

Chapter 6: A Glimmer of Hope

Leona

The silver light of Aadar's moons shined down on the forest as I trudged along with Everett coiled around my body. Every now and then I would touch his cold scales to make sure he was still breathing. He was completely unresponsive.

Even with Everett's thick vest over my shoulders, my torn dress was no match for the biting wind. I struggled to fight off the chill. It was nearly impossible to find a portal. I couldn't feel the natural energy of the planet through my own discomfort. But I knew we wouldn't survive the night in the wilderness.

"It's times like these I wouldn't mind being telepathic," I said to Everett. "Anything for a distraction."

I wondered if Everett could still hear me. The freezing temperatures had completely incapacitated my cold-blooded partner, but I couldn't bear the silence.

"Have you ever been off-world?" I asked through chattering teeth. "There are rumors of planets that have been so stripped of natural resources that all the portals close and people completely lose their abilities and skills. Can you imagine?"

No response.

"Me neither," I said. "That's why I never leave Aadar."

Everett didn't stir.

"I have a cousin who went off-world once. Of course, he was running from the law at the time..." I bit back my uncontrolled rambling. I doubted Everett wanted to hear about my family's criminal history—or why I became a trapper.

A strong gust of wind almost knocked me over. I shielded Everett as best as I could with his vest and pressed on. We hadn't prepared to spend a lot of time in the mountains. We hadn't prepared for a lot of things. I hadn't told Everett everything that had happened on the train. He didn't need to know.

The energy emanating from the portals changed a person's genetic makeup, and I was born with rapid healing abilities. The gene was strong in my family. My cells could regenerate even faster if I absorbed gold from the planet. But there were two things that could kill me. *Really* kill me. Fire... and a severed heart. Ada and Agnes had tried to rip out my beating heart. I'd never felt terror like I did on that train. I'd never felt so alone.

I swallowed hard, suppressing my raw emotions. I hadn't truly been alone. Everett had come back. He'd chosen to stay with me. The energy around us shifted. I glanced up. High above, between two large trees, I saw a glimmer. Glistening violet light. A portal. One that would transport us within the world. I circled one of the tree trunks, searching for a safe foothold. There was no easy way up.

The heavy thumping of paws hitting the ground snapped me to attention. I ran and jumped, grabbing the closest branch I could reach. Everett's limp body started to weigh me down. My foot found a sturdy gnarl, and I pulled us up onto the branch. I took a moment to steady myself against the brittle bark then started the slow ascent.

"This will be an exciting story we can tell the other trappers at the annual social," I said, trying to mask my nervousness. "If you plan to accompany me."

I fell out of a tree once. And died.

"I'm not saying you *have* to attend the social with me." My voice was trembling. "It would be nice if you did—but I'm not asking you to be my escort or anything like that."

I cautiously moved from branch to branch. Even my palms were sweating.

"Actually, forget I said anything about the social. You probably don't even enjoy dancing."

In the darkness, something slammed into the bottom of the tree. I winced. Claws frantically scraped the thick bark below us. My whole body was shaking. I didn't dare look down. We were so close. We just had to get above the portal.

I tugged on a branch to ensure it could handle our weight. It snapped. I shrieked and grabbed hold of the tree trunk, regaining my balance as the dead limb crashed to the ground. My heart pounded wildly in my chest. Everett wrapped himself tighter around me. I took a deep breath and pushed aside my fear.

With the last of my strength, I wedged my boot into a small crack and pulled us up onto a thick branch. I straddled the rugged limb, ignoring the sound of ripping fabric. My dress was already ruined. I slowly inched across the branch and positioned us over the portal.

"Think warm thoughts, Everett!" The subtle crack in my voice betrayed my lighthearted quip.

I let go. A high-pitched scream escaped my throat as we fell into the shimmering light. The portal sucked us in and propelled us forward almost simultaneously. I clung to Everett and braced myself for the painful landing. Instead, we flew headfirst into a haystack.

I gasped and clawed through mounds of straw. Both of my arms were scratched and sore from the rough climb. I crawled out of the haystack with Everett dangling from my neck. The air was stifling. My eyes stung from the bright sunlight shining directly overhead. I glanced across the acres of golden farmland. There wasn't a soul in sight. I gently lay Everett across the ground to soak up the sun's rays and collapsed beside him.

I told myself I was only going to close my eyes for a second. When I opened them again, the sun was setting... and a dark-haired woman was pointing a shotgun in my face.

"Who are you, and what are you doing on my land?" she asked.

I slowly sat up with my hands raised. "My name is Leona. My partner and I just needed a place to rest."

Her eyes narrowed. "Your partner?"

I glanced at the spot where Everett was just rousing from sleep. He slowly uncoiled his body and stretched long.

The woman stepped back. "Move, so I can kill it!"

I jumped up, grabbed the barrel of the shotgun, and yanked it out of her hands. She lunged at me. I jabbed her in the chest with the butt of the gun, knocking her to the ground.

"Are you out of your mind?" I shouted. "I said that's my partner!"

Everett morphed into humanoid form, stretching his arms and yawning. He shook the dust off his clothes.

"How long was I asleep?" he asked.

The woman stared at Everett, wide-eyed, and let out a frightened squeak.

"What's her problem?" Everett asked.

"She's clearly not from around here." I aimed the shotgun at her. "Are you an off-worlder?"

She nodded emphatically, causing her thick wavy hair to cover her face.

I eyed her carefully. "Do you know the name of a man who deals in rare merchandise?"

"I doubt all off-worlders know each other," Everett stated.

"He's not just any off-worlder," I said. "If he had close dealings with the doctor, he must be well-connected."

"I'll see what she knows," Everett said quickly.

He knelt in front of the woman and stared into her eyes. She appeared completely mesmerized by his gaze. Telepaths had an easier time reading the minds of off-worlders, but Everett rarely used his ability so openly. Neither of them spoke a word. I desperately wanted to know what he was saying—if he was asking the right questions—but I fought the urge to interrupt.

Everett slowly rose. "She doesn't know anything. It's best we move on."

I lowered the shotgun.

"Wait..." The woman shook her head, as though trying to clear her mind. "There is a man. He goes by the name of Irving—"

"This is a dead end," Everett cut in.

"We have no other leads," I reminded him. "Let her talk."

Everett ground his teeth and quietly stood by my side.

"Irving conducts business with most off-worlders," the woman continued. "But he'll only deal with wealthy Aadarins."

I glanced down at my shredded, bloodstained dress then turned to Everett. "We're going to need some new clothes."

Chapter 7: No Pair

Everett

I hated wearing suits. Clothes in general were always so cumbersome. It took everything I had not to loosen the strangling apparatus around my neck. Leona said that if she had to wear a corset, I couldn't open my mouth to complain about wearing a tie. I tried to focus on my cards instead.

No pair. Another junk hand.

"Raise," I said, bluffing.

I glanced across the poker table. Irving was the only other player left in the round. His shiny silver eyes met mine. He was like a stone, but I didn't flinch. I wasn't intimidated by off-worlders. They were usually kept in their place. Most thought they could come to Aadar and make a fortune off the advanced technology they brought from their worlds. Instead, they were often shunned and forced back. Everyone knew technology was at odds with nature. When an area became too technologically advanced, portals collapsed. Nobody wanted that. Nobody.

Irving, however, was smart. He'd made his fortune by going another route entirely. It just worked to my advantage that he was also a miserable poker player.

Irving placed his cards face down on the table. "Fold."

The dealer gestured to the pot. I casually collected my winnings, suppressing my excitement. Maybe it wasn't such a bad thing that I'd been too weak to cloud the farm girl's mind. By the end of the night, I would have more money in the bank.

The velvet curtains leading to our private room parted, and Leona stood in the doorway. I clenched my teeth to prevent my jaw from dropping. Her thick raven hair was pinned back in wavy curls, and a silk crimson gown hugged her frame. A corset cinched her waist, accentuating her curves, and long black gloves stretched up her toned arms. She cleaned up nice. Real nice.

A gentleman escorted Leona to the empty seat between Irving and Mary. Leona placed a small change purse on the table and acknowledged the other woman with a slight nod. Irving barely looked in her direction as he ordered another drink.

"I'll have the same," Leona spoke up.

Irving glanced at her and did a double take. He froze in his seat. I tossed in the ante, and all the other players followed suit... except Irving.

"Is something wrong?" I asked the off-worlder.

He swallowed hard and threw his money in the pot. "No. Nothing."

Mary started shuffling the cards, and the table fell silent. When the drinks arrived, Irving swallowed his in a single gulp and ordered another. Leona left her whiskey untouched.

The cards were cut and dealt. I examined my hand. More junk. I glanced up at Leona. She was rearranging her cards and ignoring the jittery man beside her.

"It's sure been hot," I said, pushing a gold coin toward the pot. "Bet."

"Hotter than Qlar's suns," Frank agreed. "Fold."

"Call." Daisy matched my bet. "This is nothing. Have you been out on the prairie lately?"

Irving spoke curtly. "Pass."

"I was recently on the prairie. I had to pay a visit to a doctor." Leona examined her cards then put five gold coins in the pot. "Raise four."

Mary folded. We had a job to do, but I secretly hoped I would win a few more rounds. Easy money.

I called. "A doctor's visit, huh? I hope it wasn't anything too serious."

Irving wiped the sweat from his brow.

"I'll live," Leona said flatly.

Daisy folded and tossed her cards aside. "I've been looking for a good doctor. Is he someone you would recommend?"

Leona tilted her head in thought. "I'm not sure how much longer he'll be practicing medicine."

"I don't trust doctors." Irving stared at her. "They're too unreliable."

Leona downed her whiskey and met his gaze. "Who do you trust?"

"Certainly not you... or anyone who looked like you." Irving reached for the pot, grabbed a handful of gold coins, and disappeared.

Leona and I jumped up from the table. Our chairs scraped across the wood floors, muffling the bewildered chatter of the other players. We charged out of the private room, into the crowded saloon. Frantic piano music played over raucous laughter coming from the bar. Irving was nowhere in sight.

"I see better in the dark," I said to Leona. "You search inside, I'll search outside."

She grabbed my arm. "Be careful."

I nodded and rushed to the back doors. The warm desert air filled my lungs as I made my way out into the night. I collapsed within myself and shifted into snake form. The town was buzzing with activity as I slithered through dark cracks and crevices, unseen. I could sense the off-worlder. He didn't get far.

Irving leaned against the side of a building in a dark alleyway, panting. Fortunately, there wasn't enough gold in the pot for him to maintain invisibility for long periods of time. I slowly took on a different form. One that was very familiar.

The off-worlder jumped back at the sight of me then let out a defeated breath.

"I knew you would eventually come after me, Leona," he said, winded. "I heard stories about you and your quest for justice."

I didn't say a word as I approached him.

"Well, what is it you want? Revenge?" he said. "We both know killing me won't bring back your sister."

"What did you want with Maude's body?"

Irving looked taken aback. "I didn't want anything to do with her. I was just the middleman. I handled the transaction."

"Who hired you?" I asked in Leona's voice.

"It was a trapper... goes by the name of Leroy. But I don't remember who he was working with."

"And you never will."

I shifted into snake form, bit his leg, and released some of my venom into him. His expression went blank. I took Leona's shape once more. Looking into Irving's metallic eyes, I spoke directly into his mind.

You will forget this face. You will forget everything you know about Maude and Leona. They don't exist. You don't belong here. Go find a red portal and leave this world immediately.

Irving blinked rapidly. He stumbled out of the alleyway, his mind clearly clouded in a fog. I followed behind him without a word. Out of nowhere, a drunk staggered into my shoulder and almost fell to the ground.

The old man removed his hat. "Pardon me, ma'am."

I flashed him one of Leona's sweetest smiles and blew him a kiss. He grinned broadly, revealing missing front teeth, then continued down the dark street. Frantic footsteps drew my attention toward the front of the saloon. I quickly shifted into my regular human form. Leona turned the corner and almost ran into Irving. She breathed a sigh of relief.

"You caught him!" Leona turned her attention to the off-worlder. "What do you know about my sister, Maude?"

Irving stared at her. "Who?"

"My twin sister. What happened to her?"

His brows furrowed. "I don't know you."

I stepped forward. "I don't think he's the person we should be looking for."

"I know you recognized me!" Leona grabbed Irving by his suit jacket. "What did you do to her?"

The off-worlder shook his head. "I've never seen you before in my life. Who are you people? Where am I?"

Leona's face dropped. She looked to me with pleading eyes. "I don't understand."

"It was a bad lead," I stated. I was getting too good at bluffing.

"That's impossible..." She spoke in a daze.

"I have to go," Irving muttered. "I don't belong here."

The off-worlder continued on his way, mumbling to himself. Leona turned her back to me and quickly brushed away tears with a gloved hand. A wave of guilt overcame me.

"I'm so sorry, Leona." I actually meant it.

"I need to think." Leona's voice was shaky. "I'm going back to the hotel."

"Good idea. I'll meet you there shortly."

I waited until she was completely out of view before I darted off in the opposite direction. I needed to hurry. The last thing I wanted to do was raise her suspicions. Even on foot, it didn't take me long to reach the railroad depot on the other side of town. I approached the small telegraph window and knocked on the smudged glass.

The window slid open, and a short woman with round spectacles peered out. "Can I help you?"

"I have an urgent message I need sent immediately."

The woman reached out her slender fingers. "One gold piece per word."

I hesitated. "For a night message? Surely the lines aren't that busy—"

"Is it urgent or not?" she said, cutting me off.

I ground my teeth. I'd planned to save some of the gold I'd won that night for Leona in case she got hurt again. I reluctantly dropped eight gold coins into the woman's hand.

"The message?" she asked.

"Doctor and off-worlder wiped. No trail. Crotalus."

I turned to leave, and the window slammed shut. The walk back to the center of town felt twice as long. My thoughts kept returning to the devastated look on Leona's face after her encounter with Irving. I wasn't proud of what I'd done—but we needed the money. That's what I kept telling myself. But I couldn't shake the guilt. Not after she had carried me to safety... then risked her own life protecting me from the trigger-happy farm girl.

I reached the hotel just before midnight. The empty lobby was a welcome sight, and I quickly made my way up the creaky stairs. I was hoping Leona would be asleep so we wouldn't have to get into a lengthy discussion about the failed catch.

I quietly unlocked the door and stepped into the dimly lit room. There was an eerie silence. The bed was made, and all of our belongings were neatly tucked away. The door slammed shut, and the cold barrel of a gun pressed into the back of my head.

"I'm going to give you five seconds to answer my question."

Leona's icy voice sent a chill down my spine.

"Why did you impersonate me?"

Chapter 8: Confessions
Everett

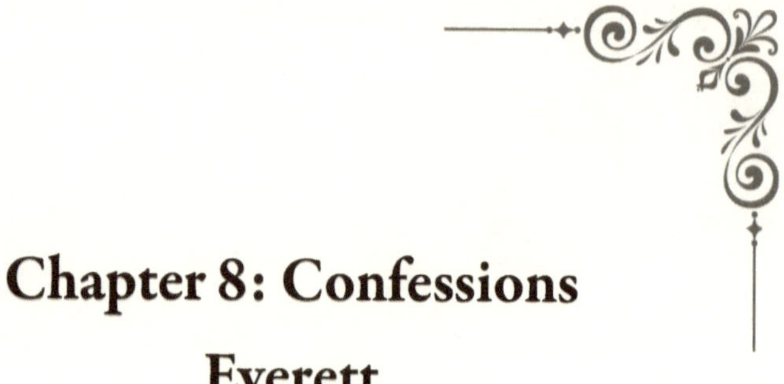

"Why did I impersonate you?" I repeated, stalling for time. "A man in the lobby said he kept bumping into me. First in the alley, then in the hotel." Leona's steady hand held a gun to the back of my skull. "I wasn't in the *alley* tonight."

I slowly turned around. Her dark eyes blazed with anger. She aimed her pistol directly at my forehead. I swallowed hard and decided to go with the truth. For once.

"I thought I could get information out of Irving," I said.

"What kind of information?" she demanded.

"Connections he might have to other trappers. I was trying to find out who we could trust."

"Did he tell you anything?" she asked.

I shook my head. "Nothing. He was just a middleman. No connections."

Leona didn't budge. She continued to stare at me without a word.

"It was wrong of me to take your form," I said sincerely. "I'm sorry."

Leona lowered the gun and pushed past me. "You can sleep on the floor tonight."

I cursed under my breath but didn't argue. She had every right to be upset, and I knew better than to cross her when she was angry.

I loosened my tie and hung my suit jacket in a wooden wardrobe in the corner. Instead of undressing, Leona paced back and forth across the room. Her red gown swished about like it was in a fury as well.

"I apologized," I said. "What more do you want me to say?"

"I don't know, Everett!" She tore off her long black gloves. "You crossed a line, and I'm having a very hard time trusting you."

"What if—" I hesitated. "Would you trust me if I shared my thoughts with you?"

She tossed her silk gloves onto the bed. "I'm not telepathic. You know that."

"I know, but I can teach you to hear me."

"That's impossible."

"Not for shapeshifters. We can project our thoughts to a nontelepathic human—if we've developed a strong connection with them. It just takes practice. And a lot of patience." I removed my tie. "Would you be willing to try?"

Leona bit her lower lip then gave a slight nod. I took the lantern from the side table and sat cross-legged on the floor. Her dress billowed out as she knelt in front of me. She flattened the fabric but couldn't seem to stop fidgeting. Not the reaction I was expecting.

"I won't be able to hear your thoughts," I assured her. "If that's what you're worried about."

"I know," she said quickly. "I'm just trying to get comfortable."

So was I. My telepathic abilities only worked when I lowered my guard. Mentally and emotionally. I half expected her to refuse my offer. But a deeper part of me wanted to regain her trust. I gently took her hands in mine and stared into her deep-brown eyes through the soft light.

"I'm going to tell you something about myself out loud," I said. "Then you tell me something about yourself out loud."

"That's it?" she said skeptically. "We're just going to have a conversation?"

"Yes. That's how it starts. If we're not comfortable talking, there's no way you'll ever be able to hear what I'm thinking."

Leona took in a breath. "All right."

I sat up straighter. "I don't enjoy riding horses because I always spook them."

Leona thought for a moment. "I haven't had a horse of my own since I learned how to drift."

"How old were you?" I asked.

"Seventeen." She paused. "Maude learned way before me."

"I learned how to wield lightning when I was fifteen."

"I almost got struck by lightning when I was out fishing once," Leona said with a slight chuckle. "I was just a kid, but I still caught three fish that day."

"So, you were always a trapper."

She smiled and looked away. "I guess you could say that."

I gently brushed my thumb across the back of her hand, and she met my eyes once more. "Before I became a trapper, I was a range detective."

Her eyes widened. "You were?"

"Yes," I continued. "It was messy work. But I was good at it."

"What made you change jobs?"

"More money."

She grinned broadly. "Of course."

I stared into her eyes. "I'm saving for something very important."

Leona leaned forward. "What?"

I'm saving to purchase my own plot of land, I attempted to speak into her mind.

She continued to stare at me intensely.

"Did you hear me?" I asked.

"No..." She moved closer and held my hands tighter. "Try again. Please."

Land. I've always wanted land of my own. To raise a family.

She took in a shallow breath without breaking her gaze.

"Could you hear me that time?" I asked.

"There was something faint—like a whisper. But I couldn't make it out."

I felt a spark of hope. "That means we're starting to connect."

Leona swayed slightly. "I feel dizzy."

I stood up and offered her my hand. "It may take some time for you to get used to it."

She clasped onto me and slowly rose. One thought had been floating around in my head the entire night, and I could no longer keep it to myself.

"You're very pretty." My jaw snapped shut, and I suppressed my emotions. *Too honest.*

Leona didn't seem to mind. Her fingers curled a little tighter around mine. "You're very handsome."

There should have been awkwardness in the silence that followed. But there wasn't.

Leona turned around. "Do you mind loosening my corset?"

Her flowery perfume filled my senses. I inhaled her pleasant scent as I carefully tugged at the delicate strings of her corset. My fingers worked up the laces, and I could feel her starting to relax. Leona suddenly spun on her heel.

"Please don't do that again without my permission."

"I won't." I doubted there would ever come a time when she would give me permission to impersonate her. "I promise."

"And you're still sleeping on the floor tonight." That time when she said it, there was a hint of playfulness in her voice.

I bowed. "The bed is yours, my lady."

Leona held back a smile. She wiggled out of her corset and left her dress in a pool of fabric on the floor as she unpinned her hair. Her dark locks fell to her bare shoulders.

"Honestly, I didn't think the old man would remember your face," I said. "He was so drunk."

Leona whipped around to face me. "He wasn't an old man. He couldn't have been more than twenty-five."

My stomach turned. "What did he look like?"

"Tall, muscular, blond hair..."

"Was he missing any teeth?" I asked.

Leona frowned and shook her head. "No. None."

"Did he have any distinguishing traits? Anything out of the ordinary?"

"There was a tattoo on his hand," she said. "It looked like four claw marks."

I stood frozen in place. No matter where I tried to hide. No matter how far I tried to run. My past always caught up with me. "We're being stalked... by a shapeshifter."

Chapter 9: Checkout

Leona

Everett's blank stare set me on edge. I rushed to the door of our hotel room and locked it. Somehow it didn't feel like enough protection.

"Why would a shapeshifter be stalking us?" I whispered urgently.

"I—I don't know." Everett went to the window, ensured that it was locked, then drew the curtains. "He's not from my clan."

"Your clan?"

"Yes, we all belong to different clans," he said. "It keeps things orderly."

I clutched my long chemise and peered under the bed. I knew very little about shapeshifters. They were highly secretive. Everett was the first one I'd ever had close contact with. He grabbed my arm, and I stood up.

"I need to do a thorough sweep of the room," he said seriously.

I nodded and climbed onto the bed, out of the way. Everett morphed into his reptilian form and started searching the dark corners of the room. He was so fast, I barely caught glimpses of his dark diamond-shaped markings as he slithered past. After a few minutes, he crept onto the bed and coiled up in front of me.

"Anything?" I asked.

Everett returned to his humanoid form. "Nothing. But I'm going to keep watch tonight. You sleep."

"I doubt I'm going to get any sleep," I said.

"You need to rest." His yellow eyes flickered in the soft light emanating from the lantern. "We'll leave at dawn, before anyone sees us."

I readjusted my thin undergarments and curled up under the covers. My nerves were so frayed, I didn't think I'd ever be able to relax. But when my head hit the feather pillow, exhaustion overtook me.

Everett's light touch on my shoulder a few hours later roused me from my slumber far too soon. I moaned.

"I'm sorry, but we have to get moving," he said urgently.

I hurried out of bed. Everett stood by the window and looked through the small sliver parting the curtains. He was dressed in his usual trapper clothes with a whip tied at his hip.

"Did you sleep at all?" I asked as I gathered my clothes.

"I'm fine."

Everett went back to keeping watch. He was anxious, which made me anxious. I rarely saw anything rattle him.

I quickly buttoned a dark shirt over my camisole and slipped on a pair of wool pants. I shoved my feet into my heavy boots and shook off the layer of dust that was clinging to them. Everett was already packed. I stuffed my red gown and corset into a leather bag and slung it over my shoulder.

"The off-worlder was a dead end," I said, tying my thick hair down with a bandana. "We need to get back to headquarters and find a new lead. There has to be someone else tied to the doctor who knows what happened to my sister."

"I'm ready," Everett said. "I'd like to get out of this town as soon as possible."

I put on my hat, unlocked the door, and peeked down the hallway. There was no noise. Not even the sound of light snoring. We crept down the stairs and into the lobby. The ornate velvet couches were empty, and the front desk clerk was nowhere to be found. Everything was too quiet.

We headed out into the street. Beams of light crept up the board-and-batten sides of the buildings as the sun rose, but I couldn't shake the hollow feeling. Even the air was still. The sooner we were back in the wilderness, the better. I couldn't open a portal in the center of town. The energy was too unstable.

"Something's not right," I whispered to Everett. "We need to get out of here. Fast."

He glanced over his shoulder. "It's only two miles, but if we try to run, we'll only draw attention to ourselves."

"We need a horse."

He lowered his voice. "I don't know if you remember our conversation last night, but me and horses don't get along so well."

"We don't have a choice." I handed him my bag. "It's easier for you to stay out of sight. Head toward the edge of town. I'll find you."

By the time I blinked, Everett was slithering away. I hurried to the livery stable attached to the hotel. I told myself it wasn't stealing. We'd only be borrowing the horse for a short time.

The familiar scent of hay and manure struck me as soon as I entered the stable. I spotted a bay mustang whose rider had left the horse's tack in the stall, and I breathed a sigh of relief. Forgoing the saddle, I quickly bridled the curious creature and led him to the exit.

"Can I help you with something?"

I jumped at the sound of a man's voice behind me. An older gentleman stood holding a bucket of water close to his chest.

"No, thank you," I said politely. "I don't need any help."

I started to lead the mustang out of the stable, but the man ran ahead of me, blocking my path. I backed away, still clutching the reins.

"Why are you leaving in such a hurry?" he asked.

"No hurry," I said. "Now, if you'll excuse me—"

The man smiled. He was missing his two front teeth. My blood went cold.

"What's wrong, drifter?"

He tried to fling the water in my direction, but I kicked the bucket out of his hands. The metal container clattered to the ground, startling the horse. I grabbed hold of the frightened mustang's thick mane, swung myself onto his back, and he bolted out of the stable.

"Your partner's not who you think he is!" the old man shouted.

My heart pounded in my chest. I clung to the reins and frantically searched for any sign of Everett. A high-pitched howl tore through the air. I glanced back to find a coyote standing in place of the old man.

"Everett!" I screamed.

He ran out of an alleyway and appeared a few yards ahead of me. I pulled back on the reins, and the horse staggered to a stop, surrounding us in a plume of dust. Everett grabbed my hand and climbed onto the back of the horse in one swift motion.

The coyote yipped and howled again, charging after us. Everett wrapped his arms around my waist, and I spurred the horse forward with the heels of my boots. The mustang broke into a full gallop. The shapeshifter's shrill barking began to fade in the distance, but I didn't dare look back. Buildings and storefronts became nothing more than a blur.

By the time we reached the outskirts of town, the mustang slowed to a steady trot. My legs were burning, and all the muscles in my abdomen felt like they were on fire from the rough ride.

"Next time I'll steal a carriage," I said when I was finally able to catch my breath.

Everett tightened his grip around my waist. "Let's hope there won't be a next time."

He was still tense. The old man's last words resurfaced in my mind despite my best efforts to block them out. Everyone knew the fastest way to take down trappers was to weaken their partnerships. But I couldn't shake my lingering doubts about Everett.

We reached a wide-open area of the barren land, and I pulled back on the reins. The tired mustang slowed to a stop. Everett dismounted first and quietly backed away, as though still worried he might frighten the horse. I gathered the reins and slid to the ground. Part of me missed riding. I took a step, and my legs almost gave out. The other part of me preferred drifting.

"Thank you," I whispered as I gently scratched the mustang's withers.

"Yes, thank you," Everett said from a distance.

I turned the mustang back in the direction of town, removed the bridle, and let him loose. Everett stood beside me with our bags.

"You're an excellent rider," he said in a sincere voice.

"Thanks."

He patted my shoulder. "It's a shame none of that talent transferred over to your drifting abilities."

I burst out laughing and grabbed a handful of the desert sand. "I have no problem leaving you here for a couple of weeks."

He smiled. "I'd miss you too much."

I stared into his eyes. "Liar."

Everett suddenly turned serious. "We should probably be on our way."

I nodded, and he positioned himself behind me. His entire body was stiff, and I couldn't tell if it was because he hated drifting—or the fact that I had struck a nerve. Either way, drifting in such a state would result in a painful landing.

I shifted slightly. "I think we travel better when you're in your more natural form."

He let go of me. "Are you sure?"

"Yes, I think it's easier. For both of us."

Everett morphed and slowly wrapped himself around me. His cool scales tickled my neck. I refocused my attention and concentrated on our destination. The sand heated up in my palm, and I extended my arm. I closed my eyes, letting out a breath.

An angry growl rumbled against my chest. My eyes shot open. The coyote clamped down on my arm. I screamed. The sand slipped from my fingers, and the ground swallowed us up. We fell through the dark abyss. A strong force dragged us down, and the coyote was flung into the unknown, ripping the flesh off my right arm. Everett squeezed me tighter, as though trying to keep me in one piece. Suddenly, we were propelled forward. I curled into a ball, and we landed in a shallow puddle of mud. I couldn't feel anything. Everett uncoiled himself from me and morphed into his humanoid form.

"Leona!" he cried, lifting me out of the muck.

Blood was pouring from my open wound, but I still felt nothing. My body had gone into shock.

I peered up at Everett. "I might need to see my doctor."

Chapter 10:
Withdrawal

Leona

Every trapper had a favorite doctor. In my case, I had a favorite bank teller.

"We need to get to town," I said, clutching my mangled arm. "I need gold."

Everett tore off what was left of my right sleeve and used it to wrap my wound. Blood seeped into the dark fabric. The coyote bite was horrific.

"Where are we?" Everett asked as he helped me to my feet.

I glanced around the lush woodlands. Light drops of rain trickled down vibrant green leaves and splashed onto my face. We were near the mines.

"We landed about a half mile north of town." I took a step and immediately felt faint. "We need to move quickly before I lose too much blood and I'm not able to walk."

"You're not walking anywhere." Everett scooped me into his strong arms and headed south.

Heat crept up my neck. "Put me down! I'm fine. It's just a scratch!"

Everett ignored me and continued trudging through the muddy forest. I twisted and turned like a petulant child. The thought of showing up at the Agency in such a weakened state was too much for me to bear. I told myself I'd rather be dead. Dead and buried.

"Let me go!" I struggled in vain to be released. "I don't need your help!"

Everett stopped and stared into my eyes. I froze. He was trying to tell me something. I could feel it. But I still couldn't hear him. I looked away.

"You carried me when I needed help," he said softly. "Now I'm carrying you."

I swallowed hard and nodded. I wrapped my good arm around his neck and hung on tightly. Despite the rain, the weather was warm. Everett's steady footsteps almost lulled me to sleep.

"I'm sorry I wasn't fast enough to stop him." Everett spoke up, jolting me awake.

"It wasn't your fault."

He shook his head. "I should have kept my guard up. Members of the Tetred clan are vicious."

"What about your clan?" I asked cautiously. "What are they like?"

He thought for a moment. "Elusive."

"So, your clan defines itself by being secretive?" It was more of a statement than a question.

"No, we just tend to be more—private than most." Twigs and branches snapped under his heavy boots. "That's why I don't open up to just anyone."

"Really? I hadn't noticed." I didn't even attempt to mask my sarcasm. "We've been together for months, and I barely know anything about you."

"Well...you know that I like to play poker."

"That was a shocking discovery," I admitted. "I figured you were too cheap to be a gambler."

He chuckled. "You also know about my former occupation."

"True," I said with a nod.

Everett's piercing yellow eyes met mine. "And you know that I care about you."

My heart started beating faster. "Actually, I didn't know that."

"Oh..." He broke his gaze. "Well, now you do."

A soft spring breeze caressed my cheeks. I curled up tighter against Everett's muscular chest and inhaled his familiar scent. He smelled like expensive leather. I couldn't deny the fact that I found his touch comforting. But a single thought still plagued my mind.

"The shapeshifter said I shouldn't trust you," I blurted out.

Everett didn't flinch. "That's fair."

"Fair?" I rested my head on his shoulder. "I don't understand you."

"You should never trust a shapeshifter," he said in a playful tone.

I closed my eyes. "Especially one with a forked tongue."

He held me closer. "Some women like my tongue."

"Are you trying to change the subject?"

"No, I'm trying to keep you from falling asleep." Everett's voice grew distant. "Leona... Leona?"

My eyes shot open. Everett's arm was wrapped around my waist, holding me upright. We were standing in the bank. Bars and glass separated us from a petite, silver-haired teller. My favorite teller. Maggie. Her wrinkled brow should have caused me alarm, but I was too numb to feel anything.

"Unfortunately, this is the last of your gold, honey." She slid a small velvet bag under a narrow opening. "I'm so sorry."

"It'll be all right." I held the bag to my chest. "*I'll* be all right. Really."

Her frown deepened. "You let me know if there's anything I can do for you. New clothes. A hot meal. A place to rest your head. All you have to do is ask."

"You're the best." My breathing was shallow. "Thanks, Mags."

"Anytime. I'm always here for you."

Maggie reached under the opening, and I clasped onto her frail hand. She gave my fingers a tight squeeze then let me go. I'd taken her up on her offer *many* times before, but this time I wasn't alone. Everett and I shuffled out of the line, ignoring the stares of the other patrons as they eyed my wounds.

"And stay away from trouble, young lady," Maggie called out in her motherly tone.

I couldn't help but crack a small smile. Everett helped me out of the bank and took me to the side of the building, out of view. I slumped to the wet ground, dropping the bag.

My voice was barely above a whisper. "I'm so tired."

Everett knelt beside me, cupped my hands, and poured the gold coins into my palms. He held my hands closed. A cool sensation washed over me as my cells regenerated. My heart beat steadily in my chest, and I could feel the blood rushing through my veins. I took in a rejuvenating breath. The coins slipped through my fingers, and I stood up.

I tore off the soaked bandage and touched my arm. It was completely smooth, but faint teeth marks marred my brown skin. More battle scars. I glanced up to find Everett watching me intently.

I cleared my throat. "Thank you for carrying me."

"You don't have to thank me. We're partners."

I nodded and straightened my shirt. "We have to get to the Agency. We need a bigger catch."

"I hate to remind you," Everett started. "But we've never made a single catch together."

"I know. But that was before. If we work together and partner up with another set of trappers, we can get a bigger payout."

Everett lowered his voice. "Are you sure that's a good idea? You said yourself there's a rift in the Agency."

"We'll just have to be extra cautious. If we look out for each other, we should be safe. It's just one job."

He glanced about. "After the incident on the train, I just don't know."

"I've depleted my savings. We need a big enough job to get us through the next couple of months." I swallowed hard. "If I get injured again..."

He placed a soft hand on my shoulder. "We'll do a job with other trappers. Just this once."

I lightly brushed my fingers across his. "Just this once. I promise."

We headed to the center of town past rows of rugged buildings. Horses splattered us with mud as they trotted on their merry way. Every now and then, a weary miner would glance up and offer a silent greeting.

The Agency was housed in a log structure with a false front. There were no signs on the windows or doors. A typical Headquarters. I knocked lightly and stepped inside. The furniture was sparse. A long desk was set up in the corner of the room, where a secretary sat scribbling away on a piece of paper.

"We need a new assignment."

At the sound of my voice, Amos looked up with a broad smile. His curly hair stood on end, and his oversized suit looked as though it had been handed down to him by a much larger older brother.

"Leona!" Amos ran up and dragged me into a hug, lifting me off the floor. I couldn't help but laugh. He was so much stronger than he looked.

"Be careful!" Everett said. "She's just getting over a coyote bite."

Amos chuckled and put me down. "A little coyote's no match for my favorite regenerating trapper." He nudged me. "Your new partner's a bit overprotective, huh?"

"I have no complaints," I said sweetly.

Amos nodded, catching my meaning. Down the hall, the three doors leading to the back offices were closed... but someone was always listening.

"What can I do for you?" Amos asked, returning to his desk.

"We'd like to take on a bigger assignment," I said. "Do you have anything available?"

Amos rummaged through stacks of tattered papers and retrieved a large envelope. "As a matter of fact, we were looking for another set of trappers to set up an ambush."

"We'll take it," I said without hesitation.

"You haven't even read the details, or consulted with your part—"

"She said we'll take it," Everett cut in.

Amos gave a nod of approval and handed me the envelope. "All the information is inside, including the names of the trappers you'll be working with."

I gave him a quick hug. "I owe you. As always."

A sly smile crept across his lips. "Enjoy the chase."

As soon as we were outside, I tore open the envelope and skimmed through the instructions.

"They want us to capture three smugglers," I said.

"Who are we assigned with?" Everett asked. "Anyone we know?"

I read the names written at the bottom of the page and breathed a sigh of relief. "I know these trappers. They're trustworthy."

"What are their names?" Everett asked.

I handed him the paper. "Otto and Leroy."

Chapter 11: The Gentleman

Everett

*L*eroy. I stood motionless, staring down at the trapper's name. The trapper we would be working with. The same name the off-worlder disclosed to me when I questioned him about Leona's sister.

By the time I looked up, Leona was already heading toward the train station at the edge of the mining town.

"Maybe we should talk about this," I called after her.

"Talk about what?" she asked without breaking her pace. "We already agreed to do the job."

A steady drizzle of rain splattered against my face. I folded the paper with our instructions and stuffed it into my bag. There was no reasoning with her. I resolved to continue with my original plan. If Leroy was the trapper involved in Maude's death, I would simply wipe his memory at the end of our assignment. No one would ever have to know. Especially not Leona.

The thought of keeping yet another secret from her pricked my conscience—what was left of it. She was just starting to trust me. I didn't want things to go back to the way they were.

Despite the nine-hour train ride, I couldn't keep my eyes open long enough to formulate a backup plan. I didn't realize how tired I was until Leona's soft fingertips brushed the side of my face. I woke with a start and found myself sprawled across her lap. I never slept that soundly.

"I'm sorry to wake you," she whispered. "But our stop is next."

I quickly sat up, relieved there was no one else in our compartment. The train rocked and swayed through the valley. The fading sun was a welcome sight after plodding through the rainy forest.

Leona smiled at me. "I didn't know shapeshifters snored so loudly."

"Pardon me. I'm not in the habit of using my partner as a pillow."

Her eyes were soft. "I didn't mind."

I resisted the urge to settle across her warm body again. Getting too comfortable with her would only serve as a distraction. I needed to keep my senses.

The train whistled as we approached the station, and I gathered our belongings.

"I can carry my own bag," Leona insisted.

"I know you can, but if we need to get away quickly, it's faster if I shift with all our gear and you drift."

"We're meeting up with other trappers. Why would we need to get away quickly?"

I tried a different tactic. "Please allow me to carry your bag—as a gentleman."

Leona bit back a grin. She brushed the dirt off her mud-stained pants, dipped into a low curtsy, and exited the compartment. Her high-pitched laughter echoed down the narrow hallway. I paid no attention to her teasing. All that mattered was having a solid escape plan.

As soon as we stepped onto the small platform, an excited voice shouted Leona's name. She rushed over to two men who were waiting by the ticket booth and practically jumped into their arms. I approached. Slowly.

"Otto, Leroy, this is my new partner, Everett," she said as I stood behind her.

"Howdy!" Otto took off his hat and shook my hand. The scraggly fellow was almost vibrating with energy. "We got the telegram from Headquarters saying you two'd be joining us."

Leroy's thick handlebar mustache twitched into a smile, and he clapped me on the back with a heavy hand. "So, you're the lucky son of a gun who got matched with Leona."

"She's one of the best," Otto said. "How many catches have you two racked up?"

Leona gave an indifferent wave, not the least bit put off by the question. "None."

The two trappers exchanged a brief glance.

"Well, we'll rectify that tomorrow, darling." Leroy wrapped his arm around Leona's shoulders and led her toward a covered wagon just beyond the platform.

I hated him already. The thought of wiping his memory no longer bothered me.

"You ain't got no bag?" Otto asked Leona.

"Everett's carrying it," she said.

Leroy stopped in his tracks and met Otto's eyes. They were both silent for a moment.

"He's a gentleman," Leona added.

Leroy looked me up and down. "I reckon so."

"The Agency set you both up good then," Otto said.

"They did..." Her face suddenly lit up. "And you three should get along perfectly as well!"

"Why is that?" I asked.

She beamed. "Because you're all telepathic."

I froze. Both trappers looked me in the eye. I forced my mind to go blank, blocking them from hearing my thoughts.

Leroy shook out his head and casually turned his attention back to Leona. "I think we'll all get along just fine."

I ground my teeth. Telepaths. I would never be able to wipe their memories, and they had the ability to communicate their thoughts to me the second I dropped my guard.

The rough trek to their base camp was a blur. I operated purely on instinct to avoid allowing either of them to slip into my mind. We reached their hideout just before dusk. Large boulders kept us hidden from the main trailway, and barren tree branches loomed overhead, casting shadows over the encampment.

Leona seemed to enjoy catching up with her old friends. Throughout dinner, their conversation was lively, and every now and then she would even try to engage me in a topic. I said very few words.

The night air was warm, but I was grateful for the crackling fire. Staring mindlessly into the flames prevented me from thinking. Leona yawned and gently rested her head on my shoulder. I relaxed slightly. I would have given anything to be back on the train with her. Alone.

Leona doesn't let anyone carry her bags.

My head snapped up at the sound of Leroy's voice in my mind. He locked eyes with me then glanced at Otto.

She don't let no one do nothin' for her, Otto said.

I glared at them.

I suppose it's just a means to an end, Leroy continued. *You pretend to have feelings for her so you can gain her trust.*

I'm not pretending! I projected loudly into their minds.

The two trappers pressed their fingers to their ears. As if it would help. I didn't care if I gave them a splitting headache.

Leroy spoke up. *We were warned someone close to Leona was destroying evidence tied to Maude's murder.*

I clenched my jaw.

Who hired you? he asked.

I remained silent.

Otto shook his head. *He don't even know who he's working for.*

I bristled. My thoughts went back to the day I received the first assignment. At the time, I had convinced myself I was protecting Leona. Wiping the trail meant she would never know the gruesome details surrounding her sister's death, and she could move on with her life. But that wasn't the only reason I took the job.

Leona and I were barely scraping by. We weren't making a single catch. I was approached by an anonymous client who promised to triple my pay if I took the job.

You didn't even begin to question your client's motives? Leroy demanded.

Images of Leona's injuries flooded my mind. *We needed the money.*

Leona stirred beside me. I wrapped my arm around her, and she drifted off to sleep. I stared into Leroy's eyes across the glowing firelight.

Why did you take Maude's body?

A blinding white light flashed into my mind, and my head began to throb. I rubbed my temples. He was blocking his thoughts from me. I blinked a few times and regained my focus.

We still have a job to finish tomorrow, so we'll make a deal with you. Leroy leaned closer. *You stay out of our business, and we'll stay out of yours.*

Otto spoke up. *It won't matter none. Leona's gonna kill him as soon as she finds out what he's done.*

True. But until then... Leroy's sharp eyes flickered. *You keep our secret, we'll keep yours. Agreed?*

I glanced down at Leona, who was sleeping soundly against my chest. "Agreed."

Chapter 12: Ambush

Everett

We were up at dawn. Leroy and Otto positioned themselves on top of a small cliff overlooking the main trail. Leona and I were the bait. She assured me her friends were reliable. I just wanted the job to be done with.

We unhitched their donkey and tipped over the wagon, blocking most of the narrow pathway between the towering rock masses. We were told the smugglers would be hauling a large load. There would be no easy way for them to pass. All that was left to do was wait. And wait.

Leona and I crouched down between the overturned wagon wheels. I glanced up at the cliff. The two trappers had completely concealed themselves within the shrubs and wild vegetation. I was almost impressed.

I projected my thoughts to them. *We're in position.*

We're watching you, Leroy replied.

I stifled my irritation. We had an agreement, but I still didn't trust them.

Leona hid a small bag of gold coins in the front pocket of her faded pants. "Are you all right?"

"I'm fine. I just hate the waiting part."

"Me too." She inched closer and lowered her voice. "What were you all talking about last night?"

"Who? What?"

A sly smile spread across her lips. "Three telepaths sitting around a campfire in complete and utter silence?"

I swallowed hard. "We were talking about your sister."

Leona's face fell. "Oh."

The crisp morning air was still. There was barely a breeze, and it was as though even the birds were afraid to fill our silence.

I continued softly. "From what Leroy said, I gather they were—close?"

"Maude and Leroy had a thing a while back."

"What kind of a thing?"

Her eyes met mine. "A bit more serious than what you and I have going on."

"Leona..." My stomach was in knots. I couldn't keep my dealings a secret forever. Not from her. The longer I waited, the harder it would be to tell her the truth. "There's something you need to know about me."

"What?"

"There's no good way to explain—and I'm not trying to make excuses for what I've done—" I clenched my jaw. Our relationship would never be the same.

"Just come out with it!" Leona whispered impatiently. "You know I hate being in suspense."

Heavy hoofs stomped in the distance.

Y'all need to quit yappin' and get ready! Otto said.

I grabbed Leona's hand. "I promise I'll tell you everything. After this job."

She nodded and squeezed my hand tighter. "Be careful."

I collapsed within myself and shrank down into a form I'd often used in the past. My hands turned wrinkly and grayish-brown, and my back curved into an arch. Taking on such a form limited my strength and movement but worked perfectly as a disguise. Most people were sympathetic to the elderly. Even outlaws.

The smugglers are in sight! Leroy shouted into my mind.

"They're coming," I whispered.

Leona grabbed her knife and looked into my eyes. "You think you can handle this?"

"I *know* I can't."

Leona smirked. Without a moment's hesitation, she slit her wrist. I cringed and looked away as her blood splattered on my face. She slumped to the ground, pretending to be unconscious. I took hold of her injured wrist and smeared some of her blood on my clothes.

A prairie schooner approached. The broad white canvas that stretched over the large wagon concealed the illegal merchandise being transported. We knew very little about the smugglers, but we were told the ringleader went by the name of Sage. I shuffled onto the narrow trail as quickly as my feeble body would allow.

"Please help!" I called out. "My granddaughter's hurt!"

A woman with sharp rectangular features pulled back on the reins, and both horses came to a stop in front of me. She whistled. Two women with rifles jumped out of the back of the wagon and flanked her.

My frail voice quivered. "Our cart overturned, and we need help."

"What are you thinking, Clover?" the ringleader asked.

A woman with long raven hair adjusted her hat as she moved closer to me. She looked me up and down then spat at my feet. "Harmless."

"Poppy?"

The petite woman gave an indifferent shrug. "We'll have to get them out of the way one way or another."

Sage's dark eyes were cold. She didn't budge.

"Please…" My bloody hand trembled as I pointed to where Leona lay motionless. "She's right over there."

Sage jumped down, tied up their horses, and walked over to the wreckage with her posse close behind. She nodded to Poppy. The woman knelt beside Leona and checked her pulse. I held my breath.

Poppy stood and stepped aside. "She's not going to last long."

"Good." Sage kicked Leona in the stomach. Hard.

I flinched.

"That's for delaying our journey." Sage turned to her companions. "Collect their valuables. Shoot the old man."

Suddenly, there was a loud sizzling sound. The horses bolted down the trail, no longer hitched to the covered wagon. The women spun around. I blinked, and their weapons disappeared.

"It's a trap!" Sage screamed.

Leroy appeared holding both rifles. The metal heated up in his palms, turned to ash, and was carried into the wind.

Tie 'em up! Otto spoke into my mind.

I blinked again, and rope appeared in my hands. I shifted into my normal human form and towered over the three outlaws. The struggle was brief. Less than a minute later, the women were bound together on the ground with their hands tied behind their backs.

Coins clattered against the rocky soil as Leona dragged herself to her feet. I let out a sigh of relief. She stumbled over to me, clutching her stomach.

"Are you all right?" I asked.

"She didn't have to kick me so hard," Leona said. "That wasn't nice."

"Ain't nothin' nice about any of them," Otto said as he skidded to a stop beside us.

"I reckon there's *one* nice thing about them." Leroy brushed the dust off his hands. "They'll fetch us a hefty payday."

Sage smiled. "If you can catch us."

"You done been caught, lady!" Otto said.

"Are you sure?" She glanced at Clover.

The woman shook off her hat and twired her long silky hair. A plume of bright-red dust enveloped us. My eyes burned, and I stumbled backward.

Leona coughed. "What was that?"

My head was spinning. Tears blurred my vision and practically blinded me. I wiped them away. The bright-blue sky turned a rusty orange hue.

"I can't feel my hands!" Leroy cried, running in the opposite direction. "My hands are frozen!"

Otto wandered around in circles. "Why's everything so slow?"

"We've got to get out of here. It's not safe." My heart raced as paranoia consumed me. "It's not safe here."

"We all just need to calm down," Leona said.

I pulled her into my arms and whispered in her ear. "They know."

Leona drew back slightly. "Know what?"

"They know about me." My forked tongue slipped out of my mouth and flicked up and down. Her scent was so strong, I could almost taste her. "That's why we can never be together."

She shook her head. "What are you talking about, Everett?"

"I want to be with you..." I gently stroked her soft face. "But you'll never forgive me for what I've done."

I had to kiss her. Just once. I leaned closer, desperate to feel her lips on mine. Leroy slammed into my shoulder and knocked me to the ground. He jumped on top of me.

"Stay away from Maude!" he shouted as he strangled me with both hands.

I struggled to breathe. "That's not Maude, that's Leona!"

"Honestly, I couldn't never tell the two apart," Otto said from a distance.

I punched Leroy in the jaw. He shook off the blow and grabbed my collar, almost ripping my shirt. We wrestled across the rough terrain, sending rocks and patches of dirt flying in all directions. Leona jumped out of the way.

"What's going on?" she yelled in dismay. "Stop fighting! What is wrong with all of you?"

I kneed Leroy in the stomach and staggered to my feet. The world tilted. I swayed. Leona extended her hand to me.

"I already lost her once." Leroy spoke through his teeth. "If you touch her again, I'll kill you."

I reached out to grasp Leona's delicate fingers. A heavy blow struck me in the back of the head. Everything went black.

Chapter 13: Mad Dash

Leona

"Leroy!" I screamed as Everett fell at my feet, unconscious. "What did you do that for?"

"Where's Maude?" Leroy's puzzled frown caused his thick mustache to rumple. "She was just here."

I confiscated the large branch he'd used to hit Everett over the head and tossed it aside. My eyes stung from the cloud of crimson dust Clover had released into the air. The three smugglers were nowhere in sight. The rope used to tie them up had been cut. I snatched up the tattered pieces of yarn that were strewn across the narrow pathway.

"Otto!" I shouted as I knelt over Everett.

The confused trapper stopped walking in circles and sat beside me. I wrapped one end of the rope around Everett's wrist and the other around Otto's left arm. I pulled Leroy down next to us and tied him to Otto's right arm.

"I need you three to stay put until that powder wears off." I grabbed Otto's face and looked into his hazy brown eyes. "Don't let him kill Everett while I'm gone."

"Riiight. No killin' your gentleman friend." Otto spoke slowly. "You ain't gotta worry about nothin'."

I took in a breath and placed the palms of my hands on the cool rocky soil. I needed to feel my surroundings. To taste the air. Absorb the land. The energy. I needed to be able to find my way back. I slow-ly exhaled. My vision became sharp.

I jumped up and took off running, following footprints that veered into the forest. Thin beams of sunlight broke through the dense foliage. I caught a glimpse of Clover's long black hair swaying in the wind as she fled. I darted around the thick pine trees, my heart beating rapidly in time with my swift strides. Clover glanced back, caught sight of me, and sped up. I was faster.

I slammed into Clover from behind, and we hit the ground hard. She rolled on top of me and clawed at my face with her razor-sharp fingernails. My cheeks burned as tiny drops of blood trickled down my skin. I grabbed a fistful of her shiny hair and yanked hard, wrenching her sideways. She yelped. I shifted my weight and pinned her face down in the dirt.

"You'll never take us in alive!" Clover shouted.

I scooped up a handful of soil. "You've clearly underestimated just how broke I am."

I squeezed my legs around her waist and let the warm sand slip through my fingers. The ground swallowed us up. Clover screamed. I probably should have warned her.

The woman was still screaming as the portal hurled us out at the edge of the mining town near Headquarters. I pulled her to her feet.

"I suggest you start walking. I would hate for you to end up drift-ing alone in a portal. Survival rates aren't very high."

Clover didn't have to be told twice. A few minutes later, I shoved her through the Agency's front door. The look of utter shock on Amos's face was the least of my concerns.

"I'll be back with the others."

Poppy put up a solid fight—but after hiking half a mile outside of town to open a portal back to the smugglers' location *and* chasing her down, I wasn't in the mood.

"Why is she unconscious?" Amos shrieked as I flipped her over my shoulder and dropped her in front of his desk.

"Don't ask." I headed out the door.

Sage had the good sense to take the high ground. But she was looking in the wrong direction as I crept up behind her. A twig snapped. She spun around.

"I'm not going to be hauled off by some filthy trapper," she sneered.

"You don't have many options," I said.

"There are always options." She flung canary-yellow powder into my face.

I coughed and backed away. "You should know, I'm not telepath-ic."

A crooked smile curved her lips. "Wait for it."

My vision went black. Completely black. I gasped and stumbled backward, groping about in the darkness. Sage's shrill laughter pierced my ears. I forced myself to stand perfectly still, trying to focus on any other sensation. I started to go numb.

"I'm not dead," I said aloud. "I'm not dead..."

I couldn't hear myself. I couldn't hear anything. My heart raced as panic set in. I was going to die alone. Like Maude...

Maude was always the one taking the lead. She was the one with the plan. She was part of my identity... and I defined myself through her. But she was no longer with me. And I wasn't weak without her. I couldn't be.

I tore my pockets inside out and grabbed a single gold coin. I clenched it in the palm of my hand. Leaves rustled in the distance. I inhaled. My heart rate started to slow down, and light flooded my vision. I glared at Sage as she came into focus.

Her laughter faded. "That's not possible."

I threw the coin aside. "It is if you're a filthy *regenerating* trapper."

Sage's eyes grew wide. I dove into her. We tumbled down the steep hill, careening out of control. The jagged rocks protruding from every angle didn't even slow us down. We hit the bottom, and my battered limbs began to throb. I bit my lip, fighting through the discomfort. Sage tried to scramble away. I jumped onto her back and wrapped my legs around her waist. My entire body weight was barely enough to hold her down.

She struggled under me. "I should have killed you when I had the chance!"

I clenched a mound of gritty sand. "Yes. You should have."

I barely registered the falling sensation. We flew out of the portal and landed directly in front of the Agency's Headquarters. I blinked. I was never that accurate. *Ever*.

Amos came running out of the building. I stood up, dragging Sage off the ground with me.

"I suggest you tie this one up. Tightly."

Drifting back to the location of the original trap felt almost effortless. I landed a few yards away from my three companions. They were sitting in a dazed stupor. I gathered all our belongings from the overturned wagon and rushed over to them.

"There she is!" Otto slurred as I untied him. "I told y'all she'd be fine."

I took Otto back first. His lanky frame was always easy to carry. Even with his mind a little muddled, he seemed to enjoy the rush and excitement of drifting. When we landed at Headquarters, he jumped off my back, turned me around, and stared at me solemnly.

"You're one of the best." His tone was serious. "Don't settle for nothin' less than you deserve."

I didn't know what he meant. I didn't know if *he* even knew what he meant. I'd never seen any of them in such a state of disarray. When I returned to Everett and Leroy, they were sitting across from each other in absolute silence. I wondered what had happened between them while I was gone.

"Leroy, I'll take you next," I said.

He stood up with his bags and gave Everett one final look. Everett nodded but said nothing.

Leroy positioned himself behind me and wrapped both of his arms around my shoulders. "I'm sorry about earlier."

"It's all right."

He squeezed me tighter. "I miss her so much."

"I know." I stifled a prickle of sadness. "I miss her too."

I'd drifted with Leroy many times, but that time felt different. We were different. Connected in a way we had never been before.

With Leroy and Otto safely back at the Agency guarding our catch, I thought I would be able to relax. But I was anxious to get back to Everett. To be with him. He must have felt the same way, because the moment I landed and came to my feet, he was by my side.

"I was so worried about you." Everett frantically examined me. "I'm sorry I wasn't there. Were you hurt? Do you need more gold?"

"I'm all right. Everything's fine."

Everett let out a sigh of relief and wrapped his arms around me. He held me tightly, as though he was afraid to let me go. My anxiety melted away. I rested my head on his chest and allowed myself to be swept under his tender embrace. All the muscles in my body suddenly began to ache.

"I'm so sore from running."

Everett massaged the knots out of my upper back. We rarely had such a calm moment to ourselves. I wasn't eager to leave, but the midafternoon sun was a silent reminder that we couldn't stay forever. I pulled away slightly.

"They'll be expecting us soon."

He peered into my eyes. "They can wait."

I smiled. Everett gently cradled my face and brushed his soft lips against mine. I closed my eyes and slowly kissed him back. My heart beat madly against my chest as he slid his hands down the curves of my body. He drew me closer. A faint whisper echoed in the back of my mind. A single word.

I gasped. "I-I think I heard you say something. Telepathically."

"That's impossible..." Everett began trailing kisses down my neck. "I didn't project my thoughts to you."

I let out a shallow breath. "Well, I think I heard something."

"What did you hear, my darling?" Everett murmured between kisses.

I tilted my head back, savoring his touch. "Crotalus."

Chapter 14: In a Fog

Leona

Everett's body stiffened. "Maybe we should rejoin the others."

My heart sank as he pulled away from me. "What's wrong? Does *Crotalus* mean something to you?"

"No." He smiled and gave me a quick peck on the cheek. "But you're hearing things, it's getting late, and you said before that you're exhausted."

I swallowed hard and nodded. The bright afternoon sun was almost blinding. I turned my back to him and grabbed a handful of sand from the dusty trailway.

"Leona..." He wrapped his arms around me from behind and whispered in my ear, "I still want to be with you. We can pick up where we left off—later."

When I didn't respond, Everett playfully nipped my neck. I smothered a laugh, and he held me closer.

"I suppose we'll have to keep this a bit of a secret from the Agency," he said.

"For now, yes." I leaned back against his muscular chest. "They'll know when they need to know. So, no pet names in front of anyone. Especially not 'darling.'"

Everett chuckled. "You don't like 'darling'?"

"Not particularly," I admitted.

"Then what should I call you?"

"I don't know yet, but we have time to sort it out."

I extended my arm, and the sand heated up in my palm. Everett grabbed our bags, morphed into his reptilian form, and coiled himself around my body. When we drifted back to the Agency, it was the first time I felt completely at ease with Everett, the first time I had no reservations about him. And it was the first time I landed on both feet.

Leroy and Otto sat in the shade under the building's broad wooden canopy. There was a sharp metallic taste in the air. The mining town was so familiar, it was the closest thing I considered to being home. The two trappers jumped to their feet when they caught sight of me approaching with Everett dangling around my neck. Amos burst out of the front door and rushed over to us.

"You survived! And your partner's still intact, albeit a little limp," he joked.

Everett slithered to the ground and morphed into his humanoid form, towering over Amos. He glared at the clerk but didn't say a word.

"What's the status?" I asked.

"The file is closed," Amos said. "You will all receive payment within the next two days."

Leroy spoke up. "The three of us agreed, and we'd like our portion to go to Leona."

I shook my head. "I couldn't possibly—"

"It's already been decided on account of what you've done," Otto said. "We want you to have it."

Everett nodded firmly. "We all agreed."

I was at a loss for words.

"I'll make sure everything's arranged!" Amos said cheerfully. "Now, if you all don't mind, I need to speak to Leona. Privately."

My eyes widened. "Amos, no!"

Amos slammed the palms of his hands into my chest, throwing me backward. I gasped for breath as time seemed to stand still. A translucent bubble formed around me and Amos. I hung suspended in midair, dreading the inevitable drop. A haze of sapphire-blue fog enveloped us. Time sped up. I squeezed my eyes shut. Pain shot through my back as I landed with a heavy thud. I stared up through the mist. Amos leaned over me with a broad grin. He offered his hand.

"You couldn't have waited until we were alone?" I demanded as he helped me up. "They just stopped hallucinating."

"A little five-second jump back in time is only going to cause a minor headache. Nothing serious," he assured me. "Besides, I'm not sure your overprotective partner would give us a minute to ourselves without getting suspicious."

Amos wasn't wrong, but I certainly wasn't going to tell him that.

Everyone in the vicinity of the bubble appeared to be frozen in time. Amos stood on his toes and looked up into Everett's intense yellow eyes. "I don't like him."

I smiled. "I'm certain the feeling is mutual."

"You seem to have warmed up to him."

I kept my emotions in check. "He's a good trapper, and he watches out for me."

"Do you want me to cancel the inquiries?"

"No." I didn't hesitate. "I still want to know why we were assigned together."

"You think it was a setup?" he asked.

My entire body ached, and I rubbed my sore shoulders. "I don't know anymore. Nothing about our match makes sense. We're not compatible on any level except—"

He raised an eyebrow. "Except?"

"Nothing."

Amos tilted his head. "Could it be that my favorite regenerating trapper is falling for her partner?"

I wrapped my arm around his bony shoulders. "If you tell anyone, I will kill you. I promise you that."

Amos burst into laughter, and I couldn't hold back a chuckle. I let go of him and straightened his baggy suit.

"You're going to have to do *so* much paperwork," Amos teased.

"There's nothing to report." I glanced up at Everett. "Yet."

Amos was quiet for a while. "Are you sure you want me to dig deeper? You might not like what I find."

"I want answers... I need answers." I was almost afraid to ask my next question. "Have you gotten any new leads about my sister?"

"I received one tip."

My mood instantly lifted.

"It's been a struggle to find information." Amos handed me a sealed envelope from inside his jacket. "And the people who were once talking aren't anymore."

"Why not?"

"I don't know." He shook his head. "People are acting like they have no memory of her. It's bizarre."

I hid the envelope in the back pocket of my pants and pulled Amos in for a tight hug. "Without you, I'd be in total darkness. I appreciate everything you've done for me."

"Don't mention it." Amos moved me back into position next to Everett. "Be careful out there. Both of you."

"We will," I said. "Thank you again."

Amos took in a deep breath then clapped his hands together. The time bubble collapsed around us. When the fog lifted, I smiled at him.

"I'll make sure everything's arranged!" Amos said cheerfully. He winked at me.

Chapter 15: Pillow Talk

Everett

Amos winked at Leona. I shook out my throbbing head. My brain felt like it was in a fog. I couldn't remember the last thing he said.

Leona rubbed her shoulders. "I need a bath and a bed."

"I'm ready to leave whenever you are." I glanced up to find Amos watching me intently. Part of me wanted to hiss at the obnoxious clerk, but I knew Leona wouldn't take kindly to me getting defensive. Especially not with her close friend.

I quietly gave Leona space to say her goodbyes to Leroy and Otto, then we headed out into the wilderness. We drifted to a remote boomtown next to Crystal Rock Canyon, and Leona checked us into a hotel we'd stayed in a few times before. I almost wished she'd chosen an unfamiliar location. Then I would have had an excuse to survey the surrounding area, instead of pretending to be preoccupied with the floorboards to prevent myself from getting too close to her.

The smuggler's powder had left me completely unguarded. I couldn't afford to let my subconscious thoughts slip into Leona's mind again. Not before I told her what I'd done.

A small bed and end table were tucked in the corner of our hotel room. Leona lay across the mattress in her thin undergarments. Candlelight flickered against the soft features of her face. Her eyes were closed, and her long eyelashes fanned out over her smooth skin. She was so beautiful. I refocused my attention to the floorboards. The dull, lifeless floorboards.

"Are you going to pace all night?" Leona asked without opening her eyes.

I stopped midstep. "I can shift, if you'd like."

"No, then your rattling will keep me awake," she said playfully. "Is there a reason you're suddenly avoiding me?"

"I'm not avoiding you."

Leona curled onto her side and watched me. "It's a good thing we're not playing poker. You can't seem to bluff tonight."

I smiled and crossed the room. Leona chuckled as I climbed on top of her and kissed her cheek. She smelled like lavender.

I stared into her eyes. "I can *always* bluff."

"Is that right?" She traced a finger down the seven diamond-shaped markings on my neck. "Did it hurt when you got those?"

"No," I said flatly. "I didn't feel a thing."

"Do you like my friends?"

"I love your friends. Especially Amos."

Leona suppressed a grin. "Do I make you nervous?"

I leaned closer and started kissing her neck. "Nothing makes me nervous."

Leona ran her fingers through my short curly hair. "Are you afraid I'll find out about your past?"

I frowned and backed away. "What do you mean by that?"

"I'm sorry, you might not even remember." Leona sat up and leaned against the wall. "When you were hallucinating, you said I'll never be able to forgive you for what you've done."

My heart pounded in my chest. "I remember..."

"If this is about when you were a range detective, you don't have to tell me anything. We all have things in our past we'd like to forget."

I shook my head. "I've made a lot of enemies over the years, and I don't want you to be one of them."

She gently cradled my face in her hand. "Why would you even think that?"

I pulled her hand away. "Because you don't know me."

"I'm trying to get to know you, Everett," she said sharply. "But you make it very difficult for anyone to get close to you."

"Maybe this was a mistake." I got to my feet. "Maybe we should go back to how things were before."

"That's fine." Leona blew out the candle with a forceful puff. Pale-blue moonlight flooded the room through the window. She slipped under the covers and rolled onto her side. Her back was to me. "You can sleep on the floor tonight."

I ground my teeth. Without thinking, I threw on my boots, grabbed my bag, and left the room. The hotel clerk took one look at me and choked back his pleasantries as I charged through the lobby. Clouds covered Aadar's moons, and a musky smell filled the night air. I was halfway across town before I even bothered to slow down. I had no business being with Leona. But I wanted her with every fiber of my being... and I couldn't keep lying to her. She deserved better.

By the time I reached the telegraph office at the train depot, I knew exactly what I had to do. The elderly operator yawned and rubbed his bloodshot eyes as I approached.

"I need to send a message. Quickly." I scrawled the words across a tattered piece of paper.

Terminate contract. Crotalus.

I paid the fee and started pacing outside of the office window.

"We'll contact you as soon as there's a reply," the older gentleman said.

"I'll wait."

"Are you sure?" He glanced at his pocket watch. "It could be hours until you hear back."

A drop of rain splattered in front of me. "I have nowhere else to be."

The reply came back less than an hour later.

Contract will terminate when Pyro is wiped. Last job. Silver.

Last job. I destroyed the telegram. I would do the job—on my terms. The sky opened up. I darted back to the hotel, unable to escape the torrential downpour in time. My soggy boots sloshed against the hardwood floors as I made my way down the hall to our bedroom. Despite my efforts to creep back into the room quietly, Leona stirred. She didn't say a word, but I knew she was still awake.

I spoke softly. "When I got my markings, the pain was so bad I couldn't shift for a week. I dislike Amos, and I don't particularly care for your other friends—but they love you, and that's all that matters to me."

Leona rolled over and looked at me through the moonlit room. Cool drops of water trickled down my neck and seeped into my matted cotton shirt. I adjusted my collar slightly.

"And yes, being with you like this makes me very nervous."

"Good." She turned her back to me once more. "Then you and I can both be nervous together."

Rain pattered against the glass window. I stripped out of my wet clothes and put on clean linens. The bed was warm from Leona's body heat as I climbed in next to her. Her familiar scent had a calming effect over me. I wrapped my arm around her waist, and she laced her fingers between mine.

"What is it about your past you'd like to forget?" I asked into the darkness.

Leona was quiet for a while. "The night my sister died. I wasn't there."

"Where were you?"

Leona shook her head. "I said I'd like to forget it."

"I'm sorry." I held her closer. "I didn't mean to upset you."

"It's all right. I'll have closure soon enough." She curled up against my chest. "I think I know who started the fire."

Chapter 16: Stormy Weather

Everett

Leona had a lead. There was no way I could talk her out of following it. The next morning, she wasted little time getting dressed, and I knew better than to raise her suspicions by stalling.

"I've never been to Onyx Springs, so there's no way for us to drift there." Leona hiked up her long, flowing skirt, strapped a leather knife holster to her thigh, and slipped her blade into its scabbard. My eyes traced the lines down her perfectly sculpted legs. She caught me watching her and flipped her dress back down with a smirk. "Are you listening?"

Barely. I rolled up my damp clothes and packed them in my bag. "What are our options?"

"We'll have to travel by stagecoach."

I didn't tell her I was relieved. Drifting with Leona was getting easier, but I still hated crossing through portals. The possibility of being left in the void, completely out of control, was unnerving.

The small town was bustling with activity. A warm breeze carried the sweet scent of iron and steel from the local blacksmith shop as we made our way down to the station. My boots sank into stiff patches of dried mud. The roads weren't ideal for traveling, but the brilliant rays of sunlight and clear skies were reassuring.

We were the first passengers to arrive. The fare was exorbitant, but I didn't care. Anything was better than drifting. I escorted Leona to the horse-drawn coach and offered her my hand. She bit back a grin, accepted my polite gesture, and climbed inside. The space was cramped. I slid into the back row next to her and placed our bags on my lap.

Leona stared out the open window, keeping a watchful eye on passersby. She seemed anxious to depart. I was in no rush. The light, flowery fragrance she wore almost made me forget where we were going—or why. She was becoming one of my favorite distractions. The stagecoach would soon be filled to capacity, and we wouldn't have another private moment to ourselves for days.

"Leona?"

She glanced at me, and I stole a kiss. Her lips curved into a smile against mine, and she kissed me back. I could taste the peppermint from her morning tea. A heavy thud rocked the stagecoach. We broke away. Luggage was loaded into the boot. Roughly.

"I'm sorry," I whispered. "I know we're not supposed to openly engage in displays of affection."

"The Agency has some of the most arbitrary rules," she muttered.

I inhaled her scent and resisted the urge to kiss her again. "I agree, but I don't think either of us wants to get reassigned right now."

She sat up straighter and cleared her throat. "No. We don't."

"All aboard to Onyx Springs!" the slender stagecoach driver bellowed at the top of her lungs.

A burly shopkeeper slid onto the bench, cramming me next to Leona. Before long the coach was stuffed with the six remaining passengers, and the journey began.

The first day was marked with sand. Dry, hot sand. Relentless winds whipped it into our faces. We breathed it in until it practically filled our lungs. On the second day, the trail took us through steep rugged terrain. The stagecoach jolted us about, rattling our bones. By the fourth day, we appeared to be on a smooth pathway. Sitting beside Leona with her head resting against my shoulder was almost pleasant. Then the rain started. On the seventh day, I couldn't remember what it felt like to be dry.

The rainstorm continued throughout the night. Leona and I found ourselves pushing the stagecoach with a disgruntled ranch hand and an irate tanner while the driver guided her team of horses through the thick sludge. Lanterns swayed inside the empty compartment. The downpour muffled the complaints of our fellow travelers as they plodded alongside us.

"Just a few more days of this and we'll never have to take this route again," Leona said cheerfully as we attempted to dislodge the stubborn coach from a small ditch.

A pool of rainwater poured down from the brim of my hat in front of my face. "I never thought I'd say this, but I'm so glad I'm sleeping with a drifter."

"Sleeping *next* to a drifter," she corrected me. "I don't let anybody in that easily."

I reached down and squeezed her firm, round bottom. "Begging your pardon, my lady."

Leona laughed. She slapped my hand away, and I tried not to chuckle. I threw my weight against the heavy stagecoach once more. The faster we got out of the mud, the faster I could be sleeping next to her.

There was a slight shift in the atmosphere. The hair on the back of my neck stood on end. My hearing became sharper, and a familiar tingling sensation spread through my fingers.

"Get down!" I dragged Leona to the ground, shielding her with my body.

Lightning struck a nearby tree. Shrill screams from the terrified passengers pierced my eardrums. A roll of thunder added to the chaos. I jumped to my feet, grabbed my whip, and swung it overhead. A bolt of lightning struck the leather cord and shot down my arm. I absorbed the electricity, allowing the warm current to run through my veins.

A deep rumble of thunder startled the horses. The storm was getting closer. The driver jumped down from the box, twirling her long, narrow whip. She absorbed a lightning bolt before it could harm the frightened creatures.

"Everybody inside!" she shouted.

The passengers scrambled to take cover. I swept Leona up out of the muck and lifted her into the stagecoach with the others. She quickly shut the door and tried to calm everyone down as streaks of lightning illuminated the dark sky. Someone somewhere had disrupted the balance of nature. Aadar was angry.

"You take that side, and I'll take this one!" the driver yelled over the rain and thunder. Her swift, steady motions rivaled my own.

I swung my whip, drawing the energy to me and away from the passengers. My only concern was keeping everyone safe... keeping Leona safe.

The storm raged on for the better part of an hour. I let out a sigh of relief when the thunder finally echoed far off in the distance and a gentle mist settled over us. My mouth tasted like I had been chewing tinfoil. I ignored the common side effect and carefully wrapped my whip as I approached the driver. She stood staring up into the heavens. Four markings were inked on the inside of her wrist. Four identical stars.

"Thanks for your help." She looked over the markings on my neck. "I don't often cross paths with members of the Diamas clan."

"You probably do without realizing it," I said.

"True." She went back to examining the sky. "A member of my clan is looking for you."

My back tightened. "I know."

"He said you were traveling with a partner." She glanced at the passengers huddled inside the stagecoach and lowered her voice. "I didn't realize she was that kind of a partner."

"We work together."

"I noticed." The driver's light-green eyes danced in the moonlight. "Quite intimately, it would seem."

I cursed my foolish indiscretion. I shouldn't have kissed Leona. Not in public.

"If Hiram finds out, he'll do worse things to her than just taking a bite out of her arm. Much worse."

"What do you want?" I asked.

"From you? Nothing. I don't allow clan matters to interfere with my employer's affairs."

"We all have to make a living," I said dryly.

"Exactly, and blood feuds are bad for business." She adjusted the reins on the lead horses. "However, if we cross paths under any other circumstance, I will not be so gracious."

My heart was racing, but I kept my voice neutral. "Understood."

She flashed me a smile, baring her sharp, canine-like fangs. "All aboard."

Chapter 17:
Pleasantries

Leona

Bathing in a cold river never felt so rejuvenating. I scrubbed layer after layer of grime and dirt from my body. And my hair. And my nails.

Everett was off surveying the area—yet again. He hadn't been the same since the night of the storm. He'd become overly cautious, almost paranoid. As soon as we'd arrived in Onyx Springs, we bought provisions and supplies to set up camp a few miles outside of town. Everett didn't want to be anywhere near other people. After spending fifteen days crammed inside a stagecoach with seven other strangers, I couldn't blame him. But something felt off.

I leaned back and let the smooth current wash over me. The river was unlike anything I'd ever seen. From above, it appeared completely black. I dipped under the inky surface and opened my eyes to crystal clear water. Fish scattered as I spun and twirled, relishing the cool sensation against my bare skin. When I emerged, Everett was standing at the shoreline with his back to me. I brushed my thick curly hair away from my face.

"Are you coming in?" I asked.

"When you're done." He hung a fresh towel on the branch of a tree. "I thought you might want some privacy."

I stifled my disappointment. "Thank you."

"You're welcome."

Pleasantries. He was hiding something. Before I could say another word, he morphed into his reptilian form and disappeared into the woods. I slowly swam to the river's edge. Jagged rocks pressed into the soles of my feet as I climbed out of the water. The towel was warm, as though it had been heated on hot stones. I wrapped it around my shivering body and hurried to our campsite.

Flames crackled in a small firepit. Everett was nowhere in sight, but he had folded my new clothes in a neat pile near my bag. I dried myself by the fire and quickly dressed. The dark cotton shirt and wool pants were slightly large for my frame, but I was used to altering my clothes to fit. Sunlight dotted the forest floor, and I went about gathering cooking utensils to make breakfast.

By the time Everett returned, the meaty aroma of fried bacon was wafting through the air. I served him a plate with fresh biscuits and poured him a cup of coffee. I felt bad everything was cooked, but I explained that I didn't know how to prepare anything else for him. Everett seemed moved by my thoughtfulness and didn't have a single complaint throughout the meal. More pleasantries ensued.

"Are you going to tell me what's bothering you, or would you like me to guess?" I asked, taking a seat beside him on the ground.

Everett sipped his coffee. "Guess."

"You're worried someone might find us, and you don't want to be caught in a compromising position."

He tilted his head. "Close."

"There's an easy solution." I took his coffee cup, placed it aside, and straddled his lap. "We just make sure we're quick about it."

"That's not—"

I kissed him. Talking was the last thing on my mind. Everett wrapped his arms around me, and his damp clothes seeped into mine. After two weeks, I was desperate to taste him. My tongue brushed against his. He clung to me so tightly, I could feel his heart racing. A bird squawked overhead. Everett pulled away.

"This is the problem," he said, exasperated.

I glanced up at the canopy of burnt-orange leaves. "I can't do anything about the birds watching us."

"That's not what I'm talking about." He lifted me off his lap in one swift motion and jumped to his feet. "I can't communicate with you."

"Yes. That seems to be a recurring theme in our relationship."

"What if it wasn't a bird?" he demanded, kicking up pebbles and twigs as he paced. "What if it was someone out to hurt you? I could be trying to warn you of danger, and you'd never know."

"What are you saying?"

He stopped short. "I'm saying I want us to practice—again."

"Telepathy?"

He nodded.

"All right... if it's that important to you."

"It is," he said firmly.

I sat on my knees, and Everett settled in front of me. Nothing about telepathy felt natural to me. Knowing I *had* to be open with Everett in order for it to work made me tense. He took my hands in his and peered into my eyes. We were both silent for a while. I could tell he was searching for something to talk about. Some sort of light conversation.

"The weather here is nice," I said randomly.

"Very nice."

Silence. I didn't know what made me more uncomfortable—pretending to act normal or watching Everett pretending to act normal.

"The trip here was long, but it wasn't all bad," Everett said finally. "The sunset on the last night was beautiful."

"It was," I agreed. "This is a beautiful region."

Everett seemed to relax a little. "This would be a nice place to settle down."

"I suppose so." I chuckled at the thought. "Drifters don't really settle down."

He frowned. "No?"

"The idea of being stuck in one place makes me feel suffocated," I admitted. "Like being buried alive."

Everett repositioned himself slightly. "Of course. Not right away... but I would like to settle down eventually. The very first day I was old enough to work, I started saving to buy land."

"I didn't know that." I swallowed hard. "Do you want children?"

He stared into my eyes. "Could you hear me?"

"No..." I inched closer. His penetrating gaze held me transfixed. There was a murmur in the back of my mind. A voice that wasn't my own. I suddenly felt lightheaded, and I closed my eyes.

"Are you all right?" he asked. "Do you want to stop?"

"No, we can keep trying."

Everett's fingers tightened around mine. I wanted us to have a deeper connection, but I was almost afraid of his reply. The voice grew distant until it was nothing more than a fading whisper. He slowly let go of my hands.

"I'm sorry this isn't working," I said.

Everett shook his head. "It's not you."

The fire sputtered and popped. I picked up his cup and took a sip of the cold, bitter coffee.

"Maybe try kissing me again," I suggested. "I swear I can hear you when you do that."

"Leona, I need you to be serious."

I handed him back his cup. "Then why don't you tell me what's really going on?"

Everett downed the rest of the coffee. "The shapeshifter survived the drift. He's looking for me."

My eyebrows shot up. "How do you know?"

"The stagecoach driver is a member of his clan."

"Why is he after you?" I asked.

"Because I did something... something terrible to him in the past."

I didn't want to know the answer to my next question. "What did you do?"

"I erased someone from his life." Everett met my eyes. "Someone he cared about."

My stomach dropped. "Erased?"

"In the worst possible way." His voice cracked. "Not a day goes by that I don't regret what I've done."

"That's what you didn't want me to know?"

He grabbed my hands once more. "I've never spoken about this to anyone."

Everett entrusted me with his past. A part of himself that he didn't share with anyone else.

"The night Maude died, we'd had a fight." The words came out so quickly, I wasn't able to stop them. "We were out of money, and I accidentally let one of our catches get away. She was mad. We both said some hurtful things. I drifted away and left her there alone. When I returned, the building had been set on fire. I found her body—what was left of it—but someone was waiting for me."

"What happened?"

"I was attacked by a man with a scar down his right eye. He left me for dead." I took in a breath. "It's taken me two years to track him down. He's the reason we're here. He's the one who started the fire."

Chapter 18: Close Encounters

Leona

Everett's silence was disconcerting. The lingering aroma of coffee and bacon hung in the air from breakfast, and I fought the urge to clean up. Anything to avoid the awkwardness. I'd finally opened up and told him one of the most personal experiences in my life, and he just sat there. Staring at me. He squeezed my hand, and I suddenly realized what he was trying to do.

I spoke softly. "I still can't hear you."

"I said, I'm sorry you went through all of that alone. I wish I could have been there for you." He brushed his thumb across the back of my hand. "Does the man who started the fire know you're looking for him?"

"I doubt it. Amos is very discreet."

"Amos?" Everett's forehead wrinkled. "He's the one who gave you the lead?"

"Of course. He's been helping me piece together clues since the beginning."

Everett nodded but said nothing. A stiff breeze stirred up fallen leaves, swirling them around us.

"You don't trust Amos," I said.

"I don't trust *anyone*." He leaned closer and tenderly kissed my lips. "Except you."

I smiled. "I should hope so. I'm your partner."

"Not just my partner," he whispered. "You're my companion and my friend."

I closed my eyes. He held me close and gently rubbed my back. I loved being in his arms. Safe and secure. His muscles began to relax, and he nuzzled against my neck.

"No one else knows we're here?" he murmured.

My eyes slowly opened, and I pulled away. "No. Why do you ask?"

He shook his head. "No reason."

"You wouldn't ask me something like that for no reason."

Auburn leaves rustled behind him as the wind picked up. "I just want to be sure we're not walking into a trap."

"What kind of a—" I saw the spark before I registered the sound of the gunshot. I yanked Everett's vest so hard the fibers almost ripped. He collapsed on top of me. A bullet flew over his head and ricocheted off a nearby log. The stump splintered, sending shards of wood in all directions. We scrambled for cover. Another shot rang out.

"Drift!" Everett shouted. He morphed and slithered deeper into the forest toward the assailant. His menacing rattle sent a chill down my spine.

A bullet whipped past my face, grazing my cheek. Tears stung my eyes. I grabbed a fistful of dirt. My heart was pounding. I couldn't focus. The warm soil slipped through my fingers. Then I was gone. Leaving Everett behind.

The portal catapulted me across a barren desert, and I landed face down in the blazing-hot sand. Gritty particles clung to my sore, bloody cheek. I squinted through blinding rays of sunlight and dragged myself to my feet, taking a moment to get my bearings. Oppressive heat radiated off massive dunes that extended as far as the eye could see. The Valley of Sand. Half a world away from civilization. And my partner.

No one survived the valley. There was no water, no recognizable landmarks, and no way to get out. Except by drifting. I scooped up tiny grains of sand, closed my eyes, and let out a calming breath. I had to get back to Everett. Nothing else mattered.

I landed by the river—but I was too far north. Our campsite was over two miles away. I broke into a sprint, dusting dead autumn leaves with sand that fell from the folds of my clothes. I was going so fast I almost didn't hear the heavy, uneven footsteps coming toward me. A man in a tattered sack coat staggered into a tree trunk, clutching his arm. I froze. He glanced up. A deep jagged scar ran down his right eye. My blood turned cold.

I still bore the wounds of our first encounter. The night of the fire. The night he'd tried to butcher me. Images flashed into my mind. The axe. My severed hand. His blade lodged in my stomach. The glint in his eye as he watched me dying—as though he was enjoying it.

"It's you..." The choked words barely escaped my throat.

He stared at me with a blank expression. "Who are you?"

I stepped closer, unable to keep my voice from shaking. "You know who I am."

"You gotta help me." The man peered over his shoulder. "I was attacked by a rattlesnake."

Rage threatened to consume me. "You started the fire that killed my sister."

"I-I've never seen you before in my life," he stammered.

"You're lying!" I grabbed him by his collar. "You have seen me. You tried to kill me! My name is Leona!"

"Leona...?" A look of sheer terror came over him. "Trapper Leona?"

"Yes," I forced out through my teeth.

"I can't go near you." He stumbled backward, away from me. "I can't go anywhere near you, or I'll have to terminate myself."

"What are you talking about?"

The man pulled out a revolver and held it to his head. "I don't belong here."

"Wait!"

I lunged. He squeezed the trigger. A stray bullet flew into the air. I wrestled the weapon out of his cold hands and backhanded him across the jaw with the butt of his gun. He slumped to the ground. Blood stained his yellow teeth and trickled down the corner of his crooked mouth. He stared up at me in a dazed stupor.

"Who are you?" he asked.

"I'm—" I paused and knelt in front of him. "A drifter passing through. Do you remember what happened to you?"

He rubbed his head. "I was attacked."

"By a rattlesnake," I filled in.

"Not just any snake. He's ruthless." The man grabbed hold of my arm. "Can you get me out of here, drifter?"

"Possibly." I unhooked his bony fingers and reminded myself to stay calm. "If you answer my questions."

"What kind of questions?" he asked.

"I'm investigating a murder."

Faint rattling echoed in the distance, and he nervously glanced about. "Ask me anything. I'll be straight with you. As long as you can get me out."

"Two years ago, the remains of a woman were found in a burned-down barn. A man matching your description was seen there that night."

"I don't know anything about a woman's remains. But I was hired to burn down a barn once." He blew out a rancid breath. "If I'd known then they were gonna send someone to cover up the trail and wipe me out, I'd have never done it."

"What do you mean, cover up the trail?"

"They're trying to make it look like it never happened. Destroying all the evidence and erasing everyone connected to the incident." He shifted slightly. "They told me I would be safe if I did one last job."

"Who hired you?" I pressed.

The rattling was getting louder. "Silver."

"Where can I find him?" I asked.

"Silver's not the type of person you want to go searching for." He shook his head. "If you're not careful, you'll end up on the list to be terminated... like us."

I frowned. "Like who?"

"Me..." His finger trembled as he pointed over my shoulder. "And Crotalus."

Chapter 19: Crotalus

Everett

Leona broke me. The way she stared up at me. Like I was a stranger—someone she didn't know. I hated myself for what I'd done to her.

"Crotalus?" Her voice cracked when she spoke. "That's the name you go by?"

"Leona, I—"

"L-Leona?" the disheveled man sitting beside her stammered. "Trapper Leona? I can't go anywhere near you, or I'll have to terminate myself."

He scrambled for a revolver that was cast aside on a bed of leaves. I shifted, sprang in his direction, and bit his arm. He wailed in agony. My fangs sank deep into his skin, and I released my venom. He fell silent.

I shifted back into human form and knelt in front of him. "You will have no memory of how you ended up in the woods today. Go stand by the river for the next five hours and don't look back."

The feeble-minded agent rose, turned on his heel, and marched toward the river without a word.

Leona was staring at me again. The wind blew grains of sand from a small wound on her cheek. I reached out to touch her face. She backed away.

"Who are you?" she whispered in dismay.

I shook my head. "I wanted to tell you—"

"Tell me what? That you've been lying to me? That your real name is Crotalus?"

I spoke calmly. "You know my real name."

"Do I?" Leona jumped to her feet. "You've been secretly destroying the evidence of my sister's murder?"

I slowly stood up. "Yes. What that man said was true. I was hired by Silver to wipe the trail."

Leona's entire body was shaking. "You've been working against me for two years?"

"I didn't take the job until after we became partners."

"That makes it worse!" she screamed.

"I know. You're right."

"I trusted you!"

"I know."

"You were supposed to be on my side!"

"You're right."

"If you agree with me one more time, I will shoot you in the face!"

I clamped my jaw shut. Leona began pacing. I could barely understand the list of grievances she rattled off to herself as she tried to make sense of everything.

It was wrong, what I did. I should have told you. I never meant to hurt you. Attempting to project my thoughts into Leona's mind was futile, but I sincerely wanted her to know the depth of my feelings. Of my remorse. If only she could hear me...

"This was all a lie." Leona stopped suddenly, and her dark eyes met mine. "You never cared about me."

She could have stabbed me in the heart with a dagger—that would have hurt less. "My feelings for you were real. They always were."

"I don't believe a single word that comes out of your mouth."

"I'm sorry..." I whispered. "I'm so very sorry."

"That means nothing to me." Leona picked up a handful of soil. A single tear rolled down her cheek. "*You* mean nothing to me."

The sand fell through her fingers, the ground opened up, and she was gone. Her scent faded. I was alone. Again.

The arduous journey back through the expansive territory was pure torture, but not because of the wretched stagecoach. Two minutes without Leona left me feeling slightly tense. After two days, I couldn't shake the restlessness. And after two weeks, I was completely on edge. The whiskey couldn't even calm my nerves.

The Establishment was full of trappers—it was the one saloon where Agency rules didn't apply. Trappers could catch up, gather information, and brawl. There was always a brawl. Leona visited the saloon whenever she was searching for leads... or whenever she was angry. I sat at the crowded bar, hoping in vain I might catch a glimpse of her.

A heavy hand clapped me on the back. I spun around and hissed. Venom dripped from my extended fangs. The Knox brothers stepped back with their arms raised.

"Whoa, there! Fred and I thought we'd buy you a drink on account of you being here without your partner," Harvey said.

I downed what was left in my glass. The bartender poured us all a round, and the flannel-loving brothers wedged themselves beside me. Either they reeked of whiskey, or I did.

"Did you and Leona have a fight or something?" Fred asked.

"None of your business," I snapped.

"It must have been pretty bad," Harvey said. "No one's seen or heard from her in a month."

I lowered my drink. "Leona didn't come back here?"

A bottle shattered behind us, and a skirmish broke out between two hotheads with telekinesis abilities. Their partners jumped into the mayhem, inciting a full-blown bar fight.

"The Willis cousins are at it again!" Harvey announced gleefully.

Fred rubbed his hands together. "I was hoping there would be a tussle!"

The Knox brothers charged into the fray. A large round table floated in midair, with two trappers wrestling on top and one haplessly dangling over the edge. I shook my head and went back to dulling my emotions. Trappers had entirely too much pent-up aggression.

An eerie presence pricked my senses. Someone was watching me. I glanced up at the broad mirror hanging behind the bartender. Amos stood in the doorway of the saloon. Our eyes locked. He flashed me a condescending smile. I spun around, and he vanished.

My barstool toppled over as I rushed after him. The scuffle spilled out of the Establishment, and no one seemed to notice me chasing the scrawny clerk into the night. Amos made a sharp right and fled down a dark alleyway. I had him cornered.

"I know who you are!" I shouted as I caught sight of him.

He stopped short and slowly faced me. "And just who am I?"

"You're the one behind the whole operation." I stepped closer. "*Silver.*"

He peered around me. "Do you really think this is the smartest place to be having this conversation?"

Before I could open my mouth, he sprinted toward me and slammed into my chest, shoulder first. I flew backward. A clear dome encased us, and everything slowed to a crawl. I dangled in the air, unable to move. The bright light of Aadar's moons was obstructed by a cloud of blue smoke. The world sped up. I dropped, landed hard on my back, and struggled to catch my breath.

Amos stood over me. "For someone with so many secrets, you're not entirely discreet."

I pushed myself upright, too groggy to stand. "What did you do to me?"

"It's just a time bubble." He knelt in front of me with a smirk. "But it usually hits telepaths a little harder."

"Terminate my contract," I snarled. "I'm done working for you."

He sighed. "You never worked for me."

"You're lying! Everything points to you. You were the only one who knew where we were going. The only one who could have led Pyro to us." I grabbed his oversized suit jacket. "You set me up!"

"I'm so glad Leona got away from you." Amos stared into my eyes through the moonlit haze. "I never liked you, Everett. But I didn't peg you as a traitor."

I slowly released my grip. "She told you?"

"Yeah. You know. Loyalty. Friendship. That's what Leona and I have." He straightened his suit jacket. "I know they're difficult concepts for you to understand."

"You're not Silver..."

"The guy who hired you to destroy the evidence? No. But I'm pretty sure Leona's looking for him."

"Where can I find her?" I asked.

Amos laughed. "She doesn't want anything to do with you. Let her go."

"Please. I need to talk to her. Just once."

Amos's face was stone-cold. "No."

His loyalty was to Leona. As mine should have been. "Will you at least give her a message?"

He nodded slightly.

"Please tell her I'm still carrying her bag." I swallowed hard. "But I will leave it where we spent our first night together."

Chapter 20: Under the Falls

Everett

Three days. I waited for Leona under the waterfall for three days. The steady sound of rushing water muffled the outside world but couldn't quiet my troubled mind. I'd been wrong about so many things. Amos. Silver. The assignment. But I didn't want to be wrong about Leona. She would come. I hoped she would come.

A fire burned brightly and warmed the musty cave as the sun began to set. I picked up Leona's scent long before she approached, and I quickly got to my feet. She slowly emerged from the darkness. A single braid was twisted over her shoulder, and her dark-green gown swayed silently with each deliberate step. Neither of us spoke a word. I wasn't expecting to be immobilized by the mere sight of her.

"Where's my bag?" Leona asked.

I slid the leather pack off my shoulder and handed it to her. She flung it into the fire. I remained motionless. The charred material smelled like burnt hair as flames licked the surface of the bag. Her icy stare shattered what was left of my nerves.

"Why did you ask me to come here, Everett?"

I straightened my back. "I've never been completely honest with you, and I know you still want answers. Ask me anything, and I'll tell you the truth."

Her sardonic laughter echoed throughout the hollow space. "You're a liar. Why do you think I'd believe anything you said to me now?"

"Because I've already lost you." I spoke the words I never wanted to admit out loud.

Torrents of water poured over the falls, causing a light mist to float into the cave. Leona stayed near the fire—where she would be dry. At any moment, she could drift away, and I'd never see her again.

"I have nothing to hide," I said softly.

She folded her arms across her chest. "Is Everett your real name?"

"Yes," I replied. "Crotalus is my alias."

"You have the ability to erase memories?"

I nodded. "And sometimes I can temporarily cloud a person's mind."

Leona shifted slightly. "How many people did you erase for this job?"

"Eleven."

Her eyebrows shot up. "Eleven people have absolutely no memory of Maude?"

"And no memory of you," I added.

Her arms fell to her side. "You just go around messing with people's minds at will?"

I spoke calmly. "No. I'm very deliberate."

"That's why the off-worlder didn't recognize me?" Her fists were clenched. "You'd gotten to him before I could question him?"

"Yes. I wiped him in the alleyway," I admitted. "The others were a little easier. Very few attempted to flee."

Leona walked back and forth in front of the fire. "You did all of that right under my nose?"

"No, sometimes you were sleeping."

"It's an expression!" she shouted.

My efforts to be open and honest had gotten the better of me. "Sorry."

Leona mumbled something to herself and began rummaging through my campsite on her hands and knees. Pots and pans clattered against the rocky ground. She was either avoiding eye-contact, or my confession had put her in a destructive mood. Probably a little of both.

"How much did they pay you?" Leona asked.

"A lot."

She stopped and looked up at me. "How much?"

"Triple my yearly pay."

Leona crawled over to my sleeping area and shook out the blankets. "So, that's how much our partnership was worth to you?"

"I didn't know you when I took the job." I restacked the battered cookware. "Really know you, I mean."

"You don't know me now," she spat.

I didn't dispute her. The distance between us was worse than the night we met... and that cold night was indelibly marked in my mind.

"This is why I don't trust people." Leona tore open my bag and tossed my clothes out one by one. "I'm better off alone."

"I'm not trying to make excuses for my—what exactly are you looking for?"

Leona huffed. "I'm hungry! I've been so mad at you I haven't eaten in days."

"I don't have the type of food you eat here."

She stood up and wiped her hands on her dress. "I'll be back in a couple of hours."

"Wait!" I refolded a wool blanket and placed it by the fire. "Please stay. I'll get you something."

She yanked up the fabric of her long skirt and settled across the stiff blanket. I shifted and slithered out of the cave just as the last light of the day began to fade. I never hunted so quickly in all my life. Leona devoured the rabbit meat. And the squirrel meat. And the fish. I half expected her to ask me for some bison. Fortunately, she was satiated after an hour.

"You make me so angry." Leona tossed a small pile of bones into the fire. "I just want to choke you."

"I know."

She glared at me.

"Sorry," I said.

"Amos didn't want me to come here," Leona said.

He was always watching out for her. "Understandable."

There was a chill in the air as darkness enveloped the forest. Leona stared into the brilliant firelight. Her soft voice could barely be heard over the sound of water cascading down from the rapids above.

"I want to know *everything*."

I started from the beginning. The night Silver contacted me. Names of all the people I was assigned to wipe. The secret telegraphs. Covert dealings with other agents. Leona listened in silence. She scarcely moved an inch. By the time I finished, the fire was beginning to dwindle, and my dry throat was hoarse from speaking.

"Is there anything else you want to know?" I asked.

Her dark eyes peered into mine. "Have you ever used your mind control on me?"

"No." The very thought of such a violation against her turned my stomach. "Never."

Leona didn't break her gaze. "Why did you really ask me to come here?"

"Because... I know how we can trap Silver."

Chapter 21: Silver and Gold

Leona

I was waiting for Everett. Like a fool. Apparently, I hadn't learned my lesson. When we were on good terms, he'd jokingly warned me not to trust a shapeshifter. I didn't listen, and I paid the price for it.

The cramped quarters of our dank hotel room left little space for me to expel the negative energy building inside me. I tried pacing but kept knocking into the edge of the bed. Meditation left me in a rage as my thoughts kept returning to the night under the waterfall when Everett divulged all the secrets he'd been hiding from me. And there wasn't anything in the room I could break. Not even a window.

I plopped down on the bed, ignoring the sharp odor of sweat emanating from the stained sheets. A small lantern barely lit the room but effectively hid the dirt and grime caked onto the walls and floors. Trying *not* to think only reminded me of what Everett had done to his victims. Wiping their memories. Altering their consciousness. He'd sworn he had never used his mind control abilities on me, but part of me didn't believe him. I'd fallen for him so fast... and something was still pulling me toward him. Something I couldn't explain.

The door swung open, and I jumped to my feet. Everett locked the door and did a quick visual sweep of the room. His yellow eyes darted over to me.

"Well? What did you send?" I asked impatiently.

Everett ripped open his bag and handed me a tattered piece of paper. I snatched it up and scanned the message scrawled in his handwriting.

L met Pyro before wipe was complete. She knows. Everything. Terminating L. Crotalus.

I folded the paper. "What was the reply?"

He handed me a telegram.

Touch L and I will hunt you down myself. Silver.

My throat tightened. "How did you respond?"

"No loose ends. Crotalus."

I stared down at the telegram. "So, you kill me, lure Silver out—"

"We trap Silver. It's just that simple."

I bit back my irritation. There was nothing simple about dying.

"I have to destroy the correspondence," Everett said. "It's not wise to have anything that can be traced back to me."

He tore the messages to pieces, lit a match, and set them on fire. His swift actions seemed like second nature, causing my anger to flare again.

"Clearly you've done this before," I said through clenched teeth.

"Many, many times."

I turned away from him. After all the lies he'd told me, his sudden honesty was becoming infuriating.

"Leona..." Everett spoke softly. "We can't do this when you're upset. You said yourself it's too danger—"

I spun on my heel. "I know what I said!"

The room fell silent. Everett didn't take his eyes from me. He didn't have to say what we were both thinking. We needed each other for the plan to work.

I blew out a breath. "I'm sorry. It just makes me nervous, no matter how many times I do it."

"What would you like me to do?" he asked.

"I don't know." Every inch of my body was tense. "I have to be in a relaxed state."

He was quiet for a while. "I could do it while you're asleep."

"No, that would be much worse." My hands started shaking, and I flattened the front of my forest-green skirt in an effort to hide them. "This is the only way."

"Are you sure?"

I nodded and turned around. Everett approached and gently rested his hand on my shoulder. Panic rose in my chest. I stepped out of his reach and faced him.

"L-last time, you did it from behind." My voice was quivering. "I couldn't prepare myself."

"We could try a different way," he suggested. "Maybe sitting down so you're more comfortable?"

I pushed my hair back. "Yes, that would be better."

Everett sat on the edge of the bed without a word. I stifled my apprehension and positioned myself across his lap. He wrapped his arms around me.

"Tell me what you need," Everett whispered.

I'd hoped our forced proximity would create some sort of awkward barrier between us—something to prove how incompatible we truly were. Instead, I felt secure, and a calm washed over me. "Can you talk to me? Until it's over?"

"Yes..." He lightly stroked my neck with the tips of his fingers. "Let me know when you're ready."

I exhaled, slowing my heart rate. "I'm ready."

Everett leaned closer, and I suddenly realized how much I'd missed him. His touch. His smell. His soft breath on my skin. I closed my eyes. A sharp burst of pain tore through my neck. I gasped. Everett's fangs plunged deeper into my throat. A warm sensation spread through my body. His venom. My limbs started to go numb, and I had difficulty breathing.

Everett lifted his head and stared into my eyes. "Everything's going to be all right."

Tears filled my eyes, but I couldn't speak.

"I'm here." Everett gently lay me across the bed and hovered over me. "I'm not going anywhere."

I blinked, but my vision remained blurry.

He brushed the tears away from my cheeks. "You're not alone."

My pulse was weakening. The darkness set in.

"I promise I'll never leave you..." Everett's voice was fading.

I hated dying—but we needed each other.

The light clanking of metal was so familiar... but I couldn't place the sound. My heavy eyelids refused to open, and after a few moments, I stopped trying. A ragged breath entered my lungs. The clanking stopped.

I could identify the smells. Fresh-cut flowers. Wood burning. Gold. Silver. My eyes shot open, and I sat upright on a plush narrow couch. I could barely choke out a word as I stared at the petite gray-haired woman sitting across from me in an ornate upholstered armchair, knitting.

"Maggie...?"

"Hi, honey." My favorite teller—the woman who had treated me better than my own mother—flashed me a warm smile. "I'm so glad you're finally awake."

I touched my hand to my heart. It was beating. Wide cuff bracelets were wrapped around my wrists, depleted of gold. I didn't know whose black gown I was wearing, but the expensive fabric clung tightly to my sore, aching body.

"What happened? What's going on?"

"You died," Maggie said calmly. "And now you're in my home."

Lavish furniture adorned the luxuriant parlor, and sheer curtains covered the tall windows. I had no idea how much time had passed, but it was well into the night. A warm fire blazed in the fireplace, and opulent floral arrangements filled decorative vases on the mantel.

Maggie continued knitting. "It took me two days to get to you. That *man* left you to rot in that filthy hotel room. But there's no need to worry. I'll take care of him myself."

"Everett?"

"I can't say I ever liked him." Maggie's frail, wrinkled fingers moved with practiced ease. "Sure, he'll get the job done, but the minute he starts asking questions, he completely loses focus."

I swallowed hard. "You're Silver."

She lowered her knitting needles. "Yes, that is a name I go by from time to time."

"B-but why would you reawaken me now?" I demanded. "You were the one who sent that madman—that butcher—to kill me!"

Maggie sighed heavily. "Pyro was only supposed to scare you."

"Scare me?" I cried.

"He went too far. Which is why Crotalus was sent to wipe him." Maggie pulled out a silver pistol and aimed it over my shoulder. "But you couldn't even get that right, could you?"

I froze. Everett was completely silent, but I could feel him standing behind me.

"You probably don't know this about me, but I was a trapper for forty years." Maggie leaned back with her finger curled around the trigger. "I know when I'm the catch."

I opened my mouth, but nothing came out.

"Back in my day, when we set a trap, we didn't let our catch live." Maggie's eyes turned cold. "I still don't."

"No!" I shrieked.

She pulled the trigger. I jumped up. A familiar warmth spread through my abdomen. Blood pooled in my mouth and spilled down my chin. I turned around. Everett and Maggie were screaming at each other—but I couldn't hear them. The ringing in my ears was too loud. I fell backward. Light began to fade. Darkness consumed me.

"Leona, please wake up!" Everett whispered urgently.

A wall of cold water flew into my face. I sat up, gasping for breath. Everett was in front of me, holding a large vase, while Maggie paced behind him.

"I said *lightly* splash her with water!" Maggie kicked Everett in his side with her tiny boot. "Not douse her with the entire container!"

A large handful of coins dropped through my fingers and fell to the thick woven carpet. My heart rate stabilized. I felt no pain... but the dress I was wearing was soaked in blood.

Maggie knelt beside me and gently patted my cheek. "Leona, this is why you're always running out of money. You can't keep taking bullets for random strangers and partners you hardly know."

I met Everett's eyes. He remained still.

"Unless..." Maggie slowly stood up. "He's more than your partner."

"He's not," I said quickly. A little too quickly.

She frowned. "This certainly complicates matters."

The walls shuddered slightly. I held my breath. I'd felt a similar sensation once before. On the train. The tremors stopped.

Maggie inhaled sharply. "There was a reason I had him scheduled for termination."

Everett glared up at her. "And why is that?"

"Because you're too careless." Maggie's small hands balled into fists. "You led them right to her."

Chapter 22: Gold and Silver

Leona

The energy in the room shifted. Even in my reawakened state, with my senses still dull, I could feel it. And I wasn't the only one. Everett's back stiffened. All the furniture in Maggie's parlor started shaking, and my aching body vibrated uncontrollably. I knew what was coming. *They* were coming.

The windows blew out, sending shards of glass flying in all directions. I couldn't move fast enough. Everett and Maggie crouched over me, shielding me from the debris. Ada, Agnes, and the two Knox brothers teleported into the parlor with their arms wrapped tightly together in a chain. The quaking stopped. Everett swept me off the floor in one quick motion and stepped behind Maggie's diminutive frame.

"What are you doing in my home?" Maggie demanded.

They unlinked their arms, and Ada stepped forward. She was no taller than Maggie, but the stocky trapper was more than double her weight and solid muscle. "You know why we came."

I clenched the silky black fabric of my gown to prevent my hands from shaking. My vision was blurry from the venom still coursing through my body, but I could see the vehemence in the four trappers' eyes. They wanted me dead. And I was dressed for my own funeral.

"I already warned you," Maggie said. "You can have any other drifter. Not Leona."

Harvey tugged on his suspenders. "We don't want any trouble with you, Mags. Just hand her over."

I'm so sorry. This is all my fault. Everett's voice echoed in my mind. *I was so focused on leaving a trail for Silver, I completely disregarded potential threats. I never meant to put you in danger. You're the only woman I've ever truly—*

My head snapped up, and I met his eyes.

You can hear me? he asked in disbelief.

I nodded slightly, trying to keep the shock from showing on my face.

Maggie spoke up. "You all know where my loyalty lies. Nothing has changed."

Can you drift? Everett asked.

My dress was soaked, and cool drops of water slid down my neck from my wet hair as I shook my head.

Everett's jaw clenched. *I'm sorry for dousing you with water. It had been over an hour, and you just weren't waking up. I panicked.*

I frowned. Reawakening always distorted my sense of time. Hours felt like mere seconds. But the gunshot wound coupled with the venom weakened my ability to heal.

"Don't make this any more difficult than it has to be," Fredrick said to Maggie.

We have to get you out of here. You're in no condition to fight. Everett glanced at the rogue trappers. *Maggie and I can hold them off. If you can get to a window, run. Don't look back.*

"Does your leader know you're here?" Maggie asked, still blocking me from their path.

Agnes's long face twisted into a scowl, and she snorted. "We don't have a leader."

Maggie cocked her head to the side. "Are you sure about that?"

The four trappers exchanged nervous glances. Windows flanked both sides of the fireplace, and I inched closer to the hearth.

Maggie's voice was deceptively sweet. "You have five seconds to get out of my home before I—"

"Before you what, *Grandma*?" Fredrick scoffed.

Maggie's entire body suddenly turned silver, from the tip of her gray hair down to the laces of her pointy boots. Firelight flickered off her shiny reflection. Her eyes were soulless. She grabbed her knitting needles from the armchair, dashed forward, and stabbed Fredrick in the neck.

"Fred!" Harvey cried in horror as his brother's blood splattered across his face.

Ada pounced on top of Maggie. The room shook, and they disappeared. Everett morphed, sprang across the floor, and bit Harvey's arm. He wailed in agony. Agnes cursed loudly and charged at me.

Maggie's gun! Everett's voice echoed.

I grabbed Maggie's pistol from the floor and fired a shot in Agnes's direction. She dove behind the long couch. The walls trembled. Ada and Maggie fell from the ceiling, smashed through the velvet couch, and landed so hard their bodies left an imprint in the wood floor.

Leona, get out of here! Everett shouted into my mind.

I rushed to the broken window. Jagged pieces of glass sliced the palms of my hands and snagged my dress as I scrambled out of the opening. I ran into the night. I had no idea where I was going. But I ran.

Moonlight shined down on barren hills that stretched as far as the eye could see, but I couldn't get my bearings. I stared up at the night sky without breaking my stride. The constellations weren't making any sense. For the first time in my life, I was completely and utterly lost. Maude had left me. Everett had betrayed me. And Maggie... Maggie...

Blood trickled down my fingers, and my shredded gown flapped in the wind. My heart pounded in my chest. The side of my face started to feel slightly numb. Everett's venom. It was still inside me.

The ground rumbled, and I skidded to a stop. Ada, Agnes, and Harvey teleported in front of me. I darted in the opposite direction and slammed into an invisible wall. Harvey. I spun around to find his arms outstretched. His force field was strong. I crouched down and snatched up a handful of dirt. Nothing happened. I was still too wet to drift. Agnes stretched long, her limbs extending over twenty feet. She grabbed my wrists and dragged me kicking and screaming across the dry terrain. They surrounded me. Harvey forced my hands up over my head, and Ada held down my legs. My eyes stung as I struggled against them. Harvey leaned over me. Liquid oozed from the bite marks on his swollen face.

"You're not even going to beg?" he sneered.

I choked back the sob that was threatening to escape my throat.

Agnes slid a dagger from her belt. "She never does."

I closed my eyes, and tears slipped down my cheeks. They were going to cut out my heart. I was going to die. My body would be nothing more than a shell. Hollow and empty. The same way I felt.

We're coming, Leona...

My eyes shot open. The hair on my body stood on end. I let out a breath. Clouds formed overhead as Maggie and Everett appeared in the distance. The three trappers jumped to their feet and scattered in different directions. Ada tried to teleport. Everett cracked his whip and sent a bolt of lightning through Maggie. She thrust out her hand, and an electric current shot through her fingers, stopping Ada dead in her tracks. She convulsed violently and dropped to the ground, unconscious. Agnes went down next. The light was blinding. Harvey managed to erect a force field around himself. Briefly. The smell of burned flesh permeated the air.

Maggie looked at me through the moonlight. Her body slowly returned to normal. In place of the silver armor was her skin. Her bruised and battered skin. She collapsed into Everett's arms.

"Maggie!" I jumped up and ran to her side.

"I don't have much longer." Her frail voice cracked, and something inside of me broke. "But you must believe me when I tell you, I did it to protect you both."

"Did what?" I cried.

Maggie grasped my hand. "I loved you both like my own daughters, and you deserve to know the truth."

I leaned closer to hear the whispered words from Maggie's dying breath.

"Your sister... is alive."

Chapter 23: Breaking Point

Everett

Leona's silence was excruciating. She said nothing as we buried Maggie at the first light of dawn. She barely made a sound when I sucked the last of my venom from her bloodstream. And when we drifted, she wouldn't tell me where we were going.

We stood staring at the charred remains of a barn. Most of the roof was missing, and the back end of the building lay in a heap of rubble. Black soot clung to every visible surface, and the hollow structure cast ominous shadows across the desolate farmland. Nothing good came out of that place.

A biting wind went straight through my clothes and pricked my skin. I couldn't imagine how cold Leona must have been in her tattered sleeveless gown, but she didn't flinch. I wanted to offer her my vest, but she scarcely acknowledged my presence. She was lost in her own thoughts. I had no idea what to say to her. The trap for Silver had gone completely awry, rogue trappers were determined to wipe her out, and Maggie's final words weighed heavily between us.

"Everyone lies to me."

The sound of Leona's voice startled me, and I glanced over at her. Her expression was blank. I remained still. She entered the barn, picked up a rusty pitchfork, and started smashing everything in sight. Splintered wood and debris went flying in all directions. The screaming came next. I thought I was prepared for any reaction she might have. I wasn't. Her high-pitched wailing left me shaken, and I didn't know if she was crying tears of sadness or anger.

"I can't trust anyone!" Leona shrieked.

She started beating into one of the wooden pillars that had actually survived the fire. I was certain she was trying to get what was left of the roof to collapse on top of her. Fortunately, I'd had the forethought to secure extra gold. There would be no more dying. Not on my watch.

The pitchfork snapped in half. Leona let out a bloodcurdling scream and hurled the broken pieces across the barn. Critters scattered but remained out of sight. She slumped to her knees and stared into nothingness. I slowly made my way over to her and sat beside her on the cold ground.

"They wanted me to beg for my life," Leona whispered.

I listened without a word. There was no way I could express how deeply I regretted leading the other trappers to her. They were relentless in their attack. Had it not been for Maggie, they would have overpowered us in a matter of seconds. Her abilities had been stronger than any others I'd encountered in the past.

"Even if I'd been able to drift," Leona continued, "I didn't know where to go."

I nodded but couldn't fully comprehend her statement. I had a difficult time grasping the mindset of drifters. The idea of not having a solid place to return to in times of crisis was foreign to me. Even I had a home—of sorts.

She wiped away tears that were drying on her face. "I've spent so long trying to track down everyone responsible for Maude's murder—death—I don't even know what direction to follow."

"What led you back to this place?" I asked, cautiously.

"Honestly, I don't even know what I'm doing here." Leona scooped up a handful of dry, crumbling dirt. "As if Maude's suddenly going to reappear from the ashes."

Wishful thinking on both our parts. Reuniting the twin sisters would put an end to a traumatic chapter in their lives. I wanted nothing more than for Leona to be happy and at peace.

She tossed the soil aside and brushed her hands off on her frayed skirt. "Why would Maggie keep something like that a secret from me?"

I had no answers. Maggie was an enigma to me. The more I learned about her, the less I knew. During our very brief time together, when she wasn't trying to kill me, there was only one thing that I was certain of about her.

"Maggie truly cared about you," I said softly.

Beams of sunlight shined down through the gaping hole in the roof but did little to thwart the icy chill in the air.

"Maggie got us through some of the roughest times in our early trapping days. She was always patching us up and mending our clothes. She'd even lend us money when we came up short... or if one of us had a fatal accident." Leona swallowed hard. "I just can't believe she's gone."

"I'm so sorry."

"If it hadn't been for you and Maggie—" Leona shook her head. "I suppose it's safe to say we're even."

Fighting off the rogue trappers couldn't compare to the fact that Leona literally took a bullet for me, and it gnawed at me that she thought I only did it to settle some sort of personal debt. Like we were keeping score. "You know that's not why I fought for you."

"Then why did you?"

Because I'm in love with you. I was almost grateful our telepathic connection had been severed the moment I drew my venom out of her. I was too exhausted to guard my thoughts.

"Because I'm your partner," I said aloud.

"Partner..." she echoed. "What does that even mean anymore?"

"It means I'm not going to leave you to fend off rogue trappers by yourself." My voice was calm but firm. "It means if you need space, I'll give you space. But I won't ever be far away."

Leona wouldn't look at me. I gently took her hand in mine.

"And it means I'll do everything in my power to help you find your sister."

She peered at me through weary eyes. "I don't even know where to start."

"I do." The wind picked up, and I wrapped my vest around Leona's shivering body. "We start with Leroy."

Chapter 24: Down and Dirty

Everett

Leroy was a difficult man to track down. Leona and I drifted so many times, I stopped keeping count. We finally received a tip that Leroy and Otto were celebrating their latest catch in a wealthy gold mining town just west of the Wispy Mountains. The last place I expected to find Leroy was attending a public theater performance, but when we spotted him amongst a flood of patrons exiting an elaborate playhouse, I breathed a sigh of relief. I wasn't sure how much more drifting I could handle.

"Leroy!" Leona called over the crowd.

Leroy and Otto turned, caught sight of her, and rushed over to us. Our plain trapper clothing looked out of place compared to their fancy three-piece suits. Otto's tie and jacket were slightly askew, but Leroy appeared perfectly at ease dressed and out in society.

"What a surprise!" Leroy gave Leona a peck on the cheek. "I didn't expect to see you here, darling."

"Did y'all catch the performance?" Otto was barely able to stand still. "It was a lot to sit through, but I ain't never seen such good actors."

"I'm fairly certain I've seen better acting in real life." Leona smiled sweetly. "From people I consider to be my friends."

Leroy's mustache twitched, and he locked eyes with me. *You told her?*

I had to. I glanced at Otto. *Things have gotten a bit more complicated than when we last met.*

What's complicated about keeping your mouth shut? Otto asked.

I thought we had an agreement! Leroy projected loudly into my mind.

Otto shook his head. *Can't trust nobody these days.*

"Out loud, please," Leona said.

I spoke up. "Maude's alive."

Leroy punched me in the jaw, and I immediately regretted being so blunt. "Don't toy with me, Everett!"

"It's true," Leona said.

"Can't be." Otto's eyes bulged out of his head. "Can't be."

I spit the blood out of my mouth. "Believe me, it came as a shock to us as well."

"T-that's not possible," Leroy stammered.

"Everett said you were the one who paid the off-worlder for Maude's—*remains*." Leona's voice was surprisingly calm, but I could tell she was holding back her emotions. "I want to know what you did with them."

"Otto..." Leroy squared his shoulders and yanked on his suit jacket lapels. "Get the shovels."

The journey to Maude's burial site took us four days by railway and half a day's trek through the Golden Forest. No one spoke much—out loud. On the train, Leona was at the point of exhaustion, and she asked me to fill Leroy and Otto in on everything that had happened since we parted company. I told them about the trap for Silver. And about the rogue trappers. And Maggie. Communicating telepathically allowed Leona to sleep, and we were able to speak candidly. A little too candidly. By the time we disembarked, I was so used to the constant chatter that I didn't bother trying to block either of them from my thoughts.

It's not much farther now. Leroy led the way through a maze of stately birch trees. Thin white bark contrasted with the brilliant-yellow foliage, and a blanket of golden leaves covered the forest floor.

I still can't believe Leona didn't kill you after all the lies you done told, Otto said.

She wanted to, I admitted. *More than once.*

You think this will get you back in her good graces? Leroy asked.

No. I glanced at Leona. On top of all the supplies each of us were hauling, she'd insisted on carrying her own bag. *I'm not sure she'll ever forgive me.*

They're both stubborn like that, Leroy said, almost to himself. *Leona and Maude...*

Leroy hadn't said her name during the entire trip. Not even once. Otto and I remained quiet. The yellow leaves beneath our boots suddenly began shimmering. They swirled into the air and whipped around us, tickling our faces. Aadar was in a whimsical mood, but none of us shared her lighthearted disposition in that solemn moment.

We hiked the rest of the way in silence and reached a small clearing just after midday. Leroy lingered behind, carefully inspecting a specific tree. He ran his fingers down the peeling bark, and I noticed a small symbol burned into the trunk. A crescent moon with two vertical lines down the center. Leroy turned on his heel, counted out twelve paces from the tree line, then stuck his shovel in the ground.

"We're here."

"You're certain?" Leona stood beside him and spoke softly. "Why did you choose to bury her here?"

Leroy's gaze was distant. "This was where I told Maude that I loved her for the first time."

Leona raised her eyes to mine then stared down at the ground. It didn't seem right. Digging up their past. But I kept those thoughts to myself.

Do you really believe what Maggie said? Leroy asked me.

I don't know. But if there is a chance that Maude is alive, Leona won't be able to rest until she finds her.

Then we'd better get started. Otto picked up the shovel. "This will be a whole lot faster if y'all let me do this alone."

We stepped back. Otto closed his eyes and took in a breath. I blinked. Mounds of dirt flew into our faces. Apparently, we hadn't stepped back far enough. The three of us scrambled out of the way as thick clumps of soil rained down over us. None of us were fast enough. I wiped the grime from my eyes. Dirt covered every inch of my clothing. I could barely catch a glimpse of Otto, but the pit grew wider... and wider.

Suddenly, Otto stopped. He climbed out of the large crater and handed Leroy a square wooden box.

Leroy's voice was low. "Maude said that if anything ever happened to her, she wanted this to be her final resting place. A place where we were once happy together. She made me promise to do everything in my power to return her to this exact location."

Leroy slowly gave the box to Leona. She stood motionless. I placed a reassuring hand on her shoulder. With shaking fingers, Leona carefully pried open the box. It was empty—except for a small handwritten note: *I'm sorry.*

Chapter 25: Tea Time

Leona

I'm sorry? I stared down at the tiny note in my sister's handwriting. Everett, Leroy, and Otto were mute. I wondered if they were even speaking to one another telepathically, as they had been the entire trip. My body was numb. I grasped the note and handed the heavy wooden box back to Leroy.

"Sorry? She's sorry?" Leroy's hands glowed fiery red, and the box turned to ash in his palms. "What does she mean?"

Everett's brow was furrowed, but he said nothing.

"That don't make no sense." Otto leaned on his shovel and shifted from side to side. He was always jittery, but even more so when emotions were high. "There ain't no way Maude was able to regenerate. No way. No how."

"Otto, can you refill the hole, so no one falls in?" I asked.

"What difference does it make if someone falls in?" Leroy blurted out as Otto quickly got to work. "Who cares about some random hole in the middle of nowhere?"

"I just need to think…" I muttered.

Otto became a mere blur as heaps of dirt disappeared from the high mound. I had trouble making sense of the chaotic thoughts racing through my mind. Maude was alive. Maggie had helped her. She'd managed to stay hidden. From all of us. But Maude knew someone would come looking for her. That *we* would come looking for her.

"I don't believe any of this!" Leroy shouted. "How could she do this to me?"

Everett's bright-yellow eyes turned to slits, and he gave Leroy a stern look.

"No, Everett, I will not be quiet!" Leroy stopped suddenly. "You couldn't possibly understand. It would be like you mourning Leona's death, dealing with the pain of having someone you love ripped away from you, only to find—"

"I said I understand why you're upset." Everett spoke through clenched teeth. "But now is not the time to get wrapped up in your own head."

Everett glanced at me, but I avoided his gaze. I couldn't think clearly with the three of them making me anxious, and Maude's message left no additional clues as to her whereabouts. There was only one logical place to go. The one place Maude and I would always go to when we needed to regroup. The Tea Room.

"A brothel?" Everett nearly choked.

We arrived well past midnight, and a bright-red light illuminated the stunned faces of my three companions as they stared up at the two-story brick building.

"Yes, Maude and I used to come here to relax," I explained.

Leroy's mustache twisted to the side. "Relax?"

"I done told you your girl was wild." Otto nudged Leroy in the chest. "You ain't never listen to me."

"And occasionally we'd come here to get information." I climbed the steps to the entrance and knocked on the door. "But mainly to relax."

The door practically flew off its hinges, and Madam Beatrice greeted me with a wide grin. "Leona! Welcome back. It's wonderful to see you again."

"It's good to see you too." I turned to find my associates with their mouths agape. "We don't have all night, gentlemen."

"Actually, you do." Madam Beatrice winked at me.

I held back a chuckle and followed her inside. Floral perfume tickled my nose as I entered the dimly lit parlor. Roses and peonies. My favorite scent. A handsome young musician played a lively tune on the piano while two ladies danced for a man seated in a large arm-chair by the window. Another man lingered in the corner with a shot glass in hand and a sultry dark-haired woman whispering in his ear. His hearty laughter lifted my spirits despite the fact that I was not privy to their conversation.

"You all look like you could use some freshening up," Madam Beatrice said, eyeing our muddy clothes.

"Do you mind?" I asked.

"Not at all." She snapped her fingers, and three ladies suddenly appeared beside Otto, Leroy, and Everett. The fronts of their ruffled skirts were cut short to reveal knee-high lace stockings and garters. Each of the voluptuous women wore a different color corset to match their vibrantly dyed hair and painted lips. Scarlet, Jade, and Violet.

Everett's head whipped back in my direction. "I'm not going any-where with her."

"You'll be fine." I waved him off. "Just watch your coin purse."

The ladies erupted in laughter. Violet linked her arm around Everett's. "We wouldn't dream of taking advantage of a friend."

Before he could utter another protest, she escorted him up the stairs with the others. Three more women entered the parlor, as if on cue.

"It's just Leona, ladies," Madam Beatrice said.

They breathed a collective sigh of relief and slowly morphed into their true forms. Their tight-fitting corsets and gowns were re-placed with camisoles and bloomers, and their cheeks were stripped of face paint. Madam Beatrice snapped her fingers again, and the entire room transformed. The men disappeared. The furniture and curtains turned from solid crimson to pink and white stripes. I blinked as my eyes adjusted to the soft yellow lighting. The musician—a gentle elderly man—started playing classical music.

"Would you like me to make you more comfortable?" Madam Beatrice asked.

"If it's not too much trouble."

Before I could finish my sentence, my damp muddy clothes were replaced with a simple cotton dress, and my hair was swept back, out of my face. I even smelled better.

I sighed and wrapped my arms around Madam Beatrice's broad shoulders. "I love benders."

Madam Beatrice and the other ladies broke into a fit of laughter. I wasn't joking. Their abilities were extraordinary. Benders were high-level telepaths. They could alter the perception of reality—or alter reality in and of itself. I plopped down on what appeared to be a long couch, and the soft cushions hugged my frame. For all I knew, it could have been a metal bench. I didn't care. The Tea Room became whatever a person desired... as long as their mind was unguarded.

"You look like you could use a drink." Madam Beatrice handed me a dainty teacup and sat beside me.

I sipped my tea, enjoying the warmth and comfort of being in familiar surroundings. "You always know exactly what I need."

"That's my job," she said gently. "What's troubling you?"

"Maude." I glanced down at my half-empty teacup. "She's alive."

Madam Beatrice's face turned serious. "You're joking."

"I think she planned to have someone dig up her remains if anything ever happened to her."

"Who?" Madam Beatrice asked.

"I have no idea." I drank the last of my tea, and the cup refilled it-self. "That's why I came here. You know us both *very* well, and you're discreet. Do you remember anyone who was that close to her?"

Madam Beatrice cocked her head. "It would be unprofessional to disclose someone else's personal fantasy."

"I know. But for Maude to go to such extreme lengths to make everyone believe she was dead, she had to be desperate."

A striped teacup materialized in Madam Beatrice's hands, and she quietly took a sip as she pondered my words. "I'm only sharing this with you out of concern for a friend. Maude was never one to openly express personal preferences, and at times she was very diffi-cult to read. But there were two particular men who often resurfaced in her mind. One looked like the gentleman who was whisked up-stairs—"

"Leroy," I said.

Madam Beatrice nodded. "And the other..."

The elderly piano player stopped abruptly. As he turned around, his frail body morphed into the shape of a tall, rugged young man. His dark hair was braided back, and a thin beard covered his strong jawline.

"Hello, Leona." His voice came out as a deep rumble.

"Who are you?" I asked.

"I go by the name of Chester."

"Where can I find you?"

"The copper mines." He turned back to the piano and continued playing his sonata. "Near Crystal Rock Canyon."

My vision became hazy, and I rubbed my eyes.

"I'm sorry," Madam Beatrice said. "That's all I know."

There was a loud thump from the second floor. I glanced up. "Was that real or in my head?"

"That was real," Madam Beatrice said.

I handed her my teacup. "Maybe I should check on my partner."

"Be my guest." Madam Beatrice made both cups disappear into thin air. "The last room on the right."

I jumped off the couch and scurried up the stairs. The hallway was quiet. Too quiet. I burst into the room. Everett lay face down on the wood floor. His shirt was missing, and Violet was standing over him with a broken vase.

"What happened?" I demanded.

"I had to do it." The damaged vase slipped from her nervous fingers and shattered at her feet. "He refused to relax."

Chapter 26: Bender

Leona

I knelt next to Everett and checked his pulse as he lay on the floor unconscious. Madam Beatrice, Scarlet, and Jade rushed to the room and stood in the doorway.

"Was there a reason you bashed my partner over the head?" I asked Violet as she timidly hovered behind me.

"T-this has never happened to me before." Violet sounded like she was on the verge of crying. "I swear."

Madam Beatrice inhaled sharply. "Explain yourself."

"I-I'm sorry, Madam," Violet stammered. "I tried entering his mind, but he kept blocking my efforts. Then paranoia set in, and he started shouting. I didn't want him to disrupt the experience of the other guests—"

"So, you had to take him out the old-fashioned way." Madam sighed heavily. "Well, we can't just leave him on the floor."

Madam Beatrice snapped her fingers. Everett disappeared then reappeared on the bed.

"Thank you." I rose and turned to the other young ladies. "Are my other friends all right?"

Jade spoke up. "Sound asleep."

"You know how easy telepaths are to subdue." Scarlet paused and looked at Violet. "Well, most telepaths."

Violet burst into tears, and I patted her on the back. "This is no reflection of your talent. I'm sure you're a highly skilled bender. Everett's like a vault. He doesn't let anyone in."

Madam Beatrice eyed me carefully. "Perhaps we should let you have some privacy."

She snapped her fingers once more, and the ladies quickly exited the room. I glanced around the intimate space. The silk bedding was suddenly more luxurious. Madam Beatrice had also made the mattress slightly larger... and rearranged the position of the candles so the soft lighting perfectly accentuated Everett's bare chest and strong physique. I swore even his pants looked tighter.

I stifled my irritation. Benders were constantly shifting reality to draw out wants and desires. But my feelings for Everett were far too conflicted. He'd broken my trust. And I didn't know how to move past the betrayal. No matter how attractive he was in that moment.

Everett moaned. I grabbed a wet cloth from the water basin in the corner of the room and sat beside him on the bed.

"I'm sorry about Violet." I dabbed his forehead with the cool cloth. "There was a slight misunderstanding."

"She was trying to get information out of me." Everett spoke in a daze. "She wanted to know who hired me to do the job."

"Silver hired you," I reminded him gently. "But that's all over now."

"Not that job. The one before it. With the shapeshifter."

I shook my head. "That's all in the past."

"It's not." Everett grabbed my wrists. "He's coming for me. I know it. I can feel it."

I patted the sweat from his brow. "Calm down. No one is coming for you here."

He slowly settled back against the pillow. My vision blurred slightly, and I blinked. Everett was quiet, but I could tell his mind was still racing. We were in for a long night. I tossed the cloth aside and curled up beside him, feeling partly responsible for his paranoia. And the nasty blow to the head.

"Most benders get people to reveal their deepest desires, not their deepest secrets," I quipped.

"My deepest desires are no one's business..." He looked into my eyes. "Except yours."

I swallowed hard. "They're no longer any of my business either."

Everett turned on his side and faced me. "I wish we could go back to how things were."

"Unfortunately, we can't," I said.

"What can I do to show you how sorry I am?"

"Not lie to me in the first place."

Everett lowered his head. "Leroy was right. You are stubborn."

I sat up. "Stubborn?"

"But that's also what I like about you." He pushed himself up and inched closer. "You're the most headstrong woman I've ever met."

"Flattery will get you nowhere," I said.

He held my face in his hand. "Will a kiss?"

"I doubt it."

"May I try?"

I peered into his eyes... his beautiful golden eyes. "You can try."

Everett leaned closer and lightly brushed his lips against mine. "Did that work?"

Something inside me fluttered. "No."

He tried again. And again. He tasted like peppermint. His fingers curled around the ruffled sleeve of my dress, and he pulled the fabric down over my shoulder. My skin tingled. I could feel the warmth radiating off his chest. He climbed on top of me and started caressing my neck with his tongue.

"Everett..."

He silenced me with a kiss that left me breathless. My body arched under him. I closed my eyes, giving in to the ecstasy. He wanted me—and I wanted him. Nothing else mattered. Nothing in the world... mattered.

I gasped and sat upright. The room was dark. I blinked rapidly as my eyes adjusted to the moonlight shining in from the windows.

Everett stirred under the covers beside me. "What's wrong?"

"Nothing." I was fully clothed, and so was Everett. "I just forgot—where are we again?"

"Crystal Rock Canyon. We drifted here to follow the lead you received about Chester."

My head was pounding like someone had taken a hammer to my skull. "That was an interesting night."

"It was *three* nights," he corrected me.

I nodded, but my mind was blank. "No one got into too much trouble, I hope."

"Not too much," Everett said. "At one point, Leroy donned a corset and was spewing poetry off the roof, and Otto was running around in his undergarments screaming about his brain overheating. It took six ladies to catch him. But for the most part, you and I were in the room."

I was quiet for a while. "Did we...?"

Everett turned and looked at me through the moonlight. "Did we what?"

"Nothing." I leaned back and stared up at the ceiling through the darkness. The benders were good. A little too good. "Did I pay them at least?"

"Yes. They took all our money," Everett said. "That's why we're sharing a room."

Leroy snored loudly, and I noticed him and Otto curled up on the opposite end of the bed.

"Worth every dime," I muttered.

"I agree."

"What?"

"Nothing." Everett rolled onto his side. "Good night."

Heat flashed into my cheeks, and I tapped his shoulder. "Which part of that was real and which part was in my head?"

I could tell Everett was smiling. "Get some rest, Leona. You're going to need it."

Chapter 27: Miner Problems

Everett

Toying with Leona wasn't right, but I couldn't help myself. I tried not to chuckle as she tossed and turned under the covers. She was itching to ask me more questions about what really happened at the Tea Room. I could feel it. By the time she finally fell back to sleep, I was wide awake—as I had been during most of our stay at the *brothel*. Leona, Otto, and Leroy had been completely out of their senses, oscillating between wild hallucinations and states of unconsciousness. Not one of them was lucid. Not one.

Violet had tried to read my thoughts and manipulate my mind, but I wasn't about to let down my guard. That was when she'd decided to hit me over the head with a vase. I had no idea how long I was unconscious, but I was relieved to wake up beside Leona. Unfortunately, she slipped into a trance halfway into our conversation. Her words became garbled, and most of what she said was unintelligible. But every now and then she would say my name. And moan.

Daylight began to creep in through the curtains of our hotel room. I was the first one out of bed, but Otto was already dressed, packed, and waiting in the lobby while the rest of us were still scrambling to tie our boots.

"You two know this area well?" Leroy asked as he threw on a long overcoat.

"Yes, we've been here before." I grabbed my hat from the edge of the bed. "The last time we stayed here was right after the smuggler job."

Leona stopped fiddling with the belt on her skirt and glanced at me. "But it's not as though this hotel holds any special meaning."

"I didn't say it did," I replied.

"Good." She slung her new leather bag over her shoulder and headed for the door. "Because it doesn't."

Leroy gave me a frown. *What the devil?*

Don't ask. I quickly followed Leona into the hallway and down the creaky stairs to the lobby.

"Y'all just takin' your sweet time," Otto said with a smile. "This is why I don't travel with womenfolk."

Leona blew him a kiss. "Not everyone can be as fast as you, Otto."

He laughed, wrapped his bony arm around her shoulder, and escorted her to the exit. Thick clouds covered the gray skies, and despite the balmy weather, I was cold. Something felt off since our arrival to Crystal Rock Canyon. I tried to stifle my apprehension. Shops were opening, and people were going about their daily activities. Nothing appeared to be out of place. I had no reason to worry.

A crow squawked overhead. I jumped back. No one else seemed startled. I quickly regained my composure. Three days of minimal sleep and constantly blocking benders from entering my mind had clearly taken a toll on me.

We headed down the main street toward the outskirts of town where a small mining camp was set up. Horse-drawn carriages trudged alongside us, splashing mud in all directions. Leona seemed slightly oblivious as she led the way. Her long skirt swayed with her hurried steps.

She's determined to find this Chester fellow, isn't she? Leroy remarked.

The miner is the only lead we have, I replied.

I ain't never seen her so focused, Otto said. *I hope she finds the answers she's lookin' for.*

Me too, I said honestly.

Through the corner of my eye, I spotted the stagecoach station. I tilted my hat down over my face. The wiry driver was busy tending to her team of horses and paid us no attention as we passed. But the shapeshifter knew who I was, and her threat still echoed in my mind. *If we cross paths under any other circumstance, I will not be so gracious...*

I walked closer to Leona.

"What's wrong?" she asked.

"Nothing."

"Then why are you tense?"

I resisted the urge to glance back at the driver. "I don't think we should stay in this town."

"We won't be here long," she assured me. "Once we find Chester, we'll be on our way again."

"You've met him before?" I asked.

"In a manner of speaking."

We approached a cluster of small log cabins scattered along a rocky hillside. The identical shelters were crudely built with flat roofs and scarcely enough room for more than one person to reside. A heavily bearded man with deep-set brows sat outside of his dwelling, cooking pork and beans over an open fire. His gruff exterior softened as soon as he caught sight of Leona, and he was more than obliging to direct her to the cabin belonging to Chester.

We quietly stood behind her as she took a moment to steel herself. I wondered what was making her so nervous. She let out a breath and knocked on the door. Seconds later, a brawny man with long, dark braids stood in the doorway, gaping at her. Before she could open her mouth, he dragged her into his arms and kissed her. Passionately. Flames burned up my neck. I leapt forward, tore him away from Leona, and slammed him against the wooden hut.

"What do you think you're doing?" I hissed, venom dripping from my fangs.

The miner's panic-stricken eyes darted to Leona. "I thought—you're not—?"

"It was an honest mistake!" Leona shouted. "He thought I was Maude."

"Maude?" Leroy echoed behind us.

Leona stomped her foot. "Let him go! He's probably just as confused as we are!"

I released the stunned miner and stepped back. Chester nearly tripped as he staggered away from us. Leona glared at me.

"I-I'm sorry." My unbridled emotions caused me to display an embarrassing lack of control. "That was completely uncalled for."

"You thought she was Maude?" Leroy knocked Chester to the ground, jumped on top of him, and started strangling him. "I'll kill you!"

Leroy was embarrassing himself as well. I grabbed hold of him and tried to pull him off Chester. "Let him go!"

"This is why I don't mess with no womenfolk!" Otto yelled as he helped me drag Leroy away.

Chester coughed and pushed himself upright. "Who are you people?"

"I'm Maude's twin sister, Leona." She calmly knelt in front of him and rested a hand on his shoulder. "We're looking for her, and we thought you might be able to help us."

Chester reached out to touch her face then stopped himself. "You're Leona?"

She nodded. Leroy struggled wildly in our grip, but we didn't let him go.

Calm down so Leona can get some information out of him! I projected loudly.

No use in fighting, Otto said. *He might be the only one who knows what happened to Maude.*

"She was supposed to come back," Chester said in a daze. "She never came back."

"You were the one who dug up her remains?" Leona said.

Chester straightened his back. "Of course. I would have done anything for her. She said if anything ever happened to her, I would know where to find her. And she insisted I leave her note behind."

"What happened after that?" I asked.

"I followed her instructions, and Maggie took over from there." He shook his head. "I didn't know if Maude would really be able to regenerate after that sort of trauma. But I waited, and when she didn't come back..."

"You and Maude were—*friends*?" Leroy spoke through clenched teeth.

Chester swallowed hard and nodded.

"Will you help us find her?" Leona asked. "I think she's in trouble."

"I'll do anything to see her again," Chester said in a low voice. "Just let me pack a few things. I'll only be a moment."

Chester pushed himself up and disappeared into his cramped living space. We let go of Leroy.

He yanked on his overcoat. *I don't want anything to do with him.*

You ain't never gonna get closure until you find out what happened to her, Otto said.

We'll need his help, I added.

Leona wandered a bit from the cabin. She seemed lost in her own thoughts. I followed after her.

"What do you think?" I asked quietly.

"Because I'm such a good judge of character?" she quipped.

"I'm being serious, Leona."

She pressed the toe of her boot into the mud and drew a half-circle with two lines down the middle. "I trust him."

A coyote howled in the distance. Leona grabbed my hand, practically digging her nails into my skin. My blood turned to ice. There was no escape. I met her wide eyes. "He's coming for me."

Chapter 28: Wild Animals

Everett

Another howl tore through the rugged hillside. The shapeshifter was close. I grabbed Leona's shoulders. "You need to drift away from here. Immediately."

"I can't." Her voice was shaking. "The mud."

I cursed under my breath. The howling turned to high-pitched barking, and a deep growl thundered in reply. A bear. The shapeshifter wasn't alone.

Otto bounced from side to side. *That don't sound good.*

What's going on, Everett? Leroy demanded.

A shapeshifter is out to kill me. Leona isn't safe. I scanned the small cabin where Chester was gathering his belongings. We couldn't outrun multiple members of the Tetred clan, but I could draw them away. "Everybody inside! Barricade the door."

They rushed to the cabin as the barking became frantic. Almost deranged.

Leona spun around to face me. "What about you?"

"Go. I'll be fine."

She shook her head. "I'm not leaving you out here alone."

"Leona..." I held her soft face in my hands. "This is not your fight. I need you to be safe."

She swallowed hard and nodded. "Be careful."

I wanted to kiss her. In case it was the last time. But I didn't. "Go, now."

Leona hurried into the cabin and shut the door behind her. Furniture scraped against the wood floor as they blocked the solitary entrance. I tossed my bag aside and charged into the woods. Dark clouds blocked the morning sun's rays, sending a chill through me. If I shifted into snake form, they would never be able to track me. I could stay hidden. But I needed them to follow me. My boots sank into the damp soil, slowing me down. I pushed myself harder. Hiram would never stop hunting me until he had his revenge. I had to keep him away from Leona.

Heavy footsteps thumped behind me, but I didn't look back. A crow squawked overhead. I kept running. My heart pounded in my chest as I made my way deeper and deeper into the forest.

A fox darted around a thicket of oak trees then jumped out in front of me. I dug my heels into the ground and came to a stop. The canine's fierce eyes were fixed on mine, and her distinctive bark sounded like a scream. I stood up straight and didn't move. Moments later, a grizzly bear lumbered up behind me. A crow swooped down from off a tree branch to my left. And to my right, a coyote quietly crept toward me, a low growl rumbling through his body.

I took in a breath. "I'm not going to run."

Hiram shifted first. His presence was menacing in both coyote *and* human form. He stood about as tall as me, but with blond hair and sharp features that were much harsher than I remembered. The grizzly bear was his brother. Ira. A broad, muscular fellow with a deep-set frown that made his bear form seem almost cuddlesome. The fox—the sinewy stagecoach driver—didn't come as a surprise to me... but the crow did. The bird shed its glossy black feathers as it shifted into the form of a woman. Violet. In place of her tight, revealing clothing from the Tea Room was a simple black gown with lace that wrapped all the way up her neck. I blinked, seeing her clearly for the first time. Four X's were inked down the right side of her face. Markings a bender could easily hide.

"Don't look so shocked, Everett," Violet said with a smirk.

Hiram spoke through clenched teeth. "You said she was with him."

"She was," Violet insisted. "Sallie can vouch for me."

"They passed the station, and I saw them both leaving town together," Sallie said. "She can't be far."

"I didn't pick up any other scent," Ira said.

"You came here for me," I said to Hiram. "Isn't this what you wanted?"

"It was..." He flashed me a sardonic smile. "But now I want you to suffer. Like you made me suffer."

"I'm sorry for what I did." I meant it, whether Hiram accepted my apology or not. "But I can't change the past."

"I know," Hiram said. "But I can destroy your future."

"Please... please leave her out of this."

"Begging for her life? That's so unlike you." Hiram turned to his brother. "Well, now we *have* to kill her."

Their hollow laughter echoed through the forest. Rage welled up inside of me. One bite would be enough to immobilize Hiram. Just one. I collapsed within myself, shifted, and sprang in Hiram's direction. He shifted before I could clamp onto his arm. The bear rose on his hind legs and growled.

Forget Everett, find the girl! Hiram projected loudly.

The bear took off running, with the fox close behind. *We'll find her, brother!*

I'm the one you want! I sprang toward Hiram's scraggly mane. Claws dug into the scales on my back, and I was swept into the air. I hissed wildly.

Put me down!

Violet flapped her wings, carrying me higher until we were above the tree line. *I'll gladly drop you wherever you'd like.*

Don't kill him! Hiram warned. *I want him to feel my pain.*

Something pricked the back of my mind, and my body suddenly felt heavy and weighed down. I fought through the fatigue and tried to block out all thoughts of Leona. *Stay out of my head, bender…*

She's hiding in a cabin with three other men, Violet said to the others.

My eyes closed. And then I fell. And fell. And fell…

"Everett? You dead?"

Otto's voice pulled me out of the trance Violet held me under, and my eyes shot open. I sat upright. Darkness surrounded us, and a cold mist permeated the air.

"Where am I? What happened?"

"We spent the last twelve hours searchin' for you." Otto carefully helped me to my feet. "We thought you was dead."

"Where's Leona?" I asked urgently.

Through the moonlight, Otto lowered his eyes and shook his head.

My voice cracked. "Take me to her."

The trek back to the miner's cabin felt like an eternity. We found Leroy limping around what remained of Chester's hut, picking up splintered beams and tossing them into an open fire. His right arm was in a makeshift sling, and blood was seeping through a bandage wrapped around his head. The firelight cast shadows across his face, but the dark rings around both of his eyes weren't an illusion. His left eye was completely swollen shut. Two bodies were covered and had been placed side by side in front of the dwelling. The muddy heels of Leona's boots protruded out of one of the sheets. Leroy stood beside me.

"We couldn't hold them off." His voice was distant. "Just before I lost consciousness, I told Otto to get help. I knew they wouldn't be able to catch him."

"And Chester?" I asked.

"Chester fought..." Otto said. "Until he couldn't fight no more."

I slowly knelt beside Leona's body. I reached for the sheet, but Leroy grabbed my arm.

It's hard to look at. He spoke directly into my mind. I could hear the anguish in his tone.

I squared my shoulders and nodded. The damp covering smelled like rust and mildew. I quickly pulled it away. My heart sank. I fought the stinging sensation in my eyes. I'd seen Leona die three times. Twice by my venom and once by a bullet. But nothing could have prepared me for what Hiram had done to her. I squeezed my eyes shut and turned away.

"He gutted her." I could barely choke out the words. My body was trembling. I'd never be able to get the image out of my mind. "We need gold. Where's my bag? I hid extra gold for her in my bag."

We tore through the wreckage and found my belongings under a heap of broken furniture near the side of the cabin. The waiting was always the hardest part. I didn't know how long I sat there holding Leona's blood-soaked hands. Minutes. Hours. Time was meaningless. I was numb. I hadn't been there to protect her. And I'd never let it happen again.

The gaping hole that was once Leona's stomach slowly began to regenerate. I signaled the others. Otto helped Leroy up from where he was warming himself by the fire, and they came to stand across from me. We watched and waited in a hopeful silence. Leona was healing, but it wasn't until the moment she drew in a breath that I began to feel again.

"Leona, can you hear me?" I asked.

She sat bolt upright and burst into tears. The gold dropped out of her hands and clattered to the wet ground. Tears streamed down her face as she spoke. "My heart. Did they take my heart?"

"No..." I gently held her hand over her heart and tried to speak soothingly. "Your heart is still there. You're going to be all right."

A coyote howled, and every muscle in my body stiffened.

Leona clung to me. "H-he'll find out what I am and kill me again. I can't—I can't do this!"

I held her close and looked up at Leroy and Otto. "Get out of here while you still can."

"But he'll getcha both!" Otto cried.

"You'll be out here alone and unprotected," Leroy said.

"We won't be alone," I said firmly. "My clan will come."

Chapter 29: The Ties That Bind

Leona

I woke up crying. I never woke up crying. Ever. The physical pain had stopped the moment the coyote ripped my insides out. The moment I died. But I found myself shrouded in darkness on a rocky hillside, curled up in Everett's arms. Crying.

Light drops of rain sprinkled onto my face, mixing with the tears rolling down my numb cheeks. I could hear what Everett was saying to Leroy and Otto, but I couldn't make sense of his words. The horrific sound of the shapeshifter's howling left me paralyzed with fear.

A sob escaped my throat. "I can't go through this again."

"I won't let Hiram near you." Everett held me in a strong embrace. "I promise."

"But how—" Leroy suddenly fell silent. He and Otto exchanged glances and nodded. "All right, Everett. We trust you."

Otto grabbed Leroy, lifted him off the ground, and bolted into the woods before I could blink. The rain picked up, reducing what was left of the fire to smoldering embers. Everett's rapid heartbeat thundered against my back, but he remained still. He was waiting for something.

Through the silver moonlight, the coyote's dark silhouette came into view. His grayish-brown fur was matted to his wet body as he watched us intently from the edge of the forest. His eyes locked on mine. The look of shock on the creature's face was slowly replaced with fury. Raw, primal fury. He charged at us. I screamed.

Everett slammed his hand into the ground. "*Diamas!*"

Everett's voice was so deep and savage it rattled my core. I glanced back just as the markings on his neck began to fade. The veins in his body turned black and bulged underneath his skin, and his glistening yellow eyes looked like they were coated in black oil. I stared up at his vacant expression, unable to recognize the man I thought I knew.

The coyote barked wildly and dove into the air. Four shadowy figures rose from the ground and surrounded us in a diamond formation. A translucent yellow force field materialized around them. The shapeshifter slammed into the barrier and flew backward across the muddy terrain. He crawled out of the muck and growled. Everett hissed back. The figures were completely silent.

Rain poured down overhead, but the force field shielded us from the elements. Heat radiated inside the small enclosure, warming my aching body. I started to regain my strength, but I didn't dare move or speak. The coyote paced back and forth, his gaze fixed upon the dark figures.

The tall, imposing figure in front of us spoke up. "The shapeshifter says he's only here for the woman. Is that true, Everett?"

Everett tightened his arms around me. "Yes. He's trying to kill her."

"She's not part of our clan," the figure behind us said in a shrill voice. "We're under no obligation to protect her from harm."

The figure to our left snorted. "Do you suggest we throw Everett's love partner to the wolves, so to speak?"

"Don't be ridiculous," the woman snapped. "If Everett had a new love partner, he would have told us."

"She is my partner," Everett insisted. "And I care about her."

"You know our laws," the tall figure said. "We will not protect her."

The figure to our right spoke in a calm, soothing tone. "However, we *could* protect Everett—while he protects his partner."

They were all silent for a moment, and I realized Everett was holding his breath.

"We will stand guard. Just this once." The figure in front of us crossed his arms. "Am I making myself clear?"

Everett's voice was low. "Yes, Father."

The coyote barked and hurled himself against the barrier, repeatedly. It didn't budge. Hiram morphed into humanoid form. His wet hair clung to his forehead as he glared at Everett.

"Next time I'll come with fire and turn your precious lover to ash."

A shudder ran through me. Everett remained still. Hiram returned to his canine form and retreated into the woods. The four figures were like stone. Rigid and immovable. They waited, as though they were expecting the shapeshifter to strike again, but he never returned.

As dawn broke, the force field lowered and the shadowy figures slipped back into the ground, one by one. Before Everett's father departed, he turned to both of us. His broadbrim hat concealed his face, but his displeasure was evident in his voice.

"You started a feud with a member of the Tetred clan?"

"I made a mistake," Everett said.

His father shook his head. "She'll be dead in a week."

There was no malice in his tone, but his words left me cold. Everett's father slipped away and disappeared.

A stiff breeze reminded me that the midsection of my cotton dress was shredded, and I awkwardly wrapped what was left of the fabric across my bare stomach. Everett found a wool blanket to wrap me in and started a fire. I was used to his silence, but his somber expression made me feel hollow inside.

"What are we going to do?" I whispered.

"I've given this a great deal of thought." Everett prodded the firewood with a long stick. "The only way you'll ever truly be safe from Hiram is if you join my clan... as my love partner."

My mouth fell open. "What are you suggesting? That I become your wife?"

"It wouldn't be anything more than a formality," Everett said with no emotion. "If you're accepted into my clan and they approve our union, you'll have the ability to seek refuge from any serious danger."

I couldn't form a coherent response. I barely knew any personal details about Everett, and after that night's encounter with four members of his clan, I realized I knew *less* about shapeshifters than I'd originally thought.

"Nothing would change between us," Everett said. "No one outside of the clan would ever have to know about it."

My throat felt like it was closing up.

Everett continued, "And I wouldn't interfere in your affairs if you were to form an attachment to someone else in the future."

My eyebrows shot up. He was already thinking up contingencies to our phantom union.

"Joining my clan is the only protection I can offer you."

Leaves rustled in the distance, and my heart nearly leapt out of my chest. Everett jumped to his feet. Leroy and Otto emerged from the forest, and I let out a breath. Leroy's face was horribly bruised, one of his arms was bandaged, and he was using Otto as a crutch.

"We were waiting until it was safe to return," Leroy said. "Otto's done a full sweep of the area. There are no current threats."

"I ain't never seen nothin' like that before!" Otto clapped Everett on the back. "The way them four people came up out of the ground last night, that coyote had no choice but to turn tail and—Leona, where you goin'?"

I'd gotten up and started wandering away without realizing it. "I-I need to think."

"Are you all right?" Leroy asked.

I met Everett's gaze. "I'm not sure..."

"Take your time," he said. "I'll find you something to eat."

Everett morphed into his reptilian form and disappeared before I could say anything else. Leroy glanced at Otto. He nodded and took off running. I frowned.

"Otto's getting more wood," Leroy explained as he settled in front of the fire. "You should probably rest. Reawakening is never easy on you."

I slowly sat beside him on the damp soil. The fire was warm, but I couldn't stop shivering. Leroy wrapped his good arm around me, and I rested my head on his shoulder.

"Everett asked me to join his clan," I said softly. "As his love partner."

Leroy nodded. "And what did you say?"

"Nothing."

"What did you want to say?"

I twisted the blanket around my fingers. "No."

"I figured as much." Leroy sighed wistfully. "I lost track of how many times I proposed to Maude."

"I've never been tied to anyone or anything."

"Except your sister," Leroy said.

"That was different."

"How so?" he asked.

"Because she was part of me. Everett and I aren't even..." I shook my head. "I don't know what we are."

Leroy took his time before responding. "Darling, I'm going to be straight with you. This is not about love. This is strictly about survival."

I sat up and looked at him through narrowed eyes. "What do you mean?"

"I saw what that shapeshifter was capable of. We couldn't stop him. The Agency would rather terminate your contract than offer you shelter. And the only family you have left is either on the run or in prison."

I gritted my teeth. "You're saying I need him."

"I'm saying he's your partner." Leroy's voice was serious. "So, let him be your partner."

I clung to the blanket and stared into the flames. My first inclination was to drift. To run away from everyone and everything. But the ground was too wet. I was still weak. And Hiram would find me.

Everett walked out of the woods, carrying two squirrel carcasses by the tail. Leroy went about busying himself with the fire as he approached. I squinted up at Everett through the hazy morning light. There was no doubt in my mind that he cared about me—the problem was everything else. The lies. The secrets. The deceit.

"It's all I could find," Everett said. "I didn't want to be away for too long."

My jaw felt like it was locked. I trusted him with my life...

"I know squirrel's not your favorite," Everett said.

But I'd never trust him with my heart.

"I can look for rabbit—"

"Yes," I blurted out.

"All right. I'll be back shortly."

"No!" I jumped up and grabbed Everett's arm before he could shift again. I forced the words out of my mouth. "Yes. I will marry you."

Chapter 30:
Introductions

Leona

Everett looked uncomfortable. He tugged at the collar of his stiff dress shirt as we stood at the edge of a broad river. I could tell he wanted to loosen his tie, but he refrained. We needed to look respectable.

I smoothed the fabric of my fitted bodice and full skirt. Despite the long sleeves and modest neckline, I felt exposed. Everett's family would determine whether or not they deemed me worthy to join their clan. They would be the ones to decide if Everett could marry me. I was at their mercy.

I glanced back at Leroy and Otto, who were closely patrolling the area for possible dangers.

"Are you ready?" Everett asked.

My head was bobbing up and down, but inside I was screaming. I would never be ready. He was taking me to a dimension parallel to our world. A place where matter and space were fluid concepts. Where shapeshifters originated. Sutorath.

Otto shook Everett's hand. "Y'all be careful out there."

"We'll send word if we receive any new information about Maude's whereabouts." Leroy pulled me in for a tight hug and whispered, "You'll be all right."

I nodded, swallowing my apprehension and sadness. If the Diamas clan accepted me, my life was never going to be the same. I was going to be bound to a man I hardly knew. But tears were inappropriate. Everett was offering me protection, and for that I was grateful.

Leroy and Otto moved back as Everett stepped into the river barefoot.

"Water connects both of our worlds," Everett explained.

The torrent rushed past his ankles, and he extended his hand to me. I removed my narrow boots, entered the icy waters, and grasped his fingers. The soles of my feet were too numb to feel the jagged rocks beneath me. Everett gently pulled me closer and turned me around. My back pressed against his chest, and he wrapped his arms around my waist.

"It might be a little hard to breathe," he whispered. "Just try to relax."

I stared down into the water, half expecting it to rise and swallow us up. Instead, a crushing weight closed around me. I opened my mouth but couldn't utter a sound. The heavy force compressed my lungs and organs. Everett held me steady, but I felt like I was folding within myself. The world flipped upside down. Then right side up. Then upside down—over and over again. I fought through the sudden nausea and squeezed my eyes shut. It would all be over soon. The pressure slowly began to ease, and I took in a ragged breath. My eyelids fluttered open.

The sky was a vibrant shade of cobalt blue, and massive sandstone cliffs loomed just beyond the forest. The red cliffs were streaked with alternating layers of pink and cream stone, creating mesmerizing patterns that almost appeared to be in motion. The raw, natural beauty of his home world stole my breath. Everett took my hand and led me out of the water.

"I don't ever want to hear you complain about drifting again," I said.

He cracked a smile. "I still think drifting is worse."

Although the ground appeared to be solid, it felt like fine powder between my toes. I couldn't connect with the land. I couldn't drift in his world. "I suppose we won't have to worry about that while we're here."

"There are bigger things we'll have to worry about," he said.

"Like what?"

"Hello, Everett."

I spun around as four shadowy figures took shape, aiming shotguns in our direction. Their broad-brimmed hats concealed their faces, but I could tell their focus was fixed squarely on me. Everett wouldn't let go of my hand.

"Hello, Cecil. It's been a long time," Everett said. "How are your folks?"

"Same as ever," he replied. "Yours?"

"We're about to visit them." Everett spoke casually—as though we were meeting them for supper.

"I reckon she's with you?"

"Yes," Everett said. "She's my—partner."

A tall slender figure tilted his hat up to get a better look at me. I gasped. He had no face. I nervously glanced about. They were all faceless. No eyes. No nose. No mouth. Their empty expressions sent a chill down my spine. My knees started shaking, and my legs almost gave out. Everett squeezed my hand reassuringly.

"I'd like safe passage for her," Everett continued.

Cecil glanced at the others, and they all lowered their weapons. The ground shifted slightly, and walls of solid rock slowly rose around us.

"I hope it goes well this time, Everett," Cecil said sincerely.

Everett gave a slight nod. The walls closed in, and darkness enveloped us. I clung to his arm. The markings on his neck began to glow, filling the space with radiant violet light. His hand was pressed against one of the craggy sandstone walls. The rough surface morphed and shifted into an archway. We stepped through the darkness into a small chamber. Candles burned brightly on a low stone table in the center of the room. The wall closed behind us. I jumped back, but Everett didn't flinch.

"We have to stay here until they send for us," he said.

"T-their faces..." I stammered, still clinging to Everett. "I couldn't see their faces."

"That's because you don't belong to our clan," he stated.

"But I can still see yours."

"No. You can't." He let go of my hand. His face tightened and stretched until his features became indistinguishable through the layers of taut skin.

I covered my mouth to prevent a shriek from escaping my lips.

"Don't be frightened." Everett grabbed my hand, and his face became visible once more. "You can only see us when we make physical contact."

I shook my head. "You didn't prepare me for any of this."

"I'm sorry," he whispered. "I never wanted it to be this way."

I noticed a glint of sadness in his eyes, and a wave of guilt washed over me. I'd been so consumed with my own doubts and insecurities, I never considered the possibility that Everett felt just as trapped as I did.

"Maybe we should take this time to get to know each other better." I tried not to wrinkle my dress as I sat on the floor near the table.

"Good idea," Everett said, kneeling beside me. The candles flickered, as though eagerly waiting for one of us to fill the agonizing silence. Neither of us did. Everett sighed heavily. "This would be a lot easier if you were telepathic."

"Well, we both know I'm not." I rested my hand over his. "So, we'll just have to talk. Quickly."

In the hours that passed, I learned the names of Everett's six older siblings and how to easily identify them. He told me that his *mother* was the one who interceded on our behalf when Hiram tried to attack us. And I learned that he enjoyed doting on his nieces and nephews. He spoke very little about his father... and even less about the woman he'd planned to marry who was rejected by the clan. I also learned that he hated parsnips.

Our conversation was cut short when a narrow archway took shape. A barn owl flew into the room and landed in front of Everett. He was silent for a moment.

"Yes, Mother."

The bird flapped its wings and gracefully glided out of the room. Everett didn't have to say a word. I took his hand and followed him down a dark, winding hallway. We emerged from the labyrinth and stepped into a spacious courtyard where a fire blazed in a large pit. Stars glistened in the night sky, but I didn't recognize any of the constellations. The massive cave dwelling stretched three stories high with walls lined in stone steps, leading to private entrances.

One by one, members of Everett's clan entered the courtyard and stood before us. I lost count of how many were in the faceless crowd. I couldn't see their eyes, but I could feel them staring at me.

"Thank you for taking the time to meet with us tonight." Everett's voice was steady despite the fact that I could feel him shaking. "I would like to formally acknowledge Leona as my love partner."

Four familiar figures stepped forward. His parents and his two eldest siblings, Alta and Ollie.

"What's her classification?" his father asked.

"Human," Everett replied.

"A shapeshifter with a human?" Alta sucked her teeth. "How dull."

"What is her natural ability?" his father asked.

I spoke up. "Regenerative healing, enhanced with the use of gold."

"Enhanced?" someone in the crowd echoed. "That means she takes from the land."

"She's not a pure-blood," someone else said, aghast.

"Your ancestors were originally off-worlders?" Everett's mother asked.

"Yes, my family settled here from another world," I said. "I'm a fourth-generation Aadarin."

"That will be a taint on the bloodline," another voice called out.

Their words stung, but I maintained my composure. "I certainly don't have anything comparable to Everett's lineage, but that doesn't mean I'm unworthy of his attention."

His father turned to Everett as if he couldn't hear me. "What is her learned skill?"

"Drifting," he replied.

"You wield lightning," Ollie said. "Land abilities and sky abilities aren't exactly complementary. You'd be binding yourself to someone who can't enhance your powers."

"She's not even telepathic," Alta muttered.

His mother shook her head, woefully. "How will you communicate, dear?"

"By talking. Quickly." Everett squeezed my hand. "It works well for us."

She sighed. "I just want to be sure you've thought this through. You know how impulsive you are."

I frowned. Everett was anything but impulsive. His need to mull over every possible scenario was almost maddening.

"What do you really want from our brother?" Alta asked me directly. "Everett's capricious and fickle. He isn't exactly suited for marriage."

"Everett's a gentleman." I had trouble keeping the edge out of my voice. "He's always treated me with dignity and respect. I've never met a kinder soul, and he would most certainly make a fine husband."

"Everett, you don't have the best judgment when it comes to these matters." His father crossed his arms. "The last one stole your money and left you for dead."

"Leona doesn't want my money," Everett said through clenched teeth.

"Does she know how much you have?" his father retorted.

I spoke up. "He doesn't know how much I have either."

"Keeping secrets from each other already?" Ollie said with a smirk.

"We don't have any secrets between us," I said firmly. "All Everett would have to do is ask. He's never asked."

"Our relationship isn't about money, or power, or ancestry," Everett said. "I love her. Pure and simple."

"Do you love him?" his mother asked me.

"We didn't always get along..." I glanced up into his eyes. "But I can honestly say the man I fell for was loyal and trustworthy. He still is. Everett cares for me, and I care for him. He's the only one I want by my side."

"Would you die for her?" his father asked.

Everett didn't waver. "Yes."

His father turned to me. "Would you die for him?"

"I already have."

Murmurs spread throughout the courtyard.

"Leona took a bullet for me," Everett said. "I wouldn't be here if it wasn't for her. I owe her my life."

The silence was deafening. Everett's father slowly approached and clasped both hands around mine. His strong features came into focus. He was almost a mirror image of Everett. He looked me up and down with his piercing yellow eyes. I stared back at him, obstinately.

He smiled. "Welcome to the family."

Chapter 31: Cold Feet

Everett

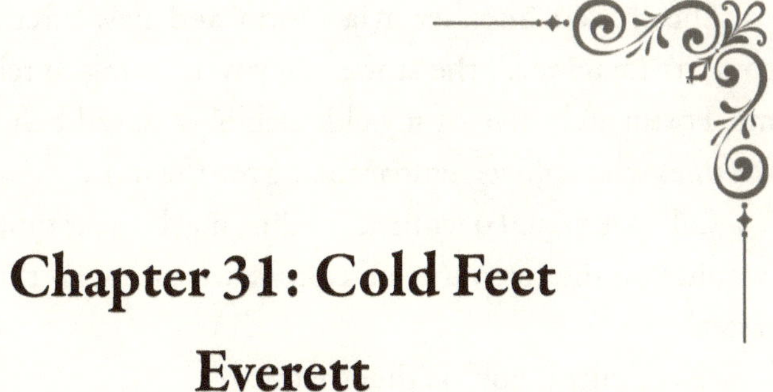

Leona and I fooled everyone. Even my father. She was welcome in the Diamas clan. We could wed, and she would be recognized as my love partner. Forever. The marriage itself would be fraudulent, but I didn't care. If Hiram ever went after Leona again, she could seek refuge with my family. We had one less problem to deal with.

Moonlight shined down on the crowd that had gathered in the center courtyard. Friends and relatives surrounded us to offer their sincerest congratulations and best wishes. The outpouring of support drowned out all the negative emotions that had resurfaced when my father started questioning Leona. I was expecting a fight. Like the last time. Like *every* time.

Leona smiled respectfully and answered a barrage of questions—half of which I didn't hear over the lively chatter. New members were always a cause for excitement. Leona's hand was wrapped so tightly around mine I could feel her anxiety rising. Before I could offer her any sort of reassurance, she was whisked away by my aunts. She looked back at me with pleading eyes.

"May I go with her?" I asked my father.

"Absolutely not."

Mother tenderly patted my arm. "I'll see that she's taken care of."

She shifted into her avian form and flew after the women. I couldn't imagine all the stories they were going to tell Leona about me. Fortunately, five of my elder siblings stayed behind. They were the ones who enjoyed embarrassing me the most.

Ollie sauntered over first. "Father, maybe next time start with the 'would you die for him' question so we can wrap things up a little faster."

"Keep silent, boy," Father snapped.

Ollie laughed and glanced at me, firelight dancing in his yellow eyes. *Congratulations, Everett. I actually really like this one.*

Thank you.

Do you need any help getting ready?

I think I'll manage, I replied.

Marion practically broke into tears when she gave me a hug. She chastised me for waiting so long to contact her, and I made plans to visit the children as soon as we were settled. My twin brothers, Dennis and Dave, said they couldn't care less if I visited more often. I still owed them money for a card game I'd lost fifteen years ago. They were never going to let it go.

A smile curved Alta's thin lips as she stood beside me. *I thought Leona was going to rip my head off when I suggested you'd make a terrible husband.*

I think she wanted to, Marion said.

Dennis chuckled. *I'd love to see that fight.*

Dave punched him in the stomach. *You would.*

From what Everett's told me, Marion said, *Leona's not one to be trifled with.*

That's good, Alta said. *It means she'll keep Everett in line.*

I wrapped my arm around Alta's shoulders. *Since when do I need a woman to keep me in line?*

Alta grabbed my face and squeezed my cheeks. *Since you were up to my knee.*

I rolled my eyes. *I'm about to get married. I hope you all realize I'm not a child anymore.*

"Everett!" Father shouted.

I snapped to attention. "Yes, Father?"

"Go to your room and get ready!"

I ground my teeth as my siblings burst into laughter. "Yes, Father."

I headed toward my bedchamber in a disgruntled silence.

"And Everett?" Father called after me.

I turned around to find him standing directly behind me.

"For once in your life, you've made a sensible choice. I'm proud of you, son." He paused, gave me a stiff hug, then stepped back. "I think you and Leona will be very happy together. You two seem well suited for each other."

My throat practically closed up. He'd never expressed approval for anything I'd done. Ever.

"T-thank you, Father."

He gave a curt nod and walked away.

Guilt consumed me. I'd lied to him and everyone else. Leona and I weren't even well suited for trapping together... let alone marriage.

I turned to Ollie. *Actually, I think I do need some help.*

He followed me out of the courtyard, and we made our way through the dark winding hallways. The stone walls felt narrower. Like they were closing in on me. Neither of us said a word until we were in my chamber and the entrance sealed behind us.

"Father approves." Ollie clapped me on the back. "You can relax now."

I stood with my hands clenched, unable to move. Despite the familiar furnishings, and the fact that Mother kept all our rooms in pristine condition, everything felt wrong. The seating area appeared cramped. The bed seemed too large for the corner alcove. And the heat coming from the fireplace was stifling. Nothing was right.

"You should've heard what Father said to me before I got married." Ollie mimicked our father's monotone voice. *"Let's hope the woman finds you half as funny as you think you are, boy."* He let out a hearty laugh. "Fortunately, she does."

I bolted across the room, grabbed a bottle of whiskey from a wooden chest, and swallowed a mouthful. "Leona doesn't love me."

"Of course she does," Ollie said. "No woman would go through what she's about to go through for a man she didn't love."

I wiped the corner of my mouth with the sleeve of my suit jacket. "I offered her protection. From Hiram."

Ollie was silent for a moment. "You're not that stupid."

"Yes, I am."

Ollie rushed over, snatched the bottle, and took a large swig. "You're about to go through the binding ceremony."

"I know."

"This isn't something that can be undone!" he cried.

"I gave her a way out. I told her I wouldn't interfere if she formed an attachment to someone else in the future."

"It doesn't matter!" Ollie shouted. "Even if she finds another mate, her soul will be bound to yours until the day you die!"

"And if she dies…?"

"Are you looking for loopholes?" he demanded. "As long as she has the ability to regenerate, neither of you will be free!"

"I had to do something. Hiram's never going to stop." My stomach was twisted in knots. "I'm the one responsible for putting Leona's life in danger. She never asked for any of this."

Ollie took one final swig, shoved the cork back in the bottle, and hid the whiskey back in the chest. "Does anyone else know?"

I shook my head.

"Good. Then I don't know either." He tore through the clothes in my dresser drawers and retrieved my ceremonial robe. "We never had this conversation."

I removed my suit jacket and rid myself of the cumbersome tie. "What am I going to do?"

Ollie looked me straight in the eye. "You're going to honor the declaration you made in front of our clan and fulfill your promise to your love partner."

"Or maybe... she could stay here." I unbuttoned my wrinkled dress shirt and tossed it aside. "Just until I sort out the blood feud."

"For how long?" Ollie demanded. "Weeks? Years? You think it's fair to lock her away just because your past has come back to haunt you?"

"You told me not to take that job," I muttered. "I should have listened."

"Everett, you never listen to anyone when your emotions are involved."

"If I hadn't been so hard up for money—"

"And whose fault was that?" Ollie raised his voice. "You fell for some random off-worlder you barely knew, tried to bring her into the clan, then decided to run away with her when we didn't approve."

"I didn't know what she was."

"Well, she made her true feelings for you clear when she stole your money and left you to freeze in the tundra."

It had taken me years to forget that woman, and I hated reliving the details. I changed out of my suit pants and wrapped a long skirt-like garment around my waist. Ollie stepped in to help when I struggled to secure the thick fabric in place. I couldn't remember the last time I'd worn ceremonial garb.

"I know how long it took you to get over that betrayal," Ollie continued. "That's why I was genuinely happy you'd found someone new... but it's all a sham."

I remained silent. Leona and I were in our situation because of my poor decisions, and there was nothing I could say in my defense. But I couldn't imagine a life with her... a home. A family. A real life.

Ollie tied a leather belt and sheath around my waist and re-trieved an ornate silver dagger from one of the floating shelves on the wall. He tried to hand it to me, but I wouldn't take it.

"I don't think I can go through with this," I whispered.

"Everett, you've made a lot of mistakes in the past." Ollie shoved my knife into its sheath. "But you will not bring reproach and shame on our family name. Am I making myself clear, brother?"

I stood up straighter. "I will marry her."

Ollie stepped behind me and lifted the heavy robe across my shoulders. The physical and emotional weight of what was about to happen made me want to retreat into my snake form. But I had Leona to think about. Her well-being had to come first, and I knew she was just as anxious and apprehensive as I was. I needed to be strong for both our sakes.

"Maybe..." Ollie's voice had softened. "Maybe you'll eventually grow to love each other."

"We started to get close. Really close. But she broke things off."

"Why?"

I cleared my throat. "Because she found out I'd taken a job from an anonymous client to destroy the evidence of her sister's murder."

Ollie whacked me across the back of the head. "You're an idiot!"

"I know."

"Now I don't know if I should warn the girl not to marry *you!*"

"I said Leona doesn't love me." I turned to face him. "I never said I didn't love her."

Ollie took in a breath. "Well, that's a start."

An opening formed in the wall, and Father appeared in the arch-way. "It's time."

Chapter 32: Honest and Open

Everett

Father led me down a series of stone hallways and narrow winding stairs to the lower levels of our clan's dwelling. The sanctuary. Small lanterns lined the pathway, creating an atmosphere of tranquil serenity. But I knew what was about to happen, and nothing could calm the rapid beating of my heart. Father paused when we reached a dead end.

"This is a very sacred moment," he said solemnly. "Honesty and openness are essential. You will not have a solid marriage without them."

I nodded politely.

"Take as much time as you need, son."

"Thank you, Father."

He placed his hand on the stone wall, and it shifted and transformed into an archway. I entered the small chamber. There was no furniture. No decorations. No embellishments. Just candles along the smooth round walls—and Leona standing on the opposite side of the room. A black strapless sheath gown was wrapped tightly around the curves of her body, and her thick hair was tied back in a single braid. Seeing her adorned in our traditional garb left me speechless. Even in such simple attire, she was beautiful. The wall closed behind me, but she stood perfectly still.

"Everett?" Leona's voice was quivering. "Is that you?"

"Yes." I hurried over and took her hand so she could see my face. "It's me."

She threw her arms around my neck and clung to me so tightly I almost fell over. "I was starting to panic. I thought maybe they changed their minds—or you changed your mind—and I couldn't even plan an escape because there are no doors anywhere. Why are there no doors?"

"I'm sorry." I could barely get a word in over her nervous rambling.

"Everett, if you ever leave me like that again, I swear—"

"We won't be separated from this moment on."

She pulled back slightly and looked into my eyes. "Don't sound so glum. It's not real, remember?"

"Sorry." I forced a thin smile. "So, you survived my family."

"Barely. They insisted I take a bath, and they scrubbed every inch of me in some sort of ritual cleansing."

They'd physically prepared Leona for the binding ceremony. The ancient waters that seeped into her pores would prevent her human body from rejecting the markings. "The water here is *special*."

"It certainly is. My skin feels incredible," she said. "And you should smell me."

"I don't think that would be appropriate."

She tilted her head. "I doubt I'm ever going to smell this good again."

I leaned closer and brushed my nose against her soft neck, inhaling her scent. Jasmine, with hints of vanilla. I was in the sanctuary for the very first time. A place where hundreds of my ancestors solidified their sacred bonds. And I was hunched over, smelling my partner.

"You smell lovely," I said briskly.

"Thank you." She smoothed back tiny strands of hair that had fallen out of her braid. "And you don't have to worry about anything.

Your mother explained the entire process, including tomorrow's wedding ceremony."

My eyes narrowed. "She did?"

"Yes." Leona stood up straighter and held both of my hands in hers. "This is the painless part where you express nice things about me, and I express nice things about you."

The vows. She didn't quite understand that we were saying our vows. My father's words echoed in my mind. *Honesty and openness...* I'd never been completely honest and open with anyone. Especially not Leona. When things were good between us, I was keeping secrets from her. When I fell out of favor with her, I closed myself off. I knew she didn't feel the same way I felt about her, and it was easier to hide my emotions than face an outright rejection. I was at a loss for words.

Leona's dark eyes were locked on mine. She spoke softly. "Are you trying to communicate telepathically? Because I can't hear you."

I couldn't seem to unclench my jaw to speak. I shook my head.

"Oh..." An awkward silence filled the chamber, and she shifted slightly. "I suppose I'll start."

Leona said nothing. I said nothing. We both said nothing.

"Well, that about sums it up," she declared.

I let out an involuntary chuckle, and she smiled. "This is serious, Leona."

"You know I don't do well when things get too serious."

"I know."

She bit her lower lip. "Should we just move on to the painful part?"

"No." I gently held her face in my hands. "I don't deserve you. I'm sorry I messed up what we had. But I promise I'll never lie to you again. You're the only woman I've ever cared this deeply about, and I'll do everything in my power to protect you from this day forward."

Leona nervously glanced about and whispered, "Are they listening?"

"No one can hear us," I said.

"Then why are you—"

"Because I need you to know my feelings for you are not superficial."

She lowered her gaze. "I never thought they were."

I slowly let go of her. *Honesty and openness.* "That's all I wanted to say."

"Thank you for telling me that." Leona's voice was sincere. "And thank you for being my partner."

I nodded and faced the wall. The marriage wasn't real to her, but it was very real to me. I placed my palm against the smooth surface, and an archway formed. I extended my hand to Leona. She clasped onto it, and we exited the chamber together.

Crisp fresh air swirled around us as we stepped into a vast underground cavern. Glistening streams flowed through pools of turquoise water so vibrant they appeared to be glowing. The energy was so strong, it almost took my breath away. Ancient utensils were spread across a wool blanket on the damp cave floor, and a petite elderly woman stood before us dressed in a long ceremonial robe identical to my own. Beulah. I'd known her since I was a child. My father had chosen an artist I was close to, and I was genuinely grateful to him.

I knelt in front of Beulah and bowed low. Leona followed my lead, kneeling to my left.

Beulah approached with a small metal bowl. I slowly removed my robe and pulled my silver dagger out of its sheath. Leona sat perfectly still, as though afraid to breathe. I handed Beulah the knife, tilted my head back, and closed my eyes. I didn't want to see it coming.

A sharp burst of pain shot through the right side of my neck. I gasped. Ink from my markings poured out of the open wound, burning like acid. Beulah pressed the bowl into my neck, collecting the thick, oil-like substance. The burning sensation spread throughout my body. I clenched my jaw, unable to stop tears from streaming down my face. Leona placed her hand over mine and squeezed my fingers. I hated her seeing me in such a weakened state, but her presence was oddly comforting.

Beulah wrapped my neck with a cool, wet cloth then went about mixing water from one of the sacred pools into the bowl. The pain subsided, and I dried my face. My focus needed to be on Leona. I took a moment to gather myself before addressing her.

"The placement of your markings is a personal choice." I met her eyes. "They don't have to be visible to everyone."

Her expression remained the same, but I knew she understood my meaning. No one outside of the clan needed to know of our union. Not acquaintances. Not the Agency. Not Hiram.

"May I have them placed here?" Leona asked, pointing to an area on her back just over her left shoulder.

"You may." Beulah knelt in front of us, holding a small bronze tool. One end was sharpened to a fine point. "Please lie down."

Leona lay across my lap. I brushed the tips of my fingers across her unblemished skin. There was no going back.

"Two will be as one. Bound by love." Beulah pierced Leona with the sharp needle.

Leona's body tensed up, but she didn't make a sound. Beulah slowly carved two overlapping diamonds down Leona's back. They were so razor-thin I could barely make them out. When Beulah finished, she wiped away streaks of blood and picked up the metal bowl.

"May you never be parted."

Beulah poured the dark mixture into Leona's open flesh. Leona let out a bloodcurdling scream. I held her close as a single tear rolled down her cheek.

"The worst is almost over," I said quickly.

Leona's shallow breaths echoed throughout the cavern. The thick concoction almost appeared to take on a life of its own, and Leona's body absorbed every last drop. Black ink spread under her skin and filled in the diamond pattern etched into her back. Marking her for life. She was one of us.

"May you never be parted," Beulah repeated.

I bowed slightly. She placed her hands on the ground, and stone walls slowly rose around us. I touched the rough surface of the transport chamber, and an archway formed, leading into my private bedroom. I lifted Leona's trembling body into my arms and carried her into the dimly lit room. My mother had seen to it that everything was comfortable and welcoming. A tray of food was spread out on a small table in the seating area, and bouquets of fresh flowers were arranged throughout the space.

I carried Leona to the corner alcove and placed her on the bed. She buried her face in the plush blankets and curled into a ball, whimpering.

"I'm going to find you some gold," I whispered, lightly patting her arm.

She didn't respond. I hurried across the room to my wooden chest. The elder members of the clan looked down on anyone who took from the land to enhance their natural abilities. But I couldn't bear to see Leona in pain. I tore through my belongings. There was no money left in my coin purse or the secret stash I kept hidden in the hollowed-out mantel above the fireplace. The twins must have raided my room as a joke.

I blew out a frustrated breath, placed my hand against the wall, and entered the private lavatory. A stone tub was situated on a raised platform at the far end of the room and filled to the brim with water and rose petals. I wasn't sure bathing would do anything to relieve Leona's pain, but it was all I could offer.

I rushed back into the bedroom to find Leona standing over the tray of food, shoving grapes and cheese into her mouth. I stopped dead in my tracks. She looked up at me.

"I'm so hungry."

My jaw dropped. "Are you all right?"

"I'm fine." She tore off a piece of bread and devoured it. "It was just a scratch."

I eyed her carefully. "A scratch?"

"If I'm not mortally wounded, my body begins to heal rapidly. It was an excruciating experience that I *never* want to repeat, but I've been through worse."

I joined her by the table and bit into a small fig. "I'm almost afraid to ask."

"Maude and I used to be pretty reckless," she said. "We almost made a game out of who could handle the most pain."

I shook my head in dismay. "It took me a week to recover when I got my markings."

"I didn't say it was a fun game." Leona drank two mouthfuls of wine directly out of the bottle. "Anyway, I should probably be preparing for the wedding ceremony tomorrow. Do you mind showing me back to my room?"

"Custom dictates we spend our first night together in my bedchamber," I explained.

She frowned. "*Before* we're married?"

"We are married." The words sounded strange coming out of my mouth. "We were bound together the moment you received your markings. The wedding ceremony is merely a formality. An acknowledgement of our union before the clan."

"B-but I thought there would at least be vows."

"There were. That was the painless part."

"We're married..." Leona began wandering aimlessly around the room. "I suppose I shouldn't be shocked. This is what we both wanted. It's just—everything happened so fast—"

"Leona..." I took her hand and turned her around to face me. "Absolutely nothing has changed between us. Do you understand?"

She swallowed hard and nodded. "Right. We're exactly the same."

Her eyes drifted down my bare chest. She caught herself and stared into the fireplace. Heat from the flames radiated between us, and I could almost feel the pulsating of her heart.

"Actually…" I pulled her closer. "One thing has changed."

Leona looked up at me with wide eyes. "What?"

I leaned closer and whispered in her ear. "I'll no longer be sleeping on the floor."

Leona burst into laughter. "Unless you make me mad."

I smiled. "Unless I make you mad."

Chapter 33: Trapped

Leona

Everett insisted nothing had changed between us. But I knew better. Everything had changed the moment we were bound together. The markings on my back that burned with every breath attested to that fact.

I stared up at the sandstone ceiling of Everett's bedchamber. The fire had long since gone out, and only a single candle remained on the table in the sitting room. I'd never been in such exotic surroundings. Skilled artisans had carved intricate diamond patterns into the walls, and every piece of furniture appeared to be handcrafted. The sharp angular designs were offset by layers of plush textiles and rugs. The Diamas clan seemed to value both beauty and function.

They were nothing like I imagined. On the surface they seemed cold and rigid. I thought they would continue to be indifferent toward me, an outsider, even after being welcomed into the family. Instead, they treated me like one of their own. Everett's mother went out of her way to ensure I was comfortable by explaining their customs and rituals. I wondered what it was like for Everett to grow up in such an environment. A close-knit community. A loving and supportive family. All the things I never had.

Everett stirred under the covers, and I glanced over at him.

"Are you awake?" I whispered.

He didn't make a sound. I quietly climbed out of bed and crept across the room. The thin cotton shirt Everett had let me borrow hung off my sore shoulders. Despite having the ability to heal quickly, the binding ceremony had taken a toll on me. Physically and emotionally. The pain from the markings would eventually go away, that I was certain, but the guilt would always remain. Putting on a façade in front of Everett's family felt wrong. They had accepted me into their clan under false pretenses. I had been so consumed with my own self-preservation that marrying Everett seemed like the right course of action at the time. But the more I thought about us—together as a couple—the harder it became to justify what we'd done. We couldn't successfully set a trap. We had opposing abilities. We had nothing in common. We didn't belong together.

"Looking for the door?"

My heart practically leapt into my throat, and I spun around to find Everett standing over me. I slapped him across his bare chest. "Don't sneak up on me like that!"

He stifled a chuckle. "Sorry. I thought maybe you were lost."

"Trapped is more like it." I yanked at the loose fabric of his shirt and wrapped it tightly around my body. "I need to use the privy."

Everett led me to the wall at the far end of the room. He gently took my hand in his and placed it against the grainy surface. The markings on my back began to tingle, and the sandstone trembled slightly.

"Do you feel that subtle vibration?" he asked.

I nodded.

He let go of my hand. "Don't think about what you see in front of you. Focus on the shape you want it to take."

I slowly let out a breath and concentrated. Heat spread throughout my body as energy flowed from my markings to the tips of my fingers. The stone shifted at my touch, and a narrow opening formed, mirroring the prominent archways of the clan's cave dwelling. I had trouble containing my excitement.

"Thank you!" I peered into the spacious washroom. "And sorry for slapping you."

"Sorry for sneaking up on you."

Everett returned to bed as I continued practicing on the wall. My abilities improved with each attempt. The sensation of shifting matter was exhilarating. It was the first time I felt truly connected to his world. Once I was confident enough to cross between rooms, I used the facilities and hurried back to the warm bed. Everett was so still I was certain he was asleep. I slipped under the covers and went back to staring at the ceiling.

"I don't ever want you to feel like you're trapped with me," Everett said softly.

The hurt in his voice was palpable, and I suddenly realized the binding ceremony had taken a toll on him as well. "It was a poor choice of words. I'm sorry."

Everett's silence was agonizing.

"Do you think we made a mistake?" I asked.

"I don't know."

I whipped around to face him. "That's the most honest thing you've ever said to me."

"Sad, isn't it?"

"Very sad."

Everett rolled over and looked at me through the flickering candlelight. "I have nothing to hide from you."

"Then can I ask you a personal question?"

He nodded.

"Why is your mother a barn owl and not a rattlesnake?"

"Shapeshifters can take on a variety of human forms, but we can only transform into a single animal. One that embodies our soul."

"Oh, I thought..."

Everett bit back a smile. "You thought you were marrying into a family of pit vipers?"

"In my defense, I know nothing about shapeshifters, and you've offered very little details."

"My middle brother, who I was very close to, was the only other person in my family who took on the form of a rattlesnake." Everett lowered his eyes. "But he's no longer with us."

My thoughts returned to Maude and the cryptic note she left behind. "So, you know what it's like to lose a sibling."

"Unfortunately, yes."

I gently ran my finger down the seven diamond-shaped markings on his neck. "That's what they symbolize? You and your siblings?"

"Yes. Family is very important to me." He grabbed my hand when I accidentally brushed against the cut that was made during the binding ceremony. "And I know I said nothing changed between us, but you're my family now too."

I slowly pulled my hand away. "It's getting late. We should probably get some rest before the wedding ceremony tomorrow."

Everett agreed, wished me a pleasant night's sleep, and was snoring before I was even able to get comfortable again. I tossed and turned, unable to get his words out of my mind. *You're my family now too*. I'd never been part of a functional family unit. Even when my mother was alive.

The walls felt like they were closing in on me, and I became acutely aware of the fact that there were no windows or doors in Everett's bedchamber. I hurried out of bed, searched the room for the nearest opening, and darted into the hallway. The wall sealed shut behind me. I ran barefoot through the maze of winding stone corridors only to reach one dead end after another. Panic welled inside of me. I couldn't get out.

My frantic steps echoed throughout the cave. Light clicking sounds clattered behind me. I was being followed. My heart raced as I stumbled around a corner, having lost all sense of direction. I slammed into a solid wall and spun around. A bat furiously flapped its wings and flew toward my face. I cringed and closed my eyes.

"Everett can't seem to keep a woman in his bedchamber."

Ollie stood over me with a broad grin. He was a striking fellow with sharp features and subtle streaks of gray in his short curly hair.

"I-I just needed some air."

Ollie nodded and offered me his arm. "This way."

I stifled my embarrassment and clung to him. He led me through the expansive dwelling until we reached an empty courtyard bathed in moonlight. The cool night air pricked my skin, but I didn't care. I could breathe again. Ollie shook off his long wool coat and wrapped it around my shoulders.

"This must be hard for you as a drifter."

I held my tongue.

"Just know you're never alone." His brilliant yellow eyes held my gaze. "If you or Everett run into any problems with Hiram, don't be afraid to come to me."

I opened my mouth, but I was too stunned to speak. I didn't know how much Everett had told him about our situation. The last thing I wanted to do was ruin the relationship he had with his older brother.

"Would you mind taking me back to Everett?" I asked finally. "I must admit, I'm a little turned around."

Ollie escorted me back inside the cave. Our brief conversation along the way remained light and neutral. Ollie was being just as cautious as I was. We stood in front of the wall leading to Everett's bedchamber.

"So, we'll see you in the morning for the ceremony." Ollie's tone reminded me of their father.

"Of course," I said politely, handing him his coat. "Everett and I are looking forward to it."

I placed my hand against the rough stone as he headed down the corridor.

"Ollie?" I called out.

He turned on his heel and faced me once more.

"Thank you," I said.

"Any time. We're family now."

Family. I allowed his words to sink in. But I didn't run. Instead, I entered the room, crawled into bed next to Everett, and closed my eyes.

"I'm glad you found your way back," he said quietly.

"So am I."

Chapter 34: For Better or For Worse

Leona

Everett and I were formally wed in front of his family and one hundred members of the Diamas clan. The ceremony was a blur. The officiant made a short speech about commitment and loyalty within a marriage—and within the clan. An ancient poem was read. Everett and I exchanged formal vows. We shared a kiss. A very brief kiss. Then it was over.

Everett's parents and siblings escorted us down to the riverbed as they prepared to bid us farewell. I trailed closely behind Everett, using my bouquet to shield my eyes from the bright morning sun. The light was almost blinding after what felt like days in the enclosed quarters of the clan's cave dwelling.

By the time we reached the water, Everett's family had exhibited the entire gamut of emotions. His mother was crying. Happy tears, she insisted. Marion was bubbling over with excitement. Alta was furious that the flowers she'd requested for my bouquet were pink instead of red. Everett preferred red. Dennis and Dave were anxious about the fact that they'd lost a bet with Cecil about whether or not Everett would actually go through with it, and Ollie was reflecting on the blissful time he'd spent as a newlywed. Everett and his father were the only ones who showed no emotion. They were like stones.

Everett and I stood by the edge of the river and politely thanked everyone for their love and support. The lace fabric of my long-sleeved gown rubbed against the sore markings on my back. Although they were no longer burning, the closer we got to the water, the more they prickled.

Marion's golden eyes sparkled as she stepped forward to present me with a gift. The petite woman most resembled Everett's mother, with her wavy dark hair and sandy-brown complexion.

"I wish you both happiness." Marion carefully hooked a dainty silver necklace around my neck. "I wore that every day for the first five years of my marriage, and I was blessed with five children. I wish you the same good fortune."

My head snapped in Everett's direction.

"Thank you, Marion." He spoke calmly. "That was very thoughtful."

"Y-yes, it's beautiful," I said, regaining my composure.

Dennis and Dave lumbered up, each carrying a small leather pouch. Thick beards covered their faces, and despite being slightly shorter than Everett, their broad shoulders and stocky frames made them appear larger. They dropped their gifts into Everett's hand.

"Don't spend it all in one place," Dennis said.

Everett shook the bag of coins. "This is the money you stole from my room."

"You're welcome," Dave said.

Their gruff laughter was almost identical. They dragged us in for a tight group hug that nearly crushed my lungs.

"Her bouquet!" Alta shrieked.

The twins let us go and examined the crumpled bouquet in my hands.

"It's fine, Alta," Dennis said.

Dave chuckled. "There are a couple of petals left."

"You brutes!" Alta shoved the twins aside, her yellow eyes blazing with anger. The sharp features of her face softened as she turned to me. "Please forgive them."

"It's all right." I did my best to rearrange the limp flowers. "I appreciate everything you've done for us."

"I'm just glad to have another sister to balance out the incompetence." She handed me an ornate wooden box. "That is a gift for both of you, but it shouldn't be opened until your one-year anniversary."

My curiosity burned, but Everett offered only a polite thank-you and took the box from my hands.

Ollie gifted me a knife. The blade was similar to the one Everett had used the night I received my markings.

"You are one of us now," Ollie said solemnly. "The Diamas clan will always protect you."

I nodded, afraid to say anything that might rouse suspicion.

He met Everett's eyes. The two were silent for a moment, and I wondered what parting advice he was giving Everett. I was certain I would never know. Everett had just started opening up to me, but some things were best left between siblings. I understood that well.

Everett's parents stepped forward, tenderly holding hands. After all their years together, they both appeared to be very much in love. Guilt pricked my heart. Everett and I would never have that. We started our relationship on a lie.

His mother gave us each a hug and kiss. "We couldn't be happier for you both."

"Our gift to you is in a very safe place," Everett's father said to him. "You're free to take it whenever you choose."

Everett bowed slightly. "Thank you, Father."

The family exchanged one final goodbye, then Everett led me into the river. Cool water rushed over my bare feet as he gently wrapped his arm around my waist.

"It's similar to the wall," he whispered. "Feel the space around you and don't fight against it."

I exhaled, allowing myself to connect with the land. My markings began to tingle. A heavy force compressed my body, but instead of resisting, I surrendered to it. The world twisted upside down then right side up repeatedly as I folded into myself. I closed my eyes, grateful that Everett was still holding me tightly. The pressure dissipated, and I took in a breath.

I blinked through a haze of dense fog. We were standing in the icy river near the canyons. The solid rocky soil between my toes was a stark contrast with the shifting sands of Sutorath. I was on stable ground. I was home.

I hurried out of the water with Everett close behind, and we retrieved our bags. We'd hidden our belongings in a tree just before we parted from Leroy and Otto. We'd only been gone for two days, but it felt like a lifetime. I was not the same woman as when I left. Something had changed in me. I didn't feel quite so alone.

"Your family is intense," I said as I stripped out of my gown and into a pair of wool pants.

"I know." Everett rid himself of his restrictive suit in favor of his trapper clothes. "I'm sorry."

"I didn't say it was a bad thing." After walking around barefoot for two days, I was happy to be in a pair of boots again. "I'm just not used to them yet."

Everett stopped buckling his pants. "Yet?"

"I assume we'll be seeing them again. Marion's planning a big family dinner. She said she already spoke to you about it."

"Oh…"

I frowned. "We are going, aren't we? Won't it raise suspicion if we don't?"

"Honestly, I always say I'll go, but I never do. I haven't spent this much time with my family in five years."

I shook my head. "That explains why your mother was crying so much. If I ever had a son who—"

Everett's eyes went straight to the necklace.

I reached around and fumbled with the clasp, but the stubborn jewelry refused to come loose. Everett came up behind me. His soft fingers brushed against my skin as he helped me unhook it.

"Thank you. You can keep it." I finished buttoning my shirt as he slipped the necklace into his pocket. "That's the last thing we need to be worrying about right now."

He gave me a sly smile. "I can't say I'm truly worried, considering we've never—"

"Well, just in case," I said briskly.

Everett raised an eyebrow.

Heat flashed into my cheeks. "Anyway, we have much more pressing matters to attend to."

"Like what?"

"Like finding another lead to track down my sister." I stuffed my wedding dress into my bag. "And figuring out how to work together before the Agency terminates our contract."

Chapter 35: Trial and Error

Everett

Leona and I were terrible at trapping together. *Terrible.* When we'd first started, I blamed it on the fact that I was keeping secrets from her. I told myself we weren't truly compatible because I wasn't being honest with her, and deep down I knew she didn't trust me. But the bitter reality of just how poorly matched we were hit me about two weeks after our wedding—when we'd failed to execute our fifth trap since returning to work.

Leona pushed herself out of a pile of manure as I ran toward her. Our catch was laughing hysterically as he fled across the barren desert. On our horse.

"If I say, 'go right,' I don't mean 'go left'!" Leona shouted.

"I was facing you!" I yelled. "How was I supposed to know you meant *your* right?"

The outlaw teleported, jumping miles ahead until he was almost out of sight.

Leona flung the muck from her hands and grabbed a fistful of dirt. "I'll get him myself!"

"That's the problem! We never do anything together—"

She drifted before I could finish my sentence. I tore off my hat and threw it on the ground.

"And you never listen to me!" I shouted into the air.

A vulture circled overhead and squawked in reply. Fortunately, the bird of prey was the only one privy to our embarrassing attempt to trap the outlaw. Had we been closer to civilization—or worse yet, the Agency—we'd have never lived it down.

I slumped to the ground and sat on the dry soil, waiting. I wasn't mad at Leona. We were both trying. Almost *too* hard. We'd barely slept. Mornings were set aside for planning new traps. Afternoons were spent gathering information and supplies. And our evenings were dedicated to practicing telepathy. But nothing worked. That was what made me mad. The constant reminder that we had no business being together.

Leona returned twenty minutes later. Empty-handed. She looked to be in worse shape than when she'd left. If that was possible. Dirt was caked onto her pants, the right sleeve of her shirt was torn and dangling off her shoulder, and scraggly twigs protruded from her thick hair. I looked into her weary eyes.

Glad you're still alive. I projected to her even though she couldn't hear me.

Leona stood over me, blocking blinding rays of sunlight. "He got away."

I can see that.

"The horse was supposed to be the bait. Not the means of escape."

Tell that to the horse thief.

"It was a terrible plan," she muttered.

I agree. One of our worst.

"We should have known something like this was going to happen."

We should have. We've been doing this long enough.

The vulture perched itself on a dead tree branch and watched us—as though waiting to see some carnage.

Leona huffed. "That's it? You're not going to say anything?"

"What would you like me to say?" I asked.

Leona mumbled something to herself and snatched up a handful of dirt. "Don't just sit there. Shift so we can leave this wretched wasteland!"

"No."

Her eyes narrowed. "What do you mean 'no'?"

"We're not going back to the Agency."

Leona spoke through clenched teeth. "We need a new assignment."

"No, we don't. We need to catch the thief who just got away. Together."

"That would be lovely." Her voice was sickly sweet. "Except for the fact that he's miles from here, and we have no way to track him."

"Then we need a new strategy."

Leona threw down the dirt. "Why are you being so difficult?"

"I'm not."

"You've been fighting me every step of the way."

"I'm not fighting you. I'm simply not going back to the Agency."

"Why not?" she demanded.

"Because we can't keep doing the same thing over and over. It's not working."

"Well, I don't know what else to do, Everett!"

I dusted off my hat and stood. "Neither do I."

"If Maude were here..." She shook her head.

I waited for Leona to finish her thought. She never did. I examined the area and found the tracks left by the horse thief. The trail would be difficult on foot, but at least we were headed in his general direction. Leona grudgingly followed behind me, stomping her feet to ensure I was aware of her displeasure. I didn't care. We had to learn to work together. No matter how frustrating it was for both of us.

I tried to keep my tone light as we trudged through the sweltering desert. "Maude was a planner, I take it?"

"Yes," Leona replied. "She had backup plans to our backup plans."

No wonder you're so annoyed with me. "Planning isn't my strong suit."

"It's not mine either."

At least we had one thing in common. "Sorry I let him get away."

"It wasn't your fault." Leona increased her pace and walked beside me. "Sorry I left you behind."

"It's all right." *You always come back.*

She plucked the twigs from her hair. "If we catch him—"

"*When* we catch him."

"When we catch him," she said, "we should celebrate."

"What did you have in mind?" *Don't say the Tea Room.*

"I was going to say the Tea Room." Leona tossed the brittle sticks aside. "But I think you and I should start our own traditions."

I tried to keep the shock out of my voice. "That would be—nice." Incredible, actually. We'd never engaged in any activity outside of work.

"Maude and I liked to visit Madam Beatrice. Leroy and Otto enjoy going to the theater," Leona continued. "It's common for partners to celebrate together after a successful catch."

"I didn't realize that," I said.

"That's because we've never had anything to celebrate."

Dust flew up from our steady footsteps. I suddenly had more incentive to catch the outlaw.

"I probably should have told you about it sooner, considering you're fairly new to the world of trapping." Leona stared down at her boots. "But to be honest, I was bitter about them pairing us together, and I secretly hoped our partnership would fall apart... until recently."

"What changed?" I asked.

"Marriage," she said flatly. "And the fact that I have a companion who's stubborn as a mule."

I chuckled. *You're one to talk, darling.*

"I didn't say I was any better," Leona replied. "And don't call me 'darling.'"

My head snapped in her direction. We both froze. She stared up at me with wide eyes.

You can hear me? I cried.

Her jaw dropped, and she nodded.

"You can hear me!" I grabbed her shoulders. "Do you know what this means?"

Leona shook her head, too stunned to speak.

"It means we have the element of surprise. For once!"

Surprise was an understatement. The look of utter shock on the horse thief's face when we nabbed him in the outhouse of an abandoned ranch was worth the grueling two days it took us to track him down.

Leona and I had the satisfaction of dragging him through the Agency doors. Together.

Amos practically jumped out of his chair when he caught sight of us. "Y-you're back! That's great. I'll take it from here."

He whisked the bound and gagged outlaw to an empty room then tried to usher us out of the building.

"Amos, I haven't even told you what happened," Leona said, digging in her heels. "Do you know how huge this is for us?"

He brushed sweat from his brow with the oversized sleeve of his suit jacket. "You two can leave. I'll telegraph your new assignment."

A door at the end of the long hallway creaked open. There was no light coming from inside. Only a voice.

"Leona. Everett. I'd like to see you both in my office."

A shudder ran through me.

"Now."

Chapter 36: Upper Management

Everett

Leona went stiff beside me. The only time I'd had any dealings with the individuals in charge of managing the Agency was the day I was hired as a trapper. I certainly never imagined being called into one of their offices. Especially not after a successful catch.

Is this normal? I projected to Leona.

She shook her head.

When neither of us moved, Amos cleared his throat. "Mr. Hall is waiting for you."

I followed Leona to the back office. She paused in the doorway and stared across the dark room. A sharply dressed man stood by a window and partially drew back the thick velvet curtains. Sunlight flooded the space, and the man flinched slightly.

"This planet's sun is still a bit too harsh for my eyes," he explained.

An off-worlder. I wondered how long Mr. Hall had lived on Aadar. Judging from his rigid posture and the way he carried himself, I suspected he'd spent some time in the Cavalry. No doubt that accounted for him assimilating into society faster. Off-worlders rarely held positions of authority.

Mr. Hall gestured for us to be seated. I was almost afraid to walk across his spotless carpet. Mud would clash with the crimson-and-gold floral pattern. Leona didn't seem to give it a second thought as she entered his office, traipsing dirt and manure across the floor. The expensive leather chairs and deep mahogany furniture were a stark contrast to Amos's sparse accommodations in the front office. I sat to Leona's left and sank into the wide armchair. I couldn't get comfortable. My aching limbs were too tense.

Mr. Hall sat behind his desk and started sorting through stacks of documents. Amos popped his head into the room.

"If there's anything you need—"

"We're fine, thank you," Mr. Hall said without looking up. "Shut the door, please."

Amos glanced at Leona then left without a word. Mr. Hall paid us little regard as he signed off on paperwork.

"Congratulations on your first catch together," he said.

Leona's voice was void of emotion. "Thank you, Mr. Hall."

He stopped suddenly and met her eyes. "Is that what we're doing now?"

She didn't reply.

Mr. Hall turned to me with a tight-lipped smile. "How do you like working with Leona?"

After spending two weeks in the sweltering desert chasing outlaws, I was in no mood for games. "I have no complaints."

"That's good to hear," he said. "Because I have a special assignment for you two."

"What kind of assignment?" Leona asked.

"We were recently made aware of a situation involving four trappers we'd suspected of going rogue."

The Agency knew about the ambush at Maggie's house. Leona remained motionless, and I kept my expression neutral.

"Our scouts found Fredrick's body," Mr. Hall continued, "but they haven't been able to track down Harvey, Ada, or Agnes."

I stopped myself from trying to enter the off-worlder's mind. Attempting to pry out exactly what information the Agency had regarding that night was too risky. If he was somehow able to block my efforts, it would only raise suspicion.

"What do you want from us?" I asked.

"There are rumors that Harvey has resurfaced near Wolf Alley. He's got few remaining allies, and he's weak without his partner." Mr. Hall slid a large envelope across his desk toward us. "We want you to find him and bring him in. Alive."

Neither of us reached for the envelope. Trappers trapping trappers. Nothing good could come out of that. At best, it would create an atmosphere of distrust amongst other trappers. At worst, it would paint a target on our backs. The ones who had gone rogue would have yet another reason to eliminate us.

"What good is Harvey to the Agency?" I asked.

"We want to question him. We want to know who's recruiting our trappers and turning them against us."

The Agency had nothing to lose. They didn't care what happened to us. Either we accepted the job or we would find ourselves in breach of contract. No legitimate organization would hire us with that sort of record.

"Why were we chosen?" Leona asked.

"You're the most qualified," he stated.

Mr. Hall went back to his mindless task of scribbling his signature on sheets of paper. His pen swept across form after form. The sound of his uneven strokes grated my nerves.

"You know they're targeting drifters." I spoke through my teeth. "And you want Leona to be the bait? After he tried to cut out her heart?"

Mr. Hall's head snapped up. "Did he hurt you?"

Leona's jaw tightened, and she shook her head.

Mr. Hall tugged on the sleeves of his crisp suit jacket, straightening them out. That appeared to be the extent of his emotional range.

"We were told there was some sort of altercation between you and the rogue trappers," he said. "However, we received very few details aside from the names of the individuals involved."

"And I'd prefer not to relive that night," Leona said.

"Understood." His stern expression remained unchanged, but his voice was tender. "I'm sorry about Mags. I know how much she meant to you."

Leona stared into her lap. "Thank you, Julius."

The room fell silent. I wished Leona had the ability to communicate her thoughts the way I could. I wished we had a deeper connection. Like the one she was clearly fighting against with Mr. Hall.

Leona picked the envelope off his desk and handed it to me. "We'll take the job."

We will? Are you sure? I projected, a little too loudly.

Leona pressed her finger to her ear and nodded. "I want to be done. With all of this."

"Everett?" Mr. Hall said. "Are you on board?"

I wasn't. But I also wasn't going to argue with Leona in front of him. "We're in agreement."

"Excellent. Then if that's all settled, I'd like to speak to Leona." Mr. Hall rose from his seat. "Privately."

Chapter 37: Different Paths

Leona

I resisted the temptation to call out to Everett as he left Julius's office. I didn't want to be alone with him, but I knew I would only be delaying the inevitable.

Julius crossed the room and locked the door. When he turned to face me, his stoic façade crumbled, and I saw the compassionate gentleman I remembered during my early trapping days. His short curly hair had a couple of specks of gray, and there were a few more creases in his face, but he was still... Julius. He rushed over, swept me out of my chair, and held me in a tight embrace.

"When I saw you, I thought my heart was going to pound right out of my chest," he whispered, rubbing my back.

My body was rigid despite his familiar touch and the spicy aroma of his pleasant cologne. Cinnamon and black pepper. A scent I couldn't get enough of—years ago. My markings began to prickle as he unknowingly brushed his fingers across them. I shifted slightly.

Julius slowly let me go and looked me over. "You're just as beautiful as I remembered."

"I'm covered in horse poop."

"I don't care." He leaned closer to kiss my lips, but I turned aside.

"Everett's waiting for me," I said.

"I'm sure he won't mind us spending a few moments catching up."

"He might." I slipped out of his grasp and headed for the door.

Julius stepped in front of me. "He doesn't know about us?"

I brushed flecks of dried dirt from my face. "No."

Julius nearly choked. "But he's your partner. I assumed you would have told him."

"There was nothing to tell," I said. "You left me five years ago."

"I promised I'd come back."

"I never said I'd wait."

"But you have waited. You're still here, and you're not married." He lightly kissed my cheek. "I spoke to Amos, and he assured me you're still very single."

"Very single," I echoed. "Did he use those exact words?"

"I believe the word he used was *unattached*."

"And I'd like to stay that way," I said.

"Please, Leona." Julius rested his forehead on mine. "I missed you so much."

"I missed you too." I slowly moved away and peered into his dark eyes. "Until I didn't anymore."

Deep sadness crept into his eyes. "I should have been there for you. When Maude died."

I shook my head and avoided his gaze, afraid his grief would overtake me.

"I should have come back." He held my hand in his. "I'm sorry."

"None of that matters now."

He brushed his thumb across my ring finger. "Did they ever find the body? Were you able to give her a proper burial?"

"Proper enough." I pulled my hand away. "I've had to move on from a lot of things. I hope you can respect that."

Julius stepped aside. "Yes. I understand."

I reached for the doorknob, but he rested his hand over mine.

He spoke softly. "If you ever need anything, I'm here."

"Thank you, Mr. Hall."

Julius forced a smile then backed away. I left his office and made my way down the hall with deliberate steps. I could feel him watching me, but I didn't turn around. I couldn't. I'd made a commitment to Everett. We were married under false pretenses, but that didn't make it any less real or valid in my mind. I respected him too much to jeopardize our relationship.

Through the window, I could see Everett and Amos standing in front of the building. They stopped talking the moment I stepped out onto the porch. The air was cool as the midafternoon sun began to wane. Everett handed me my bag but said nothing.

"Sorry I wasn't able to warn you about Julius." Amos spoke in a hushed tone. "They moved him to Headquarters two days before you arrived."

"It's fine. We were bound to run into each other at some point." I slung my pack over my shoulder. "I'm sure Everett's told you we've accepted a new assignment."

Amos's eyes darted from side to side. He was always worried about being overheard. "I think it's a bad idea."

"I do, too, but we don't have much of a choice," I said.

"Just be careful." Amos gave me a quick hug. "Wolf Alley is a rough area."

"Hopefully, we won't be there long." I glanced at Everett. "We should head out as soon as possible."

He nodded and followed me down the boardwalk. The thirty-minute trek out of the mining town felt longer than usual. My mind was a jumbled mess. Memories of Julius filled my thoughts despite my best efforts to suppress them. I'd thought I was prepared to see him again. Then I heard his voice, and I feared my heart was going to be crushed all over again. But when we were alone, something unexpected happened. I felt nothing for him. No longing. No pain. Just a void. I'd closed myself off to him.

Branches swayed overhead as the wind picked up and we headed deeper into the forest.

Everett grabbed my arm. "Leona, we have a slight problem."

I stopped short. "What?

"You're not listening to me."

"What are you talking about? You haven't said a word this entire—"

He raised an eyebrow.

"No." My bag dropped to the ground with a heavy thud. "There's no way I lost the ability that quickly."

"A telepathic connection only works when both people are unguarded."

"I-I am unguarded," I stammered. Saying it out loud didn't make it true. "I mean, I'm trying to be."

"The longer we go without interacting telepathically, the harder it will be to reestablish a connection," he said.

My voice trembled as panic crept in. "We can't go into this job without the ability to communicate."

"I know."

I grabbed his vest. "We'll be killed!"

"I know."

I let go of him and rubbed my sore shoulders. I wanted to blame Julius. For everything. For wedging himself back into my life and trying to stir up emotions I'd long since buried. But I knew that wasn't fair. We'd chosen different paths, and I didn't regret the one I was on.

Everett came up behind me and massaged my back. All the muscles in my body began to relax. I closed my eyes and allowed myself to give in to his touch.

"What happened with Julius?" he asked gently.

"Nothing."

"I don't mean today."

I slowly opened my eyes and stared out at the lush green foliage. "Julius and I started at the Agency around the same time, and we both rose in the ranks with our respective partners. We got along well. I thought we had a future together."

"But it didn't work out?" he said.

"Julius wanted us to advance within the Agency—together—but I liked things the way they were." I swallowed the lump in my throat. "So, he left... and I stayed behind. With Maude."

Everett remained silent as his fingers worked knots of tension out of my neck.

I let out a cynical chuckle. "Honestly, Maude never really liked him for me. She said he was too refined and proper. She would have chosen someone more like—you."

"Someone crude and uncouth."

I laughed. "No, you're more relaxed and unpretentious."

"And what type of person would *you* have chosen?"

I slowly turned around and peered into his eyes. "I don't know. I'm a terrible judge of character."

"So, you don't know your type?"

"Do you know yours?" I asked.

Everett didn't tear his eyes from me. "Yes. I'm looking at her."

"You're just saying that because you're married to me."

No, I'm saying it because I'm in love with you.

I took in a breath. "You are?"

Everett tilted his head. *Isn't it obvious?*

"I—I tried not to notice."

I know. That's why I never said it. Out loud.

The sudden realization that I could hear his thoughts again took me aback. I froze. He truly was being open with me, and I couldn't even formulate a response to his heartfelt declaration.

I understand if you don't feel the same way. Everett took my hand as he spoke into my mind. *But that doesn't change how I feel about you.*

I had sworn that I'd never trust him with my heart. But that was before. Before he made a vow to me. Before he made me part of his family. "It's not easy for me to say it... even when I feel it." I tightened my fingers around his. "But I need you to know I am trying."

Everett softly kissed the back of my hand. "I'll wait."

I believed him. "You love me more than he ever did. You'd never put me in harm's way."

"We don't have to do this job," Everett said. "We can find a way out of it."

"No." I reached down and picked up a handful of rocky soil. "We're going to drag Harvey's pathetic carcass back to the Agency so we can celebrate a catch. Properly."

Chapter 38: The Bait

Leona

I was used to being the bait, even when Maude was my partner. But this job was different. Harvey and I had history—way before he tried to kill me. We'd trapped outlaws together. Climbed the ranks together. And more than once, we'd shared a drink together. Or an entire bottle.

I expected to find him sitting alone in the only saloon in Wolf Alley, drinking his sorrows away. Instead, I was the one sitting alone at the far end of the narrow bar. The whiskey was watered down, but after the sixth or seventh shot, I no longer noticed.

A bartender with a scraggly gray beard poured me another. "Just passing through?" he asked.

I nodded. "Former trapper. Looking to make some extra money."

"What's your specialty?"

"Drifter," I replied.

"What's your range?"

"From the Wispy Mountains to the Valley of Sand." I drained my glass. "And as far west as Onyx Springs."

He whistled. "That far, huh?"

"I get around."

He grinned. "Apparently so. We don't get too many drifters in these parts. Especially not ones as pretty as you."

I blew him a kiss and had some difficulty containing a giggle. Perhaps the whiskey was stronger than I thought. Nothing in Wolf Alley was as it seemed. People kept to themselves and minded their own business, but there was a strange undercurrent. Like everyone was hiding something. I had to keep my guard up without *looking* like I was keeping my guard up.

"If you hear of anyone looking for a lift, I'm staying at the hotel. Room six." I peered into my empty glass. "Not tonight of course. Tonight, I'm celebrating my newfound freedom."

"Freedom?"

"From my partner." I grunted. "If you can even call him that. He was a bit of a snake. We were horribly mismatched, so we went our separate ways."

"You ain't afraid of travelin' alone with a stranger?" the bartender asked. "Folks around here ain't exactly reputable."

"What's the worst they could do? Kill me?" My laughter echoed throughout the saloon. A layer of grime coated the large mirror hanging behind the bar, but I could still see a few of the patrons eyeing me up. I had their attention.

The bartender leaned closer, a glint of curiosity sparkling in his shifty eyes. "You can regenerate too?"

I brought a finger to my lips and shushed him. "Don't tell."

He refilled my glass and poured himself one as well. "It'll be our secret."

We downed our drinks together. The whiskey tasted sweeter. The trap was set. I dropped my money on the counter, steadied myself against the bar, and bid the bartender good night. My vision was slightly blurry, but I didn't let that deter me. I had a job to do. I headed toward the front entrance, drawing just enough attention to myself without making direct contact with any of the other patrons.

I stumbled out of the saloon. The cool night air filled my lungs, and I inhaled deeply in a futile attempt to sober up a bit. Just a bit.

The last time I'd spent that much time at a bar was the night I found out the Agency assigned me with Everett. I was furious. A drifter and a shapeshifter with nothing in common. Technically, we still had nothing in common. Except our markings. And our newfound ability to communicate. And our mutual attraction to one another. But that was it.

Are you all right? Everett's voice echoed in my mind.

"Mm-hmm." I tripped off the boardwalk and landed face-first onto the dusty road.

Everett swooped up behind me, lifted me off the ground as if I weighed nothing, then disappeared again.

"You're just so fast," I mused. "And strong... much stronger than Julius."

Can you walk straight?

"Yep." I took a step and the world tilted. "Nope."

Are you sure this is a good idea? he asked.

"Trust me." I tried not to slur, but my tongue got in the way. "I know Harvey."

Wolves howled in the distance. I slowly meandered through the eerie town, away from the hotel. My steps were random and aimless, lacking any sense of purpose. Every now and then I would peek into the windows of the dark storefronts. The general store. The barbershop. The tailors. My eyes suddenly felt heavy.

Someone's following you. Everett's voice quickly snapped me back to reality.

I fought through my fatigue by humming a familiar trapper melody to myself and swaying down the secluded street.

After a few minutes, Everett spoke up again. *He stopped. He's heading back the way he came.*

I pretended not to hear Everett as I leaned against a wooden post. Patience was key. I grabbed a small bottle of whiskey from the back pocket of my pants and guzzled down what was left of it.

Where did you get that? Everett asked.

I squinted to examine the bottle. "I have absolutely no idea."

What else do you have in your pants?

"Wouldn't you like to know."

That's not what I—I didn't mean—

I chuckled. "I'll let you search me later if you'd like."

Everett fell silent. I wondered if his mind had gone blank, or if he was purposely keeping his private thoughts to himself. Most likely the latter. Which was a shame.

I'm fairly certain you're drunk, he said finally.

"Maybe." I tossed the empty bottle aside. "Or maybe I'm trying to give you a subtle hint."

More silence.

"Too subtle?"

As enticing as your offer sounds, this isn't exactly the place for it.

I laughed and staggered in the direction of the hotel. "That's why I said *later*."

The dingy hotel, with its crumbling wallpaper and meager furnishings, was most certainly a place I did not want to linger. Even if the thought of Everett's hands all over my body sent tingles through me...

I only tripped once on the way up the stairs to my room. I slowly closed the door behind me. Everything was exactly the way I'd left it. The bed was made. The curtains were parted, letting in the brilliant silver moonlight. And my bag was tucked away in a corner.

I flopped onto the lumpy mattress and accidentally knocked over the rickety side table. It toppled to the floor, sending the oil lantern crashing alongside it. Murmurs echoed through the thin walls.

"Sorry!" I yelled into the air. My head was pounding. I curled onto my side and closed my eyes.

"You were always a sloppy drunk, Leona."

My eyes shot open at the sound of Harvey's voice. I sat upright. He stood at the foot of the bed, clenching a large knife. His long, stringy hair was unkept, and moonbeams cast shadows on deep scars that ran down the side of his face. Burn marks from his last encounter with Maggie and Everett.

"When they said a drifter was passing through looking for work, and she was traveling alone, I thought it was too good to be true." His hand tightened around the handle of his blade. "But here you are. In the flesh."

My vision blurred, and I shook out my throbbing head. "What do you want from me?"

"Fred's dead because of you."

Do you need help? Everett spoke into my mind.

"No..." I whispered.

"No, what?" Harvey demanded.

I glared at him. "Fredrick's dead because he mouthed off to Maggie."

"None of this would have happened if she hadn't been protecting you!"

I leaned back and slipped my hand into the front pocket of my pants. "Listen... I'm in no condition to fight you."

"Exactly."

Harvey pounced on top of the bed as I clenched the single gold coin in my pocket. My headache lifted, my vision sharpened, and all my senses returned. Harvey brought the knife over his head. I punched him in the throat. He gagged. The knife slipped from his grasp. My heart pounded as I grabbed two fistfuls of his hair and wrestled him off the bed. He hit the floor hard, and I landed on top of him, still clinging to his greasy hair. I slammed the back of his head against the floorboards.

"Why are you trying to kill me?" I shouted.

Harvey thrashed under me, sending shards of glass from the broken lantern scattering in all directions. I balled my fist. My knuckles cracked against his jaw, and a sharp burst of pain shot down my wrist. A broken hand was worth it for what he'd done to Maggie. What they'd all done. His eyes rolled back in his head, and his body went limp.

Do you need help? Everett calmly asked again.

I flexed my sore, aching fingers. "Not yet."

I pushed myself to my feet and grabbed a porcelain basin from the opposite side of the dark room. Harvey lay sprawled across the floor, moaning. I dumped the entire container of water into his face. He gasped and sputtered, trying to catch his breath. When he finally sat up, I was kneeling in front of him with his knife pointed at his throat.

His eyes narrowed. "You were never really drunk, were you?"

"No, I was very drunk. Everett can attest to that."

Everett slithered out of the shadows and coiled up beside me.

"All those drinking games..." Harvey spit blood out of the corner of his mouth. "You and Maude were cheating."

"I wouldn't call it cheating," I said. "You and Fredrick lost your money fair and square. But you two were no match for us."

Harvey snorted. "I hate you so much."

"The feeling is mutual," I said sweetly.

He nodded in Everett's direction. "At least you got what you deserve."

"Everett?" I glanced at him. "He's an excellent partner."

A wicked smile exposed Harvey's jagged teeth. "You really don't know, do you?"

I refused to let him unnerve me. "Know what exactly?"

"Why they matched you two together."

I gave an indifferent shrug. "Does it matter?"

Harvey broke into uncontrollable laughter. "You really *are* the dumb twin!"

Heat burned my cheeks. I placed his heavy knife on the floor and slowly rose. "You can take over from here so I don't kill him. The Agency wants him alive."

All the color drained from Harvey's face. "The Agency?"

Everett sprang in Harvey's direction, bit his arm, and returned to my side. Harvey lost consciousness for a second time that night.

Everett morphed into his humanoid form and stared down at Harvey's crumpled figure. "What do you think he meant by that?"

"I honestly don't know. But this marks our second catch together as partners." I placed my hand on his broad shoulder. "And nothing's going to get in the way of us celebrating."

Chapter 39: Dance Partners

Everett

Dancing. That's how Leona and I decided to celebrate our successful catch. After turning Harvey over to the Agency, we cleaned ourselves up, donned our fanciest outfits, and found a lively dance hall where the music was loud, and the crowds were rowdy.

Leona could barely contain her laughter as I swept her across the dance floor. The band played a fast-paced jig, and even the timid patrons who spent most of the night hugging the walls couldn't help getting caught up in the excitement. Dance hall girls, with their painted faces and knee-high ruffled skirts, provided an extra layer of entertainment.

"If I wasn't a trapper, I'd be one of them!" Leona shouted over the music as one of the colorfully dressed ladies waltzed by with her eager dance partner.

I twirled Leona around. "I'm not sure where you'd keep your knife."

"In my bodice," she said without missing a beat.

I pulled her closer. "I might get jealous of all the other men who would have your attention."

"No, you wouldn't. I'd be making more in one night than we could in a month."

I glanced about. "Where can I sign you up?"

I relished the sound of Leona's laughter. Her long cotton gown flared out as we leapt about. I honestly couldn't remember the last time I'd felt so free. In that moment, I could forget about trapping. And the Agency. And Hiram.

The music shifted to a slower tempo. I led, and Leona swayed with my steady movements. I enjoyed having her in my arms. For once, we were completely in step with each other. But she avoided my gaze.

"What are you thinking about?" I asked.

She looked up at me with a thin smile. "I'm still trying to wrap my mind around the fact that you're such a good dancer."

"Have you met my sister? Alta spent hours drilling us. She made sure all of us could dance so we wouldn't embarrass the family at functions."

Leona gave a nod of approval. "She obviously took her job very seriously."

"She did. But I never told her that I actually enjoyed it. No need to give her the satisfaction."

Leona chuckled slightly. Her amusement faded as she appeared lost in her own thoughts again. The violinist's passionate solo was haunting and beautiful at the same time. Like Leona. After a few moments, I caught her eye.

What were you really thinking about? I projected into her mind.

"Harvey," she said quietly.

Her answer didn't surprise me. When we'd dropped the unconscious trapper at the front door of the Agency, Leona cursed at him, kicked him in the stomach, and walked away. Julius, Amos, and I pretended we didn't notice her outburst.

Leona shook her head. "I used to hate that, you know."

"What?" I asked.

"Being called the dumb twin."

I spoke only loud enough for her to hear. "Leona, there's nothing dumb about you."

"Growing up, everyone used to say it. Teachers, schoolmates, my older cousins... even my mother would jokingly remark that Maude was the brains, and I was the brawn." Leona paused. "Although I can't say she cared much for either of us."

"I'm sorry." I was at a loss as to what else to say. Leona rarely opened up about her childhood.

"After all these years, it shouldn't still bother me."

"Words can cut deep. Especially coming from people we care about."

"Maude never made me feel that way. She never said it—except for the night she faked her own death..." Leona stopped suddenly. "I was so mad. That's why I left her there in the barn. That's what set everything in motion."

"What are you saying?"

"I'm so naïve. She did it on purpose, so she could go into hiding."

I frowned. "What do you think she's hiding from?"

"I have no idea." Leona let out a heavy sigh. "I'm always two steps behind her. That's why they call me—that's why everyone thinks I'm a dolt."

"Harvey's an idiot. And so is anyone else who underestimates you."

"You're only saying that because you've never met her. Maude is—"

"Maude is not you. And she will never be you." I tenderly squeezed Leona's hand then spoke telepathically. *You're special.*

She turned away with a bashful grin. "Thank you."

Her fingers tightened around mine. I gently slid my hand up her back, pulling her closer as we danced. I wanted to know her. Intimately. Her wants and desires. Her fears and insecurities. Her deepest thoughts. And she was finally letting me in.

"It's a little crowded in here," Leona said.

I glanced at the other couples crammed onto the dance floor. *Do you want to go somewhere private?*

Leona nodded. I broke away, stepped back, and bowed. She curtsied politely. I clasped my hands behind my back as we made our way out of the dance hall. We were in public. Trappers were required to maintain a sense of decorum amongst law-abiding folks. Someone was always watching.

We slipped out into the night and found a secluded spot behind the building. Under the stars, the prairie's wild vegetation rolled in the breeze, creating the mesmerizing illusion of waves on land. Aadar was in good spirits.

Leona pressed her back against the building's wood planks and took in a breath. "I hope you don't mind. I was feeling a little confined."

"I don't mind." The sweet smell of grass permeated the air. "Thank you for dancing with me tonight."

"It was my pleasure," she whispered.

The wind swept her dark ringlets into her face, and I brushed her hair aside. I spoke into her mind, too afraid to say the words out loud. *May I kiss you?*

Leona shook her head. I respectfully backed away, stifling my embarrassment. She reached down and grabbed a handful of dirt.

"Not here." She made a gesture around her neck.

I blinked in surprise. She held out her arm. I quickly shifted into snake form and coiled myself around her body. The ground opened up. The brief falling sensation was replaced by an invisible force, propelling us forward. The portal hurled us out. Leona's boots scraped against the rough surface of a cave floor as she skidded to a stop. A cool mist enveloped us. Beams of moonlight shined through crystal clear water that cascaded from the falls above.

I slithered to the ground and shifted back into human form. "I suppose it couldn't get any more private than this."

Leona smiled and stared out at the waterfall. "It's breathtaking, isn't it?"

"Stunning." The steady, rushing water held me entranced by its raw power and beauty. "Honestly, this is the first time I've had the opportunity to enjoy it. The last two times we were here—"

"I know."

She shivered, and I wrapped my suit jacket around her shoulders.

"Thank you," she said.

I considered building a fire because she didn't stop shaking. "Are you still cold?"

Leona's dark eyes met mine. "I'm... nervous..."

I cradled her face in my hands. "What are you nervous about?"

She took in a shallow breath. "Doing something that can't be undone."

"Like binding yourself to a shapeshifter?" I said with a slight chuckle.

"A fake marriage is one thing." Her voice was serious. "This is quite another."

I brushed my thumb across her full lips. "We don't have to do anything. I just wanted to kiss you."

"All right..." She spoke softly. "Just once. For now."

Water poured down, muting out the rest of the world. I inched closer, inhaling Leona's floral perfume. She closed her eyes. I gave her a quick peck on the lips.

"There. That's all." I stood up straight. "One kiss."

Leona's eyes turned to slits. She grabbed my shirt and dragged me down until my mouth was pressed against hers. I laughed and tried to scramble out of her clutches. She clung to me, and we both fell to the rocky ground. Water from the damp cave floor seeped through the back of my clothes as she climbed on top of me.

"Don't toy with me, Everett."

I reached up and traced a finger down the side of her diamond-shaped face. "I wouldn't dream of it, my lady."

She bit back a smile. I pulled her closer and kissed her. The way I wanted to kiss her all night. My tongue swept across hers as I devoured her. Leona's legs tightened around my waist, and I wrapped my arms around her. I loved soaking in the warmth of her body. I loved the feeling of her heart beating against mine. I loved... her.

For a second time that night, I held Leona in my arms. And we were in complete harmony.

Chapter 40: Catch and Release

Everett

After our tenth successful catch, Leona and I were getting good. Good at trapping. Good at dancing. Good at kissing...

"Everett?" Leona's voice was sharp. "Are you listening to me?"

My attention snapped back to the man I was tying to a tree. Ray was neat and clean-shaven, unlike most of the outlaws we captured. "Yes. Of course, I'm listening."

"Ma'am, I don't think he heard a word you said. I caught him staring at your—"

I yanked the rope hard. "That's enough out of you."

Leona gave me a sly smile and turned away. "I said don't bother tying him up. There's a storm coming. I'll take him back to headquarters and come back for you."

A drop of rain plunked onto the brim of my hat. I glanced up at the gray, overcast sky. She had mere minutes to get him out before the storm rolled in. I quickly released Ray from the tree and bound his hands behind his back.

"Much obliged," he said.

I squeezed the back of his stiff neck. "Don't give her any trouble."

"I don't mess with drifters," he said. "They're liable to drop you into the void."

Leona picked up a handful of dirt. "That's right, and don't you forget it."

"Although… you seem kinda sweet." His eyes swept up and down her figure. "Like your sister."

Leona froze. Another thick drop of rain hit my hat.

I spun the man around to face me. "What do you know about her sister?"

"Who? Maude?" Ray shrugged. "I know she's alive."

The dry soil slipped through Leona's fingers, and she stepped closer. "Please. If you have any information—"

"You'll let me go?" he said.

I met Leona's eyes. *We can't.*

"We might be able to arrange something," she said.

I spoke into her mind. *You know as well as I do the Agency isn't going to take kindly to us releasing outlaws.*

"They don't have to know we caught him."

That's even worse! I projected loudly. *Our reputation is hanging by a thread as it is.*

She folded her arms. "When did our reputation become more important than family?"

Nothing is more important to me than family. Nothing. My jaw was tight. *I shouldn't have to tell you that.*

Leona looked away. Rain splattered between us as the sky went dark. She'd struck a nerve, but I wasn't about to blindly put my trust in a man who was accused of robbery and extortion. He was out to save his own skin.

I hovered over Ray and made myself slightly taller. "If you cross us, the void will be the least of your concerns."

He nodded fervently as Leona came to stand beside me. Cool drops of rain began to soak through my clothes, but I didn't move a muscle. If Ray suddenly decided to do something foolish, I was ready to strike.

"How do you know Maude?" Leona asked.

"Our paths briefly crossed over a year ago when she was working as a ranch hand. She wasn't much of a talker, a real private type. But I'd never forget her face. Or her story."

"What story?" I asked.

"Just your typical lonely drifter trying to make ends meet—except she was hiding from someone. Someone trying to cut out her heart."

"Did she say who?" Leona asked.

He shook his head. "She wouldn't say. But I've never seen such fear in a woman's eyes."

I glanced at Leona. She maintained her calm exterior, but I knew she was aching inside. Her sister was in danger, and there was nothing she could do about it. I knew that sense of helplessness. I'd felt it once for Leona. When Hiram gutted her.

"Did Maude tell you anything else?" I asked.

"Like I said, she was a real private type." Ray chuckled. "She barely gave me the time of day, but when I jokingly asked if she had a sister, she said she had a twin. I had no idea she was serious until you two had the gall to ambush me."

"You're wanted in twelve territories," I said.

"Thirteen," he corrected me.

Leona wiped rainwater from her face. "Do you know where Maude went next?"

"She mentioned something about the mountains."

"The Wispy Mountains?" I asked.

"No, somewhere much more remote," he said. "The tundra."

A shiver ran through me. The tundra. The last place in the world I ever wanted to return. I blocked out memories of the coldhearted woman who left me there to freeze to death. I didn't want to remember her face. That was my past. My old life. I had a new life. With Leona.

"I told you everything I know." Ray twisted around, and the rope dangled from his bound wrists. "Now I'd appreciate you keeping your end of the deal."

I hesitated. *I still don't trust him.*

Leona sighed heavily, grabbed her knife from the holster on her hip, and cut him loose. "A deal's a deal."

"That's what I love about you trappers." He shook off the fetters. "Always so honorable."

Ray slammed the palms of his hands into our chests. The explosive force knocked the wind out of me. I clawed the air, struggling for a single breath. Every inch of my body went rigid and cold, like stone. My eyes darted to Leona. She too was suspended in place. Unable to move. Unable to breathe. And with a look of sheer panic on her face.

Ray yanked Leona's knife out of her hand. The cracking sound was horrifying. A tear rolled down her cheek. I tried to scream, but nothing came out.

"There's an underground organization paying good money to anyone willing to dispose of drifters affiliated with the Agency. It's unfortunate you and your sister share such similar traits. I hate having to cut out people's hearts. It's just so—messy." He turned to me. "You might want to close your eyes for this. Oops. That's right. You can't."

Ray's laughter was muffled by the downpour, but nothing could stifle the rage building inside me. I collapsed into myself, forcing my body to take on another form. I rapidly shifted into every physical shape I could remember. A frail old man. A buxom barmaid. A lanky train conductor. Someone different. Every second. My muscles were on fire. They tore and stretched as I ripped myself out of the stasis field. I shifted into snake form, hissing wildly at the stunned outlaw. He stumbled backward.

"They matched a drifter with a shapeshifter?" he shouted. "What kind of sense does that make?"

I sprang toward his face. He threw the knife. I dodged the blade, and he took off running. I shifted into human form, grabbed my whip, and swung it overhead. I barely felt the electricity flowing through my throbbing limbs. Ray glanced back and dove to the ground. The bolt of lightning struck a tree beside him. He scrambled to his feet and sprinted through the dense forest.

Leona gasped violently. I spun around. She fell to her knees, shaking. Ray's stasis field crumbled as he faded in the distance. I hurried to her side.

"Are you all right?" I brushed her wet, matted hair out of her face. "Are you in pain?"

"I'm fine." The fingers on her right hand were completely contorted. She grabbed her knife with her good hand and dragged herself out of the muck. "If you get a clear shot, take him out."

I jumped in front of her before she could dart away. "I need you to stay behind me."

"And I need you to let me do my job."

I gently cradled her broken hand in mine. "I don't want to hurt you."

"Everett, there's a reason the Agency frowns upon partners becoming lovers." There was no emotion in her voice. Or her gaze. "I need you to view me as your partner. Not your wife."

I released her mangled fingers. "Go get him."

Leona raced through the woods. Water pelted me in the face as I followed behind her. She was fast. I always knew she was fast. But somehow it felt like I was watching her for the first time. She dashed around trees and hurtled over rotting stumps without breaking her pace. She was a trapper. And she was in her element. Ray didn't stand a chance.

Leona pounced onto his back, and they fell into a murky puddle of sludge. I planted my feet firmly on the ground and twirled my whip. Clumps of mud flew in all directions as Ray struggled to free himself from her grasp.

"Now!" Leona cried.

I cracked my whip. A blinding flash of white light tore through the air, striking them both. The convulsions were jarring to watch, but I didn't look away. Ray fell to the ground first. Then Leona. I rushed to her side. She was unconscious. Her limbs were shriveled, and dark branchlike scars marred her face and neck. I was petrified to see what the electric discharge had done to the rest of her body. What *I* had done to her.

I scooped Leona into my arms and held her close. I knew she was right about the Agency. About us. But I didn't have to like it. She let out a quiet moan, as though privy to my thoughts.

"Leona?"

No response. She slipped away from me again. Our profession was dangerous, but it wasn't the only thing that filled me with dread. I feared just how far Leona was willing to go—for family.

Chapter 41: Natural Habitat

Leona

Everett was murmuring something to me. His lips were moving but his face was a blur, and I couldn't hear him. I closed my eyes. The pungent odor of sulfur lingered in my nostrils.

I coughed. "It burns."

I'm so sorry, Leona.

The comforting sound of Everett's voice in my mind drew me back to reality. Back to him.

I never meant to hurt you, my love.

I forced my eyes open. Everett was holding me in his lap, and small coins were strewn all around us. I didn't want to know how much gold it took to revive me. I felt guilty enough.

"Did we get him?"

"Yes." Everett's voice was muffled. "I tied him to a tree. Again."

My throat was raspy. "We have to get back to the Agency."

"You need to rest. There's no sense in pushing yourself. The ground is soaked, and the nearest drop is twenty miles from here. We'll never make it before nightfall."

A dense fog had replaced the heavy downpour from earlier when we were chasing down our catch. The one I'd foolishly released. I glanced over at Ray. His head was drooping forward, his body resembling a beaten and worn ragdoll. He was unconscious. The rope was the only thing keeping him upright.

"Do you think Ray was telling the truth?" I whispered. "About Maude?"

"No. I don't."

Everett was straightforward, as always. I usually appreciated that about him, but the thin thread of hope I'd been clinging to evaporated with his words.

"I shouldn't have let him go." I waited for Everett to chastise me for my imprudence, but he did nothing of the sort. His sole concern seemed to be keeping me dry and warm. I nestled closer to him, and two stray coins slipped off my lap. "I'll pay you back after this job."

He chuckled, but his expression shifted abruptly when he realized I wasn't joking. "I didn't think we were doing that anymore."

"It wouldn't be right for me to take your money. I don't want people thinking I'm just using you for your resources."

"People, like who?"

I remained silent.

"Is this about what my father said?" he asked.

"I don't want anyone in your family to think poorly of me."

It's our *family.* He spoke telepathically. *And you're nothing like Nell.*

"Nell?"

His jaw clenched slightly. "The woman I almost married... who deceived me."

He'd never spoken her name before. The last thing I wanted to do was dredge up bad memories. His former romantic partners were none of my business.

"I still think it would be appropriate if I paid you back."

"That's fine," he said. "I'll just save the money you give me for the next time you're injured."

I sighed. "You're so stubborn."

Everett gently ran his finger down my neck. My throbbing veins were still bulging from the bolt of electricity. I tried not to flinch. Every inch of me hurt.

"How long will it take you to fully heal?" he asked.

"Not long." I tried to sound optimistic. The burning sensation hadn't subsided, and I feared my hearing might never return to normal. "Once we're out of the woods, we'll need to find private lodging for a couple of days. I heal faster when I'm able to sleep."

"Really? You never told me that."

There were a lot of things I still hadn't told him. I was never one to be forthcoming about my abilities—or my limitations. Fire could kill me, and lightning was fire's distant cousin. Electrocution took a terrible toll on my body. Every time. If Everett had known that before we caught Ray, he never would have agreed to it. I was going to be sore for days, but I certainly wasn't going to show it. Or ask him for more gold.

"I need to start a fire before it gets dark," Everett said. "You rest."

He carefully lifted me off his lap and went to gather wood. I sat on the cold clumpy soil, propped up against a tree. A stiff breeze blew straight through my damp clothes, and I desperately wanted Everett near me again. I was getting comfortable being in his arms. Especially when we were alone. I craved the precious moments we shared when all our problems seemed to fade into the background. When it was just us. In bed. Talking. Or kissing...

I closed my eyes and clung to that thought as Everett slipped deeper into the forest.

"I didn't lie to you about Maude."

The sound of Ray's voice jolted me awake. A devious smile was plastered on his boyish face as he watched me intently. I yanked on my tattered wool shirt. "Why should I believe you? The second I let you go, you tried to kill me."

He shrugged awkwardly in the tight bonds. "I'm opportunistic. That doesn't mean I'm a liar."

"I don't want to hear another word out of you." I pushed myself into a standing position and fought through the dizziness. I stumbled forward, scanning the muddy forest floor.

"What are you looking for?" he asked.

"Something to gag you with."

Ray laughed. "You can try to silence me, but that doesn't change the facts."

"What facts?" I said through clenched teeth.

"That your sister is in danger." There was no mirth in his dark eyes. "And she desperately needs help."

Before I could respond, a faint howl echoed in the distance. A coyote. My blood turned cold. Hiram. A sharp pain tore through my abdomen. I clutched my stomach, waiting for the phantom pain to dissipate. My body had healed from the coyote attack, but part of my soul was still in shreds. Fear consumed me.

"Everett!" My shrill cry tore through the air. "Where are you?"

Frantic rattling replaced my screaming. Everett slithered in front of me, morphed back into humanoid form, and scooped me off the ground. "We have to get out of here."

"Wait! What about Ray?"

"Yes, what about me?" he asked.

Everett barely glanced in his direction. "We leave him."

I gasped. "What if he's killed?"

"Yes, what if I'm killed?"

"Stop talking!" I shouted at Ray. The dreadful howling was getting closer. I met Everett's panic-stricken gaze. "We can't leave him."

Moments later, we were running. *Everett* was running. I was in his arms, and Ray was tethered to his wrist, struggling to keep up.

"This would be a whole lot easier if you'd just untie me!" Ray yelled.

How did he find us? Everett's thoughts spilled into my mind. *I've been so careful. I've*

been erasing our trail.

I tried to focus on the energy surrounding us, but my nerves were too frayed. "I can't sense any portals nearby."

The steady patter of footsteps behind us turned my stomach. We were being hunted.

We're trapped. Everett's thoughts were spiraling. *There's nowhere to hide.*

"What are you two so afraid of?" Ray shouted. "A little coyote?"

I clung to Everett's neck. His rough, uneven strides were erratic as he weaved around broad tree trunks.

"Surely this isn't the first time you've encountered a wild animal in its natural habitat," Ray said, panting. "What kind of trappers are you?"

Everett slowed to a stop and put me down. "I'm cutting him loose. He can fend for himself."

My boots sank into the mud. "But—"

Everett unsheathed his knife, sliced the rope, and flung it at Ray.

"Much obliged," he said, tipping a hat he wasn't wearing.

Twigs snapped behind us. We spun around. The coyote was barreling toward us. Everett pulled me closer.

"Oh, for goodness' sake." Ray charged forward and slammed into the beast, shoulder first. The coyote hung in midair, frozen in Ray's stasis field. Ray regained his footing and dusted off his clothes. "See? Nothing but a harmless furry animal."

Everett cautiously stepped closer, staring into the coyote's frightened eyes. "It's not him..."

"Of course it's not a *him*," Ray said. "This here is what you would call a 'female.' She was probably protecting her pups. What did you do? Get too close to her den?"

"I-I might have," Everett stammered. "I don't remember. It happened so fast."

I let out a shallow breath and collapsed to the ground. Everett slumped beside me, shaking.

Ray knelt in front of me with a sad smile. "I reckon your sister's not the only one in danger."

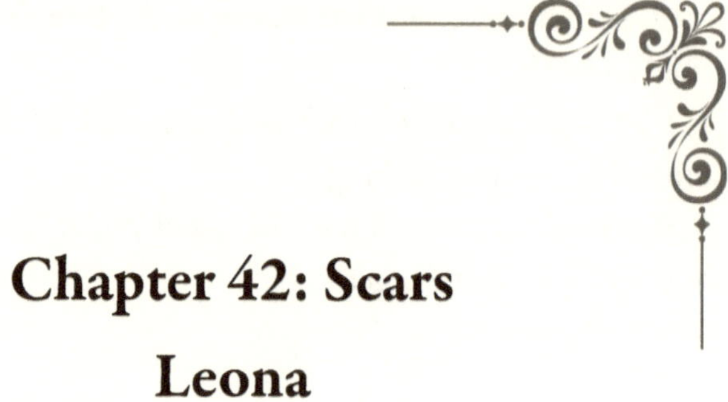

Chapter 42: Scars

Leona

Everett and I trudged up the worn wooden stairs to headquarters with Ray trailing closely behind. Normally, walking through the Agency doors with a catch filled me with a sense of pride and accomplishment. Not that day. After the twenty-mile hike to the drop location and the five-hour train ride, I was an absolute wreck. The look on Julius's face confirmed that.

"What happened to you?" he asked, his mouth agape.

The singed sleeve of my shirt flapped about as I waved him off. "Mild electrocution."

His eyes darted to Everett, who offered no further explanation. Everett was stone-cold and unemotional—on the surface. I swiped chunks of dried mud off my wrinkled clothes and cleared my throat.

"You're right. None of my business." Julius tugged on his dark suit jacket. "Amos!"

Amos came running down the hallway. "Sorry, sir. I was just securing the other—why isn't he shackled?"

I glanced back at Ray, who had a cocky grin plastered on his face. "He's all right."

"All right?" Julius nearly choked. "He's wanted in twelve territories."

"Thirteen," Ray chimed in.

Everett elbowed him in the chest.

Ray chuckled and held out his arms. "I'm sorry. I promised to behave so these two wouldn't try to roast me alive again. I'm all yours, my good man."

Amos's face was twisted in confusion, but he dutifully bound Ray in chains and led him to a holding area.

Julius hadn't taken his eyes off me, and when he spoke, it was almost a whisper. "Are *you* all right?"

I wasn't, and not just because of the lingering physical pain I was trying to mask. My nerves were shattered. Hiram was still out there. Somewhere. Waiting for us. Tears stung my eyes.

Don't cry, Leona. Everett's soothing voice entered my mind. *I'm here. We'll get through this. I promise.*

I took in a breath and regained my composure. "I'm fine, Julius. Thank you for your concern."

"Always." Julius reached for my hand then stopped himself. He clasped both hands behind his back. "I trust I'll see you and Everett at the trapper social?"

"Yes, we plan to attend," I said.

"Good. I can't tell you how relieved I was to see you with that ruffian. One more failed catch, and both of your contracts would have been terminated."

"Terminated?" Everett said.

"It's not anything you have to worry about now." Julius spoke directly to me. "Your relationship appears to be strong. Stronger than *most.*"

I smiled and pretended not to know what he was insinuating. "We look forward to seeing you at the social."

I hurried out of the building before he could say anything more, and Everett followed on my heels. My stomach was in knots. I'd almost let Ray go in exchange for information about my sister. Everything Everett and I had worked so hard for would have been for nothing. Our partnership would have been destroyed over a lead, and I would have been to blame.

The mining town was bustling with trappers, and Everett waited until we were deep into the wilderness before speaking.

"Was that his way of threatening us?"

"No. That was a friendly warning," I said. "And Julius isn't one to exaggerate. If he says we're one failed catch away from being terminated, he means it."

Everett matched my steps. "He's still in love with you."

"I know." I stared straight ahead. "Does that bother you?"

"No." Everett's voice was solemn. "If something ever happens to me, at least I know you'll be with someone who genuinely cares about you."

I stopped abruptly. "Something like what?"

Everett looked into my eyes. *Hiram.*

He wouldn't say the shapeshifter's name out loud. Memories of the savage coyote attack flashed into my mind. I could almost feel Hiram's fangs. Neither of us had openly acknowledged how scared we were, but I could no longer hide it.

"I-I'm terrified of him," I said.

"So am I." Everett shook his head. "It's only a matter of time before he finds us."

The forest was still. An unexpected respite. I absorbed the calm energy surrounding us. The silence. The tranquility. Everett rarely voiced his true fears. I needed to stay grounded for both our sakes.

"We can't live in fear of the future." I laced my fingers between his. "We can only live in this moment. And right now, we're together. We're safe."

Everett nodded. He wrapped his arms around my shoulders and held me close. I clung to him, and the tension in his body released. He buried his face in my neck. Julius wasn't wrong. Everett and I had a bond that was stronger than a mere partnership. Stronger than anything Julius and I ever had. Everett never left me, even when times were hard, and I would never leave him. The deep affection we had for each other was real. Tangible. And I could no longer deny my feelings for him.

"Let's go somewhere far away from here," I whispered.

Everett slowly let me go, and I picked up a handful of dry soil. He morphed into his reptilian form and wrapped his body around me like a warm blanket.

"Just so you know, I don't fault Julius for the choice he made." I let the hot crumbling dirt fall through my fingers. "But you're the only man I'd ever give a second chance."

Before we could settle anywhere, we drifted to the place that had become our secret hideaway. Under the waterfall. We collected only the necessities. Clean clothes and coins. A lot of coins. We drifted to the Emerald Desert, a wealthy city built on sand. The luxurious hotel I'd chosen was isolated from the rest of the town and offered the three things I was looking for—seclusion, privacy, and running water.

Everett did a thorough sweep of our spacious suite as I leaned against the locked door. The lavish gold and burgundy furnishings were more extravagant than I remembered. Sheer drapes cascaded down an intricately carved canopy bed, and candlelight shimmered off the flocked damask wallpaper. I closed my eyes and hugged my sore body. My muscles ached from the arduous journey, and I hadn't fully healed from the bolt of lightning.

"What hurts?" Everett was standing over me with concern in his eyes.

I smiled wearily. "Everything."

"Do you want to take a bath?"

I removed my sweaty bandana, liberating my matted curly hair. "A bath would be lovely."

Everett disappeared into the adjoining room. I kicked off my heavy leather boots and tucked our bags into a mahogany wardrobe. Three nights. That was all we could afford. But I was determined not to squander a single moment of our time together. Steam floated up through the open door, filling the bedroom with the rich, sensual scent of jasmine. I entered the bathing room as Everett finished filling a large claw-foot tub. He placed a plush white towel and bar of soap on a small stool next to the tub. I started unbuttoning my shirt, and he turned to leave.

"I didn't say I wanted to bathe alone."

Everett's piercing yellow eyes met mine. *You're sure?*

"Yes." The candlelit room suddenly seemed too bright, and I fumbled with an obstinate button that refused to come undone. "But—I have a lot of scars."

"I understand..." Everett slowly unclasped the button and took over undressing me.

My shirt dropped to the marble floor, and he slid my thin camisole up over my head. Light flickered against my deep-brown skin, and his eyes went to the exact spot I knew they would. The jagged scars across my abdomen. The vicious coyote bites. Everett knelt in front of me. He slid my mud-spattered pants down my hips and helped me balance as I stepped out of my clothes. A slight chill in the air pricked my naked body. Every blemish was exposed. Every imperfection.

Some of my scars were faint. A minor stab wound. A rope burn. A thin line from a severed limb that had regenerated. But the bad wounds—the ones that had killed me—they were darker. More defined. They never left me.

"I told you." I fought the urge to cover myself. "It's not pretty."

Everett gazed up at me. "You're beautiful, Leona."

My eyes were fixed on the floor. Other men had seen my scars. Some were shocked. Others were fascinated. But Everett....

He slowly rose and cupped my face in his hands. "You're beautiful in every way."

Everett leaned closer and kissed my lips. Gently. Tenderly. He brushed the tips of his fingers down my bare back and pulled me into him. My body melted at his touch. I wrapped my arms around his muscular frame, desperate for his comforting embrace. Everett loved every part of me, unconditionally. I didn't have to hide myself from him. Anymore.

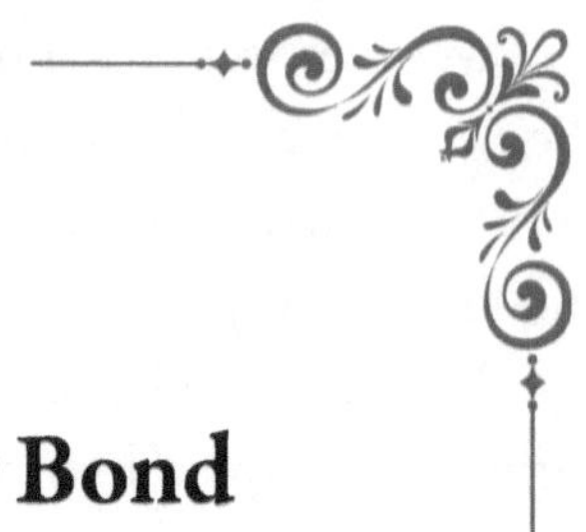

Chapter 43: Pair Bond
Everett

Leona's body was so soft. And warm. I tightened my arm around her waist and curled up closer, my bare chest pressing against her back. We hadn't slept on a real mattress in weeks. Not since our wedding night.

A thin layer of fabric surrounded the canopy bed, allowing us to enjoy a sense of privacy we were rarely afforded. All but one candle had burned out through the night. Leona shifted, and her thick hair tickled my nose. Pleasant floral notes filled my senses. I brushed her hair aside and nuzzled my face into her neck. I wanted to explore every inch of her silky skin with my tongue. Again.

"You're so quiet," Leona whispered. "You're not even in my head."

I grinned and lightly kissed her cheek. "My thoughts aren't appropriate to share with a lady."

Leona laughed and turned to face me. "I'm not a lady. I'm your wife."

You'll always be my lady. I spoke into her mind.

She suppressed a smile. "Then I suppose you'll just have to show me what you're thinking instead."

I ran my finger down the side of her face, memorizing every detail. "I suppose so."

I leaned closer and kissed her. She parted her lips, and my tongue instinctively found hers. I loved the way she tasted. Like the sweet strawberries we'd shared earlier. I climbed on top of her. Leona slid her hands up my back and clung to my shoulders, drawing me nearer. My heart pounded against hers, and I was overcome by a flood of emotions. I wanted her. Desperately. The blood pulsing through my veins suddenly felt like acid, and the markings on my neck started burning. I gasped and pulled away.

"What was that?" Leona asked, breathless.

"I—I'm sorry." I should have warned her.

"My markings felt like they were on fire. You felt it too?"

"Yes." I peered into her eyes. "I didn't think it was going to happen this quickly."

"What?"

The single flame fluttered slightly. "It's called a pair bond. The markings tied us together. But the connection gets stronger each time we—each time we're intimate."

She tilted her head. "Why didn't you think it would happen tonight?"

"Because it usually takes love partners a year before the pairing even begins." Sometimes longer. I was embarrassed the pair bond hadn't even crossed my mind. "I should have opened Alta's gift."

"You knew what was in the box your sister gave us?" Leona asked.

"It was a tonic. To help us through the transition."

Leona gently stroked the markings on my neck with her fingertips. "We hid all the gifts under the waterfall."

"I know."

"I could drift back and get it."

I rested my forehead on hers. "And waste what little time we have left before we go back to trapping?"

"What's the alternative?" she asked.

I did a mental sweep of our hotel room. Lotions and ointments would have no effect. Another bath would be utterly useless. And no amount of whiskey or wine could dull our senses enough.

"From what others have told me, it's going to feel really, really bad...." I looked into her eyes. *And then really, really good.*

Leona smiled and pulled me closer for a kiss. "I don't mind a little pain."

I didn't either. But halfway through, I had to admit Leona's pain threshold was higher than mine. Much higher. However, once the worst of it was over, the euphoric tingling sensation that coursed through my body for almost an hour afterward made me forget. Everything.

Leona returned from the lavatory and draped herself across me. "See? That wasn't so bad."

"Sure." I dragged the covers up over us. "The screaming was perfectly normal."

"It's all right. I don't think anyone heard you."

I stifled a chuckle. Leona made herself comfortable and rested her head over my heart. Our markings were glowing, emitting a bright purplish-blue hue. I softly traced the diamond pattern across her upper back.

"Why do you think the pairing happened so quickly with us?" Leona asked.

"I don't know." I wished I had answers for her. I barely had answers for myself. The pair bond had caught me completely off guard. I wasn't prepared for the intense physical and emotional connection it had forged between us. I desired more than Leona's body. I yearned for her love and affection. "The fact that we have opposing abilities makes all of this even more confusing."

"Because we shouldn't be together?" she asked quietly.

"No. I never said that." I repositioned us slightly. "Why? Is that how you feel?"

She paused. "Not anymore."

"Me neither." None of us could choose what abilities we acquired from the natural energy Aadar emitted. The planet's portals altered the genetic makeup of humans and shapeshifters alike. But those with a strong connection to the land, or water, or sky chose similar romantic partners. That was the way it had always been. "Before we met, I refused to court anyone with land-based abilities. And I avoided drifters like the plague."

Leona smiled. "Why?"

"The void terrifies me."

"You're afraid of the unknown."

"Isn't everyone?"

"To some extent, I suppose." She lifted her head to look at me. "I'm more afraid of... this."

I ran the back of my finger down her cheek. "And what is this?"

"Security. Stability. Certainty."

I projected my thoughts to her. *That's what love is.*

"I know, and it scares me."

"You're afraid to have it, or you're afraid to lose it?"

Leona rested her head against me once more. "Nothing lasts forever."

"It doesn't have to last forever to be real."

The radiant glow from our markings slowly began to fade, but there was a warmth between us that remained steady.

Her voice was a whisper. "Do you love me, Everett?"

I held her close but couldn't still the rapid beating of my heart. *You know I do.*

Leona sat up and blew out the candle. In the darkness, she settled beside me and wrapped her body around mine. "I love you too."

Chapter 44: Blind Man's Buff

Everett

Three nights in a private hotel room with Leona wasn't nearly long enough. Neither of us wanted to leave. But we had obligations. A few days later, we found ourselves mingling amongst nearly a hundred trappers at the annual social. Colorful flower garlands hung from cedar posts, sectioning off a large grassy clearing in the woods. The hidden location was known only to those in the Agency.

Across the way, rows of long tables were covered in white linens with huge platters of food arranged on top. Crispy fried chicken. Pickles. Boiled ham. Potatoes. Fresh biscuits. Human food. Not particularly to my liking. However, I knew Leona was in her own personal paradise. She was by the dessert table sampling an assortment of pies with Elsie. Her long floral dress swayed in the wind as a light breeze swept through the open field.

Leona looked up. I caught her eye. She smiled, glanced about to ensure no one was watching her, then blew me a kiss. I tried to contain the rush of excitement that swept over me. Despite wanting to whisper words of love and adoration directly into her mind, I prevented myself from communicating with her telepathically. I didn't know which trappers were pure-bloods. Telepaths. Opening my mind meant they could potentially hear me as well.

Keeping our relationship a secret was proving to be far more difficult than I'd imagined. Leona consumed my thoughts. The way her eyes sparkled in the sunlight. Her infectious laughter. How she could go from chasing down outlaws to picnicking in a dainty frock. Effortlessly. I loved everything about her. We'd spent the majority of the social away from each other, and I was counting down the seconds until we could be together again.

A heavy hand clapped me on the back. "You're not even listening, are you?"

I turned to find Leroy standing beside me with a broad grin. He was in much better shape than the last time I'd seen him. His mustache was perfectly trimmed, and the dark wounds on his face had healed. We were both wearing suits, but his looked new and professionally tailored whereas mine had seen several seasons.

"Sorry. I didn't hear you," I said.

"I understand." His eyes drifted to Leona. "Your mind is elsewhere."

I stood up straighter. "Just keeping to myself."

"Of course." Leroy lowered his voice. "It's smart to maintain your distance. We're all here to have a good time, but the less people know about your personal business, the better."

"Especially those higher up."

Leroy's eyes widened. "She told you about Julius?"

I nodded.

"I figured she would—eventually." Leroy turned me around, and we started walking. "Did she fill you in about the other trappers here?"

"No. We've been preoccupied with other affairs." It wasn't a lie.

"Not to worry," Leroy said, leading the way. "I'll introduce you."

There was Stella and Jim. Partners with an almost flawless record. Eliza and Jane. Second-generation trappers. Dorothy and Mack. Cousins. Sort of. Adam and Owen. An excitable pair with short attention spans. Gilbert and Bess... the introductions went on for the better part of an hour. Leroy was just like Leona. He knew *everyone*. And somehow, they all knew me. Rather, they knew *of* me. Apparently, Leona and I had been the topic of some very lively conversations.

"How does that work, exactly? A lightning-wielding shapeshifter and a regenerating drifter?" a pale-faced trapper with long sideburns asked. Leroy said he went by the name of Jasper. "What do you do? Electrocute outlaws and throw them into the void?"

"Don't be ridiculous," his partner Tillie said as she sipped a beer. "They probably just hide and pounce on people—like they did in the old days before they started matching trappers based on abilities. Everett, you'd be better off paired with someone like me, sugar."

I smiled at their good-natured ribbing. "Would I?"

"Absolutely!" Jasper wrapped his arm around Tillie's bony shoulders, almost spilling his liquor. "They call her 'the Chameleon.' Blends in with her surroundings. Show him."

Tillie eagerly handed Jasper her bottle, dropped to the ground, and curled into a ball. Every inch of her, from her light-brown skin to her navy-blue dress, turned vibrant green as she blended in with the landscape. After a few moments, I couldn't even see the outline of her body. She was good.

I clapped. "Impressive."

"Jasper's abilities are remarkable as well," Leroy added.

Tillie jumped up and returned to her original color. "He's able to bend light. Outlaws never see us coming."

"You two seem perfectly matched," I said.

"We are." They spoke in unison and burst into laughter.

"The Agency doesn't make mistakes," Leroy said with a broad grin.

They raised their glasses and echoed the mantra. "The Agency doesn't make mistakes."

I forced a smile and tried not to appear uncomfortable. The last thing I wanted to do was draw more attention to myself. Trappers seemed to feed on that kind of energy.

"Are you all ready to play?" A stout trapper named Floyd approached with his muscular partner, who went by the name of Kate. "The game's about to start."

"What game?" I asked, genuinely intrigued.

"Blind Man's Buff," Kate replied.

I directed my frown at Leroy. "A children's game?"

"This is the trapper version," he assured me.

I followed them to the center of the field where everyone was gathering. I scanned the crowd for Leona. Her back was to me, and she was carrying on a private conversation with Amos.

"Who wants to start?" Floyd asked.

"We will," Leroy said.

Suddenly, Otto appeared by his side, rubbing his hands together. "Word is they got some new prizes this year."

Floyd handed Kate a blindfold, and she escorted Otto to the opposite end of the crowd. The other trappers were humming with excitement as Leroy and Otto were blindfolded.

"Spin them around!" someone shouted.

Floyd grabbed Leroy's shoulders and spun him in place.

"Is this as fast as y'all can go?" Otto shouted. Two other trappers laughed and joined in with Kate to help spin him faster.

"And stop!" Floyd yelled.

Everyone backed away from the two blindfolded trappers. I followed suit, still not clear on the rules. I couldn't ask Leona. She wasn't close enough. But she appeared to be eagerly awaiting the start of the game as she whispered to some of her friends.

"Find your partner using only your abilities. But no speaking and no telepathy." Floyd whipped out a brass pocket watch. "Go!"

Otto bolted. Leroy planted his feet and stayed in place. Other trappers playfully shouted at Otto and threw rocks, trying to disorient him. Leroy squeezed both his hands into fists until they started to glow red. Otto was a blur as he went from person to person, patting them down. Every time I blinked, he was in a different spot. I didn't even see him when he got to me. I felt a light frisk down my arms, then my hat almost flew off as he blew past me. Suddenly, Otto got to Leroy. He grabbed his partner's burning hand and lifted it up.

"Found him!" Otto yelled.

"Ha!" Leroy shouted triumphantly as he ripped off his blindfold. "What was our time?"

Floyd flipped his watch around. "One minute, sixteen seconds!"

The crowd erupted in cheers.

Otto flung his blindfold into the air. "Which one of y'all wanna try and beat that?"

Stella and Jim beat it. By two seconds. Eliza and Jane came in a close third. The Nelson brothers would have outdone everyone had they not accidently disqualified themselves when someone teased them about all the pudding being gone. They both tore off their blindfolds and made a mad dash for the dessert table. Apparently, it wasn't the first time their stomachs had gotten the better of them.

Claude and Elsie were blindfolded next. Claude was silent, and Elsie barely flinched as they were spun around. A moment after the timer started, they both stood perfectly still.

"What are you waiting for?" someone shouted.

"One of you has to move at some point!"

Elsie faced her palms toward the ground. Seconds later, Claude thrust out his hands, emitting a heavy burst of wind across the field. I fell hard and landed flat on my back, joining the chorus of grunts and groans from all the other trappers who had been thrown to the ground. Elsie was the only person left standing. Her gravity field was strong. Claude calmly stepped over us as he wandered through the clearing with his arms outstretched. His hand brushed across Elsie's shoulder.

"Found her!" Claude said.

"Nice job, sweetie." Elsie untied her blindfold and gave him a peck on the cheek. "What was our time, pray tell?"

"Fifty-nine seconds." Floyd propped himself up on his elbow. "Claude, you almost broke my watch!"

Claude smirked. "No matter. I doubt anyone will be able to beat our time."

I dragged myself to my feet and dusted bits of grass off my pants.

"Wait!" someone cried out. "Everett and Leona haven't tried yet."

I stiffened. "There's no need."

Leona stood frozen at the opposite end of the field. We locked eyes, and she shook her head. We were going to lose. Badly. Elsie rushed over to her, excitedly waving the blindfold.

Claude approached me. "Come now, it's all in good fun. If you do beat us, I'll buy you a drink."

"The whiskey here is free."

"I know." Claude tied the blindfold across my eyes.

I lost count of how many times he spun me around. The raucous chatter overpowered all my other senses. I stopped moving, but the world still felt like it was rotating beneath me.

"Go!" Floyd shouted.

I took a step and stumbled. Laughter ensued. I didn't let it deter me.

"It usually works better if one partner stays put!" Mack suggested.

I staggered a bit and slowly continued in the direction I was facing.

"Lordy." Dorothy tsked loudly. "They're both gonna be walkin' around in circles for hours."

Even with my heightened sense of smell, I couldn't seem to pick up Leona's scent.

"Try drifting to him, Leona!" Jasper called out.

I blocked out their playful taunting and focused solely on Leona. On the connection we shared. Heat rose from my markings. I walked a bit faster. My steps were even and steady. I sensed her. I was drawn to her. The lighthearted chiding started to die down. My neck suddenly became cool. The connection was starting to fade. I stopped, made a sharp turn to the left and continued walking. The markings heated up again. Chatter turned to hushed murmurs. My neck was almost burning. She was close. I could feel her. I raised my hand and held out my open palm. Her fingers curled between mine, and I clasped her hand.

"Leona?" I didn't have to say her name. I knew her touch. And she knew mine.

"Forty-seven seconds," Floyd said in dismay. "A new record."

The crowd broke into wild applause.

"How is that even possible?" Jim demanded.

"I want a new partner!" Stella joked.

"Forget the drink," Claude said. "I owe you a bottle, Everett!"

I slid the covering from my eyes without letting go of Leona's hand.

She tossed her blindfold aside and gazed up at me in amusement. "Not bad, partner."

Chapter 45: Rankings
Leona

Night had fallen. Lanterns dangled overhead, casting soft yellow light across the grassy field where Everett was dancing with a trapper named Dorothy. I had insisted we spend the majority of the social apart, but I never told him why. If anyone found out about our union, I would be ruined—and after our time together at the hotel, I didn't trust myself around him. I couldn't. The markings on my back were like flames that ignited whenever he was near. My body burned for him.

I downed the last of the wine in my glass, hoping to extinguish some of the longing I felt, but it had no effect. Frustrated, I placed the empty glass on the edge of a table and searched for something stronger. Dorothy giggled, and I glanced up in time to see Everett twirling her around. His face was expressionless, but his brilliant golden eyes met mine. A wave of excitement washed over me, and a tingling sensation spread throughout my body. I bit my lower lip and forced myself to look away.

"Focus on your ranking and get a grip," I muttered to myself as couples waltzed past me.

My ranking. The only thing preventing me from rushing over to Everett and claiming him with a kiss in front of all the other trappers. Everett was new to the Agency, but he ranked as a level three, no doubt due to his previous experience as a range detective. Maude and I had risen to level nine. Expert. The moment a couple formally acknowledged their relationship to the Agency, both of their rankings dropped to level one. Couples had to rise through the ranks together, as equals. I couldn't afford that. My current wages were barely enough to keep me alive, and I wasn't *nearly* as reckless as I had been during my early trapping days. But part of me feared Everett wouldn't see it that way. Family was truly important to him, and in a way, I was choosing money over our relationship.

"That partner of yours is a good dancer." Bess fluffed her dark curly hair as she strolled up and stood by my side. She took note of the empty glass behind me and handed me her copper flask. "But he sure don't say much."

I sipped some of her whiskey and handed it back. "Everett's telepathic."

"So am I." Bess swallowed a mouthful. "He nearly blinded me when I asked him about you. Completely blocked his thoughts from me. Now I have a splitting headache."

"I'm sorry." I wrapped my arm around her narrow shoulders. "He doesn't know you and I are friends."

"He did the same thing to me." Stella approached with a sly smile. She flipped her wavy red locks over her shoulder, and her hair cascaded below her waist. "He must not know that we're friends as well."

I gave her a cold stare. "You and I *aren't* friends."

She met my gaze and didn't budge. Bess fidgeted with the cap of her flask. Stella and I burst into laughter, and I dragged her into a hug with my free arm.

"I've missed you all so much," I said.

Stella squeezed me tight. "We missed you too. Jim was worried you wouldn't be here after what happened with Harvey."

"Harvey?" Bess asked. "What happened to him?"

I freed them of our group hug and sighed wearily. "We're not on the best of terms anymore."

"Harvey and Fredrick went rogue and attacked Leona," Stella said in a hushed tone. "Fredrick was killed, and the Agency sent Leona and Everett after Harvey."

Bess's eyes went wide. "They sent trappers to trap a trapper? That's just not done."

"Harvey was a special case." I wanted to believe my own words, but more importantly I wanted to make sure anyone who overheard us knew I wasn't speaking ill of the Agency. My loyalties were to them.

"Good riddance," Stella said. "One less traitor in our midst."

Bess's shoulders relaxed. "I never much liked him anyway."

"It wasn't an easy assignment," I admitted. "But I'm glad it's over."

"You travel anywhere new lately?" Bess asked.

I shrugged. "Onyx Springs."

"What was you doin' out that far?" she asked.

Stella rolled her eyes. "That's a stupid question. She's a drifter. The further out she goes, the more jobs she can snatch up from the rest of us."

I tilted my head. "Are you still mad about losing Blind Man's Buff?"

Stella grabbed my shoulders and shook me. "How did you do it? Tell me your secret!"

I chuckled and slipped out of her clawlike grasp. "I never tell my secrets."

My hearing was muffled, and I barely registered that another song had ended until couples stepped apart and bowed. Elsie caught sight of us and pranced over, furiously waving her lace fan to prevent any perspiration from forming on her brow.

"Where, pray tell, are your partners?" Elsie asked. "Why aren't any of you dancing?"

"We're not all blessed to have partners with a decent amount of coordination like you and Leona," Stella teased.

Elsie playfully whacked Stella's arm with her fan. "I'm sure Claudie would be more than willing to dance with such refined ladies as yourselves."

"*Claudie* only likes dancing with you," Stella stated bluntly.

I remained silent, knowing better than to broach that topic with Elsie. She was sweet and innocent on the outside, but the feisty blonde had a tongue sharper than the dagger she kept hidden in her fan.

"What ever do you mean?" Elsie asked Stella.

"I mean if you don't want other trappers spreading rumors about you and Claude, you both need to stop flirting so much in public."

"Yeah, treat him like Leona treats Everett," Bess chimed in. "Pretend he don't exist."

My mouth twisted to the side. "What are you talking about? Everett and I have a wonderful relationship."

"Is that why he's danced with every woman here except you?" Stella asked.

I pursed my lips. "He hasn't danced with the Gilroy sisters."

"I declare," Elsie said. "She's keeping track."

"I am not," I said defensively.

"All this time I thought you hated him," Stella said. "But the truth is so much worse."

"What truth?" I asked.

"You don't know how to entice him."

Bess shook her head. "That's a cryin' shame."

I brushed nonexistent dust from my floral dress. "Maybe I'm not trying to attract *anyone*. Maybe I'm not the type to settle down."

"Who said anything about settling down? I'm talking about—" Stella made a gesture that caused Elsie to blush.

Her fan snapped closed. "I know your mama raised you better than that."

"She didn't." Stella turned her attention back to me. "Come on, Leona. You're not foolish enough to marry your partner and risk losing your ranking, but that doesn't mean you can't have a little fun once in a while. Take it from Elsie."

Elsie smiled sweetly and flashed a dagger between her middle fingers. "It's such a shame that mouth of yours doesn't match your face. You could be really pretty."

Stella laughed, and Bess gulped down another mouthful of whiskey.

"Did I mention how much I missed you ladies?" I said.

They all snickered, but I was being serious. Our assignments with the Agency kept us scattered throughout the territories and often stretched on for weeks. Sometimes our paths crossed, but we were rarely all in the same place at the same time. That was the nature of trapping, and it was one of the reasons I always looked forward to the annual social.

The song faded, and Everett broke away from his dance partner. Stella nudged me then shouted his name and waved him over. Everett headed in our direction.

"What are you doing?" I demanded.

"Helping you out," Stella whispered. "We all know how hard it is for you to get a man."

Elsie nodded. "It's like she purposely repels them."

I stomped my foot. "I can get a man."

"The Tea Room don't count," Bess said.

My heart beat wildly in my chest as my markings started to heat up. I was going to give us away. *Typical trappers!* They would know by my body language, or my tone of voice... or by the sexual desire that was seeping out of every one of my pores.

Everett walked up without making eye contact with me. "Good evening, ladies."

We all curtsied. His tantalizing scent consumed me and caused my body to shudder. I held my breath. My markings felt like they were on fire. Like they could burn a hole right through the thin fabric of my dress. I wanted to scream, but before I could utter a sound, Stella shoved me into Everett's arms.

"Leona wants to dance with you."

Chapter 46: Tongue-Tied

Leona

Everett politely escorted me across the field to the center of the makeshift dance floor. I had difficulty hearing the soft music or the lively chatter of the other trappers, but I pushed that thought aside. I had bigger issues to worry about.

Act natural, I repeated to myself. I found it unnerving how easily my hand fit into Everett's as we began to sway to the music. I was never that comfortable with anyone. Never. The other trappers were bound to suspect there was something going on between me and Everett. They were going to find out we were in love. That I had given my heart and soul to my partner... and I wanted him desperately.

My markings heated up, and I sucked in a breath.

"Stop thinking about me," Everett whispered.

I blinked. "What?"

His expression remained neutral. "Trust me. The burning will subside."

I cleared my mind and prevented myself from dwelling on my intense feelings for Everett. The warm sensation started to fade.

"Is that how you've done it all night?" I asked quietly. "You've blocked me from your thoughts?"

"Yes." His voice was flat. "Otherwise, I wouldn't have been able to stop myself from taking you on the dessert table."

"Why the dessert table?"

He cocked his head. "I like sweet things."

I stifled a chuckle, and he smiled.

"Your friends seem nice," he said.

"The busybodies?" I rolled my eyes in feigned irritation. "They think I can't get a man on my own."

Everett slowly twirled me around. "I heard you have a bit of a reputation."

My eyes narrowed. "Who did you hear that from?"

"Trappers like to talk. A lot."

"What do they say about me?"

He shrugged. "Nothing I don't already know."

I flashed him a sly grin. "You think you know me so well?"

"I think I know certain parts of you well." Everett slid his hand a little lower down my back. "And there's still a lot left to be explored."

Invisible flames started licking up my back again. I spoke only loud enough for him to hear. "You should probably stop toying with me. I don't have the same level of restraint as you do."

"Mine is faltering," he admitted.

"What do you suppose we do about it?"

His gaze drifted across the field. "It's dark in the woods."

My body began to ache. I wanted nothing more than his soft lips caressing my skin.

"May I cut in?"

Julius startled me, but Everett barely flinched. He slowly let me go, bowed politely, and allowed Julius to take his place. Over Julius's shoulder, Everett readjusted his tie and traced a finger down the markings on his neck. He cracked a small smile, and subtly mouthed the word, "*Mine.*" I bit my lip to prevent my own smile from escaping, and Everett swiftly departed from our company.

Refocusing my attention on Julius, I followed his lead as we danced to the slow tempo. His form was perfect and precise. Just like everything else about him.

"You're looking—" He lowered his voice. "Beautiful. As always."

"You look handsome as well, Julius." I meant it, even if I felt nothing for him. "Are you enjoying your evening?"

He snorted. "You know how much I hate dancing."

"I know." I stared into his deep brown eyes. "Almost as much as I hate games."

Julius tightened his hand around mine. "Why didn't you tell him?"

I glanced across the way at Everett. Both of the Gilroy sisters were trying to coax him into a dance.

"Because it wasn't important," I said finally.

"Everett could have killed you."

He has *killed me. More than once.* But I kept those thoughts to myself. What we'd done was far more dangerous than a mere snake bite. "I'm fine."

"How long did it take you to recover from his lightning bolt?" Julius asked.

"I appreciate your concern, but it's really none of your—"

"How long?"

Julius used the voice. The one that was tender and kind. The one that could get me to divulge my deepest thoughts and feelings. "I still haven't fully recovered. My hearing is a little off."

"I knew it," Julius muttered. "I have extra gold I can give you. Enough for you to heal and still have some left over in case of an emergency."

"No."

Julius accidentally bumped us into another couple. He apologized and quickly regained his footing.

"What do you mean, *no*?" he said.

"I don't want to owe you anything."

"You wouldn't owe me. Consider it a gift."

I shook my head. "I can't accept gifts from you."

"The Agency wouldn't have to know." He spoke quietly. "I'm not doing this as your superior. I'm doing this as your friend."

I pulled away slightly. "We're not together anymore."

Julius looked as though I had slapped him across the face. "You think this is about us? You and Everett are one failed catch away from being terminated."

"I know. You don't have to keep reminding me that the Agency will terminate our contracts."

"I don't think you understand." Julius drew me closer. "Too many trappers have gone rogue and turned against us. The Agency isn't taking any more chances. They will send someone to terminate *you* and *Everett.*"

I clenched my jaw to prevent it from dropping. After all the years I sacrificed for them. All the pain. The blood. The tears. I was nothing to the Agency. Just another warm body that could be disposed of when it no longer served a purpose. My eyes swept across the jovial faces of my fellow trappers. People I considered my family. The only family I'd ever known aside from my sister... and Everett.

"Your record with Everett is shoddy at best. What would happen if you encountered a disgruntled outlaw in your current state?" Julius discreetly slipped a small leather pouch into the pocket of my full skirt. "Use the gold, Leona."

My mind was in a whirlwind. "I-I'll need a couple of weeks."

"Take a month. Once you've fully healed, I'll have Amos give you and Everett a new assignment." Julius leaned down and whispered in my ear. "I never liked when you kept secrets from me. I'm sure your new lover doesn't either."

Heat flashed into my cheeks. "Everett's not—"

"You don't have to lie to me. You've been avoiding him the same way you used to avoid me at these functions."

My throat tightened.

"You needn't worry. I'd never say anything to compromise your ranking." The music faded. Julius bowed and kissed the back of my hand. "Thank you for the dance."

I curtsied and tried to regain my composure. "Thank you, Julius."

He smiled thinly, and we parted in opposite directions. I clung to the front of my skirt to prevent my hands from shaking. The open field was crammed with trappers. A blur of yellow lights shined down from overhead, and I suddenly felt the urge to retreat into the darkness. My three friends nearly accosted me as I rejoined them by the rows of empty tables lining the edge of the dance floor.

Stella clapped gleefully. "I stand corrected. You were able to attract *two* men in one night!"

"Julius don't count. He was probably talkin' business." Bess handed me her flask. "Here. You're lookin' like you need this more than I do."

I guzzled down a mouthful of whiskey as Elsie fanned me.

"Jules has the worst timing." Her brow was furrowed. "Are you all right?"

"Fine." I wiped my mouth with the back of my hand. "Has anyone seen Everett?"

"I saw him by the dessert table," Stella said.

"No tellin' why." Bess shook her head. "Ain't nothin' over there. The Nelson brothers ate every last bit."

I gave her back the flask. "I have to go."

Before they could protest, I quickly said my goodbyes and promised to meet up with them again if our assignments overlapped. Everett was conversing with a longwinded trapper named Ed but cut the conversation short when I signaled him over. We slipped away from the gathering and headed into the forest.

The crisp night air did little to settle my nerves. I wanted to get as far away from other people as possible. Everett kept up with my steady pace and didn't say a word until we were well past the lights and the raucous laughter of the other trappers.

"Leona..." Everett grabbed my arm and spun me around.

Before I could utter a sound, he kissed me. I wrapped my arms around his neck and gave in to my desire. I could pretend everything was fine. Just for that moment. I didn't have to tell him.

Everett backed me against a tree without taking his lips off mine. He slid his hands down my body and clenched the fabric of my skirt.

"I wanted you all night," he whispered in my ear.

"I wanted you too."

Everett didn't have to know. My secrets didn't hurt him—they were there to protect me. To prevent me from getting too close in case the relationship fell apart. Like it always did. Sooner or later.

Everett clung to me and trailed kisses down my neck. I was overwhelmed by his unbridled passion. I'd never been loved so intensely. By anyone. Heat rose from my markings. We were connected... I shared a bond with him. If something hurt me, it hurt him.

"Lightning has the potential to kill me," I blurted out.

Everett pulled away and looked at me through the silver moonlight. The strong lines of his face cast shadows over his serious expression. "*Kill* you, kill you?"

"Yes."

He took his time before responding. "So, let's agree we'll never do that again."

I nodded. My jaw was tight. That was all he needed to know. Nothing else.

Everett slowly started kissing me again. I tried to relax. His body pressed against mine, and I could feel the rapid beating of his heart. He loved me, and he trusted me. If he found out any other way,

I would lose some of that trust. Our relationship would begin to erode... and I would be to blame.

"Julius gave me extra gold so I can heal," I said quickly.

Everett tore himself from me. "You haven't fully healed?"

"No. My hearing was badly affected."

His bright-yellow eyes widened.

"You probably didn't notice because half of the time we were at the hotel you were speaking to me telepathically."

"I'm so sorry. I had no idea." Everett gently cradled my face in his hands. He leaned closer to kiss my lips then stopped. "Is there anything else?"

I clamped my mouth shut and shook my head.

Everett buried his face in my neck. I held my breath, willing myself to remain silent. He slid his hand up my skirt and squeezed my thigh.

I couldn't stop the words from pouring out of my mouth. "If we lose another catch, the Agency is going to send one of their hunters to kill us."

Chapter 47: Kindling

Everett

I didn't think it was possible for Leona to kill my mood. But she did.

"The Agency employs hunters?" I asked in dismay.

"Unofficially, yes. They're reserved for highly secretive assignments." Leona leaned her back against the broad tree trunk behind her. "Trappers and hunters never mingle. Otherwise, things would get—messy."

The dark forest was still, but all my senses were on high alert. The slightest change in the wind caught my attention. I started pacing.

"The Agency is growing increasingly paranoid about trappers going rogue," Leona continued. "Julius said they're not taking any more chances."

The hair on the back of my neck stood up, and I stopped short. "They're watching us."

"That's nothing new."

"No..." Moonlight glistened in her eyes as I projected my thoughts to her. *I mean, someone's watching us right now.*

Leona quickly crouched down and grabbed a handful of dirt. I shifted into snake form, wrapped myself around her body, and braced myself for the falling sensation.

We drifted and landed in our secret hideaway, under the falls. I slithered to the damp rocky ground, and a cool mist pricked my cheeks as I returned to my human form. Our base camp was exactly the way we'd left it. Minus a fire. I went about gathering the dry wood we'd stacked along the cave's craggy walls. Mindless tasks kept me from dwelling on the uneasy feeling lingering in the pit of my stomach. I was certain Leona felt it too because she was busying herself with our laundry, refolding our clothes into neater stacks. As if that was a priority.

"We have to be more careful," Leona said without looking at me.

"I know." I struck a match, and the kindling caught fire. "I don't think they saw us kissing."

"You're sure?" she asked.

I wasn't. But we had much bigger problems to worry about. "I'm guessing Julius knows."

Leona spun around. "Knows what?"

"About your injuries. Why else would he give you the gold?"

"Oh... yes." Leona cleared her throat and went back to folding clothes. "Julius insisted I take time off to recuperate. We don't have to report to the Agency for a month."

"It will take you that long to recover your hearing?" I felt like a cad for not noticing she hadn't fully healed.

"No, it will only take about a week if I rest."

I tossed another log on the fire. "*If?*"

She kept her back to me. "We have a rare opportunity. No one will be looking for us or expecting us to check in for the next four weeks. I want to travel to the tundra."

The mere thought of that frozen wasteland made me shudder. "There's nothing out there."

"Exactly. It's the perfect place for Maude to hide. Like Ray said."

I silently cursed Ray for even mentioning his brief dealings with her sister. I regretted not gagging that outlaw when I had the chance. "Ray's the last person I would trust."

"Under normal circumstances, I'd agree. But he's the only person we know who has seen her alive since the fire." Leona moved on to sorting our cooking utensils. "Chester was the one who dug up Maude's remains, but he never saw her regenerate, and she never returned. He genuinely believed she was gone forever... until we showed up."

Chester. A wave of guilt came over me at the mention of the miner's name. He would've still been alive had he not gotten entangled with us. I blamed myself for his untimely death. The blood feud spilled into every corner of my life and had severed yet another link to her sister.

I spoke up. "What about Amos? He was the one helping you piece together clues about who killed her. Does he have any leads?"

"Amos doesn't know Maude's alive. I didn't tell him we went to her grave."

"Why not? He's your friend." Even *I* was beginning to trust Amos.

"Because he's tied too closely with the Agency. At the moment, we don't know which trappers have turned, and I don't want the wrong people discovering she's alive."

"You think that's the reason Maude's afraid to come out of hiding?"

"It has to be. She cut ties with everyone she knew." Leona fiddled with the silverware. "Everyone she cared about."

"Do you think maybe..." I chose my words carefully. "She doesn't want to be found?"

Leona turned on her heel and looked at me. "What are you saying? That I should stop looking for her?"

I prodded the logs with a long stick. "The tundra is dangerous."

"You've navigated it before."

"Not by choice." Sparks flew up from the flames. "The landscape is treacherous. There's no easy way to travel in or out. Have you considered the fact that you can't drift when you're wet, and we'd be trudging through mounds of snow?"

"I've been to areas where I can't drift." Leona went back to tidying up. "We'll just have to be more cautious and avoid unnecessary risks."

The entire endeavor was an "unnecessary risk," but I kept that thought to myself. "I don't function well in freezing temperatures."

"We can travel at a slower pace so you can acclimate to the weather. And I was told there are outposts scattered across the territory where we can rest and gather supplies."

She was impossible to reason with. "What if we get out there and it's another dead end?"

Leona inhaled sharply. "Then I can rule it out as a possible hiding place."

"Then what?"

Pots and pans clattered as Leona restacked them. "I keep looking."

"Then what?"

"What do you want me to say?" Leona whipped around to face me. "I'm not going to stop looking for my sister. Ever."

"I know," I muttered. "That's what I'm afraid of."

Her reply was so soft I almost didn't hear it over the crackling fire. "You don't have to come with me."

My jaw tightened.

"I've been alone before." Her voice trembled slightly. "I can do this by my—"

"That's not how a partnership works, Leona."

My loud voice echoed off the hollow cave walls, and Leona turned away. The steady sound of rushing water filled our agonizing silence. I slowly rose and stood beside her. She glanced up at me through the hazy mist, and I spoke directly into her mind.

That's not how a marriage works.

Leona nodded and held my gaze.

"I promised you I would do everything in my power to help you find your sister." I gently stroked the side of her face with the back of my finger. *I have no intention of going back on that promise now.*

"I know you think I'm too trusting," she whispered. "But my sister's still out there, and she's in trouble. I can feel it."

There was little emotion in Leona's tone, but I saw a glimpse of her anguish in her eyes. She never showed her true pain. Not even to me. And it hurt my soul. "What's your plan?"

Chapter 48: Familiar Faces

Everett

The journey north to the tundra was just as grueling as I'd remembered. Two days after the social, Leona and I loaded up our gear and boarded a train that took us all the way through the Wispy Mountains. The only advantage to us *not* being able to drift to the tundra was the fact that my body was able to adjust to the frigid temperatures slowly, day by day. My worst fear was stepping into unknown territory and being completely incapacitated. If the weather didn't kill us, scavengers surely would. Leona had stubbornly refused to use the gold Julius had given her, but I didn't press the issue. She wasn't going to rest until she had answers.

The train tracks ran out in a sleepy little town called Dusty Hollow, and we found the one stagecoach heading toward Glacier's Peak. We were grateful there were few passengers on board, five of us total, but our comfort was short-lived. The temperature dropped. Clouds rolled in. Wind and snow relentlessly whipped into the stagecoach. For nine days. I huddled next to Leona, shielding her from the brunt of the storms. By the time we reached the final station, the snow had stopped, but we were chilled to the bone. Leona didn't complain. Not once.

I squinted through the bright afternoon sunlight as I climbed out of the stagecoach. A blanket of powdery snow covered the entire town. If it could even be called a town. Most of the buildings were boarded up. But there was a blacksmith, a run-down general store, a dilapidated stable, and a cemetery.

Leona jumped down beside me and readjusted her thick wool hat. "Not exactly what I was expecting."

Two men rushed over to assist the stagecoach driver with the team and luggage. The three remaining passengers slowly made their way out of the coach, clearly in no rush to be exposed to the elements.

"Where should we start?" Leona asked.

"The general store," I said. "Everyone needs supplies at some point or another."

One of the young men hauling a leather suitcase clumsily bumped into Leona. She stumbled backward. Her bag slipped from her shoulder and landed in a mound of snow.

"Beg pardon, ma'am—" The man's eyes widened at the sight of her. He quickly lowered his head, his broadbrim hat concealing his face.

"It's all right." Leona didn't give him a second glance as she scooped up her bag and dusted off the snowflakes.

I watched the young man intently. He dropped the suitcase and hurried to the opposite side of the stagecoach to assist with the horses.

Strange, don't you think? I projected to Leona as I kept my eye on the jittery fellow.

"What?"

"Nothing." We made our way down the broad pathway. Something was strange about the entire town. There was an undercurrent. Energy surrounding us that I couldn't identify. Part of me wondered if I was being paranoid. I'd nearly died the last time I was so far from civilization. But the other part of me knew better than to ignore my intuition.

We entered the general store, and it took a moment for my eyes to adjust to the dim lighting. There were no windows aside from the storefront, and no other visible exits. The smell of feed and dried meat lingered in the air, and the potbelly stove in the center of the room provided much needed warmth from the bitter cold outside. I tore off my gloves and rubbed my hands close to the heat. Leona wandered around the store, eyeing various barrels of pickles and potatoes. I thought about replenishing some of our canned goods, but the floor-to-ceiling shelves were somewhat bare. We'd have to rely on my hunting.

An elderly gentleman with a long silver mustache emerged from a back room and stood behind the counter. He flashed us a broad smile.

"Howdy, folks! How can I help—" His smile faded when he caught sight of Leona.

That time she noticed.

"Maude, what're you doing here?" the man whispered urgently. "You know it ain't safe."

She squared her shoulders. "My name is Leona. I'm looking for my sister. Do you know the last time she came through here?"

"I don't know nothin'." The man turned to me. "I swear. I'm not even from 'round here."

That was all I needed to hear. I lowered my guard and stared into his hazy brown eyes. The off-worlder's expression went blank, and he stood transfixed. Random thoughts whispered through my mind. *A twin. Ranch hands. Gold. The cook.* His mind was incredibly sharp, but one thing was certain.

"He's lying about not knowing anything," I said to Leona.

She rested her hands on the cluttered countertop. "Please. I'll pay you for any information you have."

My jaw tensed. That was the real reason she hadn't used Julius's money to heal. She was hoping to barter with it. Risking her well-being for the sake of her sister's. Again.

The elderly gentleman blinked hard and shook out his head. I felt bad for the mild headache he was surely fighting through, but I'd been careful not to probe too deeply into his mind. There would be no lasting damage.

"Got no use for your money," he said finally. He leaned closer and lowered his voice. "But you shouldn't be here. Not after what happened between them fellas and Maude."

The front door swung open, and a dusting of snow blew across the worn wooden floors. The skittish young man stood at the threshold, but his nerves had been replaced by something sinister. His dark gaze fell upon Leona. He whistled.

"I may have a crate in the back," the shopkeeper said loudly, drawing our attention back to him. "Y'all can take a look if you want."

Leona and I hurried behind the counter and followed the man down a dark narrow hallway. Heavy footsteps echoed at the front of the store. From their angry voices, I counted at least four men. We rushed out a back door. A dense forest of evergreens loomed over us.

"Head toward the mountains. Stay off the main pathways." The man grabbed Leona's hands. "Find Cookie. She'll help you."

"How do we find her?" I demanded.

"Follow the white flags."

"Thank you." Leona reached for her coin purse, but he stopped her.

"Keep it. You'll probably need it." Glass shattered inside the store, and his eyes pleaded with us. "Run."

We darted into the woods. I didn't dare look back. My boots sunk into the snow, and I cursed under my breath. There was no way to hide our tracks.

I absently projected my panicked thoughts to Leona. *They're going to kill him.*

"They're after us, not him," Leona said quickly as we charged up the slippery hillside.

Everyone knows your face. Your sister's *face.*

"I realize that."

The icy air stung my lungs each time I inhaled, but I kept pace with Leona. *If Maude's alone out here, she's in more danger than we are.*

Leona stumbled slightly.

We're trapped. There's no way out.

"Everett!" Leona shouted without breaking her stride. "I love you, but I need you to get out of my head so I can think!"

"Sorry, love." I closed myself off from her and retreated into my own mind. We weren't prepared. For any of it. I'd been so worried about getting through the physical aspect of the journey, I overlooked the possibility that we might encounter the very same people who caused Maude to go into hiding.

When Leona finally slowed down, we were a good three miles away from the wretched little town. We slumped behind a large boulder to catch our breath. My hands were numb, and my face burned from the wind. Exhaustion threatened to overtake me. I wanted to curl into my snake form and go to sleep. Leona wrapped her arms around me, sharing her warmth. I buried myself in her tenderness.

"Do you need to shift?" she asked gently.

"If I do, I'll have an even harder time shifting back into human form."

She nodded. "Then we keep moving. Maybe Cookie will offer us shelter."

I mentally prepared myself for the long trek ahead. Forward was our only option. Leona slowly let go of me. I tried not to focus on the biting chill that tore through my clothes and consumed me. As a shapeshifter, I was acutely aware of my body. I had to be in order to maintain various shapes and forms. But in that moment, I wished I was any other sentient being on the planet. Preferably one in a warmer climate.

We trudged through the snow in relative silence for the better part of an hour, but when I spotted a tattered white flag flapping in the wind, I nearly cried out in joy. Then we spotted another. And another. Bolstered by the silent markers, we hurried through the forest, following the trail until we reached a small clearing where a tent and chuck wagon were neatly arranged side by side. A large cast-iron pot dangled over an open fire, and the heady smell of meat and herbs floated through the air.

A canvas awning hung over the back of the wagon, and a slender woman stood under it, chopping vegetables on a flat hinged work surface. Her knife was fast. She didn't bother looking up as we approached.

"Make yourselves comfortable. The stew will be ready in a couple of hours. If you're low on coin, I'm willing to trade."

The melodic sound of her voice pricked something in the darkest recesses of my mind. I froze. She turned to face us. My breath caught in my throat. Our eyes locked. I couldn't hear any other sound over the rapid beating of my heart. Her expression remained neutral. She didn't recognize me. But I recognized her. The wavy black hair. The youthful facial features...

Her gaze shifted to Leona, and a broad grin spread across her face. "Maude! You're back!"

"I-I'm not—"

"Wait right there." She dashed inside her tent and began rummaging through her belongings.

I projected my thoughts to Leona. *We have to leave. Now!*

"Why?" she whispered urgently.

Because her name isn't Cookie. It's Nora. She's the woman I wiped. My entire body was trembling. *Hiram's woman.*

Chapter 49: Echo in the Woods

Leona

Everett's words echoed in my mind. *Hiram's woman.* I stifled the panic that was slowly creeping into my soul. We were there for one reason, and one reason alone.

"We can't just leave." I spoke in a low voice. "She obviously knows something about Maude."

Everett's eyes darted to the canvas tent where Nora was preoccupied with her intense search. *We get the information, and we get out. Quickly.*

I nodded.

Nora emerged from the tent holding a small wooden box. Her warm smile and soft features made her appear younger than I assumed she was, but she carried herself with poise and confidence. I wanted to trust her. I needed to trust her. We'd come so far without any answers, I couldn't bear the thought of returning to my normal life without knowing what had happened to my sister.

Nora attempted to hand me the box, but I didn't take it. "I'm sorry. That's probably meant for Maude. I'm her twin sister, Leona."

Nora's expression shifted from slight confusion to sheer delight. "Leona!" She threw her arms around my shoulders and gave me a tight hug. "I've heard so much about you. I feel like I practically know you."

Words escaped me as I hugged her back. Everett stood behind me, stiff as a board.

"And I take it he's your partner?" Nora slowly released me. "You're still with the Agency?"

"Yes..." I said cautiously.

"Please, sit." She gestured toward the uneven stumps and logs surrounding the fire. "I'll get you both something to eat."

Nora trotted off to her chuck wagon, where she'd abandoned the vegetables on her makeshift workstation as soon as she caught sight of us. She put the box on the edge of the table and continued dicing potatoes.

A large pot of stew simmered over open flames. The pleasant aroma of thyme and rosemary made my mouth water. I dusted snow off a log, dropped my leather bag, and sat beside Everett. His silence was unnerving. I was desperate to know what he was thinking, but I knew seeing Nora again had shaken him to his core. He rarely spoke about the events that led to his feud with Hiram. If he didn't want to share the details, it wasn't my place to press the issue.

"How do you know Maude?" I spoke casually, holding back the barrage of questions I really wanted to ask Nora.

"I met her a while back on the ranch," she said.

"You worked together?" I asked.

"Sort of. My daddy owned the ranch. I helped out wherever I could and got to know most of the ranch hands." Her steady chopping didn't waver. "Maude is by far one of the hardest working people I've ever known. She could run circles around just about anyone."

I was taken aback by Nora's openness. "That sounds like Maude."

"We spent a lot of time together, and after Daddy's tragic passing, she was kind enough to let me travel with her. I inherited the ranch, but it wasn't safe for me to stay behind."

"Why not?" I asked.

Nora stopped suddenly and faced us. Fear flickered in her deep-brown eyes, and her words were choked. "The shapeshifter."

Everett was so still, I wondered if he was breathing. "You were being pursued by a shapeshifter?"

"Stalked." Nora shook her head and scraped the vegetables into an empty bowl. "He was completely deranged. He had this wild notion that we were lovers, but I'd never seen him before in my life."

Hiram was persistent. Everett and I could attest to that, but I stopped myself from glancing at him. Nora walked over to the pot, added the potatoes, and stirred the stew.

"At one point the shapeshifter dragged me to a secret hideout. He held me captive for weeks." Nora shuddered. "I don't know what would have happened if Maude hadn't rescued me."

Everett's voice was quiet. "The shapeshifter harmed you?"

"Not—physically." Nora wrapped her arms around her body, as though trying to shield herself from the bad memories. "It was a relentless attack on my mind. I'm not telepathic, but that didn't stop him from trying to penetrate my thoughts. It was almost like he was trying to unlock something in my brain."

I sat silently, but she revealed no further details. When Everett and I first started trying to connect telepathically, I was left feeling lightheaded and listless each time we practiced. But he'd warned me about the effects of prolonged attempts. Debilitating headaches. Severe nausea and vomiting. Bouts of vertigo. And in extreme cases, loss of consciousness. My natural ability to regenerate and heal allowed me to withstand longer sessions—but Everett never pushed me too far. I couldn't imagine what Hiram put Nora through. The darkness in her hollow gaze attested to her unspeakable pain.

"I'm so very sorry," Everett whispered.

"It wasn't your fault." Nora forced a weak smile. "Besides, I can't even remember the man's name or what he looks like. I think I've subconsciously blocked him out of my mind."

It is my fault. All of it. Everett lowered his head as he projected his thoughts to me. *Her father hired me to erase Hiram from her mind. He said it was for her protection. I didn't realize they were in love until it was too late.*

I placed my gloved hand over his and gave him a gentle squeeze. "You and your father were close?"

"Very. Momma died when I was just a little girl." Nora held her hand to her heart. "I was his whole world... and he was mine. After Maude saved me from the shapeshifter, Daddy vowed never to let me out of his sight again."

He lied to me. Everett spoke into my mind. *He was just trying to control his daughter.*

"Your father died suddenly?" I asked.

Nora nodded and turned her attention back to the stew. "Not long after I returned, he had a bad fall while trying to fix the roof of our barn."

"I'm sorry for your loss," I said sincerely.

"I don't know what I would have done without your sister." Nora quickly brushed a tear away. "I was terrified the shapeshifter would find me again, so she brought me out here and helped me get settled. Very few people dwell this close to the tundra. I'm free to live however I choose."

"I'm glad you found a measure of peace," Everett said.

Nora's voice was solemn. "It's only because of Maude. I owe her my life."

"Does she come through here often?" I asked. "Do you know where I might find her?"

"I wish I knew. She comes back to check on me every so often. But you know how drifters are. Rarely in the same place for too long."

The wind shifted, and Everett's head whipped around. *Someone's coming. I just picked up their scent.*

"If I left a message for Maude, would you relay it to her?" I asked Nora quickly.

"Of course. Anything for a friend."

We have to go! Everett projected loudly as he jumped up.

I scooped up my bag and scrambled to my feet.

"You're not leaving, are you?" Nora asked. "You haven't even had a proper meal."

"We can't stay. Some men from town are after us."

Nora's eyes widened. "The Ellis Gang."

Everett shot me a worried frown.

Nora rushed over to her wagon and grabbed the box that was intended for Maude. "Take this. She would want you to have it."

Heavy footsteps plodded through the snow in the distance. I shoved the box into my bag and gave Nora a hug.

"Tell my sister she broke her promise. But I have no intention of breaking mine."

Nora gave me a firm nod. I slung my bag over my shoulder, and Everett and I ran deeper into the woods. I followed his lead. He was much better at evading danger due to his heightened senses. The thin air burned my lungs, but I didn't break my stride.

Gunshots rang out. Everett and I dove to the ground. We shuffled across the powdery snow and sought shelter under a fallen tree. Everett pulled me into him, our bodies pressed close together in the tight space. Snow seeped through layers of my clothes. A constant reminder that I couldn't drift. I was trapped.

I'd convinced Everett that I wasn't afraid of the frozen wilderness. That I wasn't afraid to be powerless. But I was. The only thing that kept me from unraveling was knowing that if I was attacked or injured, I still had the gold from Julius. I could heal quickly. But I feared for Everett's safety. I'd been so blinded by my quest to find Maude, I hadn't truly considered the danger I was putting him in.

We lay shivering and helpless, waiting for the inevitable. They would find us.

"We have a better chance of escaping if we split up." I spoke between chattering teeth. "We could meet back at Nora's after nightfall."

I'll draw them away from you then shift.

"But it's too cold. You won't be able to shift back into human form."

I'm willing to take that risk if it means protecting you, he projected softly.

The wind howled overhead, and I wondered if Everett would be able to hear my whispered words. "I'm sorry for dragging us out here."

Everett rested his forehead on mine. *We finally have a solid connection to Maude. That's all that matters.*

We. I knew in that moment he would follow me anywhere. That he would put me first, above all else... and I couldn't let him.

"I love you, Everett." I kissed his icy lips, tore myself from his grasp, and darted out into the open.

Leona! Come back!

Everett's frantic pleas echoed loudly in my mind as I sprinted away from him. I swerved around broad pine trees, dropped my bag, and increased my pace.

"She's over here!"

Another deafening shot rang through the air.

"Where's her partner?" a gruff voice called out.

I glanced over my shoulder, willing Everett to stay hidden. My body slammed into the solid mass of a man. A sharp pain tore through my abdomen. I yelped. The pile of snow I landed in did little to break my fall. I clenched my stomach. I should have been freezing, but all I felt was warmth spreading down my body. A burly man towered over me. His thick grubby facial hair partially hid the crooked grin that was plastered on his face. Blood dripped from his blade, marring the white snow.

My vision blurred. "I'm not who you think I am."

The man snorted and crouched in front of me. "If you're telling the truth, you'll stay dead this time."

He looked past me and gave a signal. I barely registered the explosion of pain from the heavy, jagged rock as it collided with my skull... because all I could hear was Everett's voice in the back of my mind.

I'll kill every last one of them.

Chapter 50: At the Water's Edge

Leona

"I'm telling you, Clint..." A husky voice broke through the haze of my cloudy mind. "Something's not right about that woman."

"You're being paranoid," Clint said through his teeth.

I struggled to open my eyes and realized one of them was swollen shut. My face was numb. My arms were numb. Every inch of my body was numb. But I was alive. I could still hear the men who ambushed me.

"You think she was tellin' the truth about being Maude's twin?" a shaky voice asked.

"Are you afraid, Sam?"

"I ain't afraid of nothin'!" he replied.

"Good." Clint stomped across the room and tightened the rope around my wrists. "We need to finish this and find some way to get off this stupid rock before the planet starts altering our genetic make-up."

Off-worlders. The worst kind of enemy. They relied heavily on weapons and brute force. Most resented Aadarins—until they became like us, which was only a matter of time.

I forced myself to focus as I tried to regain my bearings. After being dragged out of the woods, I'd woken up tied to a chair in the windowless room of a dank cabin. They gagged me when they got tired of my screaming. The beatings came next. As I slipped in and out of consciousness, I couldn't gauge how much time had passed. Or if it was even the same day.

I bit down on the gag. The metallic taste of blood almost caused me to retch.

"She's moving!" Feet shuffled away from me. "She's still alive!"

I opened my good eye and glared at the figure in front of me. A tall, stout blob. My vision was too blurry to make out any other details, but the knife-wielding outlaw went by the name of Jed. The young man to my right was the baggage handler from the stagecoach. Sam was skittish and jittery, but he had a nasty right hook. Clint, the ringleader, was constantly in motion and made sure I could never get a good look at his face. The fourth man, Leo, barely said a word. He stood in the shadows, watching.

I let out a high-pitched screech. Clint knocked me across the back of the head, but not as hard as last time. A warning, not a threat.

"We've had quite enough of that," he said into my ear. "There's nothing I hate more than a whiny female..."

I could barely make out the string of insults and curses he hurled at me. My hearing had been damaged well before we made the journey north, and it had only gotten worse. After being in their clutches for hours on end, I couldn't even begin to calculate how much gold it would take for me to fully recover from all my new wounds on top of the old ones. But I wasn't dead. That was all that mattered. As long as my heart was beating, I still had a fighting chance. Everett could find me. Our markings tied us together, and our connection was still strong.

The sound of rattling coins drew my attention to the corner of the room where Leo was going through my leather bag. I let out a shallow breath. They found my bag but didn't find Everett. My haphazard distraction worked, but now they had the one thing I desperately needed. Gold.

"Whatcha got there?" Sam asked.

Leo ignored him, tossed the coin purse to Clint, and continued digging through my bag.

Clint poured some of the gold coins into his hand and stared down at them. A deep frown wrinkled his brow. He clenched his fist and knelt in front of me. I saw his eyes for the first time. They were hollow and soulless.

"Why do you have gold on you?" he asked. When he couldn't make out my muffled reply, he ripped off the gag. "Talk."

I spit slivers of yarn out of my dry mouth. "I said, it's how I regenerate, you ignorant fool."

A sharp burst of pain exploded across my cheek as Clint backhanded me, but I didn't flinch. It was worth it just to raise his ire.

"See what I mean?" Jed stepped forward, pointing his dagger in my direction. "She doesn't act right. Maude wouldn't give you a straight answer like that. She'd make you guess."

Clint pondered Jed's words for a moment. He looked me up and down, as though searching for a crack in my façade.

"What you see is what you get." I spoke sweetly to grate on his nerves. I would have blown him a kiss if my battered hands weren't tied behind my back.

"You're not Maude." Clint spoke as though unable to believe his own words.

"I'm not." I wiggled a loose tooth in the front of my mouth with my tongue. "I'm her sister. Leona."

Sam shifted uncomfortably. "What are we gonna do?"

Clint shoved the coins back into the pouch. "I'm thinking."

"You best be thinking fast." Leo lifted the box Nora had given me. An eerie silence filled the room.

Clint's jaw tightened. He turned to Sam, who was staring at him, wide-eyed. "Get rid of that box. Get rid of anything that could tie us to her."

Sam grabbed the coin purse from Clint. He rushed over to Leo, stuffed everything back into my bag, and ran out of the room. The front door of the cabin slammed shut, and moments later the sound of Sam's boots crunching in the snow faded in the distance.

Clint turned his attention back to Leo. "Kill her. Then burn the body."

Before I could scream, a rope was around my neck. I gasped and thrashed about, unable to free myself of the bonds. Leo was swift and silent. The two other men left the room without so much as a glance in my direction. They were done with me—and I hadn't been clever enough to stall them. I was going to die again... because I wasn't smart enough. I wasn't Maude.

The rope tightened around my neck, and helpless tears stung my eyes. There was no air left in my lungs. My body started to go limp. *Everett.* I wanted Everett to be the last thing I remembered. His tender kisses. His undying affection. His unconditional love...

"Everett..." The soft plea barely escaped my lips.

I'm here, Leona. His words jolted me back to reality, but I feared I wouldn't be able to hold on much longer.

A shotgun fired. Clint let out a bloodcurdling scream. Leo dropped the rope, shoved my chair backward, and charged into the other room. My head slammed against the wood floor, and I stared up at the ceiling, gasping for breath. The room was spinning, and I felt like I was floating. More shots were fired. Bodies slammed into the walls. There was the sound of shattering glass. Then there was nothing.

My voice was raspy. "Everett...!"

The door burst open. Everett stood over me clutching a stab wound on his left arm. Thin lines of blood ran down the sides of his face, and shards of glass protruded from his dark, curly hair. He rushed over and cut me loose.

"Hurry!" Nora shouted. "The fourth one could be back at any moment."

Everett scooped me into his arms and shuffled out of the cramped room. The cabin was in shambles. A squeaky lantern swayed overhead. Shadows of overturned furniture and broken bottles danced about the room. Nora's bottom lip was busted, and her clothing was tattered, but that was nothing compared to the three shriveled corpses that lay at her feet. I shuddered. I couldn't fathom what she'd done to them.

"I'm forever in your debt," Everett said to Nora.

She cracked a small smile. "I don't collect often. Now go. Follow the trail I told you about."

Everett gave an appreciative nod and hurried out of the cabin. He carried me into the cold, dark wilderness and picked up his pace. Wind and sleet whipped into my face. I curled up in his arms. My safe haven. But I could feel my heartbeat slowing down.

"I'm not going to make it."

"I need you to hang on just a little longer," Everett murmured as he clung to me. "Please don't die."

Everett's boots sank into deep mounds of snow, but he didn't slow down. I closed my eyes, willing my battered body to continue functioning. Time seemed to stand still. When Everett finally stopped, my eyelids felt like they were frozen shut. I forced them open.

Moonlight glistened off the mirrorlike surface of a frozen lake. Aadar was a mix of emotions. Sad and beautiful and lonely all at the same time. Everett gently lowered me to the ground. He kicked off his boots and tore off his socks. Before I knew what was happening, he yanked off my boots and socks as well. Without a word, he carried me onto the ice. I shivered uncontrollably, yet I was unable to feel any sensation in my extremities. I was teetering on the edge of life and death.

The ice cracked ever-so-slightly. Everett stopped. He slowly put me down and knelt beside me. He pounded his fist against the solid block of ice. It didn't budge. He hit it again. And again. And again... until blood dripped down his knuckles. There was another crack. The ice shifted under us. Everett grabbed me by my waist and held me close.

"Leona..." A faint voice echoed in the woods.

I glanced up and peered across the glassy lake. My vision blurred. A woman stood at the water's edge, her long trench coat swaying in the breeze.

"Maude?"

She pressed both hands to her heart. Her voice was like a soft melody floating in the wind. "I've missed you, Leona. Terribly."

The ice splintered. I gasped. We plunged into the frigid water, and the current swept us under the ice. Everett wrapped himself around me. There was a tightness in my chest as a heavy force compressed my frozen body. I wanted to fight for Maude, for Everett... for myself. But I had nothing left inside. Darkness consumed me. My heart stopped beating.

And then... there was no sound.

Chapter 51: Dark Tears

Everett

Leona died in my arms. Again. But it wasn't like the times before. Her soul was bound to mine, and when she died, I felt it. An emptiness that consumed every part of my being. Tears blurred my vision as I walked out of the shallow riverbed and onto dry land carrying Leona's frozen body.

"Everett?" Cecil stood in front of me with his mouth agape.

Three other members of the Diamas clan surrounded me, but none of them drew their weapons. Ice-cold water dripped down my matted and tattered clothes, and I couldn't stop trembling. Blinding rays of sunlight shined down from overhead, but even the sun's warmth couldn't reach me.

My bare feet sank into the familiar terrain. Sutorath. I was home. Under the worst possible circumstances.

"What happened to—is she dead?" Cecil asked.

"S-she's..." A sob escaped my throat. I couldn't form a rational thought, let alone a rational sentence.

Cecil spoke quietly. "How can we help?"

"I need Alta and Ollie," I managed to choke out.

Cecil gave a signal, and two of the guards made a swift departure. I stared down at Leona's bruised and battered face. If I'd gotten to her sooner, before the Ellis Gang beat her, she might have survived the plunge into the icy lake. But she went into shock. Then she was gone.

I looked away, unable to suppress the waves of emotion that threatened to drown me.

"Welcome home," Cecil said in a formal tone that belied the concern wrinkling his brow.

He stepped back. There was a slight tremor. Walls of solid rock slowly rose from the ground and surrounded us.

I caught Cecil's eye and projected my thoughts to him. *Please don't tell my father we're here.*

Cecil nodded firmly. *Not a word.*

The transport chamber closed around us, cutting us off from the outside world. I pressed my cold fingertips against the sandstone wall and concentrated. Nothing happened. I inhaled sharply and tried again. My markings began to glow. Faint purplish-blue light illuminated the cramped compartment. A curved archway took shape, and I entered my private bedchamber. When the opening sealed behind me, I collapsed in the center of the dark room and wept.

Gold wasn't easily accessible in the Diamas clan. Anyone who used the land's resources to enhance their powers without first going through the council brought reproach on their family. But a hearing could take weeks. Or months. The longer it took to revive Leona, the more gold she'd need to regenerate. We were stuck. And I was utterly alone.

I clung to Leona's corpse as I sobbed uncontrollably. The sound of my muffled crying was foreign to me, but I couldn't stop. No matter how hard I tried. My heart ached so badly it hurt to breathe.

The markings on my neck began to tingle. Thick tears burned my eyes and obstructed my sight. I gasped. They weren't normal tears. I sat up and swiped the black oily substance from my face. Searing pain pulsed through my neck as ink seeped out of my markings. I grabbed my throat in a futile attempt to stop the burning liquid from gushing out of me. Suddenly, all the muscles in my body stiffened. My heart raced as panic set in. I couldn't shift.

My body started shaking. Violently. I fell to the floor beside Leona, unable to speak or cry out for help. My jaw was clenched shut.

Footsteps pattered toward me. An iron lantern came into view above me, and I caught a glimpse of Alta's and Ollie's petrified faces.

"Get him to the tub," Alta said.

Ollie lifted me under my arms and dragged me into the adjoining room. He tore off his trench coat and gathered fresh linens. Alta placed the lantern on the floor and hurried to fill the stone tub with water. They spoke over me, but I couldn't understand their garbled words. I attempted to communicate with them telepathically, but my mind was too muddled.

I fought to remain conscious as they stripped me down to my undergarments. It took both of my siblings to hoist me into the tepid bath. Water spilled over the edge, but they were careful not to submerge my head. Ink from my markings swirled in the water, turning it from clear to black. The burning sensation immediately subsided, and my muscles began to relax. I exhaled as my skin absorbed the soothing minerals that connected me back to the land of my birthplace.

Ollie sat on one side of the tub, holding me upright, while Alta sat on the other, dabbing my forehead with a cool, wet rag.

When I tried to speak, my voice was raspy. "Leona..."

"We can't help her until we help you," Ollie said gently.

I leaned back against my brother's arm and closed my eyes. "I'm numb."

"Your love partner just died." Alta wrung out the cloth. "Your connection has been severed."

My eyes shot open.

"Temporarily," Ollie added quickly.

"Y-you mean this is going to happen to me every time she dies?" I stammered.

"Yes. Your souls are entwined." Alta spoke with no emotion. "Honestly, Everett, you act like Father never had 'the talk' with you."

"He didn't," I said through clenched teeth.

"Well, then you're going to get a kick out of this." Ollie leaned closer. "Babies come from—"

"I know where babies come from!" I shouted, my nerves on edge.

Ollie chuckled, and Alta suppressed a smile.

"We're not trying to make light of the situation," she said. "But we assumed you knew all of this before you married her."

"I thought—since she has the ability to regenerate—it wouldn't affect me."

Ollie turned serious. "Everything Leona does affects you. She's your life mate."

I stared across the dimly lit room in a daze. "How am I going to deal with this?"

Alta frowned. "How often does she die?"

Too often. But I kept that thought to myself. I had other issues to worry about.

"I don't have any gold here," I admitted. "I took all of it with me after the wedding. We were struggling, and I used it to keep us afloat. The council—"

"Isn't an option." Alta locked eyes with Ollie then projected her thoughts. *Tell him.*

Ollie tilted his head toward his trench coat that was lying in a heap on the floor. *We brought you gold from our private collection. This is strictly a family matter.*

We keep this between the three of us. Alta's light-yellow eyes bore into mine. *No one in the clan can know about this. Do you understand?*

I nodded and struggled to keep my emotions in check. *I understand. Thank you both.*

"All that matters is that you and Leona are safe," Ollie said aloud.

"We'll bring you meals, and I'll find some clothes for Leona." Alta neatly folded the cloth as she spoke. "You don't have to worry about a thing."

Despite their assurances, I couldn't shake the uneasy feeling in the pit of my stomach. "They'll know we're here."

"But they won't know why," Alta said. "We'll cover for you."

"Stay out of sight for the next few days," Ollie said. "And mask your scars when you're around other people."

I reached up and touched the tender spot where one of the men had smashed a bottle across the side of my head. I dreaded looking in the mirror to see all the other damage from the fight.

"When Leona wakes up, I don't want her to know about this." I massaged my sore neck. "About what happens to me when she dies."

Alta and Ollie exchanged glances.

"She needs to know," Alta said. "If *you* die, she'll be completely unprepared. Just as you were."

"That's not fair to her," Ollie said.

I sagged. I hated it when they were right. "Fine. I'll explain it to her. After she has time to recover. I don't want to overwhelm her." I attempted to push myself out of the tub, but I was still too weak. "I wish being with me didn't cause her pain."

Alta cradled my face in her soft hand. "Surely she doesn't mind the sacrifice, considering how much you had to give up to be with her."

My voice was low. "Actually... I never told Leona. Any of it."

Ollie took his time before replying. "Your love is—strong?"

"Of course it is," Alta said sharply. "Why would you ask him something like that?"

I knew why he asked. He was the only one who knew the real reason Leona and I got married. "Leona loves me as much as I love her."

Ollie searched my expression as though he feared I might not be telling the truth.

I didn't waver. "We're in love."

"Then you should tell her." Ollie squeezed my damp shoulder. "Everything."

Chapter 52: One, One Hundred

Everett

Wait. That was all I could do. Sit and wait. I held Leona's stiff hands in mine, hoping the amount of gold Alta and Ollie gave us would be enough. My heart fluttered the moment Leona took a breath. Her eyes shot open, and she sat bolt upright on the floor of my bedchamber.

"Leona?"

She gasped for air. "That was unpleasant... and cold."

The coins slipped through Leona's fingers and scattered across the ink-stained rug. Burning wood crackled in the fireplace, and she glanced around the room as I gently rubbed her back. Her face had completely healed, and she appeared to be back to normal. But something felt—different.

"Are you all right?" I asked. "How do you feel?"

She let out a cynical chuckle. "Like death."

Well, at least you haven't lost your sense of humor, I projected to her.

Leona pulled up her shirt and examined her stomach. She saw me watching her and quickly covered herself again.

"Sorry," she said. "I got stabbed and wondered if it left a scar."

"Nothing to be sorry about."

Leona twirled her finger around the fabric of her bloody shirt. "How long was I gone?"

"Six hours," I said. *The worst six hours of my life.*

"Thank you for saving me," she said quietly. "I'm sorry for putting us in a bad situation."

"You don't have to keep apologizing."

I leaned closer to kiss her lips. We both hesitated. I gave her a quick peck on the cheek. She fidgeted slightly, and I cleared my throat.

"Do you want to take a bath?" I asked.

"Why?" Leona sniffed her clothes. "Do I smell? Is it that bad?"

"No, I just thought it would make you more comfortable. You smell fine."

She fluffed her matted hair. "Maybe it will help me to relax. I'm a little on edge."

I led the way into the private bath. Candles lined the two stone basins that flanked the room, providing just enough light to illuminate the intimate space. I stepped up on the raised platform and began filling the tub.

Leona stood near one of the sinks and examined her reflection through the wrought-iron mirror. She didn't get undressed.

"Is it bad?" I asked.

"What?"

"The new scar."

Leona wrapped her arms across her stomach and gave a slight shrug. "It's not horrible."

I gathered a bar of almond-scented soap and fresh towels. When I first arrived home, Alta and Ollie had helped me through the most difficult part of the *transition* so my full attention could be on Leona. But I couldn't tell what she needed from me.

"Do you want me to leave?" I asked.

"I—" She pursed her lips together and shook her head. "I don't know what's wrong with me. You've already seen me naked."

"But I'm making you nervous?"

"Yes." She avoided my gaze. "It doesn't make any sense."

It made perfect sense to me. I was just as uneasy around her. "Alta will be here in the morning with clothes for you, but I need to find something for you to wear tonight. Take as much time as you need."

With that, I made a swift departure out of the room. When the wall closed behind me, I let out a breath. She wasn't the same woman I married—*that* I was sure of—and my disquieting thoughts left me restless. I gathered the gold-depleted coins Leona dropped and tidied up the sitting area to give myself something to do.

By the time Leona emerged from her bath, I was so anxious I couldn't think straight. I sat in front of the fireplace, staring into the flames. Through of the corner of my eye, I caught a glimpse of Leona as she quickly got dressed in the cotton shirt I'd laid out for her. The large garment swallowed her small frame and hung off one of her shoulders. She was so beautiful. And tantalizing...

I focused my attention back on the fire. Leona lingered by one of the side tables and sampled the assortment of fruit, cheese, and bread my siblings were kind enough to provide for us. When she finished, she came to join me on the floor. We didn't speak. We just sat there. In silence. Until even the silence became agonizing.

"Our connection was severed when you died," I said softly. "That's why things between us don't feel like they did before."

"What does that mean?"

"The pair bond, our ability to sense one another when we're apart. All of it is gone."

Leona frowned. "We're no longer love partners?"

"We are. Physically we're still bound together through our markings," I said. "But the separation caused a rift between us."

Leona swallowed hard. "How do we get things back to normal?"

"I don't know." Private matters between love partners weren't openly discussed in the Diamas clan. Or acknowledged. "I suppose we need to get—*reacquainted.*"

Leona smoothed the fabric of her shirt. "That seems logical."

I didn't move. Leona didn't move. Even the fire appeared to be uncomfortable. Logs split and tumbled as they burned down, adding to the awkward tension in the room.

I stifled my apprehension. "May I kiss you?"

Leona nodded. I took in a breath. We both leaned in too fast and headbutted each other. Leona yelped and rubbed her forehead.

"Sorry." I shook off the blow but was unable to shake off my embarrassment. "Maybe we should just go to bed. I'm exhausted."

"Me too."

I stood up and grabbed Leona's hand, pulling her next to me. She fit into my arms, like she always did, but everything felt new and unfamiliar. Like I was touching her for the first time.

I guided Leona to the alcove where my bed was situated. Our bed. I pulled back the blanket, and she climbed in with her back to me. She was so distant and aloof, I had trouble keeping the hurt out of my voice.

"You can have the bed if you want. I don't mind sleeping in the other room."

Leona didn't turn around. "I'm cold, Everett."

Without a word, I slipped under the covers beside her and wrapped my arm around her stomach. She pressed her back against my chest and curled up close to me. The steady beating of her heart slowly melted away some of my doubts and reservations.

"I lose a little part of myself every time I die." Her somber tone tugged at my heart. "I'm disconnected from my body. Disconnected from life. So when I come back, it takes me a while to feel whole again."

"I think I understand," I said.

When Leona was gone, I was completely numb. That was hardly the worst of it, but I didn't want to burden her with all the things I still needed to tell her. In that moment, I just wanted to be with her. I brushed her thick hair aside and buried my nose in the back of her neck. Her scent was the only thing that felt vaguely familiar. I clung to the memories of our nights together. When we were alone. And unguarded.

"Tell me you need me," Leona whispered.

"I need you..." I tenderly kissed her warm cheek. "Desperately."

"Tell me we'll be together forever."

I drew her closer. "We'll be together. Forever."

"Tell me..." Her voice cracked, and I suddenly realized she was crying.

I gently turned her around, but she wouldn't look me in the eye. I cradled her face, wanting nothing more than to take away her pain.

"We'll get through this." I brushed her tears away with my thumb. "I promise."

Leona sniffled and nodded. She slowly leaned closer and kissed my lips. "I love you, Everett."

I rested my forehead on hers. "I love you too."

Leona closed her weary eyes. I held her close and lightly stroked her back with the tips of my fingers. Her features began to relax as she drifted off to sleep. I took in the delicate curves of her face, memorizing every detail. Again. She wasn't the same woman I married. She was so much more. If she died a hundred times, I would get to know her. A hundred times over.

And something told me that I just might.

Chapter 53:
Reacquainted

Leona

Everett held me. He held me the first night. And the second. And the third. Despite my fatigue, I relished being in his arms. Where I was protected—and wanted. Pieces of me still felt like they were missing, but his love and affection made me feel complete.

Everett stirred beside me, and I moaned. "Do we have to get up so soon?"

"It's almost midday, and Alta will be here soon with lunch." Everett kissed my cheek. "You sleep. I just need to talk to her for a moment."

He slipped away before I could protest, and I quietly fell back to sleep. I didn't dream. I rarely did after reawakening. My thoughts were hazy, and my memories were a tangled mess of events I couldn't remember clearly. It would all come back to me. Eventually.

I woke to the soft clanking of teacups. Everett's side of the bed was cold. I rolled over and slid out from under the covers. My bare feet were just about the only part of my body that weren't sore. The gold Everett used was just enough to revive me, but not enough to reverse all the damage of my compounded injuries.

I crept out of the alcove and found Everett and Alta sitting by the fireplace. They stared at each other intensely as they sipped their tea, but neither spoke a word. Telepaths. I didn't want to interrupt their private conversation, but before I could slip out of sight, Alta rose.

"There you are." The tall, slender woman hurried over and gave me a warm embrace. "It's so wonderful to see you again. Everett tells me you'll both be joining the family for dinner tonight."

I hugged her back, too dumbfounded to reply. Everett and I hadn't left his bedchamber since we arrived.

Alta let me go and gave Everett a pointed stare. "Don't be late."

"I won't," he said firmly.

She crossed the room and pressed her palm against one of the walls. An archway formed, and moments later she was gone. I waited until the wall closed behind her before addressing Everett.

"I'm not prepared to see your family," I said.

"Neither am I."

I wrapped his large shirt tighter around my body. "I don't even have any clothes."

"My sisters brought some things for you to wear."

"I thought you said no one can know we're here."

"No one can know *why* we're here," he said. "But we have to make an appearance. Otherwise, it will look suspicious."

Everett got up and prepared a small plate of food for me. The assortment of cheeses and the freshly baked bread looked delicious, but I'd lost my appetite the moment Alta mentioned the family dinner.

"I'm so confused," I admitted.

"We're part of a clan, which means we do a lot of things as a collective." Everett spoke patiently. "Dinner with my immediate family is the bare minimum. We can't come and go as though we're separate entities. It's not our way."

I shook my head and slumped down on a long, narrow couch. "How am I supposed to know what to say or how to act? You haven't taught me any of your customs."

"I know. I honestly didn't think we would be back so soon. There are a lot of things I still need to explain about us."

Everett handed me the plate as he sat beside me, and I took a bite of the warm rosemary bread.

"Shapeshifters are connected—to everything," Everett began. "We're connected to the land, which is why we can manipulate matter. We're connected to water, which is how we travel between our world and yours. But more importantly, we're connected to each other. Our markings don't just identify us. They link us together. You're now part of that link."

"What do you mean?"

"As a member of our clan, you have the ability to beckon any one of us to you if you're ever in mortal danger."

"Like you did the night Hiram attacked me?"

"Exactly. I'll teach you how to do it in case we're ever separated." He paused for a moment. "But the real reason I need to be with my family right now is because of you."

The thick piece of bread in my mouth became difficult to swallow. "Me?"

"Your death took a greater toll on me than I anticipated. It not only severed our connection. It weakened my link with the rest of the family."

I frowned. "What exactly happened to you when I died?"

Everett told me about the seizures. And the ink pouring out of him. And the excruciating pain. The physical and emotional turmoil he endured left me shaken. I pushed the plate aside, unable to finish my meal.

"I'm not telling you all this to upset you," Everett said. "But you need to know what happens when one of us dies in case I—in case our roles are ever reversed."

I struggled to comprehend the magnitude of our situation. Or why he was so calm about it. "You're going to go through this every time I die?"

"Yes."

I got to my feet. "What are we going to do?"

"There's nothing we can do," he said. "We're bound together."

"We could get divorced." I knew those were the wrong words even before they slipped out of my mouth. The flash of shock and hurt in Everett's eyes tore my heart to pieces.

His voice was low. "Divorce changes nothing—for me."

"I don't understand."

"Most members who marry outside of the Diamas clan don't go before the council to be recognized as love partners. Their spouses don't become part of our clan." He paused. "I brought you in... which means I can never bring another soul into the clan."

The seriousness of his words weighed heavily on my mind. "When you proposed, you told me it was just a formality. That we would be free to pursue other people if we chose to separate in the future."

"I said *you* would be free. Even if I were to remarry someone in my own clan, I would never be able to form a pair bond with them for as long as you are physically able to regenerate."

"So... I could move on, but you would be stuck."

"Essentially."

"And you knew all of this going into our arrangement?"

"Yes." Everett stood and towered over me. "I chose to be with you."

He was so close, I could almost feel the beating of his heart.

"I made a sacred vow," he continued. "And I will not dishonor you by casting you aside when things get difficult."

I didn't know what to say. No one was ever that loyal to me. The one person I cared about most... would suffer the most every time I died.

Everett leaned closer and spoke softly. "I will be with you for as long as you will have me."

I wrapped my arms around him and rested my head on his chest. "I'll never mention it again."

Everett slid his hands down my back and held me tighter. Silence enveloped the room. He pulled away suddenly and looked in my eyes. His face fell.

"What's wrong?" I asked.

Everett searched through me. "You can't hear me."

My eyebrows shot up. "Impossible. Try again."

His deep, penetrating gaze held me transfixed. But there was nothing. Not even the hint of a whisper in the back of my mind.

"It makes sense," he said, half to himself. "All this time I thought you were a little withdrawn because you were still recovering, but really you haven't heard anything I've said."

"What were you trying to say?"

"It doesn't matter now, love." Everett grabbed two throw pillows and placed them on the floor in front of the fireplace. "We have to practice. Otherwise, dinner with my family is going to be a disaster."

He knelt on one of the pillows, and I settled across from him.

"Now you're making me nervous," I said.

"There's nothing to be nervous about." Everett's voice was a little too high.

I placed my hands in his. We took slow, calming breaths together, but it all felt so forced.

"It's just like the times before," he said.

Except, it wasn't. My mind was jumbled. My emotions were oscillating between paranoia and panic. And I wasn't even wearing my own clothes.

"I can't get comfortable," I said.

"Focus on me, not your surroundings."

Everett straightened his back and started a casual conversation about the weather. We talked about baking. And plants. Mundane topics. Every now and then he would brush his thumb across the back of my hand, as though trying to restore our connection through sheer will alone. After several failed attempts to communicate telepathically, we started to run out of things to talk about, and I could tell he was struggling as much as I was.

"I'm sorry," I said quietly. "But it's still not working."

Everett sat back, dejected. He was starting to pull away from me. I could feel it.

I laced my fingers between his. "Maybe try kissing me."

"We need to be serious, Leona. We only have a few hours before we see my parents."

I shrugged. "It worked that one time."

He sighed heavily. "Fine."

Everett gently held my face and pulled me toward him for a kiss. I let go of everything and allowed myself to be in the moment. With him. Mint tea and honey lingered on Everett's lips. I wanted to taste more. My tongue swept across his, and he dragged me closer until I was on his lap. His hands slipped under my thin cotton shirt, and he explored every inch of my bare skin with the tips of his fingers. I moaned into his mouth.

Everett squeezed my thighs, and in one swift motion he stood up without letting me go. My legs tightened around his waist as he carried me across the room. I broke our kiss momentarily to claw the shirt off his back. There was a primal need inside of me. I craved his touch. The growing heat that radiated from my markings told me Everett felt it too. My pulse thundered in my ears as he shoved me against the wall and pressed his firm body against mine. He dipped his head and hungrily kissed my neck. A rush of excitement washed over me, and I closed my eyes. Everett's palm slammed into the sand-stone. The entire wall shuddered, sending strong vibrations down my back.

"What are you doing?" I murmured breathlessly.

"Sealing the entrance so no one can come inside while I'm rav-ishing my wife."

Wife. Everett often called me his love partner, but that was the first time he ever referred to me as his wife. He claimed me... and I surrendered to him. Completely. It didn't take long for us to get reacquainted. But as the hours stretched on, we took our time dis-covering new ways to please each other, and I learned about some of the advantages of being married to a shapeshifter who could take on multiple forms.

After we bathed together, Everett put on dark trousers and a crisp white dress shirt. He reclined on the couch and watched me get dressed as he sipped a glass of whiskey. The scarlet cap-sleeve dress I squeezed into was a little too long, but the material was nicer than anything I'd ever owned.

I turned in a circle, and Everett gave me a silent nod of approval. Before he could finish his drink, I hiked up my skirt and climbed on-to his lap. He handed me his glass. I swallowed down the rest of the burning liquid in one gulp without taking my eyes from his.

"I'm sorry it didn't work," I said.

"We both tried. Very hard."

Everett couldn't keep a straight face, and we burst out laughing.

"How bad is this dinner going to be?" I asked.

Everett lightly kissed my lips. "Worse for me than for you."

Chapter 54: Ready or Not

Leona

"Are you ready?"

I grasped Everett's hand. We stepped out of the long, winding hallway of the cave dwelling and into the spacious courtyard where members of the Diamas clan stood in clusters socializing and sharing a light communal meal.

My skin soaked up the last of the remaining rays of sunlight as the sun began to set. After three days in the private sanctuary of Everett's bedchamber, it was difficult to adjust to the natural light... and the surprised expressions. People's faces lit up at the sight of us, and within a matter of seconds, we were surrounded. I squeezed Everett's fingers, and he gave me a reassuring kiss on my forehead.

Everett told me it was customary for individuals to gather and mingle before dinner with their respective families, but I wasn't prepared for such a large group. Several children darted around the adults, unable to control their wild laughter as they played together. A small boy bumped into the back of my leg then took off running. I tried not to appear too startled. I seemed to be the only one who was uneasy. Everett took it in stride, but I couldn't remember the last time I'd been around kids.

I readjusted my gown, hoping I would make it through the night without damaging his sister's expensive garment. Everyone was dressed in what I considered formal attire, but Everett assured me there was nothing formal about the affair. Nothing formal to *him*.

I tried to focus on the excited chatter surrounding us, but I had difficulty keeping track of the overlapping conversations.

"You're looking well, Everett," someone said.

"Marriage suits you, my boy," an elderly voice added.

I glanced up at Everett. There wasn't a trace of bruising or scars on his face from the incident with the Ellis Gang. In fact, Everett looked perfect. Too perfect.

"Thank you," he said graciously. "We're truly enjoying our time as newlyweds."

It wasn't a total fabrication. We did enjoy our time together... when we weren't being threatened, chased, or beaten. I maintained a pleasant smile, suddenly grateful for my inability to share my thoughts telepathically.

As dusk set in, the crowds began to thin out. Everett politely escorted me across the courtyard to another maze of hallways. When we were alone, I was finally able to exhale.

"That wasn't so bad," I said as we arrived at a dead end.

Everett looked at me, puzzled. "Of course not. *They* were all happy to see us." He placed his palm against the grainy wall, and an archway formed.

"You're late," his father barked, causing me to jump.

Everett stepped inside his parents' private residence without letting go of my hand, and I followed closely behind. My eyes widened. Their home was massive, at least five times the size of Everett's space, with a partially concealed kitchen on one side and an entirely separate room containing a long dining table on the other. I was afraid to touch anything. The intricately carved furniture was laden with gold, from the angular side tables to the legs of the three couches that surrounded the fireplace. Two identical daggers hung above the mantel as though suspended in midair. Ceremonial blades.

Everyone was already seated in the dining room. Black diamond-shaped crystals dangled from an elegant two-tiered chandelier that hung over the table. The candlelight illuminated colorful desert flowers that cascaded out of a large centerpiece, and the soft light flickered off silver serving trays that were filled with an assortment of delectable dishes. My mouth began to water as I inhaled the fragrant spices. Everett's mother rose and crossed the room to greet us, the shiny threads of her navy-blue gown shimmering as she approached.

"Leona, you look wonderful. It's so good to see you again." Everett's mother gave me a tight hug before turning her attention to Everett. Neither spoke aloud, but he flashed her a small smile.

"Hurry up and sit down so we can eat," Dennis said.

Dave shook his head. "We're always waiting for the baby."

They broke into laughter. Everett wasn't amused. He was even less amused when his mother seated us on opposite sides of the table. Alta and Ollie sat to my left and Marion sat to my right, while Everett found himself wedged between Dennis and Dave. The seat across from Alta was empty, yet there was still a formal place setting arranged in front of it. Once we were settled, Everett's parents each took a seat at the heads of the table.

"It's so wonderful to have all the children here at once, isn't it?" his mother said.

His father didn't reply.

"And it's so lovely to have you join us, dear," Everett's mother continued, turning to me.

"Thank you," I said. "We're—happy to be here."

I nervously reached for a piece of bread in the center of the table, but Everett shook his head slightly. I quickly folded my hands in my lap.

Everett's father spoke up. "Now that we're all here..."

Everyone joined hands, and Ollie and Marion took hold of mine. They closed their eyes as they bowed their heads, and I followed suit. After several excruciating seconds of utter silence, I peeked across the table. Everyone was still. Without warning, the markings on my back started pulsing. I shuddered, and Everett's siblings held my hands tighter. The ink from my markings began to swirl under my skin, as though taking on a life of its own. An energy passed through me, and I bit down to prevent myself from gasping.

Everett's family uttered a foreign word in unison then released hands. The strange sensation faded, but I suddenly felt invigorated. My focus was sharp, and even my hearing had improved.

Everett took in a slow breath, as though centering himself. His voice was low. "Thank you."

His mother spoke up cheerfully. "Shall we eat?"

The weight in the room lifted, and his family broke out in lively chatter. They passed around the platters of leafy vegetables, hearty legumes, and exotic fruits—some of which I'd never seen before. Everett's father waited until everyone was served before he put a single morsel on his plate.

"You're certainly looking well, Everett," Dennis said. He and Dave began to chuckle.

Alta roughly cut her food into pieces. "Don't start, you buffoons."

"What?" Dennis threw his thick arm around Everett's neck. "I'm just saying, you can hardly tell he was in a fight."

Everett shrugged off his brother's arm but didn't say a word.

"Obviously he can't go around with scars on his face," Dave said. "But we didn't think he'd be so proper he'd hide them from *us.*"

Everett's eyes shifted to his father, but his father didn't look at him.

"You were in a fight?" Marion's dainty face was pinched with worry. "Who would want to fight someone as sweet as you, Evey?"

Dave roared with laughter. "Do you seriously not know what they do for a living?"

"Something about furs?" Marion asked.

"Trapping," I said. "Outlaws."

Everett's eyes shot to mine, and I closed my mouth. He stared at me as though he was trying to tell me something telepathically, but it was futile. His gaze shifted to Ollie, who leaned over to me.

"What Everett's trying to say is, he rarely discusses the topic of his employment."

"Usually because he's in trouble," Dennis said.

I was unable to remain silent. "This wasn't his fault. I was the one who insisted we go to the tundra. We were looking for my sister, and we were ambushed by a gang of—"

Everett glanced at Alta.

"No need to explain, Leona," she said quickly. "All that matters is you're both alive."

"Yes." Dennis raised his fork. "We must keep the baby safe. So he can continue to drain the rest of us."

I frowned but knew better than to ask any questions.

"*Drain* is a bit harsh, even for you, Dennis," Ollie said casually as he reached across the table at his brother's plate. "Are you going to eat all of that?"

Dennis whacked Ollie's hand. "Don't touch my food, scavenger!"

"Dennis doesn't like anyone touching his food," Everett's mother explained to no one in particular.

I shifted uncomfortably. Despite the enticing meal, I couldn't bring myself to eat anything. I moved food around on my plate to distract myself from the awkwardness.

"I didn't ask you to be here," Everett said to Dennis.

His brother shoved a buttery roll into his mouth. "Now you're just being ungrateful."

"Excuse me." Marion raised her hand, and the black polish on her nails shimmered in the candlelight. "But I'm still confused about the whole trapping thing."

Dave snorted. "Of course you are."

"Next time make sure you're hurt," Dennis continued. "I mean, *really* hurt. Near death even. Then you'll have my sympathy, and I'll gladly come to your aid."

Everett glared at him. "We all know you're just here for the food, you pig."

Dennis let out a hearty laugh. "You're right about that, little brother. *Oink. Oink.*"

I blinked, and Dennis had Everett in a choke hold. I jumped up, but Ollie motioned for me to sit back down.

"They're fine," he said. "Let them fight it out."

I gaped as Everett struggled to free himself and Dave egged his twin on. Everett's mother poured herself more red wine, and his father continued eating his meal as though none of us were there.

Everett morphed into a feeble old man, causing Dennis to lose his grip, and he shoved back from the table. His wine fell to the floor. I cringed at the sound of shattering glass.

"The old man routine, huh?" Dennis rushed Everett as he scrambled out of his chair, and the two brothers wrestled across the elegantly woven carpet.

Alta slammed down her fork, grabbed a cloth napkin, and went to the other side of the table to clean up the mess. I didn't know whether to help her, help Everett, or help myself.

Everett morphed into his reptilian form, his tail rattling loudly as he slipped across the room and out of Dennis's reach. Dennis got on all fours. His snout elongated and his lower canine teeth protruded out of his mouth as he morphed into a wild boar. My jaw dropped. Dennis squealed and chased after Everett.

Marion sighed. "I don't know how we went from furs to *this.*"

Dave's lips curved into a smile. He morphed to take on Marion's form and mimicked her singsong voice. "What's a trapper again? I like to pretend I'm too dumb to follow along."

Marion's expression turned dark. She hissed, and I moved a bit closer to Ollie.

"They've gone and upset Marion," Everett's mother said gravely.

Marion's long nails curved into claws, and she morphed into a feral black cat. Before Dave could react, she pounced. I gasped. Marion clawed at Dave's face, and he screamed. His arms flailed about as he tried to fight off her vicious attack. His plate went flying and crashed to the floor beside Alta. He morphed into a boar and took off running with Marion still clinging to his neck.

"You see, Mother?" Alta shouted. "This is why I said we should have the dinner outside!"

"Don't fret, my dear." Everett's mother calmly sipped her wine. "A couple of broken dishes won't spoil the entire evening."

My head snapped over to Ollie, but he was no longer beside me. He had morphed into a bat and was eating all the mangos and avocados off Dennis's plate while Alta was under the table scrubbing the floor. Ollie bounced around and accidentally knocked a glass of water onto her. When Alta rose, she was in the form of a swan. Her loud bugle-like cry echoed throughout the dining room, and she furiously flapped her wings at Ollie. He made a clicking sound in response then went back to nibbling on the fruit.

"Umm..." My mind was reeling. "S-should I go?"

Everett's father looked up, acknowledging me for the first time that evening. "Go where? You're part of this family."

"I believe the children are making Leona uncomfortable," Everett's mother said over the squealing, rattling, and hissing noises.

Everett's father glanced about the room at the mayhem. "Understandable."

He locked eyes with his wife. They stared at each other with such intensity it was almost mesmerizing. My eyelids felt heavy, and I was suddenly lightheaded. Ollie fell off the table. Then Alta crumpled to the floor. They all dropped one by one and morphed back into their humanoid forms, wailing in agony. Everett was the last to shift, and I rushed over to him.

"It's so wonderful to have all the children here at once, isn't it?" his mother said sweetly.

His father spoke with no emotion. "Wonderful."

Everett moaned and laid his head in my lap. I wasn't ready. I wasn't ready for his family… and the night had only just begun.

Chapter 55:
Assimilation

Everett

The. Pounding. In. My. Head. That was all I could think about even as Leona gently stroked the side of my face. My siblings and I lay sprawled out on the dining room floor after our parents incapacitated us by joining their minds. It hurt to move. Or breathe. Or think.

The food's getting cold, children, Mother projected softly to all of us.

There was a collective groan, but no one moved.

Get up! Father projected—less softly.

I gritted my teeth and forced myself upright. Leona stared at me with wide eyes. I wanted to reassure her that everything was all right. But it wasn't. My brain felt like someone had stomped on it. Someone with boots.

Alta and Ollie were the first to drag themselves to their feet and stagger to the table. Marion shook out her head and rose with more poise than the rest of us could muster. She helped the twins off the floor. They kissed her on the cheek before stumbling to their seats.

With Leona's assistance, I managed to get myself into a standing position, and I straightened my wrinkled dress shirt. My pulse thundered in my ears as I escorted Leona back to the table. I pulled out her chair, and she reluctantly sat between Ollie and Marion. I rounded the table and plopped down between the twins.

Dennis eyed me up and down. "You look rough, brother."

"Thanks," I said dryly. I didn't have the strength or the mental capacity to try to mask my injuries anymore. Shifting or altering my appearance was nearly impossible when I was in that much pain. The scars from my fight with the Ellis Gang were on full display.

Ollie slowly sipped his water, still trembling from the effects of the mind-bend. "I told you, Dennis. Everett was in serious trouble."

"How was I supposed to know it was a real emergency?" Dennis said.

"Yeah," Dave chimed in. "Everyone was being all secretive about it."

"That's because the matter was *delicate*," Marion said. "And you two don't seem to understand the meaning of that word."

I stifled my irritation. I never meant to have such a private conversation out loud. But none of us could communicate telepathically after the mental beating we took from our parents. I fought through the incessant throbbing. "I wouldn't have come back here unless I truly needed help."

"Alta came to us asking for gold," Dennis said. "We assumed you'd gotten yourself into some sort of gambling debt and had crossed the wrong people."

Alta rubbed her temples. "The gold was for Leona, you imbeciles."

Even through their thick facial hair, Dennis's and Dave's frowns mirrored one another.

"Well, why didn't you just say that to begin with?" Dennis demanded.

"How bad were you hurt?" Dave asked Leona.

Her eyes darted to mine. "I... I..."

"She was dead." My words hung in the uncomfortable silence that followed. I was rarely so blunt. Or honest. Even with my family. But I had nothing to hide, and I couldn't pretend our actions didn't have an effect on everyone else. We were all connected. We were part of a clan. And we needed them. "Leona's sister is in trouble. We went looking for her and ran into a gang who mistook Leona for her twin. It didn't end well, but we managed to escape. Almost."

Leona fidgeted with a cloth napkin. She was restless, and I knew she wanted to run away. We both did. But we couldn't.

"After Leona died, I lost my connection with her." I could feel Father's eyes on me. "And my link with the rest of the family was weakened in the process."

"Were you able to find your sister?" Dennis asked Leona sincerely.

She hesitated. "My memory is a bit hazy, but just before I lost consciousness, I thought I saw her at the edge of the lake."

"You did?" I sat up straighter. "When? Why didn't you tell me?"

Leona spoke between her teeth. "We haven't really had a chance to talk."

"You two have been holed up for three days," Ollie said with a sly smile. "What have you been doing?"

"Mind your own business, boy," Father snapped.

Ollie chuckled and picked over the fruit platter.

Father turned his attention back to me. "Life is sacred. It's not something you should be gambling with."

"I know, Father." I had no intention of arguing. Not when he was right.

"Respecting the sanctity of life means you respect the clan," Father continued, "because we are all tied together."

"You're both incredibly fortunate," Mother said. "Most don't get a second chance to be with their love partner, let alone a third, or a fourth."

"We don't take any of this for granted," I said. "We were in a bad situation. I couldn't think of anywhere else to go."

Mother flashed us a sympathetic smile. "You can always come home."

"I—I've never had a home or a family like this." Leona's voice was almost a whisper. "It's never mattered to anyone, aside from my sister, whether I lived or died."

"Well, you're part of this family now." Father was firm but kind. "And your life matters. Very much so. If you die, part of Everett dies. If part of Everett dies... it affects all of us."

"I'm sorry for being so reckless." Leona shook her head in dismay. "I honestly didn't know."

"It's not your fault. It's mine." I glanced around the table at the scattered plates and overturned drinks. Another mess I was responsible for. "Leona joined our clan with very little knowledge about shapeshifters, and I never took the time to properly assimilate her."

Mother put down her wineglass. "Not even after the binding ceremony?"

"No..." I admitted, reluctantly.

"Then I suggest you rectify that situation." Father rose from the table. "Tonight."

Father wasn't joking. He dismissed us before dessert could be served. Leona and I found ourselves in a secluded area just outside the cave dwelling. A crisp breeze rushed through the clearing, causing long strands of grass to sway and dance under the moonlight. The skirt of Leona's bright-red gown whipped around her shapely legs as I knelt in front of her. I held her hands in mine.

"Is this going to hurt?" she asked.

"No." I tried not to smile at her innocent question. "Not everything we do is painful. It should feel—pleasant."

Despite my reply, I could still feel the tension in her body rising. "Relax," I whispered. "I promise everything will be all right."

She nodded and closed her eyes, taking in a slow breath. I did the same, absorbing the energy around me. I could feel the microscopic life-forms beneath me. The subtle rumblings and vibrations of the land. My homeland. I was a part of Sutorath. And Leona was a part of me.

Leona gasped. I opened my eyes. Vibrant specks of violet light rose from the ground and surrounded us. Heat radiated from the translucent orbs, and I relished the warmth. I felt weightless. Our markings were aglow. The light intensified. I wrapped my arms around Leona's waist, holding her close. She clung to me, and for a brief moment, everything was still and silent. The world stopped. We were one.

The light faded. All at once, the spheres burst and disappeared. Tiny drops of icy cold water trickled down over us. Gravity tugged at my limbs. Leona collapsed into my arms and stared up at me in wonderment.

"That was beautiful," she uttered softly.

You're beautiful, I attempted to project to her.

She didn't respond.

"I'm sorry about dinner. Mother told me you were slightly uncomfortable."

Leona smothered a chuckle. "Yes. I certainly wasn't prepared for a brawl, but I think I love your family."

My heart swelled. "I think they love you too."

Leona reached up and stroked the markings on my neck. "Now I truly understand how important your siblings are to you."

"I think you always understood." I grasped her delicate fingers. "Did you really see Maude that night?"

She swallowed hard. "I'm almost certain I did."

I kissed the back of Leona's hand. "Then we're one step closer to finding her."

Chapter 56: Respectful Distance

Everett

Leona's assimilation into the Diamas clan was complete. She was one of us. And she had the power to summon anyone she shared a strong link with from Sutorath to her dimension. She was truly part of the family. My family.

I was grateful for the two weeks we were able to spend within the safe haven of the clan. It gave us the time we needed to regroup. And recover. By the time we said our goodbyes and departed, Leona's hearing had completely returned. My personal link with the family was strengthened. And my telepathic connection with Leona was restored.

When we finally returned to our hideaway under the waterfall, I took my time packing. I wasn't eager to get back to the Agency. But we'd spent exactly one month away, and soon they'd be looking for us. With our track record, it was best that we didn't draw any undue attention to ourselves. If our search for Leona's sister had taught us anything, it was that we had to be cautious moving forward. Very cautious.

"Let's hope they send us someplace warm," I said as I rolled up a pair of pants and put them in my bag.

"You read my mind. Maybe I can beg Amos for something near the Valley of Sand," she quipped.

I chuckled. "Maybe not *that* warm."

Leona knelt by our cooking utensils and gathered basic supplies. "I wouldn't mind being away from civilization for a little while. A place where we wouldn't have to worry about being discovered."

I crossed the damp cave floor and pulled her into my arms. "Would it really be so bad if the Agency found out we're married?"

"You seriously didn't read your contract, did you?"

I kissed her cheek lightly. "I saw a number I liked at the bottom of the page and signed immediately."

She hesitated. "If we formally acknowledge our relationship, both of our rankings will drop—to level one."

"What?" I stood up straight. "You're joking."

"It's in the contract."

I gaped at her. "We can't afford that."

"Exactly."

I cursed myself for not taking the time to thoroughly read my agreement with the Agency. Although it wouldn't have changed anything. A piece of paper wouldn't have stopped me from falling in love with Leona. I could take the hit. A drop from a level three wasn't a huge issue. But Leona was a level nine. She was an expert with far more trapping experience than me. I'd never jeopardize something she worked so hard for.

I slipped my hands into the back pockets of her wool pants. "Well, since I won't be able to touch you in front of anyone..."

I leaned down and kissed her soft lips. She wrapped her arms around my neck and pressed herself into me. I loved the feeling of her warm body against mine. The subtle motion of her hips. Every single thing about her was intoxicating. I couldn't undress her fast enough. I needed to feel her silky skin beneath my fingers.

Water rushed down from the falls and muffled the sound of Leona's moans as I caressed her body and explored my favorite parts of her with my tongue. Each shudder of pleasure caused my heart to race. I wanted to satisfy her every desire. I knelt in front of her naked body, taking in all her feminine beauty. She stared down at me, breathless.

We don't have to go back today. I couldn't stop the thought from slipping out of my mind.

"Unfortunately, we do…"

I brushed my lips across her stomach, lightly kissing her navel. *Not this very hour.*

Leona smiled and stroked the side of my face with her fingertips. "No… not this very hour."

Three blissful hours later, we drifted to the mining town. Leona's scent still lingered on me as we climbed the worn wooden steps to the Agency. I kept a respectful distance between us. Just in case someone was watching. She opened the door, and Amos practically leapt out of his chair.

"Leona!" He rushed over and gave her a tight hug, lifting her off the floor. "Julius said you'd be here today, but I was skeptical because I hadn't heard from you. Where have you been?"

"Out and about," she said when her feet touched the ground again.

"Typical drifter." Amos shot me a grin. "I bet you all were half a world away."

"Something like that," I replied.

Leona casually glanced about the sparse office. "Did we miss anything?"

Amos shook his head. "It's been pretty quiet around here. Well, except for a couple of bizarre incidents with some random trappers, but I'll tell you about that the next time we go out for a drink."

Amos returned to his desk and began shuffling through his files.

I caught Leona's eye. *What do you think he meant by that?*

She shrugged, but her curiosity was clearly piqued as well. However, we weren't foolish enough to ask him any questions. The back rooms were eerily silent. As always. But that didn't mean the people behind those doors weren't listening to our conversation.

Amos retrieved a thin envelope and handed it to Leona. "Here's your new assignment. A real easy one."

"Easy?" She tore open the envelope. "As in, low pay?"

"Great pay. Easy target," he clarified.

Leona scanned the paper and froze. I peeked over her shoulder and caught a glimpse of the outlaw's name. The blood in my veins went cold. Nora Vance.

What could they possibly want with Nora?

Despite Leona's obvious shock, her voice was even. "It says she's the daughter of a deceased rancher. What is she wanted for?"

"Did I not include that in my report?" Amos asked with a frown.

"No, it's here..." Leona said.

Theft? I projected loudly. *What could she have stolen to draw the attention of the Agency?*

"It says her last known location was near the tundra," Leona continued.

"A bit far, I know," Amos said remorsefully.

My mind was in a whirlwind. *We can't take this job. Nora saved our lives. We can't turn her in.*

"There are no other available assign—?"

A door down the hallway creaked open, cutting off Leona's words. Julius strolled down the long corridor with his hands clasped behind his back. There wasn't a single wrinkle in his dark suit. Or a crease in his emotionless face.

"Everett. Leona. I'm glad to see you're in good health." He addressed both of us, but only looked at Leona. "Is there a problem?"

Amos spoke up. "No problem, Mr. Hall—"

Julius raised a hand, and Amos shrank back behind his desk.

"We were just going over the details of our new assignment," Leona said.

"Ah, yes..." Julius straightened his cuff links. "A sheltered young woman raised by a wealthy rancher should pose little trouble to experienced trappers. Such as yourselves."

I didn't budge. Neither did Leona.

"Do you require anything else?" Julius asked.

Leona held up the single sheet of paper. "It's a small file. I wanted to be sure we weren't missing anything."

"Thorough, as always," Julius said. "But rest assured, everything *you* need to know is in that file. Any additional information is—above your ranking."

Leona forced a smile. "Thank you, Mr. Hall."

Her voice was sweet. Too sweet. I half expected her to curtsy. Then curse him out. Amos pretended to be preoccupied with his paperwork. Leona turned on her heel and stomped out of the building. Julius's jaw tensed. I tilted my broadbrim hat to him and quickly followed after her. The sooner we left the mining town and the watchful gaze of the Agency, the better.

We were four buildings away when Julius called out to us.

"Wait!"

Julius ran through the compacted mud, soiling his expensive shoes as he approached. When he reached us, he peered over his shoulder. No one had followed him out of the Agency.

"Leona, I gave you an easy assignment on purpose. As a favor."

Her expression was icy. "I didn't ask you for a *favor*."

Julius tugged on his suit jacket. "Forgive me. The last time I saw you, you were in no condition to fight, let alone chase down vicious outlaws."

If Nora's not vicious, why are we bringing her in? I projected to Leona.

"What is this really about?" she asked Julius.

He glanced at me then focused his attention back on her. "Perhaps we can speak privately."

"We are speaking privately," she said. "You, me, and Everett."

For a split second, I detected a flicker of emotion in Julius's eyes. Jealousy. He quickly smothered it.

"I desperately want to see you. Succeed." Julius lowered his voice. "If that means pulling rank to keep you out of harm's way, so be it."

A rickety horse-drawn carriage creaked past, filling the silence that hovered over us.

Leona finally spoke up. "There's nothing else you can tell us about our catch?"

"No." Julius looked taken aback. "It's a straightforward job. Why?"

"No reason." Leona repositioned her bag over her shoulder. "It will take us at least two weeks to travel to her location. We can't afford to delay, so if there's nothing else..."

"Of course." Julius bowed slightly. "Safe travels."

He headed back to the Agency, and we went the opposite direction, into the woods. I kept the torrent of questions that were running through my mind to myself until we were deep in the forest.

How long has he known about us? I spoke into Leona's mind.

"Since the trapper social."

Why hasn't he reported us?

"Because he doesn't know it's serious," she said. "He thinks we're just casual lovers."

Do you trust him?

"I want to trust him." Leona's steps were hurried. "But Nora? A thief? Yet, they refuse to tell us what she's stolen?"

"Maybe the Agency made a mistake," I said aloud.

Leona's tone was flat. "The Agency doesn't make mistakes."

In that moment, I finally understood what trappers meant when they recited that familiar mantra. The Agency was established to maintain law and order. At all costs. Mistakes weren't corrected. They were erased.

"There's nothing easy about this job," Leona said through her teeth. "If we take it, we'll betray an ally. If we don't, our contracts will be terminated, and the Agency will send hunters to kill us."

I stopped in my tracks. "And even if we don't do the job, they'll send someone else to trap Nora instead."

"Exactly." Leona leaned back against the jagged surface of a rotting tree trunk and folded her arms. "She's not safe, and we're not safe."

"What if—we trap Nora. Then bust her out?"

Leona's eyes grew wide. "Are you insane?"

An involuntary smile crossed my face as I put all the pieces together in my mind. "I have a plan."

Chapter 57: Rumor Has It

Leona

I trusted Everett. Even though I thought his plan was absolutely ludicrous. Exactly two weeks after we received our new assignment, I led Nora up the steps to the Agency with a firm grip around her frail arm. There was little resistance. Her wrists were tied tightly behind her back, limiting her movement, and a gag muffled any attempts she made to speak. The blindfold was for good measure.

"This is a bad idea," I muttered. My words were met with rattling.

Stick to the plan, Everett spoke into my mind.

I soothed myself by brushing my fingers across the familiar scales that were draped around my neck. Taking in a breath, I pushed Nora through the front doors of the Agency.

Amos's head whipped up from the notes he was scribbling. "Leona! Everett! You made it back in record time."

"Everett's not a fan of the cold," I said. Nora tried to wiggle out of my grasp, and I shook her hard until she stopped. "We got in and got out as quickly as possible."

Amos laughed and rounded his desk. "I suppose that comes with having a cold-blooded partner."

His attempt to pat my reptilian companion on the head was met with hissing. Amos jumped back and clutched his hand to his chest.

"Everett's going to need some time to thaw out," I said apologetically.

"Too bad." Amos shoved his hands into the oversized pockets of his suit jacket. "I was going to invite you both to the Establishment tonight. Drinks on me."

I grinned. "You know I'll never turn down free whiskey."

Suddenly, a door closed loudly down the hall. Julius. My heart began to race as he approached.

Everett's soft voice echoed in my mind. *Be calm, Leona. We've gone over every scenario a hundred times.*

Julius entered the room, and the scent of his strong, spicy cologne twisted my stomach in knots.

"You're back. So soon." Julius couldn't seem to mask the shock in his voice.

"Like you said..." I shoved Nora forward, trying to ignore her high-pitched whimper. "It was an easy job."

"Quite right." Julius straightened his suit jacket. "Amos. If you please."

"Yes, Mr. Hall." Amos led Nora down the dark corridor, and they disappeared into one of the back rooms.

"When will Everett and I receive payment for the job?" I asked Julius.

"I'll be sure to have the money in your account today."

"Excellent." The cool scales began to tickle my neck, and I stroked them gently. I met Julius's eyes.

He looked away and cleared his throat. "Job well done."

"Thank you. Is there anything else you need from us?" I asked.

"No. Have a nice evening." Julius spoke curtly. "You as well, Everett."

I smiled politely and made my way out of the Agency. The pleasant dry air and the sun's warm rays weren't enough to quell my anxiety. By the time I reached the edge of the mining town, my nerves were completely frayed. I slipped down an empty alleyway, ensured no one was watching, then uncoiled the heavy rattlesnake from around my neck. I placed him on the warm ground. He disappeared in the shadows and slithered under a building.

My voice was barely a whisper. "I hope you know what you're doing, Everett."

———— ⬥ ————

The Establishment was bustling with excitement, but I was too restless to enjoy the lively piano music or entertaining card games. Amos and I weaved around crowded tables and headed to the back of the saloon. A couple of trappers who were hovering over a group playing a game of faro stopped me to chat. Everyone wanted to know where my partner was. I told them all the same story. We'd had an exhausting journey north. Yes, we got our catch. No, we weren't fighting. Everett was back at the hotel—resting. I received dubious glances, but no one questioned me further. I tried not to let it irritate me. Trappers were always getting into other people's business, and I'd be just as curious if the roles were reversed.

Amos and I finally made it to two empty seats at the far corner of the bar. I lifted my skirt up a bit and hopped onto the wooden stool. I tried to get comfortable, but I was too tense. Everett consumed my thoughts. I hated not knowing exactly where he was or how to reach him, but we couldn't deviate from the plan. No one could know he was posing as Nora. If the Agency found out, I had no doubt they would immediately send trappers to find her. I only hoped the message we sent to her reached her in time.

Amos ordered us a round of drinks, and I quickly swallowed down my first shot. It didn't stop me from worrying about Everett, but it did help me to relax slightly. Ever so slightly.

We talked about everything and nothing, just like old times. I always enjoyed Amos's company. He was easy to talk to, and easy to drink with. No theatrics. No drama. Just honest conversation.

I was on my fifth shot of whiskey when I handed Amos a small pouch of gold coins.

"What's this for?" he asked, slurring.

"I need you to give that to Julius. It's money I owe him."

Amos peeked into the bag, and his jaw dropped. "This is almost as much as you made on your last three catches."

"Yes, I know." I'd practically depleted my savings, but after the Ellis Gang robbed me of the money Julius had given me, I had no other choice. I refused to be indebted to him.

Amos didn't ask me any questions. He hid the money in the pocket of his suit jacket and finished his drink.

I fanned myself. The alcohol coursing through my bloodstream made me feel like I was on fire, but I was no longer anxious. That alone was worth the mild discomfort.

"So what's really been going on at the Agency?" I asked, ready to catch up on the latest rumors and gossip.

"Multiple trappers have been attacked..." His glossy eyes met mine. "By a coyote. Isn't that wild?"

I felt the blood drain from my face. "Where? When?"

"Random attacks all over the territories." He waved his empty glass as he spoke. "No rhyme or reason. But a couple of telepaths who were mauled swear it's a shapeshifter."

My throat tightened. "Why do they think that?"

"They said it was trying to probe their minds and get information out of them about the activities and whereabouts of trappers. Isn't that the craziest thing you've ever heard?"

I couldn't speak. My head was spinning. The room tilted slightly, and I grabbed hold of the bar.

Amos signaled the bartender for another round then paused. "Hey... weren't you bitten by a coyote a while back? Like, waaay back, before the smuggler job?"

I frantically snatched a gold coin from the pocket of my skirt, immediately sobered up, and jumped off the stool.

Amos glanced about. "We're leaving? I was about to have another—"

I hauled Amos from the bar and dragged him to the stairs. A few trappers clapped as we shuffled up to the second floor where the private bedrooms were located.

"Good for you, Amos!" someone shouted.

"Don't let her get too rough with you!" another person teased.

I ignored their drunken laughter and kicked open the first door on the landing. Dorothy and Mack scrambled off the bed, startled.

"Get out."

I didn't have to tell them twice. They scooped their clothes off the floor and hurried out in their undergarments. Mack started to complain, but Dorothy put her finger to his lips and hushed him.

"Leona needs this more than anybody. She's wound up."

I slammed the door and locked it. Amos was staring at me, wide-eyed.

"Where are they taking Nora?"

"Wha—?" His face twisted in confusion. "What does Nora have to do with anything?"

"Never mind that," I said, impatiently. "I need to know where they're taking her."

Amos swayed then regained his balance. "I can't tell you that."

"Amos..." I fought to hold back my emotions. "Please, I need your help."

He pursed his lips together. "It's confidential."

"I wouldn't ask you something like this if it wasn't serious." I grabbed Amos's shoulders. "Everett's in trouble."

"Everett... Nora...?" Suddenly, understanding washed over his face. He clamped a hand over his mouth.

I spoke calmly, despite the fact that my heart was thundering in my chest. "Where does the Agency take the prisoners?"

"Leona, I can't." Amos's voice cracked. "I'm sorry."

Tears of frustration stung my eyes. "Everett's not just—he's more than my partner."

Amos was still. "*More* than?"

I turned around and slid the ruffled sleeve of my dress off my left shoulder, exposing the diamond-shaped markings on my upper back. I caught a glimpse of Amos through the corner of my eye. The ruckus and commotion coming from downstairs seemed to fade into the background as he stared at me in a stunned silence.

"We're married," I whispered.

Amos exhaled. He quickly repositioned the sleeve of my dress over my shoulder and covered me up. I faced him once more. Neither of us said a word. When he finally spoke, his voice was somber.

"They take the prisoners to a place no one can get out of..." Amos shook his head in sorrow. "The Valley of Sand."

Chapter 58: Blocked

Leona

The Valley of Sand. I struggled to process Amos's words. The vast, uninhabitable desert was a death sentence, and my partner—my soulmate—was going to be trapped there. With no way out.

I hurried to the door, but Amos blocked my path.

"What's your plan?" he asked.

"I don't have one." Panic rose in my throat, and the private bedroom started to feel cramped. "I just need to get to Everett."

Amos was calm despite the slight haze over his eyes due to the alcohol. "You can't go rushing out of here without a plan. When the Agency finds out what you and Everett have done—"

"They'll come for us. But at least we'll be together."

Amos took his time before speaking again. "I'll saddle my horse. You'll need to ride out of town. Quickly. The sooner you're able to open a portal, the better." He squinted at his watch. "It's eleven now. They transport prisoners to the Valley exactly at midnight, and you might be able to catch Everett in time."

I wrapped my arms around him. "I can't thank you enough."

He hugged me back and whispered in my ear, "This conversation between us never happened. Agreed?"

"Agreed..." I slowly pulled away. "I'm going to leave here quickly and quietly."

Amos gave a firm nod. We slipped out of the bedroom without another word. The clamor and commotion coming from downstairs in the saloon wasn't enough to drown out my panicked thoughts, but the racket provided a perfect distraction. No one would think twice about my swift departure.

A door slammed down the hall, and we both spun around. Elsie, dressed in a checkered blue gown with puff sleeves, stood fanning herself. There wasn't a single blond hair out of place. I breathed a sigh of relief at seeing a familiar face, and she lit up at the sight of me.

"Leona!" Elsie snapped her lace fan closed. "Fancy meeting you here."

"I had no idea you were in town," I said.

"Just passing through." She paused when she spotted Amos, and her eyes widened.

Amos cleared his throat and muttered, "I'll be waiting out front, Leona." He bowed slightly to Elsie then hurried down the stairs.

Elsie pranced over to me and playfully whacked my arm with her fan. "I declare!"

"It's nothing like that," I insisted.

"None of my never mind," she said with a casual shrug. "Where, pray tell, is that partner of yours?"

"Everett's back at the hotel," I lied. I glanced over Elsie's shoulder, and curiosity got the better of me. "Who were *you* just with?"

"No one important." She smiled innocently. "Just a dark-haired gentleman who wanted to show a lady a good time."

I let out an involuntary chuckle. "What's Claude going to say about that?"

Elsie cocked her head to the side. "Who?"

My heart skipped a beat. Her pale-blue eyes flashed bright green. I gasped. Elsie grabbed me by the throat and strangled me with both hands. I yanked her wrists and kneed her in the groin as hard as I could. Grunting, she released her grip. I snatched a handful of her long hair and shoved her head against the wall. She spun and punched me in the jaw. I barely felt the blow, but I tasted the blood. I grabbed her by the collar and dragged her to the top of the stairs. My pulse thundered in my ears. I knew how much it was going to hurt. I'd done it before.

I threw myself from the top step without letting go of Elsie. We tumbled down the stairs. Head. Heels. Head. Heels. Head... I swore every bone in my body was going to be fractured.

"Leona and Elsie are fighting!" someone shouted.

We hit the bottom of the stairs, and I landed on top of her. Streaks of red blood marred her blond hair. I forced myself to my feet. The room was still spinning. A wave of nausea washed over me. Elsie pushed herself up, let out a guttural roar, and dove into me. I flew backward, and we smashed through a wooden table. Trappers scattered. Poker cards and coins went flying in all directions. There was a chorus of shouts and rebukes.

"Break them up!"

Elsie spit blood at me as Dorothy and Mack pulled her away. I hurled a heavy glass at her and missed. Two gangly trappers dodged out of the way, and it shattered behind them.

Ed stood between us and stared down at me. His massive size shielded Elsie from my view. "You both need to calm down! You're supposed to be friends. What kind of example does this set for younger trappers?"

"That's not Elsie!" I screamed. "It's—"

Ed was struck over the back of the head with a bottle of whiskey. His eyes rolled back, and he fell to the floor, unconscious. My head snapped up in time for me to see Leroy holding a broken bottle. Only it wasn't Leroy. His eyes glowed green... another shapeshifter.

"What did you do that for?" Ed's partner swung at Leroy and struck him in the gut.

Two other trappers joined the fight, and within a matter of seconds, half of the trappers in the saloon were embroiled in a violent brawl. The other half were spurring them on.

I'd lost sight of Elsie. I scrambled to my feet and charged out of the Establishment. Despite the chaos inside, the night was eerily still. I staggered down the boardwalk, scanning the dark street.

"Amos!" I called out.

A heavy body slammed into my back. My scream was cut off as I flew headfirst into a horse trough. Lukewarm water enveloped me. I tried to sit up, but a strong hand gripped my neck, forcing my head back down. I squeezed my eyes shut in the murky water.

I will not drown again. I will not drown again…

My long, flowing skirt billowed out as I reached for the dagger hidden on my thigh. My lungs begged for oxygen. I yanked my knife from the holster and stabbed my attacker in the arm. There was a muffled yelp. He recoiled and released me. I sat upright in the trough, gasping for air and clutching my weapon. I whipped around to face my attacker, but there was no one in sight. Amos rode out of the livery stable on his gray thoroughbred and cantered toward me.

"Leona!" he cried. "Are you all right? What happened?"

I wiped the slimy water from my battered face and sputtered. "He's after me."

"Who?" Amos hastily dismounted and rushed to my side. "Who's after you?"

"The shapeshifter. Hiram…" I choked out. "The coyote."

I tried not to gag as I hauled myself out of the trough with Amos's help.

He glanced about nervously. "I don't understand."

"I know. And I don't have time to explain." I wrung out as much water as I could from my soiled garments, but it was pointless. I couldn't drift. "I have to get to Everett before he does."

Amos held his horse steady, and I climbed into the saddle.

"Do whatever you have to do," Amos said. "You know how to contact me."

I nodded, clutching the reins. I turned the thoroughbred around and took the fastest route out of town.

My limbs ached, but all I could think about was Everett. Hiram was no longer toying with us. He didn't want us to suffer. He was out for blood.

I rode through the dark woods, trying to remember the way back to the Agency by land. The horse kept a swift, steady pace, and I secretly hoped he knew where we were going. I was so used to drifting, the landscape almost felt foreign to me.

Through the moonlight, I spotted a figure in the distance—broad and menacing. A grizzly bear. The beast reared up on its hind legs and roared. The frightened thoroughbred turned and bolted in the opposite direction. I crouched down and clung to its mane. My grip began to weaken. I couldn't hold on. The horse threw me from the saddle and galloped in the direction we'd come.

I lay on the ground in a crumpled heap, my wet clothes matted to my sore body. Deep in the forest, a bird squawked wildly. I couldn't move. The bear was joined by a coyote, and together they stalked toward me.

They were going to rip me to shreds—then burn my body.

Everett would lose his love partner...

Tears burned my eyes.

Our love would die.

I slammed my hands into the dry soil, summoning every ounce of strength I had left. "Diamas!" I cried.

The markings on my back came alive. I felt the ink slip through my veins. The ground was teeming with life. There was a connection between worlds, between dimensions, that I'd never felt before. My vision turned black. In my mind's eye, I saw Ollie.

He blinked in surprise. "Leona?"

"I need your help," I whispered.

He closed his eyes and took in a slow breath. My vision returned. The coyote and the bear were getting closer. Suddenly, Ollie rose from the ground in front of me.

"Ollie..." I reached out to him, but my hand went through his leg. He was there—but he wasn't there.

He did a quick scan of the woods. The two beasts increased their pace.

Ollie shouted the clan's name in such a ferocious tone, I shuddered. Four other figures came forth and surrounded us in a diamond formation. In a matter of seconds, we were completely encased in a translucent, gold structure.

The coyote howled and charged forward, leaving the bear behind. I couldn't control my trembling hands as Hiram morphed into his humanoid form. Blood dripped down his arm, and his face was badly bruised, but his wounds didn't even seem to register. His eyes were fixed solely on mine.

"Give her to me!"

Ollie stood over me with his arms folded. "We won't let you harm her."

"She's not part of your clan!" Hiram shouted. "You can't protect her!"

Alta was in front of us, Miriam was behind, and Dennis and Dave were at our sides. No one moved a muscle.

"Ira!" Hiram shouted.

The grizzly bear morphed into a hulking form of a man and hurried to stand to Hiram's right. A black crow swooped out of the sky and landed to Hiram's left. She morphed, and my jaw dropped. Violet. From the Tea Room. I suddenly understood Everett's mistrust of everyone and everything. With shapeshifters, nothing was as it seemed.

"This matter doesn't concern you," Hiram said to Ollie.

"Ahh, but it does," he replied.

"She's our sister," Alta stated plainly.

Hiram's face fell. Ira and Violet exchanged glances but said nothing.

"Impossible," Hiram said through his sharp teeth. "I don't believe you."

I gathered my courage and stood. I was with my family—my clan. "It's true. I am Everett's love partner. I belong to the Diamas clan."

Hiram ran up and pounded his fist against the barrier. He shot a vicious look over his shoulder at his companions. They both winced and covered their ears. I was grateful I didn't have the ability to hear his thoughts, but I wondered what he was saying to them.

"There's no reason to get all emotional about it," Alta said.

Miriam tsked. "Such language."

Dave snorted. "I've heard you say worse, Mir."

"Out loud too," Dennis added.

"That's only when you two make me mad," Miriam said sweetly.

"It's never good to make anyone in our family mad," Ollie said to Hiram. His voice was like their father's. Calm, cold, and calculated. "So why don't you and your little posse move along—before your blood feud turns into a clan war."

Ira's deep voice was almost a rumble. "Your quarrel is with Everett. He's the one you want. If you kill him, the blood feud is over. If you kill Everett *and* his love partner, they'll have grounds to retaliate. I won't be able to support you, brother."

"Me neither," Violet said. "You know how the Diamas clan is. They'll wipe out an entire bloodline in the name of family and honor." She spit the last words out like they tasted foul in her mouth.

"I don't care. Everett took everything from me when he erased Nora's memories of me." Hiram clenched his fists. "She would still be alive if he hadn't forced me to take such drastic measures to make her remember me."

I shifted slightly and clamped my mouth shut.

Violet stared at me intently. "Leona knows something we don't know."

"Get it out of her," Hiram demanded.

My vision blurred. A sharp pain tore through the back of my head. Violet forced her way into my mind. Into my memories... and I couldn't stop her.

I was standing in front of a telegraph office. The bright afternoon sun was blinding. Heat radiated off every surface, almost suffocating me. Everett paid the teller. The message was short: Trappers heading north. Hide at ranch.

"It's abandoned." Everett's words echoed in my mind. "Nora will be safe there..."

The light intensified. I was surrounded in it. Consumed by it...

"Leona?" Ollie's soothing voice drew me back to the dark forest. "Can you hear me?"

I blinked, and the fog clouding my mind began to lift.

"She's coming out of the trance," Alta said with relief.

"Thank goodness," Miriam said.

I found myself lying on a bed of leaves with Everett's siblings hovering over me.

Hiram, Violet, and Ira where nowhere in sight. My head was throbbing, but my damp clothes were almost dry. *Almost dry.*

I shot up. "What time is it?"

"Three in the morning," Dennis replied.

"Three thirty, to be exact," Dave said.

"No..." I struggled to keep my emotions from pouring out of me. "It can't be."

Ollie knelt in front of me. "Leona, where is our brother? Where is Everett?"

Chapter 59: Worst-Case Scenario

Everett

Leona and I had gone over every possible scenario. Except the one I found myself in...

Posing as Nora had been the easy part. Leona brought me into the Agency bound, gagged, and blindfolded. Amos ushered me to one of the back rooms, cut the rope from my wrists, and replaced the bonds with metal handcuffs that were attached to the wall. He removed the blindfold but never looked me in the eye. The tiny, windowless room was sparse. There was a cot, a small square table with a pitcher of water, and a chamber pot. That was it. Amos locked the door behind him. Then I waited. And waited. And waited. Night fell.

I expected an interrogation. Or a beating. But there was nothing. After a few anxious hours, I decided to try to get some sleep. But I was restless, and my dreams were scattered.

"Just the one prisoner?"

"Yeah. It's going to be a quick drop."

I woke to the sound of unfamiliar voices and sat upright on the cot. Footsteps plodded up the hallway. I found myself holding my breath as keys rattled in the lock. The door flew open, and two slim trappers stood in the doorway. One held an oil lantern, the other a rope. Soft yellow light flickered off the weathered bandanas that concealed their faces, and their eyes were hidden by the broad brims of their hats.

I didn't resist when they tied my wrists in front of me and led me out of the Agency. A mule was hitched to a small wagon, and they hoisted me onto the flatbed before loading a few bags next to me. They worked quickly and quietly. Experienced partners. The driver hopped in the box and took the reins while the other trapper sat next to me, keeping guard but without any visible weapons.

"Where are we going?" I asked in Nora's timid voice.

The trapper wouldn't look at me. Or respond. I wrapped my long skirt tighter around my ankles and stared up at the pale moons as we rode out of the mining town. It had to be close to midnight. I wondered how Leona was faring. I'd assured her that as soon as I found out where the Agency was holding the outlaws and criminals, I would make my escape. Knowing the location gave us the upper hand. One less secret the Agency could hide from us.

I wasn't familiar with the dusty road the trappers took into the wilderness, and soon the beaten trail ended, and the path turned rugged. A dense canopy of leaves blocked out the light of Aadar's moons as we traveled deep into the forest. The strained creaking of the wagon's wheels filled the ominous silence. Despite the warm night air, I suddenly felt a chill. My markings—the ones I was concealing—were cold. Something was wrong. With Leona.

"Right here." The trapper beside me spoke up, and his partner brought the mule to a halt.

Before I had time to react, the trapper dragged me off the wagon, scooped up a handful of dirt, and grabbed me by the waist.

"Off we go, sweetheart," he mockingly whispered in my ear.

The sand fell from his fingers, and the ground swallowed us up. I gritted my teeth as we fell. And fell. Just as suddenly, we were propelled forward and thrown out of the portal. We landed on top of a large sand dune. The drifter held me upright, preventing me from tumbling over the side. Moments later his partner landed beside us, carrying the four bags.

The trapper released his grip on me. "She didn't even scream," he said to his partner in dismay.

"No? That's unusual." He started down the steep incline. "Must not be her first time."

"Pity," the man said.

They laughed. I wanted to punch their teeth in. Instead, I kept my mouth shut and my temper in check.

"We don't have time to waste." The lean young man took hold of the rope and yanked hard, dragging me along like an animal.

I struggled to get my bearings. The brilliant sunlight burned my sensitive eyes, and the dry air was like a furnace. I was barely able to breathe. Let alone speak.

"T-the Valley of Sand...?" I choked out.

The two trappers ignored me. They continued down the sand dune with me struggling to keep up. My thoughts began to spiral out of control. The Valley was a death trap. No one would be able to find my body. I couldn't let them leave without me. No matter what. I had to get back to Leona. Somehow.

As we approached the narrow valley, the ground became more stable and solid. For the first time, I noticed what looked to be hollow openings in the mounds of sand. Caves.

We reached the bottom, and I squinted up at the towering desert mountains. We were like specks of dust in the vast wasteland. At the complete mercy of the elements. I was in awe of the raw beauty that encompassed the harsh landscape. And terrified at the same time.

The trapper gave my rope one final tug then shoved me into the mouth of a cave. I gasped. Pain shot up my left arm as I landed hard, unable to break my fall. The bags flew in my direction. I scrambled to my feet and dashed forward as the drifters prepared to leave. I just needed to grab hold of one of them to make it into the portal. The two trappers moved in unison, each hurling a fistful of sand directly into my face. I shrieked and stumbled backward, momentarily blinded. The butt of a gun came down hard against my skull. I didn't remember hitting the ground. But when the ringing in my ears stopped and I was finally able to gather enough strength to wipe away the rough, sandy grains that were stinging my eyes... the drifters were gone.

I lay there in a dazed stupor. Alone. Not knowing what to do next. Leona and I had gone over every possible scenario. Except the one I found myself in.

"Nora?" a familiar voice croaked out.

I twisted around to find a gangly figure stumbling toward me.

I blinked hard. "Ray?"

He looked worse than the day I electrocuted him and tied him to a tree. Much worse. His tattered clothes hung from his skeletal frame, and his usual clean-shaven face was covered in a scrubby, uneven beard.

Ray hurried over and untied the rope that was cutting off my circulation. The bonds fell to the ground, and I rubbed my tender wrists. When he helped me stand, his weak limbs trembled from the exertion. I tried to mask the shock of seeing him in such a deplorable state.

"They left food this time?" Ray asked, motioning behind me.

"I-I'm not sure."

Ray tore open one of the leather bags, and his eyes lit up. Moldy bread. I frowned, but his mouth was visibly watering.

He quickly closed the bag and slung it over his shoulder. "Come. We'll share this with the others."

"Others?" I asked. "What others?"

"Prisoners. Like us."

Ray attempted to grab the other bags, but I could tell it was a struggle. I lifted them up and carried the rest of the food and provisions on my back.

We didn't have to go too far into the cave before we reached "the others." Emaciated bodies were curled up on old ratty blankets, forming a circle around a firepit that held no fire.

"The days are scorching," Ray explained. "But the nights are unbearably cold."

I stared down at the beaten and worn faces of the other prisoners. I recognized—all of them. The horse thief. Sage, Poppy, and Clover from the smuggler job. The doctor. Harvey. Every successful catch Leona and I had ever made. All together. In one place. Heat rose up my neck.

"What's going on?" I asked Ray. "Why did they bring us here?"

Ray frowned. "You must be in shock. Why don't you have a seat in my spot?"

He guided me around the other prisoners. Some were sleeping. Others were conversing quietly. And a couple of them were rocking back and forth, clearly in some sort of pain. Mental or physical. I sat on a ripped blanket in the sand while Ray and the doctor went about distributing the meager rations the two trappers had left. There was hardly enough food and water to go around.

"No real medicine this time," the doctor grumbled. He pulled a small bottle from a bag and took a sip. "I suppose this will have to do to calm my nerves."

He joined Sage and Poppy in a corner where they were attending to Clover. Her once silky black hair was coarse and lifeless, and tangled strands were matted to her gaunt cheeks. Her cough was horrific. And when she wasn't coughing, I couldn't understand the incoherent string of words she mumbled.

"Fever," Ray whispered as he sat beside me.

I looked away from her. "How long has she been like that?"

He shrugged. "Since before I got here."

"And the Agency does nothing?"

Ray placed the back of his hand on my forehead. "Are you sick? Or did they hit you over the head too hard?"

"I just don't understand it."

"There's nothing to understand." Ray offered me a dried piece of bread.

"No, you have it," I said.

"You're always so selfless, Nora." He took a small bite. "Do you remember the nights we used to sneak food from the cook and sit out under the stars?"

"Those were good times." I flashed him a weary smile. "I miss the ranch. How long have you been here?"

Ray hesitated. "Hard to say. Time is difficult to judge in this place."

"None of this makes any sense," I said. "Why are we all here together?"

"Why do you think?" Harvey's voice was so raspy I almost didn't recognize it. "Leona... and Everett."

I froze. I hadn't noticed the rogue trapper watching me until that moment. Harvey crawled closer and planted himself beside me. I turned my head slightly in an effort to avoid his foul body odor.

"What do you mean?" I asked.

Harvey looked me up and down. "They were the trappers that brought you in, weren't they?"

"Yes..." I said cautiously.

"I'm here because I tried to kill that whore. Twice." His scornful laughter was cut off by a coughing fit that rivaled Clover's. "You ever have any dealings with her sister?"

My eyebrows shot up. "Maude?"

"Of course she has." Ray nudged my arm. "Her old man hired Maude to work on his ranch around the same time he hired me. Isn't that right?"

"That's right." I forced a smile then turned my attention back to Harvey. "Maude and I became very close."

Harvey smirked. "Then you know Leona will get what's coming to her for trapping us all here."

I wanted to knock the smug grin off his face, but I kept Nora's voice level. "What do you mean?"

"I got friends high up in the Agency. They're looking for Maude. That's why she went into hiding. She learned too much about their *practices*." He gestured around the cave. "About this place, and what they do to prisoners. She was going to expose them."

I shook some of the sand out of my long hair and tried to sound casual. "What does that have to do with Leona?"

"She's the bait..." Harvey leaned closer. "To trap Maude!"

My throat went dry.

"Leona and Everett were set up to fail," Harvey continued. "Opposing abilities. Conflicting skill sets. Completely incompatible."

Ray chuckled. "A drifter and a shapeshifter. Absolutely ludicrous."

"Their partnership was doomed from the start. They couldn't make a single catch together. The Agency thought it was a sure bet. Then the two of them started to get good. Real good." Harvey rested his weight on his elbow. "But it's only a matter of time before they slip up. Then the Agency will send out their hunters, and Maude will do what she always does—rescue Leona."

My mind was racing, but I remained silent.

"And you know what the Agency will do to Leona and Maude once they've caught them?" Harvey spoke with a hint of glee. "They can't confine them here, so they'll have no choice but to cut out their hearts."

His choked laughter sounded so deranged it made my skin crawl.

"That'll be a shame for Everett," Ray said remorsefully.

"He'll be dead too!" Harvey's cackling was suddenly cut short. "Wait, why do you say that?"

"Because he's in love with Leona." Ray looked me in the eyes. "Isn't that right?"

I met his gaze. "I wouldn't know."

"Sure you would."

My heart hammered in my chest. Ray knew. I started to get to my feet. He grabbed my wrist and twisted it hard, forcing me back down.

"Where are you going, Nora?" Ray asked.

My voice trembled. "Nowhere..."

"Exactly." He dug his sharp, uneven nails into my skin and lowered his voice. "You're not going anywhere."

Chapter 60: Trance

Everett

I didn't dare move a muscle. Ray released his grip on my wrist and calmly went back to eating his stale bread. Harvey appeared to be lost in thought and didn't notice the interaction between me and Ray.

"Everett's in love with Leona?" Harvey spoke half to himself. "Then he's a much bigger fool than I thought."

"Why's that?" I asked, discreetly rubbing my sore wrist.

"She's got nothing to offer him. Except a drop in rank."

It astounded me that after everything Harvey had been through, a bit of trapper gossip still held his interest.

"Leona's very attractive," Ray said.

I kept quiet. He was trying to get under my skin.

"She's not as attractive as Maude," Harvey scoffed. "Not by a long shot."

They're identical twins! I wanted to shout.

"Everett's never met Maude," Ray said.

Harvey snorted. "Well, if he did, he'd drop Leona in a second."

"I doubt that," I muttered.

Ray leaned closer. "Did you say something, Nora?"

"No." I brushed sand from the folds of my skirt. "I think I need to go for a walk. I'm feeling restless."

"This place will do that to you," Harvey said, settling back on his blanket.

Ray stood. "I'll go with you."

I smiled politely and rose. We headed toward the opening of the cave, away from the other prisoners. Away from listening ears.

"How did you know?" I asked under my breath.

"There was only one other person who wanted to escape the ranch more than me," Ray said. "Nora."

I cursed myself for the slip-up.

"And I worked there *four* years before Maude was hired."

We reached the entrance of the cave. A burst of wind whipped sand into my face, but the warm breeze did nothing to cool me off.

I spoke up. "Are you going to try to kill me?"

"I'd love to kill you, Everett," Ray said. "But alas, I don't have the strength."

I stared up at the towering sand dunes. Running wasn't an option. I wouldn't survive a day in the scorching heat. There was no water. No living plants. No... life.

"It would be a terrible shame if the others found out," Ray continued. "They'd probably smother you in your sleep."

I had no doubt of that. "What do you want?"

"Can you get us out of here?"

"No," I admitted.

"Then I guess I'll just silently torture you until I get bored and expose your secret."

I understood his bitterness. And frustration. What the Agency did—what we did—was inhumane. I couldn't unsee the anguish and misery on the faces of the other prisoners. They were mere shells of the people they once were, and I was responsible for their pain and suffering. I never asked any questions. I blindly carried out the Agency's wishes. The same Agency who used me... and Leona.

"There might be a way for me to contact Leona." I looked Ray in the eye. "But I'll need your help."

I told Ray my plan. If it was going to work, we needed to move fast. We headed back into the cave to rejoin the others. I was putting my life in Ray's hands, despite the fact that he'd betrayed me once before. I steadied my breathing and pushed that thought aside. I had a plan, and I couldn't do it alone.

We reached the makeshift firepit, and I stood a few paces behind Ray.

He clapped his hands together. "I need everyone's attention, please."

Those who were sleeping stirred and opened their weary eyes. Others rolled over to face him but didn't seem to have the energy to do much more than that. Sage gently hushed Clover, who was murmuring incoherently, and Poppy wiped sweat from the sick woman's forehead.

"What's this all about?" the doctor demanded. "I'm trying to keep my patients comfortable."

"I understand, but this concerns all of us." Ray gestured grandly in my direction. "*That* is not Nora. It's Everett."

There was a stunned silence. Nobody moved.

"Show them," Ray said to me.

I slowly shifted. My body shuddered as I shed Nora's appearance and stood at my natural height wearing my weathered trapper clothes. It had been a while since I'd spent that much time in the form of another person. Jaws dropped. Outside the cave, the high-pitched howling of the wind died down. All was still. And then chaos ensued.

Sage charged at me first, screaming like a vixen and wielding a stone knife. Ray rushed forward and slammed the palm of his hand into her chest. She froze midstep, suspended in his stasis field. Poppy ran up and tried to sidestep Sage, but Ray knocked her back, trapping her in place. Two individuals who were too weak to stand started hurling rocks in my direction. I dodged out of the way, only to have three nimble prisoners pounce on my back. I dropped to my knees. Fortunately, the sand broke my fall. One of them tried to bite my arm. They fought with all their might, but the frail captives were easy to shake off. Harvey wasn't. He managed to sneak up from behind. His tight choke hold cut off the air going into my lungs. I gasped for breath.

"Ray!" I called out.

His head whipped around as he struggled with the horse thief. "Harvey, now's not the time!"

Harvey squeezed tighter. I slammed my head back as hard as I could, smashing into his face. He grunted and let go. Ray lunged forward and knocked Harvey off his feet. The stasis field prevented him from hitting the ground. He hung in midair, two inches above the sand. I crawled away from him and caught my breath.

Half of the prisoners were suspended in place and the other half were neutralized. The doctor stood in a corner sipping some sort of concoction from a glass bottle. Apparently, he preferred being a spectator.

Ray stood over me in a protective stance. "You were right. They didn't take the news very well."

I dragged myself up and dusted off my pants. Those who could still move about freely spit and shouted curses at me.

"I understand why you all want to kill me," I said, addressing the entire group. "I'm sorry. I truly am. This wasn't what I signed up for when I became a trapper. But there may be a way I can contact Leona. If you give me the chance."

Ray looked around. "We have nothing to lose. If he succeeds, we have a shot of getting out of here alive. If he fails, we kill him."

"Thanks, Ray," I said dryly.

"You're welcome."

Ray went from person to person and released them from his stasis field. No one made a move toward me. The negative energy seeping out of every one of the prisoners was suffocating.

Sage cracked her neck as she glared at me. "What happens now?"

"I need to induce a trance," I said. "So I need a space where I won't be—disturbed."

"You won't be harmed." Ray turned to the others. "Agreed?"

Everyone nodded. They settled back in their respective spots around the firepit, but no one spoke a word. Harvey dabbed his bloody nose with a frayed rag, never once taking his eyes off me.

I cleared a small area in the sand then unbuttoned my vest and cotton shirt. The last time I went into a trance, it didn't end well. But they didn't need to know that. I placed my shirt and vest on the ground and sat on them, cross-legged. My breathing was slow and controlled.

"I need something sharp," I said.

Ray approached Sage. "Do you mind?"

She blew her long bangs out of her eyes and grudgingly handed him her stone knife. Ray brought the crude weapon over to me. The blade was heavy.

I can do this. I can do this, I repeated to myself.

My fingers tightened around the knife. There was no turning back. I jabbed the side of my neck with the pointed tip of the stone blade. There were gasps. The sharp burst of pain faded. Ink from my markings rolled down my neck and across my bare chest.

I closed my eyes and cleared my mind of everything but Leona. Her scent. The curves of her body. The melodic sound of her voice...

The world faded around me. I could almost feel her soft touch. The tips of her fingers stroking my skin. My markings began to tingle.

Suddenly, I felt weightless. I opened my eyes, but there was only darkness. Beautiful darkness.

Leona...

My mind reached out to her. Time seemed to bend and fold into itself. Every moment we shared flashed before my eyes. The first time we met. Our first job together. Our first kiss. The argument. The waterfall. Her death. My family. Our wedding. Trapping. Dancing.

Leona...

Our souls were entwined. She filled me with love and happiness. Euphoria. Ecstasy. We were one. I could feel her heart beating with mine.

Leona...

There was a whisper. *Everett?*

"He's shaking! Do something!"

"You heard the doctor! Back away! Nobody touch him!"

Ray's petrified voice tore me from the darkness. I gasped. My vision returned. I lay flat on my back, staring up at the troubled faces of the other prisoners. A fire crackled behind them. Ray and the doctor knelt beside me and slowly helped me sit up. Someone wrapped a blanket around my shoulders.

"That was horrifying," Ray said.

The cave felt like it was spinning, and I fought back the urge to vomit. "What happened?"

"You morphed into this—*thing*." Ray wiped sweat from his brow. "Not quite human. Not quite reptile."

"Then there was the shrieking," the doctor added. "It went on for hours. Suddenly, you fell silent. We thought you were dead. Then the seizures started."

A chill went through me. I glanced behind me. There was no light coming from the mouth of the cave. It was well into the night.

I swiped wet patches of black ink from my body. "I have to try again."

The doctor rested his bony hand on my shoulder. "I'm not sure your body can handle it so soon."

"I have to try." My breaths were shallow. "Every second Leona and I are apart, our connection gets weaker. I don't know how much time we have left."

Ray stood. "Get him the knife."

Chapter 61: Through the Darkness

Leona

Everett was in my mind. Ever present. He was calling to me, but I couldn't reach him. For two days and two nights I drifted in and out of the Valley of Sand. I drifted until my body ached. Until my legs gave out and I lay in a crumpled heap on the cold forest floor near our hideaway.

Leona... go through the darkness...

"I don't understand," I cried into the night. "What does that mean?"

I clung to the thin threads of Everett's consciousness but couldn't grasp what he was trying to say.

We bleed together... we fall together...

"*Fall together.*" I struggled to make sense of his words. "Do you mean drift?"

Everett's voice was growing more and more distant. I reached into the pocket of my dusty pants, grabbed a gold coin, and regained my strength.

I'm lost without you...

"I'm coming. I promise. Just stay with me, please." I scooped up the dry soil and inhaled slowly, calming my nerves.

Everett said my name—softly. He was fading.

"Through the darkness," I repeated to myself. The warm sand fell from my fingers, and I drifted.

I hated the Valley with every fiber of my being. On more than one occasion, when I drifted in a highly emotional state and without a destination, I ended up in that wretched wasteland. My mother was to blame.

The day Maude and I turned eighteen, Mother dragged us to the Valley of Sand... and left us there. Hundreds of miles apart from each other. Maude was able to get back home within a day. I wasn't so fortunate.

I tried to bury the memory as I was propelled forward, out of the portal. I landed in a mound of scorching-hot sand. There was no sign of life—anywhere. I tried to sense Everett with my markings, but there was nothing. Not even his voice whispering in my head. Frustration and anger welled inside of me.

"Everett!" I screamed. "Where did they take you?"

The bright, early-morning light cast shadows in the curves of the sand. The temperature was already unbearable. I drifted again. The landscape shifted and changed with the wind, but it all looked the same. Desolate and lonely. I called out to Everett, screaming until my throat went dry. I drifted again. And again. Going deeper into the Valley. When I exhausted every single location I'd ever physically been to in the stark desert, I began to walk. I wandered across dune after dune. Aimless. Just like my life had become.

Everett had once spoken about his desire to own land and raise a family. The very idea sounded ludicrous to me at the time. An absurd dream. I'd never given any thought to a lifestyle like that. I was a drifter. Tied to no one place and no one person. Yet in that moment, I wanted nothing more than to be with Everett... in a safe place we could call our own.

"Everett! Can you hear me?"

Only the wind responded, whipping around me with a high-pitched wail. When Aadar was enraged, the Valley of Sand was where she took out most of her aggression. My boots sank into the heavy sand as I trudged along. Minutes stretched into hours. The heat was oppressive, but I knew better than to strip off the protective clothing that helped to shield me from the scorching sun. I'd made that mistake once before.

By midday, my stomach began to rumble. I ignored it. There wasn't time to concern myself with hunger or thirst. Every second I was away from Everett meant he was in greater and greater danger. I didn't know what the Agency had done to him, or how long he would be able to survive in the harsh elements. Sweat poured out of me. My drenched clothes clung to my skin, weighing me down and adding to my exhaustion. I pushed through the dizzy spells and the throbbing headaches. But then the vomiting started.

I stood hunched over with my hands on my knees, expelling what was left in my stomach. There was more than I imagined. When I finally stopped retching, I wiped my mouth with the back of my sleeve. My pulse was racing, but I didn't dare sit for fear I'd never get up again.

"Everett..." I could barely get the words past my parched throat. "Where are you?"

I pressed on. Each time the heatstroke set in, I used a gold coin. When my skin blistered and peeled off in clumps from the sunburn, I used two. There were moments I swore I saw Everett in the distance, reaching out to me, but then I would blink, and he was gone. A mirage. He wasn't the only one I saw. There was my mother. With her expressionless face. Staring at me as I begged her not to leave me there alone.

Leona...

My heart leapt at the sound of Everett's voice.

"Yes! I'm here!" I shouted into the air.

He went silent again. It was just me and the wind. I gazed across the endless mountains of sand. Emptiness consumed me. A dark abyss I couldn't crawl my way out of. I dropped to my knees, unable to fight the tears that were stinging my eyes. I curled up in a ball and sobbed uncontrollably.

"Everett, please don't leave me here alone," I whispered. "I don't want to go through life without you..."

Bleed...

I sat up straight. "What?"

Markings... Everett's voice faded.

I attempted to piece together his message. "Bleed markings?"

My vision became hazy. I fought another dizzy spell. I was out of gold, but I couldn't go back. I was too close.

I tore off my sweaty button-down shirt and tossed it aside before grabbing my knife. Without thinking, I sliced my upper back. I bit down to prevent a shriek from escaping. The ink stung like acid as it poured out of my body and soaked into my cotton chemise. The burning sensation was almost unbearable. I sheathed the blade, grabbed a handful of sand, and closed my eyes, focusing solely on Everett. The grains of sand trickled between my fingers.

The ground opened up, and I fell. Suddenly, there was a sharp tugging sensation, pulling on my markings. A heavy force yanked me back, like a fish caught on a line. I gasped. I careened through the void. *Backward.* Completely out of control.

A portal opened, and I was hurled into a cave. The wind was violently knocked out of my lungs as I landed flat on my back. I struggled to breathe. Pain pulsed through me, and my wide eyes remained fixed on the cave ceiling.

"Leona!"

I heard frantic shuffling in the sand, then Everett was hovering over me with a look of sheer astonishment on his face.

"It worked! It really worked!"

I took in a ragged breath. Everett scooped me into his arms and held me in a tight embrace. Relief washed over me. I closed my eyes and buried my face in his neck. His bare chest was covered in oily black ink that seeped into my clothes, but I didn't care. I never wanted to be parted from him again.

"When I couldn't hear you anymore, I was afraid—" I squeezed him closer. "I thought you were gone."

"I wasn't gone. Just weaker." Everett's entire body trembled as he whispered in my ear. "I love you so much."

I didn't try to hold back the tears. I couldn't even if I wanted to. We were together. We were safe. That was all that mattered.

"I knew you'd come for me." Everett gently stroked my back as he spoke. "They didn't think it was possible, but I never gave up hope."

I froze. "They?"

I slowly pulled away from Everett and looked behind me. Skeletal figures stood at a distance, staring at us in an anxious silence. I felt the blood drain from my face. All the outlaws Everett and I had ever caught were in that cave, watching us—and waiting.

I couldn't formulate a coherent sentence. "Everett...?"

"Yes, my love," he said calmly. "You and I have a couple of pressing issues we need to discuss. Quickly."

Chapter 62: Falling

Leona

I sat there in the cool desert cave and listened to Everett without so much as flinching, despite the warning bells ringing in my head. The only thing I wanted to do was grab him, drift out of the Valley of Sand, and never return again. Instead, I listened silently as he spoke to me telepathically.

When he got to the part about my sister, I went numb. The watchful gaze of the outlaws faded into the background. All I could hear was Everett's voice in my head.

We're the bait for Maude.

"So, the Agency purposely set us up to fail." I said the words aloud, not wanting to believe them, but knowing deep down they were true. Everett and I were never meant to be together. We were meant to drag each other down. Yet, despite our differences, we'd become more than partners. We were friends. Lovers. Mates. Bound forever... and I would destroy anyone who tried to keep us apart.

We have to get these people out of here. Everett buttoned his shirt over the dried ink that was smeared across his chest. *It's not right, what the Agency has done.*

Everett wasn't exaggerating about the deplorable conditions the outlaws were forced to endure. I saw it firsthand. Suffering and deprivation. The Agency barely provided enough food and water to go

356

around, but it was their blatant disregard for the sick that turned my stomach. They didn't care about anyone, and I'd had enough.

"I know a place we can go," I said to Everett.

Whatever you do, take me and Harvey last. I don't trust him. And I don't want you to be alone with him. Not even in the void.

"Agreed," I said quietly.

I pushed myself up and took in the sunken faces and frail bodies that were huddled together. There were fourteen people, not including Everett. I made my rounds, assessing the physical condition of each prisoner. Five were too weak to stand, and Clover was incoherent.

"I need to get the weakest people out first," I said.

"You'd better be quick about it," Harvey said with a scowl. "The Agency's transporters return every three days. They're due back here soon. And if they find anyone missing, they'll kill us. One by one."

"I can stand watch at the entrance, like I always do," Ray said. "They won't find that suspicious."

Sage spoke up. "I volunteer to stay until the others are out. I'm not afraid of a fight."

"You're sure?" Everett asked.

Sage pulled a makeshift knife from her pocket. "All that matters is my girls are safe."

No one argued with her. I had the distinct feeling it wasn't the first time she'd risked her life for her close-knit posse. The three smugglers were inseparable, but I feared Clover wouldn't make it through the drift. Her life was hanging by a thread.

Poppy wiped sweat from Clover's forehead as she coughed violently. I stood beside her and stared down at her fragile figure. "She's the worst off, but I can't take her first. She'll need someone who can tend to her."

"Take the doctor," Everett said.

My eyebrows shot up. Aside from Harvey, he was the *last* person I trusted. The man sold my sister's body parts—and seemed to like it.

"He'll make sure she's cared for," Everett reassured me. "I'll help the others get ready."

I reluctantly approached the scraggly doctor. During his imprisonment most of his hair and beard had turned gray, and his loose shirt looked like it was struggling to hang onto his bony shoulders. I assumed he of all people would be eager to leave, but I was mistaken.

The doctor stepped back. "I'm sorry, but who are you?"

I glanced at Everett.

That one's my fault, Everett projected to me remorsefully. *I wiped his memory of you. You'll have to reintroduce yourself. Convince him he has nothing to worry about.*

I calmly turned to the doctor. "My name is Leona. I'm a drifter, and I'm going to take you somewhere safe."

"Leona..." The gray-haired doctor squinted as he looked at me. His features softened. "Has anyone ever told you, you have beautiful eyes?"

I ground my teeth and forced a smile. "No. Never."

I scooped up a handful of sand, and he followed me and Everett to the mouth of the cave.

Everett said nothing. He even held back his thoughts. He was just as nervous as I was, and I knew we were both thinking the same thing. We didn't want to be apart, but there was no other way.

When we reached the entrance, a wall of heat nearly knocked me back. The blazing sun was almost directly overhead. I was utterly exhausted, but I kept my focus on the task in front of me. There wasn't time to worry about my needs. With enough gold, I could easily recover from the ordeal, but Everett and the others weren't as fortunate. I had to get them to safety.

Everett gave me one final hug and whispered in my ear. "Come back to me."

"Always." I kissed his cheek. "I love you."

Everett let me go and backed away, giving us space. I stepped out into the open and positioned the doctor in front of me with my arm wrapped firmly around his skinny waist.

"Where are we going?" the doctor asked.

I let the hot sand slip through my fingers. "Maggie's."

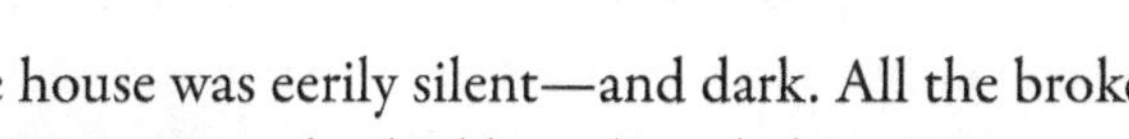

The house was eerily silent—and dark. All the broken windows in Maggie's parlor had been boarded up. The once elegant furniture was in shambles and strewn about the room from the fight. A layer of thick dust blanketed the mantel and every visible surface. No one had set foot in the home in months. A perfect place to hide. We just had to stay one step ahead of the Agency.

A grandfather clock chimed in a corner, jolting me from my thoughts. Thirty minutes to midnight. I cursed under my breath. Amos said the Agency transported prisoners and supplies to the Valley exactly at midnight. We had to move quickly. The doctor and I set about lighting candles and lanterns. Once a proper space was cleared for the others, I hurried into the night, grabbed a handful of dirt, and drifted back to the cave.

Everett carried Clover out, with Sage and Poppy nervously lingering behind him.

"Please be careful with her." Poppy's shallow voice quavered. The once stoic outlaw was on the brink of tears.

I wondered just how many people the Agency had broken. Too many, I was certain. I gently squeezed Poppy's shoulder and assured her everything was going to be fine. Lying was better than facing the unpleasant possibilities.

They lay Clover in the hot sand outside of the cave. The coughing had stopped, but so had almost everything else. She was practically comatose. I carefully straddled her limp body and wrapped myself around her. Poppy covered her face and buried herself in Sage's open arms.

I'd never lost anyone in the void, and I didn't want Clover to be the first. I didn't want any of them to be the first. I hesitated.

Just twelve more after this one. Everett spoke into my mind. *You can do this. I have complete faith in you.*

Bolstered by his words, I clung to Clover, focused solely on my destination, and drifted. The vortex sucked us in, and it took all my strength to keep her from being pulled out of my arms. The landing wasn't pretty. Clover and I lay in a heap of weeds and rotting vegetation. She was unconscious, but still breathing. I hoisted her into my arms and carried her through Maggie's overgrown garden. The doctor came rushing out of the house and helped me bring her inside.

"Just twelve more to go," I said, mimicking Everett's confident tone. I didn't quite feel it.

However, by the time I had nine trips left, I was feeling a bit more positive. When I got down to six, I was somewhat hopeful. And when I got to three, I was downright optimistic.

"You're light. You can get on my back," I said to Ray as I grabbed yet another handful of sand. He was tall, but due to his time spent in captivity, he barely had an ounce of fat left on his bones.

Sage, Harvey, and Everett were deep within the cave, waiting. I planned to take Sage next, then drift with both Harvey and Everett. I could see the end in sight.

Ray hopped onto my back. "I'm so glad you and Everett have that weird connection with the little drawings on your skin."

I held back a grin. "Me too."

"Don't take this the wrong way, but I hope I never see either one of you again after this," he said playfully.

I laughed. "I'm fairly certain our paths won't ever cross again."

The sand heated up in my palm. Ray wrapped his long legs a little tighter around my waist, bracing himself for the fall. The energy surrounding us suddenly shifted. I glanced up. There, at the top of the dune, stood two trappers. Ray froze.

"Everett!" I screamed. The grains of sand turned black and began to burn my hand. "They're here! Hide before they—!"

A shot rang out. Smoke rose from my burning flesh. I couldn't hold on. The sand slipped from my fingers, and seconds later, we were gone.

Ray and I flew headfirst into the garden. He collapsed beside me, spitting dandelions out of his mouth. I brushed clumps of dirt from my face and dragged myself up. My head was spinning. I couldn't think straight as I stumbled through the darkness, struggling to get my bearings.

"Hurry!" Ray shuffled away from me, trying to give me enough space to open a portal.

My heart was racing. I drifted back to the Valley of Sand—but landed in the wrong location. Frustration welled in my throat. I forced myself to calm down and breathe. Steady, calming breaths. I drifted again. The portal threw me out at the entrance of the cave. Everett's frantic rattling echoed off the walls. I charged inside.

One of the trappers was firing round after round at Harvey, who had erected a force field around himself in the far corner of the cave. I dodged out of the way as stray bullets ricocheted off the enclosure. Sage grappled with the second masked trapper, who was desperately trying to confiscate her knife. Everett sprang from the sand and latched onto the man's arm with his sharp fangs. He wailed in agony. Sage stabbed the trapper in the neck. He crumpled to the ground and lay motionless in the sand. I rushed toward them.

The first trapper spun around and started firing wildly at the three of us. We dove in different directions, scrambling for cover.

Leona, get Sage! Everett projected into my mind. *Harvey and I can hold him off!*

"No!" I shouted. "We leave together!"

There was a hollow clicking sound. The trapper had run out of ammunition. He turned to me, and our eyes locked. My stomach dropped. I knew him. I knew him well. He hurled his gun in my direction, grabbed a handful of sand, and drifted. A strong force dragged us toward the portal, but it closed before it could suck us all under. I took in a breath. Harvey's translucent force field quivered and vanished, and he slumped to his knees in exhaustion.

"He's going to get reinforcements." I unbuckled my belt with trembling fingers. "We have to leave. Now!"

Everett and Sage hurried to my side. Harvey sat in a daze, swaying back and forth.

"Harvey, get up!" I shouted.

Everett slithered up my body and coiled himself around my neck. I positioned Sage behind me, looped my belt around hers, then fastened it around my waist as tightly as I could. She gasped. I looked up.

The wounded trapper was no longer on the ground. He was standing with a gun raised to my forehead and a smirk on his exposed face. "I get to be the one to kill Leona."

He pulled the trigger.

I cringed. My heart stopped. But there was no pain. No blood. I peered over my shoulder. Harvey stood with his arms outstretched, shielding us with a protective wall. He slowly made his way in front of me, glaring at the trapper.

"You wanna kill Leona?" Harvey sneered. "Get in line, pal."

The trapper roared and fired at us in a fit of rage. Bullets bounced off the barrier and flew in all directions. I grabbed a fistful of sand.

"Everybody hang on!" I shouted.

I wrapped myself around Harvey, Sage wrapped herself around me, and Everett clung to my neck. The force field shuddered. I let go of the sand.

And then we fell.

Chapter 63: Out of the Shadows

Everett

Leona landed. Hard. I uncoiled myself from around her neck and slithered across mounds of weeds and dead plants. Harvey and Sage lay beside her, moaning. I knew exactly how they felt. Every inch of my body hurt. The thought of shifting and stretching into my normal human form caused my muscles to ache. But I also knew Leona felt worse. Much worse.

Panting, she stared up at the dark sky but didn't attempt to move. I fought through the pain and forced myself to shift. The crisp night air was a refreshing change from the sweltering desert, and I couldn't get enough of it into my lungs. I crawled over to the others and unbuckled Leona's belt from Sage's.

Ray barreled down the steps of Maggie's front porch and came running over. "You're alive! I thought for sure you all were goners."

He skidded to a stop and knelt beside Sage as I helped Leona stand upright.

"How's Clover?" Sage asked Ray.

"Stable," he replied. "The doctor's optimistic, now that he can properly treat her."

Sage shook sand out of her tangled hair and turned to us. "I hate trappers with a vengeance."

I remained still. So did Leona. We were outnumbered and no longer necessary for anyone's survival.

"The so-called *code of conduct* and self-righteous bull you all feed into makes me sick," Sage continued. "But we all know you two could have just left us there—and you didn't. For that, I'm grateful."

We both gave a brief nod, and I had to mask my shock. I'd been almost certain Sage and the others would turn on us as soon as they were freed from the Valley. But something had changed. In all of us.

Sage dragged herself out of the weeds and dusted off her faded trousers. "You coming, Harvey?"

Harvey didn't get up. He sat there staring at the house. Moonlight shimmered in his glossy eyes. I'd blocked out memories of that vicious fight with the rogue trappers, but I was certain the final moments with his brother still haunted him.

His nostrils flared. "I never wanted to come back to this place."

"Neither did I." Leona reached down and offered him her hand. "But here we are."

Harvey stared up at her for a moment. I watched him intently, ready to pounce if he made any attempt to harm her. Instead, he clasped onto her hand and stood.

"What now?" he asked.

"I won't try to kill you, if you don't try to kill me," she said.

Harvey glanced at me then back at her. "That's fair."

It was more than fair, but I kept my mouth shut. Leona and Harvey had history, and it wasn't my place to butt into their affairs. But that didn't mean I trusted him. No matter how devastated he was over the loss of his brother.

Maggie's home was situated on a lonely stretch of land, miles and miles away from prying neighbors and curious townsfolk. Sage leaned on Ray as they headed into the house, and Harvey followed behind them, limping. When the front door creaked closed and

Leona and I were finally alone, I swept her beside me, and she buried herself in my arms.

"I thought we were going to die," I murmured.

She laid her head on my chest. "So did I."

"The Agency's going to kill us for sure now."

"Yes." Leona's voice was emotionless. "They'll be coming for us."

I pulled away and examined her face through the silver light of the moons. "Why are you so calm?"

"Because the Agency is the least of our concerns right now. After we get these people food, medicine, and proper clothing, you and I have to go to the ranch and get Nora out of there."

I frowned. "What are you talking about?"

"She's in danger... and it's all my fault."

My stomach twisted in a knot. "What happened while I was gone?"

Leona shook her head and looked away. "I couldn't stop them."

I cradled her face in my hand and rested my forehead on hers. "Tell me everything."

Leona didn't leave anything out. I almost wished she had. The events she recounted kept replaying in my mind in a silent loop. We spent three solid days acquiring food and provisions for the former prisoners, but I could barely stomach a piece of bread. Sleep wouldn't come to me, so I spent my nights patrolling the surrounding area. Our final evening at Maggie's was spent securing the house like a fortress to keep everyone safe while they recovered and regained their strength. But it only reminded me of the fact that I couldn't even keep my own wife safe from Hiram and the Tetred clan.

Everyone had spread out and claimed spaces throughout the three-bedroom house. As night fell, we went to our respective areas.

Leona and I were in a private corner of Maggie's former dining room, and Ray and the horse thief were on the opposite side, sound asleep.

The grandfather clock chimed twelve times, but I continued pacing in the dark.

"You need to sleep," Leona whispered.

I'm not tired, I projected to her.

"Let me rephrase that," she said quietly. "I need you to sleep with me."

I held back a smile and curled up behind her on the floor. She rolled over to face me and wrapped a blanket around us.

"There was nothing you could have done differently," she said, "and dwelling on the past won't change it."

"How do you know that's what I was thinking about?" I asked.

Leona brushed her nose against mine. "Because your thoughts keep slipping into my mind."

"Sorry." The lack of sleep made it harder for me to remain guarded.

"I don't mind. I like when you're in my head." Her eyes drifted from mine. "Silence scares me."

My morbid curiosity got the better of me. "Is it always quiet? Before it happens?"

"Yes." Her voice was low. "That's what I hate the most about dying."

After being trapped in the desert, I couldn't shake a lingering thought. "I don't know how I'll face death," I admitted.

"No one does. But then you're staring it in the face."

I ran my fingers up and down her back as I spoke. "You're braver than I am. And stronger."

"Flattery," she said with a sly grin.

I'm being serious. I spoke directly into her mind. *I don't know what's on the other side of this life, but just knowing you're here with me now, in this moment, that's the only thing that keeps me from falling apart.*

"I'll..." Leona's voice cracked. "I'll always be with you. Even when we're apart."

There was a longing between us. An indescribable pull to be near one another. I leaned closer and tenderly kissed her soft lips. Heat radiated off her body, and I hungrily soaked in her warmth. My tongue brushed against hers. I lost myself in the love and desire I could no longer suppress. The fleeting time we had together was precious, and I took nothing for granted. She was mine, and I was hers.

I'd never kissed that deeply before, and when we finally broke away, a single tear rolled down her cheek. Leona briskly wiped it away.

"Now, will you please go to sleep?" she said in feigned irritation.

I smiled and gently kissed her forehead. "Yes, my lady."

While I was grateful we befriended the horse thief, the four-day journey to the ranch was still grueling. On top of the dreadful horseback ride, the terrain was rough and unforgiving with long stretches of flat land and dust that whipped up from every direction. Leona and I maintained a steady pace, and when we finally arrived at the winding dirt path leading to Vance Ranch, I breathed a sigh of relief.

Thick clouds blocked out the afternoon sun, and the estate was shrouded in a dull gray hue as we rode up to the dilapidated buildings. The barn was missing part of its roof and was leaning precariously to one side, and the main house, a once pristine and inviting home, looked as though it was ready to crumble. There didn't appear to be a soul in sight.

We dismounted, tied up our horses, and cautiously made our way to the two-story house. I was surprised the porch's rotting wooden planks were still able to support our weight. We crept to the door, and the loose handle practically came free in my hand when I turned the knob. Leona stood beside me at the threshold. There were no lanterns or candles burning in the dark, musty space.

"Hello?" I called out. "Is anyone here?"

Light footsteps pattered away from us, then everything went silent. There were numerous places for a person to hide. Formal rooms flanked the entryway, stairs led up to the second floor, where the bedrooms were located, and the long hallway in front of us led to the kitchen.

"Nora?" Leona stepped forward. "It's just us. Leona and Everett."

The room was still, but I could feel the tension in the air. I spoke up softly. "You're safe. There's no one else with us."

Moments later, Nora's petite figure emerged from the shadows. Her long prairie dress was muddy and faded, and a thick crochet shawl was wrapped around her shoulders. Relief washed over her weary face. She rushed over to Leona and gave her a hug.

"I arrived yesterday." Nora quickly ushered us inside and shut the door. "Thank you for your warning about the Agency."

We entered what was once the parlor. I did a visual sweep of the room as Nora pulled back the heavy curtains and let in the light. The inside of the house looked to be in the same poor shape as the outside. Small animals had chewed through bits and pieces of the furniture, a layer of dust was caked onto a neglected piano in the corner, and the moldy floral wallpaper was peeling off the walls. Nora seemed to notice my gaze.

"It didn't always look like this," she said with a sad smile.

"I'm sure it was lovely when you lived here," Leona said politely.

Nora ran her fingers across a carved antique secretary. "Daddy loved this house, but I couldn't wait to leave. Now I'd give anything for things to go back to the way they were."

I listened without interrupting, despite the feeling of urgency that constantly gnawed at me since we'd left Maggie's. Gaining her trust was essential. I was the one responsible for upending her life, and I wanted to set matters right in any way that I could.

Nora sighed wistfully. "When I was young, I didn't realize what I had. No one wanted to leave the ranch more than me." She paused and chuckled. "Except maybe Ray."

"We recently met him," Leona said.

Nora whipped around with a delighted grin. "You're kidding! How did you—?"

"Through our line of work," I replied.

Nora's face fell. "Oh…"

"He's actually doing a lot better than we are," Leona assured her.

"What do you mean?" she asked.

"We're not entirely sure this place is secure," I said.

Nora visibly tensed up. "I have nowhere else to go."

"You don't have to worry." Leona approached Nora and put a re-assuring hand on her shoulder. "We're going to take you with us."

Nora wrapped her shawl tighter around her body. "What does the Agency want with me?"

Leona flashed me a concerned look. We'd both agreed not to add any undue stress on Nora, but she deserved to know the truth.

"It's not just the Agency," I said. "Hiram—the shapeshifter who kidnapped you knows you're here."

"No…" Nora's knees gave out, and Leona caught her before she slumped to the ground.

I darted over, lifted her up, and carried her to the couch.

Leona sat beside her and spoke soothingly. "You're all right. We won't leave you."

"W-what if he's out there right now?" Nora stammered.

I locked eyes with Leona and projected my thoughts to her. *I'll do a perimeter check. Keep her calm. Have her pack whatever possessions she has left and be ready to go when I return.*

Leona nodded. I hurried out the door and shifted into snake form before I even reached the bottom step of the porch. I started my search behind the main house before moving on to the bunkhouse then the barn. The property was an eerie reminder of a life I'd left behind. I remembered the late-night meetings with Nora's father. How he'd enjoyed flaunting his wealth and success. I didn't care, as long as I got paid. He was more than happy to double my fee so long as I held up my end of the bargain. He told me he was building a life for his daughter. An empire. He'd no doubt be turning in his grave if he ever saw what had become of his precious ranch. Or the daughter he tried to control.

I finished in the barn and shifted so as not to spook the horses as I returned to the house. The fact that I didn't encounter any potential threats or signs we'd been followed should have brought me a measure of comfort. But it didn't. The silence was unnerving. There were no animals skipping about. Birds didn't chirp. There was no breeze. No rustling leaves. Everything felt—lifeless.

I reached for the front doorknob, but the door slowly swung open of its own accord.

"Leona?" I called out. There wasn't a sound.

I headed up the stairs and grabbed hold of the banister. My hand swept across something slick, and I froze. Through the corner of my eye, I noticed red splotches along the wall. Blood. My heart raced as I took the steps two at a time. I followed the gruesome trail and burst into one of the bedrooms. Leona lay motionless in a pool of blood in front of a brick fireplace.

Before I could cry out, a metal rod struck me in the back of the head. The explosion of pain temporarily blinded me. I landed beside

Leona, unable to move. My head lolled to the side, our faces inches apart.

Leona...

Her eyes fluttered open.

I'm so sorry...

Tears rolled down her cheeks. I desperately wanted to reach out and hold her. But I couldn't. I was struggling to maintain consciousness.

A dark shadow hovered over us. Nora's figure shifted into its true form. Through my blurred vision, I saw Hiram—staring down at me with a sinister smile. His voice was the last thing I heard before my world went black.

"This ends where it began..."

Chapter 64: Murky Waters

Everett

I couldn't remember being dragged down the stairs. Or out the front door. Or across the pasture. As I faded in and out of consciousness, all I remembered were the scattered oak trees overhead. The prickly grass against my back as I was pulled along by my ankles. And the sound of Hiram's deep, menacing voice.

"Nora belonged to me. I knew her inside and out. Until you erased her memories. Made her forget me."

My throbbing head was too heavy to lift as Hiram dragged me through an open field.

"I did everything in my power to get Nora back. I had to break her just to try and reverse what you did. But your venom…" Hiram inhaled sharply. "It was too strong. After she escaped, I followed her trail to the edge of a ravine. I saw her clothes at the bottom of it—and the bloody heap that was left. I thought she took her own life. That I'd lost her forever. Then I find out, from your precious partner, that Nora's alive and has been in hiding all this time—and that you've been in contact with her."

My hands were tied together over my head. I tried to shift, but the pain shooting from my bruised limbs was excruciating.

"We were happy once," Hiram continued. "I could have given her everything she ever wanted. A life away from her tyrannical father and his wretched little ranch."

My eyes fluttered as I struggled to remain conscious.

"We had plans to elope." Hiram stopped and glared down at me. "We were going to start a family."

My thoughts drifted back to Leona. She was dying. Alone. In the farmhouse. Because of me. "I'm sorry..." My muffled speech was slurred. "For what I did to you."

Hiram snorted. "You're not nearly sorry enough. Not yet."

I stared up at the overcast sky. The world began to dim again.

Through the darkness of my mind, I heard the sound of rushing water. My eyes shot open. It was midafternoon. We were more than two miles away from the house, at the edge of the property. By the river. And Hiram was ripping off my boots and socks. Panic overtook me, but I could barely move.

No! You can't do this! I frantically projected into his mind. *It's forbidden!*

"My brother said the same thing." Hiram's lip curled up. "But I'm not afraid of starting a clan war. You know why?"

I thrashed about, and Hiram kicked me in the ribs.

"I have nothing to lose." Hiram grabbed my ankles once more and dragged me along as he stepped into the river barefoot.

Rocks scraped against my back, and the shock of cold water made my muscles tighten. He waded deeper into the river. I gulped in a lungful of air seconds before my head went under the water. I started sinking.

Hiram grabbed me around the waist. I tried to wriggle out of his grip, but I was too weak to break away from him. A heavy force compressed my entire body. My bones felt as though they were going to snap. I couldn't fight it. He was taking me to his clan. The world twisted and folded around me as we crossed dimensions into Sutorath. The water no longer felt cold. It was boiling. Searing my skin. My scales. I couldn't maintain my human form no matter how hard I tried. I wasn't part of their dominion. I didn't belong there.

Hiram stood upright, knee-deep in the water and clutching me by the neck. Instead of towering cave dwellings in the distance like those of the Diamas clan, giant redwood trees stretched to the sky. Spiral staircases wrapped around the massive trunks and led to treehouses that were cradled in vines. Bright rays of sunlight shimmered off the mirrored windows and doors. I froze for a moment and gaped up at the intricate web of bridges that connected the private homes together. I'd never seen another clan's dwelling. And I was certain I never would again. They would kill me the moment they detected my presence. I writhed about, my tail rattling uncontrollably as I struggled to free myself from Hiram's grasp.

A silent figure approached from the dense forest. She carried no weapons. Just a glass jar. I couldn't make out any of her features. She was faceless. I was Diamas, and she was Tetred. Shielded from my sight.

"Hurry!" Hiram shouted. "I paid off the guards, but the second wave could be here any moment."

The figure rushed forward into the lake, splashing water in all directions. I hissed wildly, suddenly understanding what was about to happen. They were going to take my venom. Before I could react, the figure leapt behind me, grabbed the base of my head, and shoved my open mouth against the glass jar. The pressure she exerted on the back of my head was almost unbearable, and my vision blurred. Venom dripped down my fangs. But it wasn't like the times before. My life force—my soul—felt like it was being drained from my body. All of my physical senses began to dull. My vision wasn't as sharp. Sound was muffled. I could no longer taste the air. It was like being in the void. I should have been terrified, but I wasn't. I was numb.

When the final drop of venom fell from my mouth, the figure backed away, quickly sealing the jar. "What about the woman you told me about? Leona?"

"I'm going to make him watch as I burn the house down." Hiram tightened his grip around my throat. "With her in it."

Something inside of me snapped. The last thread of sanity. The only thing that prevented my primal side—the serpent—from taking control of my mind. Hiram could take my venom. He could take my life. But I wouldn't let him take Leona's. Not again. Never again.

My savage instincts took over. I twisted around, sprang from Hiram's grip, and clamped down on his forehead with my sharp teeth. Hiram shrieked and stumbled backward with me dangling from his face. I tasted his salty blood and bit harder. The woman scrambled away, making no attempt to help her fellow clansman. I whipped my body around Hiram's neck, throwing him off-balance. We fell into the scalding-hot water, and I dragged him under, forcing us back across dimensions.

We broke through the surface of the icy river, and Hiram gasped for breath. He clawed at my peeling skin with his jagged fingernails. My scales still felt like they were on fire, but I wouldn't let go. I couldn't. I stared up at the gray sky, channeling the very last of my strength. Clouds formed overhead. There was a familiar charge in the air. I closed my eyes and drew the energy toward me. A bolt of lightning tore through my body. Then another. And another. And another. Hiram was unable to choke out a scream. It happened too fast.

Thunder rumbled in the distance, and the haze lifted from my mind. *Burned flesh.* That was the sickening scent I couldn't get off my tongue. Hiram was no longer twitching in my grasp. I uncoiled myself from around his neck, and he floated face down in the clear water. Lifeless. The weight of what I'd done came crashing down on me all at once. I'd never killed another shapeshifter before. My chest ached, and I struggled to breathe.

I shifted into human form and stood waist-deep in the river. Tears streamed down my face as sobs racked my body. I couldn't stem the flood of conflicting emotions that poured out of me. Relief. Guilt. Shame. Anger at Hiram. Anger at myself. Sadness...

Hiram began to shift, and I froze. The transmutation. I knew what happened to a shapeshifter's physical body when it died, but I'd never witnessed it personally. Every form Hiram had ever taken flashed in rapid succession. Elsie, an old man, a cavalryman, Nora... so many individuals I lost count.

Finally, Hiram shifted into the animal that embodied his soul. The coyote. I watched in horror as the stiff corpse melted into a puddle of black ink, staining the water.

I clambered to the edge of the riverbed. They were coming. The undertakers. And there was only one way to avoid retaliation. I grabbed the sharpest rock I could find, braced myself, and slit the side of my neck. I bit back a yelp. The previous wounds from the Valley of Sand were still raw, and I winced at the stinging sensation. I had one chance to set matters straight with the Tetred clan. One.

Ink from my markings pooled in my cupped hand. When I couldn't hold any more, I released the oily substance into the river. It drifted upstream, instantly drawn to the dark waters. My ink intertwined with Hiram's and spread. I hurried to dry land and knelt beside the river's edge in a respectful posture. I waited. And waited. Time seemed to stand still.

Four figures slowly emerged from the murky waters. Three were cloaked, and I couldn't see their faces through the dark shadows cast by their hoods. The fourth person I recognized immediately. Ira. Hiram's older brother. He locked eyes with me, and I bowed low.

I acted in self-defense, I projected to Ira. *I swear on my markings and on the blood of my family. I wish no harm on the Tetred clan.*

The cloaked individuals spoke amongst themselves, telepathically. Bits and pieces of their conversation slipped into my mind, their urgent voices overlapping and mingling together.

Laws were broken... He was still one of us... A technicality... A life for a life... Where does that end? It ends with him...

I held my breath for what felt like an eternity. Four individuals would determine my fate. Retribution or redemption. The sky was still cloudy, blocking the warmth of the sun, and I shivered.

Finally, the undertakers nodded in unison and looked to Ira.

He bowed, ever so slightly, and addressed me directly. *The Tetred clan wishes no harm on you.*

I nearly wept, but I kept my composure. The undertakers placed their palms on top of the rushing water. Black ink swirled up into their hands. They absorbed every last drop of the dark liquid until the river was clear once more. One by one, they disappeared under the water, their solemn task complete. Ira was the last to leave. There was a flicker of hatred in his green eyes.

May we never meet again, Everett. Ira slipped under the water and vanished without a trace.

I exhaled and collapsed onto my back in the grass, holding my sore neck as ink continued to ooze from my markings. Blood rushed to my head. My heart had been beating so fast I couldn't prevent the dizzy spell from overtaking me. I lay on the ground, drenched and barefoot, unable to move.

But then I thought about Leona. *Saw* Leona... standing over me in a long trench coat that swayed in the wind.

I shot upright and faced her.

"Hello." Her voice was melodic, her smile warm and inviting.

My jaw dropped.

"You must be Everett." The woman knelt beside me, pulled an ivory handkerchief from her pocket, and gently pressed it against my slashed neck. "I'm Maude."

I glanced about, searching for any sign of Leona.

"Leona's fine," Maude said, as though reading my mind. "Or at least, she will be once she's conscious again. Nora's tending to her right now. I was hoping I would finally meet you in person. Just not under these circumstances."

I was too dumbfounded to speak.

"This all must come as a bit of a shock," Maude continued. "Nora told me about the message you sent her, but she was worried it was a trap. I promised to come along, and we got to the ranch as soon as we could."

I sat there, gaping at her.

Maude tilted her head. "Wow. You really don't say much, do you? Leona must tease you mercilessly." Her laughter was almost identical to Leona's. "She can't handle silence."

I cleared my dry throat. "I'm telepathic."

"Ahh..." Maude nodded. "You have a lot to say about everything, but you live inside your head. Only a select few really get to know you."

My mouth opened then shut again.

She waved her free hand. "No matter. I enjoy the company of telepaths. It's familiar to me."

Maude quietly went about tending to my wounds, wrapping my neck with a clean rag that seemed to materialize out of thin air. She was prepared. For everything.

"How did you find me all the way out here?" I asked.

Maude cracked a smile. "Once a trapper, always a trapper. The real question is, who ambushed you?"

I shook out my pounding head. "Hiram."

Her eyes widened. "The shapeshifter?"

"How did you end up having dealings with him?" I asked.

Maude finished with the bandage and settled beside me in the damp grass. "Two years ago, I made the decision to leave the Agency, but I knew doing so would put my sister at risk. So I faked my death and went into hiding, thinking it was the best way to keep Leona safe. Nora's father hired me as a ranch hand, and for a while, things were good. I lived a quiet life, and nobody bothered me."

"But it didn't stay that way," I said.

"No. Nora was secretly seeing a young man—a shapeshifter—her father didn't approve of. She was in love. Those of us who knew her well were happy for her, but we stayed out of it to avoid a confrontation. Her father had a violent temper, and their fights never ended well. The next thing we know, Nora has no memory of the man she was courting and suddenly she's getting along with her father like he's her entire world."

I listened quietly, feeling foolish for having been duped by Mr. Vance.

"One night, her father boasted to me that he'd hired you to erase Nora's memory of Hiram."

I spoke up. "It was a mistake. A terrible mistake."

"It was a bad situation all around. Nora was living a lie, and none of us could say a word about it," Maude said. "Months went by then suddenly Nora disappeared. Her father knew I was a former trapper, and he paid me to find her. I located the hideout and staged an elaborate scene so Hiram would think she was dead. He was so distraught he went on a rampage. I secretly returned Nora to her father, and he began making arrangements for her to stay with some distant relatives down south, but he died from a fall shortly after that."

"Then you left?" I asked.

"Yes. Too many people started asking questions about this place... and about me. I went back on the run soon after that and took Nora with me." Maude buttoned her trench coat as the wind picked up. "I have allies in the Agency. People I still trust. The Agency found out about what happened to Nora. They knew you and I were both hired by her father, and they thought we might be connected somehow. They recruited you and paired you with Leona in the hopes that it would lead to my whereabouts—"

"And if it didn't, we were both so horribly mismatched they knew they could still use us to get to you," I said.

"Exactly. That's when I approached Maggie. She hired you to wipe my trail. To keep Leona from finding me. To keep her safe."

I pondered her words for a moment. "Does Nora know? About what I did to her?"

"No, and there's no sense in telling her. You fell victim to her father's lies and paid a heavy price." She gestured toward my bandaged neck.

I pushed thoughts of Hiram's final moments out of my mind and put on my socks and boots. "I have to get to Leona."

In one graceful motion, Maude rose and offered me her hand.

"Thank you," I said, clasping onto her for support. I was anxious to know if Leona was awake, but my balance was off, and my steps were unsteady. Nothing felt right. Not since the moment they took my venom.

Maude eyed me curiously. "What exactly happened between you and Hiram?"

"There was an altercation," I said with little emotion. "But the matter was settled."

"Settled?" She paused, as though waiting for me to elaborate. When I remained silent, she laughed and linked her arm around mine as we walked through the field. "A man of many secrets. You're perfect for Leona. She trusts everyone, and you trust no one."

Before I could respond, the sound of heavy hoofbeats pounded through the air. Far off, across the open pasture, Nora raced toward us on horseback with Leona's body draped in front of her.

"They're coming!" Nora screamed. A gunshot rang out.

Maude grabbed me by the collar and shoved me to the ground. I was barely able to break my fall. She jumped onto my back, straddled my waist, and snatched up a handful of dirt. We dropped into the void before I could even gasp. She clung to me, and seconds later we were propelled forward. Our feet hit the ground, and I stumbled ever-so-slightly. Maude rushed past me, crouched down to grab a fistful of sand, and hurled it in front of her. The ground opened up. She jumped into the portal and disappeared. Just like that.

It took me a while to realize my mouth was hanging open. The cramped dugout I found myself in was warm, despite the snow flurries that floated in from the single entryway. I stumbled about in a dazed stupor. I had no idea where I was. Or which way was up, for that matter.

A sudden burst of cool air pushed me back against the wall as a vortex swirled into existence. Maude emerged carrying Leona. My heart leapt in my chest. I hurried over and scooped Leona into my arms. She was unconscious, but her breathing was steady.

"I have to get Nora." Maude hastily picked up a handful of sand and headed to the doorway. "Please take care of my sister."

"Wait! You're not coming back?" I asked in dismay.

"No. I have to stay on the move." Her voice was emotionless, and I noticed blood seeping through the front of her trench coat near her heart. "It's safer for everyone this way."

I held Leona closer. "Please. She'll be devastated if she doesn't get to see you."

Maude remained still with her back to me. "Tell her to meet me in three days. At dawn."

"Where?" I asked.

Maude glanced over her shoulder at me. "The place where we buried our mother."

She opened a portal, and without another word, she was gone.

Chapter 65: Gold Mine
Leona

I wasn't dead. I couldn't figure out how I wasn't dead… or why Everett was trembling uncontrollably as he cradled me in his lap.

I pushed through the throbbing headache and slowly opened my eyes to find Everett staring down at me. His back was against a dirt wall, and soft candlelight flickered off his bruised face.

"Where are we?" I asked.

"I-I don't know," he said.

The heady smell of mud and sod filled my lungs. I glanced around the unfamiliar dugout. Thick snowflakes were falling just outside the entrance—a stark contrast from the balmy spring weather at the ranch. "How did we get here?"

Everett clung to me tighter. "Maude."

I shot upright. The world tilted, and I held my head as I fought a dizzy spell.

"Be still," he said soothingly. "Maude couldn't stay, but she gave us a location to meet up with her again in three days."

A torrent of questions swirled in my mind as I settled against his chest once more. "How did she find us? Where did she go? What happened after Hiram ambushed us?"

Everett took in a shaky breath. "It was *unpleasant*."

As my vision sharpened, I noticed faint streaks running down both of his cheeks. Dried tears. My eyes narrowed. "What did he do to you?"

Through chattering teeth, Everett recounted the events I'd missed while I lay bleeding half to death in the farmhouse. I kept silent as he described being forcibly dragged across dimensions into Sutorath—to the Tetred clan's dominion. He struggled to get through the part about what he did to Hiram... and about the undertakers.

"So... he's gone." I almost had trouble believing my own words.

"Yes." Everett closed his eyes and rested his head against the dirt wall. "We're finally safe."

Almost. I reached up and stroked the side of his face. "Everett, you're shaking. We have to get you out of this cold."

I scooped up a handful of cool dirt, absorbing as many details of the fine soil as I could to ensure I'd be able to find my way back if I needed to. I slowly rose and waited for Everett to morph so we could drift, but he remained on the ground.

"I can't shift," he said quietly.

A stiff breeze blew snow into the dugout. "It's too cold?"

"No." He swallowed hard. "They took my venom. Something that was a part of me. Part of what embodied my soul. And it's trapped in another dimension."

I knelt in front of Everett as the reality of the situation started to sink in. "We have to get you back to your family, immediately. They'll know what to do."

"I can't cross back into Sutorath, which means I can't seek help from the Diamas clan."

"What do you mean?" I asked. "Why not?"

"Leona, I can't shift," he repeated. "I'm not able to leave this dimension. That was Hiram's master plan. To leave me here. Alone. Without you... and without my family."

The bitterly cold wind that swept through the dugout started to prick my skin. We only had one option. "We need to get back to our hideaway."

Our landing was rough. Horribly rough. It had been so long since I drifted with Everett in his human form, I couldn't figure out a comfortable position for both of us. Mist from the waterfall hung in the warm air as we lay panting on the floor of the cave. I lost count of how many new bruises I suddenly felt.

Everett moaned. "If I didn't know how much you loved me, I'd swear you were trying to kill me, darling."

"Next time you try being on top," I choked out.

"No. I like it better when you're on top." He dragged me back onto his muscular body. "I get a better view."

I smirked and pushed myself up. We needed to get a fire going, and I was more than ready to get out of my filthy clothes. My smile faded as I looked around our hideaway. Our sanctuary. "Everett..."

The rushing water muffled my quivering voice.

"Everett!" I spoke louder, more forcefully.

He rolled over and saw what I saw. He sat frozen in place. Every article of clothing we owned was scattered across the cave floor. Dishes were overturned, and the canned goods were smashed to oblivion. All the firewood was bobbing up and down in the pool of water under the falls. There didn't appear to be a single item left untouched.

I rushed over to the dark corner where we'd hidden the gifts from our wedding. The box and the knife Ollie gifted me were both intact. I quickly grabbed a bag and packed it away along with my clothes.

Everett stood staring at the wall. "I've seen this symbol before."

I glanced up. My stomach dropped. Sweat began to bead up on my forehead. There, on the wall, was a crescent moon with two lines down the center. Drawn in blood.

"I've seen you trace it. And it was on the tree leading to Maude's grave," he said. "What does it mean?"

My throat was so dry it was difficult to speak. "When partners reach the rank of level nine, the Agency brands them, so to speak. Each pair is given a unique symbol. They use ciphers to discreetly communicate information to us, either to warn us of threats or relay instructions. That symbol was the one given to me and Maude."

"Why is it written in blood?"

"It's a message. A courtesy." I couldn't stop my hands from trembling. "The hunters are giving me a head start."

Everett backed away.

"We need to pack whatever we can and get out of here. Quickly."

He didn't argue. Minutes later, we were running out of the cave and into the woods. My heart was racing. Everett stumbled a couple of times, but I thought nothing of it. When he complained of dizziness and he started falling behind, I realized he still had a concussion. He wouldn't be able to maintain that sort of pace. The sun was just beginning to set, and we were completely exposed. I grabbed the first patch of dry soil I could find, and we drifted.

We landed on a hillside in a dark forest, but I knew exactly where we were. Not far from our location was a hideout Maude and I used in our early trapping days. I hadn't been back in over eight years. We dropped our bags, and I helped Everett get settled near a small outcrop of rock where he'd be shielded from view.

Where are we? he projected as he propped himself up against the stone wall.

"An old gold mine," I whispered, covering him with a blanket. "I'm going to check it out to make sure it's clear. You rest."

He curled up in a ball. *Be careful.*

I kissed him on the forehead then cautiously headed down the steep incline. Thick clouds blocked out most of the moonlight, and I hoped with every fiber of my being we could take shelter before a storm rolled in. The entrance to the abandoned gold mine was tucked deep within the side of the massive hill.

I crept inside the narrow tunnel. My footsteps echoed throughout the dark passageway, and I ran my fingers along the craggy walls to maintain my balance. There was barely enough room for more than one person to enter at a time. I reached a T-intersection and stopped. There wasn't a sound or any other signs of life. I let out a breath.

A large hand clamped around my nose and mouth. I screamed, but the sound was muffled as I was overpowered and dragged out of the mine. Panic welled inside of me, and I flailed about, trying to free myself.

"You're too predictable, Leona."

I stiffened at the sound of Julius's voice.

He spoke through his teeth. "If I can find you, *they* can find you."

A drop of rain splattered in front of me. Julius let go of me, and I spun around to face him. He looked different in his old trapper clothes. Like he was pretending to be a version of himself that he was no longer comfortable with.

"I came here to tell you that they've got Amos. They think he's working with you, and they're trying to use him to draw you out."

I didn't say a word.

"I've got a pair of my most trustworthy trappers searching for him as we speak. I'll find him. Don't fall for their trap." Julius stared at me as though waiting for me to crack.

I kept my expression blank. "Why are you pretending to be on my side?"

"I've always been on your side."

"Really? How long did you know the Agency was using me and Everett as the bait to trap Maude?"

Julius didn't respond.

"What did you think? That you and I would rekindle what we once had? That I'd confide in you and eventually lead you to Maude?"

"I truly wanted to be with you," he insisted.

"But you wanted my sister more—because trapping her would increase your ranking."

Julius remained still as raindrops plunked down around us.

"Well, at least that's one thing that hasn't changed about you. Your ambition always comes before your heart."

Julius lowered his head. "I'm sorry."

"Don't be. Apparently, you're not the only one." I folded my arms, ignoring the rain as it seeped into my clothes. "I ran into your old partner in the Valley of Sand."

"He told me."

"Did he also tell you he tried to kill me?"

"He was working under orders."

I snorted. "Is that the new Agency mantra?"

"Leona, I admit I've made some mistakes." Julius raised his eyes to mine. "But I'm here now. Even though I know it's too late."

"Way, *way*, too late."

"I wish things could have been different," Julius continued. "I wanted to protect you. But then you and Everett did the very same thing that caused us to go after Maude."

"What the Agency does to those people..." I shuddered thinking back to the sunken faces of the prisoners. "It's not right."

"That's not for either one of us to decide."

I ground my teeth. "Well, Everett and I decided that it's not right."

Julius stepped closer and lowered his voice. "Do you love him?"

I glared up at Julius. He didn't deserve to know my private thoughts.

"It's a simple question." His tone was gentle. "Do you love him?"

"Yes." Rain trickled down my eyelashes, but I didn't flinch. "I love Everett."

Julius swallowed hard and nodded. "Then I suggest you both run."

I didn't hear the arrow as it sliced through the air. I only saw the stunned expression on Julius's face as it slammed into his back. He dropped to his knees, clutching his abdomen. I screamed, and a second arrow narrowly missed my left cheek. I ducked, grabbed hold of Julius, and dragged him into the mine. The stone walls protected us from the hunters, but we were trapped. I sat Julius upright and tried to examine his wound. The tip of the arrowhead was protruding from his stomach. Through the darkness, I couldn't see all the blood, but I knew it was ghastly.

Julius pushed me away. "Run..."

"I can't just—"

"Run! While you still can."

I bit back tears of frustration and pounded my fist against the ground. I started to stand, but Julius grabbed my wrist.

"Leona..." He gasped for air. "I am sorry. For everything."

I squeezed his bloody hand. "I'm sorry too."

I rushed to the entrance and waited. Another arrow whizzed past. I bolted into the rain and charged up the hill.

Everett was already poised to run. We darted through dense ferns, climbing higher and higher. He followed my lead without question. My eyes burned as I struggled to get the last image I had of Julius out of my mind. I had to focus. Without being able to drift, our only option was finding a portal.

I inhaled deeply. The energy surrounding me felt heavier on my right. I veered in that direction. Rain pelted me in the face, but I didn't slow down. The trees thinned out as we reached the top of the hill and found ourselves standing at the edge of a cliff. Even the light of Aadar's three moons couldn't reach the bottom—because there was no bottom, only a shimmering violet light that faded in and out of existence.

Everett hunched over with our bags and struggled to catch his breath. "We have to go back."

"No." I swiped the raindrops from my face and backed away from the edge. I needed a running start. "Please know I'm not trying to kill you."

The rain muffled the string of expletives Everett muttered as I sprinted forward and dove into him.

We careened over the edge of the cliff. I bit back a scream and wrapped my arms around him, clinging to him as we fell. The glistening purple light intensified. A heavy force sucked us into the portal, and I squeezed my eyes shut.

Where we landed didn't matter, because deep down I knew... the hunters would always find us.

Chapter 66: Rocky Soil
Leona

I never visited my mother's grave. There were things about my past that I didn't want to remember. She was one of them. Yet that was the location Maude chose for us to meet up.

Everett and I stood on top of a massive canyon overlooking the Valley of Sand. The sun crept into the sky, painting the pillowy clouds soft shades of pink and violet. Under any other circumstance, the sunrise would have been breathtaking. A rebirth. Instead, the vast emptiness of the desert reminded me of death, and it left me feeling hollow inside.

"Are you all right?" Everett asked.

I realized my fists were clenched, and I quickly stretched out my fingers. "I'm just worried she won't come."

Everett wrapped his arms around me, and I rested my head against his chest. The steady beating of his heart calmed my frayed nerves. He gently rubbed my back without a word. We hadn't spoken much since the night we escaped the hunters. I told him about Amos. My friend knew the inner workings of the Agency better than anyone, and I knew full well he could handle himself, but I was still worried about him. After I recounted the horrific incident with Julius, we both agreed it was too dangerous to seek allies within the Agency. We couldn't risk getting anyone else entangled in our lives. The remainder of our time spent in the wilderness consisted of one of us sleeping while the other stood watch. After almost three days, we were exhausted—but we were together, and that was all that mattered.

"How are you feeling?" I asked gently.

"Not great," he admitted. "It's disorienting to remain in a single form for long periods of time."

I couldn't fathom what he was going through. "I'm sorry."

"I'll get used to it." His voice was strained. "Eventually."

"No..." I knew he was masking the emotional pain he was actually suffering through. "We'll find a way to get your venom back. I promise."

Everett ran his fingers down my back. "I'm glad you're the one by my side through all of this."

I nuzzled closer. "So am I, love."

A vortex swirled into existence behind us, and my heart practically skipped a beat. Through the maelstrom, a dark form materialized. My sister emerged from the portal, the tails of her trench coat floating behind her as her feet softly touched the ground. Her dark eyes locked on mine. My throat was so tight I couldn't utter a sound.

Everett's hands slowly fell away from me as his gentle voice entered my mind. *I'll give you some privacy.*

He walked across the dusty canyon and tipped his hat to Maude as he passed. She flashed him a small smile then turned her attention back to me. Her hair was braided into two thick locks, and there wasn't a single blemish on her deep-brown skin. She looked flawless.

"You broke your promise," I said with little inflection.

"You didn't get my apology?"

"The note you left in the box where Leroy buried you?"

She nodded.

"I got it."

"Yet, you're still mad," Maude said.

I folded my arms across my chest.

"Do you want to hit me?"

"I should."

Maude opened her arms wide. Taunting me. My façade crumbled. I ran up and hugged her so tightly I almost knocked her off her feet. She laughed and squeezed me back.

"I missed you, Lee." Maude clung to me as she spoke. "There were so many times I wanted to come back… but I couldn't."

"Because of the hunters?" I asked.

"The hunters, the Agency—all of it. But just so you know, technically I didn't break my promise."

I slowly pulled away. "You most certainly did. We agreed if there ever came a time we had to go our separate ways, we would say one last goodbye."

"I was dead."

"You were *pretending* to be dead."

Maude turned solemn. "If I had said goodbye, would you have let me go?"

"Absolutely not."

"Exactly."

We stared across the horizon as beams of sunlight began to illuminate the desert. Memories I'd kept buried deep inside came rushing back. "Mother always said I was too clingy."

Maude sighed. "And that I was too detached."

An image of our mother flashed into my mind, her tall silhouette hovering over me like a dark omen. It was the last time I saw her alive. When she dropped me in the Valley of Sand. Alone. Right after she'd done the same thing to Maude.

"She just left us. Without a word." I struggled to keep my voice from quavering. "Like we didn't even matter to her."

"I think I finally understand why she did it," Maude said softly.

"Really? You know why our mother dumped us hundreds of miles away from each other in a sweltering desert only so we could return to an empty house?"

Maude looked me in the eye. "She wanted to make sure we were strong enough for this world without her... and without each other."

Tears stung my eyes, but I held them back. I swore I'd never cry over my mother's grave. "Well, congratulations, Mother!" I shouted at the ground. "You succeeded in raising two strong women who are only mildly damaged!"

Maude tapped me on the shoulder. "I think we buried her ashes over there." She pointed to an area where thistles and cacti were protruding out of the rocky soil.

"You're right." I stomped over to the actual burial site and repeated my tirade. Louder. My voice echoed off the canyon walls as though shouting back at me.

Maude walked up and threw her arm around my shoulder, holding back a chuckle. "Feel better?"

"A little."

"Good." She glanced over at Everett, who was wandering about pretending not to hear us. "I hope you didn't scare off your partner."

"Everett?" I shook my head. "No, he's fine. He's seen much worse out of me."

Maude raised a single eyebrow. "You seem to like him."

"I do. He's my husband."

Maude burst into laughter.

I didn't flinch.

She caught a glimpse of my expression, and her face fell. "Oh... you're serious. Are you pregnant?"

Maude patted my stomach, and I slapped her hand away. "No, I'm not pregnant."

She cocked her head to the side. "You—really love him."

"I do."

She blinked. "I'm... speechless..."

I glanced over at Everett as he settled beside our bags to rest. "I suppose that's one thing the Agency did in my favor."

"Always looking on the bright side," Maude said half-mockingly.

"Not always. I'm not delusional enough to think they had my best interests at heart. They just underestimated us."

"Just make sure *you* don't underestimate the Agency. They'll do everything in their power to break you."

I eyed her up and down. "I think I'm seeing that firsthand."

"I was broken long before I joined the Agency." Maude flashed me a sly smile. "I just hid it really well."

I chuckled despite myself.

"I get the feeling you two don't hide anything from each other," she said, nodding to Everett.

"We don't. Not anymore."

"And you're—happy?"

"Yes." I spoke with all honesty. "We're both very happy together."

Her expression softened. "Then I'm happy for you as well."

"Oh, and get this..." I nudged her and whispered, "He likes to dance."

Maude gasped. "You lie. He doesn't seem like the type."

"I know." I paused briefly. "Of course, I found out about the dancing thing *after* we got married, but that's beside the point."

"Well, it's just good you really got to know him before you made any sort of serious commitment."

Our collective laughter echoed throughout the canyon.

Far off in the distance, sunlight shimmered off a mirrorlike surface in the desert. A vortex. Two figures landed in the sand, and the portal closed behind them.

Maude grabbed my hand as if trying to hold on to the moment.

Everett approached and stood by my side as we peered across the barren land. The hunters split up and began searching the area.

"They came close to capturing me once," Maude said bitterly. "It didn't end well."

My thoughts went back to the night at the gold mine. "Julius said we should run."

"He's right." Maude moved away from the edge. "And we have a better chance of surviving if we're apart."

I turned to face my sister. Her vacant stare was unnerving. In the two years we'd spent apart, we'd both changed, but there was something different about her I couldn't quite put into words. A feeling I couldn't explain.

Maude picked up a handful of sand and continued backing away. I knew what was coming, and I didn't try to stop her.

"This isn't goodbye," she said.

"I know."

Maude retreated farther away from us, released the sand, and let the ground swallow her up.

My gaze fell upon the cluster of thistles and cacti. For my entire life, I felt like I was thrown about by the whims of others. I swayed this way and that, never once feeling grounded or in control. The instability of my family was replaced with the instability of the Agency... an organization that knew nothing of loyalty.

But I was no longer beholden to anyone or anything. Everett and I could determine our own path. Our own future. The emptiness that lingered inside of me was replaced with something I'd never felt before—purpose. I could choose the direction I wanted to go, and for once, I wasn't adrift.

The two figures in the sand reconvened. They opened a portal and drifted away, disappearing into nothingness.

Everett spoke up. "They're coming for us."

"Let them come." I stared into his golden eyes as they flickered in the morning light. "We're done running."

Acknowledgments

To the Red Adept Team: I can't thank you enough for your hard work and creativity. It's a pleasure working with all of you.

To Erica: Thank you for allowing me to bounce ideas off you at random hours of the night when we both should have been sleeping.

To Lynn: I'm eternally grateful for your support and truly appreciate your guidance. I promise not to go too far off the rails with the next book.

To my critique partner: Thank you for challenging me to always make my writing better and my characters stronger. I seriously couldn't have done this without you. Just know you're stuck with me for life.

To my siblings: I know y'all are busy. With actual lives. I'll text you when book 2 is done so you can binge read them both in one sitting.

To my mom and dad: Mom, you can skip this one; I know how you feel about snakes. Dad, I'll be getting back to the dragons soon. I promise.

To my son: Thank you for coming into my life. You're actually the reason this book came about, but Mommy's going to write you something more age appropriate.

To my husband: Thank you. For everything. For listening attentively as I worked through plot holes. For supporting my dreams. For always encouraging me to keep doing what I love. You never once complained about our Netflix queue being glutted with westerns, and you'll be happy to know we'll be moving on to rom-coms in the coming weeks.

About the Author

Rashida T. Williams has been crafting stories for as long as she can remember. Over the years, she developed a passion for writing, in part because it allowed her to combine her two favorite genres: romance and fantasy.

When Rashida is not writing, she can be found playing video games, binge watching romantic movies, and attempting to hone her baking skills. She lives in south Florida with her husband, son, and two cats.

Read more at www.rashidatwilliams.com.

About the Publisher

Dear Reader,

We hope you enjoyed this book. Please consider leaving a review on your favorite book site.

Visit https://RedAdeptPublishing.com to see our entire catalogue.

Check out our app for short stories, articles, and interviews. You'll also be notified of future releases and special sales.